DATE DUE

Thaddeus Kościuszko

Thaddeus Kościuszko

The Purest Son of Liberty

James S. Pula

HIPPOCRENE BOOKS
New York

For information, address:
Hippocrene Books, Inc.
171 Madison Avenue
New York, NY 10016

Library of Congress Cataloging-in-Publication Data:

Pula, James S., 1946-
Thaddeus Kościuszko : the purest son of liberty / James S. Pula.
p.   cm.
Includes bibliographical references.
ISBN 0- 7818-0576-7
1. Kościuszko, Tadeusz, 1746-1817.   2. Nobility--Poland-
-Biography.   3. Generals--Poland--Biography. 4. United States.
Army--Officers--Biography.   I. Title.
DK4348.K67P85   1998
943.8'02'092--dc21
[B]   98-44025
CIP

Printed in the United States of America

For my father
who enjoyed reading about his Polish heritage
and helped me to appreciate the lessons of history

Contents

Illustrations following page 192

Acknowledgements

The research necessary for this work was greatly aided by a number of individuals and institutions. I am particularly indebted to Mr. Jacek Galazka for his support and encouragement throughout this project; to Dr. M.B. Biskupski who read and offered invaluable suggestions for the chapters dealing with the protagonist's European experience and translated the Połaniec Manifesto from Polish to English; to Mr. Kenneth Gallagher who read and critiqued the entire manuscript; to Mr. Joseph Gore, president of the Kościuszko Foundation and Ms. Elizabeth Koszarski-Skrabonja, Curator-in-Residence at the Kościuszko Foundation, for their invaluable assistance in locating illustrations and granting permission for their use of items held in their exceptional collections, including the painting used as the cover illustration; and to Ms. Carmen E. Gonzalez, the best research assistant in the world. Others who offered materials and assistance included Dr. Stanislaus A. Blejwas, Ms. Adele Chwalek, Mr. Lawrence A. DeLong, Mr. Eugene E. Dziedzic, Dr. Thaddeus V. Gromada, Ms. Jane Kedron, Mr. Shelby J. Marshall, Ms. Sarah Ringer, and Dr. Robert Szymczak.

Institutions which offered their research facilities with professionalism and courtesy included the Albermarle County [Virginia] Circuit Court, the American Antiquarian Society, The Kościuszko Foundation, the Library of Congress, the Maine Historical Society, the Maryland Historical Society, the Massachusetts Historical Society, the Mullen Library at The Catholic University of America, the New-York Historical Society, the New York Public Library, the Polish Institute of Arts and Sciences of America, the Saratoga National Historical Park, the Society of the Cincinnati, the United States Military Academy Library and Archives, the University of Virginia Library, the William L. Clements Library at the University of Michigan, and the Yale University Library and Archives.

To all of these, and to everyone else who assisted in any way, I am appreciative and greatly indebted.

Foreword

*T*o every Pole, Tadeusz Kościuszko is a hero. His legendary figure in "Krakowian" dress with its red four-cornered hat adorned with a bright feather, stands for duty, honor, liberty, and freedom as the Polish people understand it. Tadeusz Kościuszko took the oath to free and liberate Poland of its oppressors on a stone in the central square of the city of Kraków called the "Rynek," where today every visitor can see it and read its inscription.

But, Kościuszko was an equally important hero in America. Americans, led by George Washington, were fighting to liberate their country from its colonial oppressor. The Continental Army contained few men of skill in the military arts; its motivating spirit was its patriotism and desire for freedom and liberty. And, the Red Coats were coming. Organized, disciplined, with generals educated in the martial arts, they were ready to put down American aspirations for independence.

The Continental Congress understood the problem created by a lack of trained military specialists, so when Kościuszko arrived and offered his services, it offered him a commission in the army with the rank of colonel. His military credentials were excellent. He had graduated from the top military academy in Warsaw with a specialization in building fortifications. Afterwards, he completed four years of training and study in France. Kościuszko was a professional soldier who came to America's help just at the right time. His greatest achievement was the fortification of West Point, which, if captured by the British, would have given them full access to the Hudson Valley and would have put the outcome of the revolution in doubt. By succeeding in building proper defenses and fortifications, West Point was saved. According to Lt. General Howard D. Graves, Ex-Superintendent of The United States Military Academy at West

11

Point, every cadet in the Academy learns who and what Tadeusz Kościuszko was.

On the Polish side, Kościuszko had to use his other skills. Leadership was required to lead a "Peasant Army" in combat. Fighting with scythes and pitchforks, supported only with their courage and patriotism, Kościuszko led a force that, benefiting from his leadership, achieved the famous victory at Racławice—a small village north of Kraków which today tourists can easily reach by car.

Unfortunately, blood and courage were insufficient and, at Maciejowice, his army was defeated and he was captured by the Russians. Czarina Katherine the Great had him imprisoned in St. Petersburg, but later released him—all to the ultimate benefit of the United States.

Today, two bridges in the United States are appropriately named after him. Since Kościuszko bridged the Atlantic, naming bridges is a befitting memorial. There are also monuments erected to him—including the one at West Point overlooking the Hudson.

Perhaps the most fitting monument, however, is The Kościuszko Foundation, a non-profit educational institution located at 15 East 65th Street in New York City which seeks to maintain cultural and educational ties between the two nations its namesake considered his two homes. Founded in 1925 under the leadership of Stephen Mizwa, the Foundation embarked on an ambitious program of providing scholarships for Polish students to study in the United States and American students to study in Poland. One of its early successes was a grant that made possible publication of *The Trumpeter of Krakow* by Eric Kelly which won the Newberry Medal as the outstanding American literary work for children. During the Second World War it provided assistance to refugee Polish scholars, while after the war it was able to increase its assistance to scholars, host frequent meetings and lectures, initiate a program of artistic and cultural events, and encourage the publication of books dealing with Polish and Polish American history and culture. Today, true to the ideals of the Pole who placed so much value on education, the Foundation maintains a strong scholarship and publication program, as well as supporting other cultural events and scholarly research.

It is appropriate and very useful, at this time, that a biography by Professor James S. Pula is published. As I share in Dr. Pula's work, together with other Trustees of the Polish Institute of Arts and Science of America, I am proud to introduce his biography which appropriately deals more extensively with the American accomplishments of Kościuszko, and which will permit the reader to learn and evaluate what he did for this country. I also hope that the reader will appreciate the historical importance of a man whom Thomas Jefferson labeled the true "son of liberty." As ex-Polish President Lech Wałęsa remarked: "Kościuszko understood freedom as complete, not only from the outside oppressor, but also from internal tyranny." In this spirit, upon leaving liberated America, Kościuszko left his remaining fortune to help emancipate the slaves so that everyone in this beautiful country could enjoy its full freedoms.

Michael G. Sendzimir
Honorary Chairman of
The Kościuszko Foundation

Chapter 1

"I and My Nation Are One"

*C*reaking timbers proved a sharp contrast to the gentle breeze filling the canvas sails as the small ship moved slowly toward the vague outline on the horizon. Gradually, with a slow steadiness that almost seemed to defy time, the distant shape took form. Hills emerged, then trees and beaches. The traveler's first view of the unfamiliar land may have caused him to reflect on the dangerous new adventure he was about to undertake in a land whose language, culture, and society were as foreign to him as he was to the inhabitants. He was a Pole, chancing the dangerous ocean journey to help a colonial people fight for their freedom against one of the world's greatest military and naval powers. With him he brought little save his education and the traditions of his own land. "I and my nation are one," wrote Adam Mickiewicz, one of the greatest poets of the traveler's homeland. And so it was that the young man had imbued in him as immutably as his very character the traditions of his native land. These prepared him well, for the history of his homeland was a history of struggle against foreign control, the development of a heterogenous society, and the movement toward internal political reform, the same values motivating the rebellion he was about to enter.

An ancient land, Poland lies along the vast Central European plain bordered on the north by the Baltic Sea and on the south by the Carpathian Mountains. At various times during its long history it has stretched from the Oder and Neisse Rivers in the west to the gates of Moscow in the east and Turkey in the south. In ancient times the area was populated by a group of agricultural tribes ranging from western Asia to the banks of the Elbe River in modern Germany.[1] The Polish people are generally considered to be descended from the

Polanie, a branch of the Slavs that inhabited the upper Warta River region, whose name is thought to derive from the word *pole* meaning "field," probably a reference to the fact that the tribe lived in the plains area as an agricultural society. Legend has it that Lech, a ruler of the Polanie tribe, formed the first "Polish" government at Gniezno when he found an eagle's nest on that spot and determined it would be a good place for his people to settle.

The Poles first formed a modern nation state in 966 when Mieszko I united six Western Slavic tribes located in a region centered on the Vistula River and agreed to accept Christianity as a means of protecting his people from the relentless invasions of his German neighbors, launched on the pretext of converting the "pagans" to Christianity. To the Germans, however, the conversion meant little and Mieszko spent much of his reign resisting their aggression, trying to unite the various tribes, and clearly defining and stabilizing the borders of the Polish state.[2] From that time on, the nation struggled to maintain its independence.

Wars against the aggressive Teutonic Knights, bent upon spreading German overlordship to Polish lands, continued almost unabated from the time of Bolesław Chrobry [the Brave], who came to power in 992, until the crushing defeat of the Teutonic Order by a Polish-Lithuanian force under King Władysław Jagiełło at Grünwald in 1410 ended the early Germanic *Drang nach Osten* [Drive to the East].[3] During the thirteenth century further pressure against Polish borders came with the beginning of the Mongol invasion in the southeast, while intermittent border and dynastic conflicts with Russia flared frequently during the succeeding centuries. The sixteenth century brought invasion by the Turks from the south, while the seventeenth century was fraught with destructive wars against Sweden, Russia, and the Ottoman Empire, as well as a major uprising against Polish control in the Ukraine led by the Cossack Hetman Bogdan Khmelnitsky. To any educated Pole, the nation's struggles against these incursions, depicted in literature, poetry, and art, formed a basis for patriotism and national pride, as well as empathy for other peoples seeking to gain or protect their own independence.

Another characteristic of Polish life was the multi-national, multi-religious nature of the state. Although Poland was placed under the protection of the Holy See as early as the reign of Mieczko I, and has remained largely a Roman Catholic nation ever since, it also has a long-standing tradition of religious toleration. As early as the eleventh century large groups of Jewish refugees migrated to Poland to escape persecution by the Crusaders in Germany. In 1264 Jews were specifically granted civil rights. As a result, according to Oskar Halecki, Jewish refugees began to settle in Poland "in rapidly growing numbers, thus escaping from persecution in the Western countries."[4]

Other religious accommodations followed. In 1569 the Union of Lublin guaranteed equality for the Orthodox ecclesiastical hierarchy. Later, following the advent of the Reformation, while religious warfare tore Europe asunder the liberal religious and ethnic policies of the Polish-Lithuanian Commonwealth caused it to become a haven for minorities, a society that included many different national, religious, and cultural groups: Byelorussians, Ukrainians, Ruthenians, Slovaks, Latvians, Germans, Moslem Tartars, Jews, Armenians, Greeks, Italians, Scots, Uniates, Orthodox, Protestants, and others who sought religious freedom and the right to practice their own native culture.[5] During the wars of the Reformation and Counter-Reformation, Poland emerged as the most tolerant nation on the continent. Lutheranism gained headway among the burghers in the cities, while gentry and magnate converts usually leaned toward Calvinism. Another popular movement in some circles was the Polish Brethren, known also as the Socnians, who promoted a belief in social equity.[6] Unlike Western Europe, the political and religious contests of Poland were conducted without ruinous civil wars or mass persecutions and inquisitorial murder. In 1573 religious toleration became a legal requirement of the nation in the Warsaw Confederation, the first document in European history to include religious freedom as a legal guarantee.[7] Thus, by the time King Zygmunt II August was called upon to demand religious conformity within his realms the king could, with legal and popular support, refuse, stating "I am the king of the people, not the judge of their consciences." Throughout this period, the Polish-Lithuanian government proved very liberal for its time by granting equal civil and religious rights to all religious and national minorities as long as they maintained their allegiance to the crown, a principle both well-established and well-known by the time our protagonist made his appearance in eighteenth century Poland.[8]

The third major theme in Polish history the traveler brought with him was a tradition of political liberalism. From its inception, the Polish state moved increasingly toward reform that limited royal power and increased the influence of the magnates and gentry, a course that may have begun with the traditional right of participation accorded members of the tribal societies existing prior to Mieszko's conversion. In Polish society the *szlachta* or gentry class was not an "aristocracy" in the western European sense of exclusivity. Rather, anyone could be ennobled for particular deeds or contributions, and there were even instances where entire villages were ennobled for some special joint act. Thus, the gentry, which numbered as much as ten percent of the population by the end of the fifteenth century, contained, in addition to the magnates who held vast amounts of land, families of humbler means including some descended from knights, burghers, or even peasant families. Some had major landholdings, while the acreage of others was modest and some were landless, living an existence little better than the bulk of the peasantry. Despite one's economic status, within the gentry there was a remarkable degree of equity of rights and privileges that were jealously guarded by each member of the class.[9]

As early as the fourteenth century the Polish monarchy began losing internal power to the magnates. The gentry increasingly exercising its independence with the result that as western Europe moved toward absolutism, Poland moved toward an elective monarchy and guaranteed gentry rights and privileges which they exercised through collective action in the *Sejm* [Parliament]. While government by the gentry may not appear particularly democratic to modern Americans, compared to its contemporary European neighbors the Polish system was indeed liberal for, as James Miller concluded, "despite this hierarchical stratification, participation in national political affairs was still more broadly based in Poland than in any other early modern country (except Sweden)."[10]

In 1374 the Charter of Košice granted the *szlachta* extensive political liberties including the provision that the king could not levy taxes without their consent. According to Oskar Halecki, this legally established "the privileged position of the *szlachta*, which had been developing throughout the preceding centuries" and was thus "the origin of parliamentary government." By the end of that century the first national elected assemblies were meeting.[11] A law passed by the *Sejm* [Parliament] in 1425 guaranteed personal liberty to all citizens, and in 1430 further legislation guaranteed the state could not imprison citizens without a lawful verdict of the courts. This Polish statute was an early statement of the principle of *habeas corpus*, a major legal tenet that was lacking even in the celebrated British parliamentary democracy. In fact, some 350 years later the failure of the British system to provide this protection was one of the causes which led to the American Revolution.

In 1454 the Statute of Nieszawa, sometimes called the Magna Carta of Poland, limited the power of magnates and gave the *szlachta* extensive privileges. Among its provisions, no laws could be enacted, or wars declared, without the consent of the gentry, provisions that greatly strengthened parliamentary government while limiting royal authority.[12] Additionally, the *Nihil Novi* decree issued at the Convention of Radom in 1505 made the *Sejm* the nation's supreme legislative body, rendered the king powerless to legislate or raise taxes without its consent, and provided for the election of the members of the Lower House at district councils.[13] Indeed, Poland established at an earlier date than in any western European nation the principle that no important decision could be made without the approval of the *Sejm*. Such guarantees, along with its cultural and intellectual development, were largely responsible for the sixteenth century being considered Poland's "Golden Age."[14]

Under the *Pacta Conventa* of 1574, all Polish citizens were given the legal right to withdraw their allegiance from the king if he broke any law passed by parliament or the specific conditions of his election.[15] Though certainly not "democratic" in the contemporary sense, this was, by sixteenth century standards, a unique democratic reform. In the same century, Andrzej Frycz Modrzewski's *De republica emendanda* [On Improving the Republic], a seminal work of political, social and educational reform, argued the right of all citizens, including the downtrodden peasantry, to equality of treatment under law. These, and other poets, literary figures, scientists, and political philosophers tested the validity of old assumptions and stretched the limits of knowledge.[16]

The principle of an elective monarchy was likewise firmly entrenched in Poland at an early date, with the first general election of the king by all of the *szlachta* taking place in 1573. Polish kings were thenceforth elected democratically by the *szlachta*. Thus, the Polish throne was not hereditary as in western Europe; rather, over the course of time Swedes, Saxons, French and others sat on the Polish throne through open election.[17] "Whatever its flaws," concluded historian M. B. Biskupski, "gentry democracy bequeathed to subsequent generations of political speculation deeply ingrained notions of parliamentary participation in public affairs, limitations of executive authority, the rule of law, freedom of speech and conscience, the rights of the individual *vis-á-vis* the state, and perhaps most profoundly, the essential disposition to believe that the state exists to serve the nation and not the inverse."[18]

During the seventeenth century, the writings of Polish philosophers and political theorists began to appear in western Europe. One of these was Wawrzyniec Goślicki, Bishop of Poznań, who published a book titled *De Optimo Senatore* in Venice in 1568. In this, Goślicki espoused the limitation of royal authority, equality of opportunity based upon merit, and freedom of religious worship. At a time when the divine right of kings and religious *in*tolerance were commonplace in western Europe, this book was considered extremely radical. In fact, when it was translated into English as *The Counsellor* in 1598, Elizabeth Tudor ordered all copies destroyed.

Despite the growth of liberalism and tolerance in Poland, the middle of the seventeenth century was fraught with destructive wars. Unable to respond quickly or effectively, the Sejm soon found itself in the midst of a major political crisis. During the lengthy debates in the legislative body, Władysław Siciński voted against extending the session of the Sejm beyond its legal limit to continue the debate. Supported by those who feared resurgence of absolute monarchy if the sovereign were able to rule by influencing the votes of a simple majority, this act, and the attending debate which affirmed the principle of unanimity of decision, firmly established in the Polish political system the *liberum veto*, the constitutional principle that a single negative vote could veto any positive decision.[19] Of the next 55 Sejms, 48 were dissolved by exercise of the *liberum veto*. King Jan Kazimierz, in trying to convince the Sejm to rescind the *liberum veto*, made a remarkably clairvoyant prediction: "Would God I may prove a false prophet! But I tell you that if you do not find a remedy for the present evil the republic will become the prey of foreign countries." In practice, as Robert I. Frost explained, "The *liberum veto* proved to be a useful tool in the hands of foreign ambassadors anxious to block the influence of their rivals or to prevent the restoration of political health to the Commonwealth, potentially so powerful. Consequently, the *Sejm* was paralyzed more and more frequently."[20]

Under Jan III Sobieski, elected king in 1674, the Poles rallied from the disastrous series of wars to defeat the Turks at Lwów in 1675. Regrouping, the Turks next launched a massive invasion of Europe aimed at the strategic city of Vienna deep in the Austrian Empire. Perhaps the crowning achievement of Polish arms occurred in 1683 when a joint European army under the command of King Sobieski inflicted a decisive defeat on the Turkish force besieging Vienna, thereby solidifying in the minds of Poles the claim to be the bulwark of Christianity.[21]

Despite the victory at Vienna, the *liberum veto* left Poland politically weak and the Great Northern War of 1700-1721 devastated much of Poland's territory. During the conflict, King August II of Saxony, who had gained election with the support of Czar Peter the Great, was deposed in favor of Stanisław Leszczyński who was related by marriage to Louis XV of France and supported as the candidate of Charles XII of Sweden. The Russians, however, allied themselves with the Austrians to support their candidate's return. To effect his "election," Russian troops invaded and drove Leszczyński into exile. With the death of August II, the nobles once again elected Stanisław Leszczyński as king, but Russia and Austria intervened on behalf of August's heir, August III. France, unwilling to see its influence in Polish affairs thus diminished, allied itself with Spain and declared war, igniting a general European conflict known as the War of Polish Succession (1733-1735). Although most of the war was fought outside Poland, the ruinous discord and the weakness of the Saxon kings left the nation politically and economically weak, its administrative, financial, and legal systems in chaos.[22]

August III, in particular, proved a very weak monarch who spent little time in Poland, allowing the Russians to increase their influence dramatically. In the face of this foreign control, two reform parties emerged after 1740. The Czartoryski group, known as "The Family," sought Russian, and occasionally Prussian, support for strengthening the king's power by eliminating the *liberum veto* and through other reforms. The "Republican" group, led by the Potocki and Radziwiłł families, sought French support to establish a strong aristocratic constitution limiting royal authority.[23] Thus, by 1746 Poland enjoyed an historical tradition already centuries old, a tradition of ethnic and religious diversity, of limiting the absolute power of monarchs while vigorously defending its lands from foreign invasion and Christianity from the threats to Mongols, Tartars, and Moslems. Yet, politically divided and beset from outside, Poland now languished in a state of political decay.[24] The once-powerful nation found itself mired in the muck of internal dissention and anarchy, its resources and liberties bled by its stronger neighbors to the extent where it had become a virtual Russian satellite state. It this depressing atmosphere of national humiliation, the youthful ocean traveler entered the world.

Born February 12, 1746, Andrzej Tadeusz Bonawentura Kościuszko was the son of Ludwik Tadeusz and Tekla Ratomska Kościuszko, the youngest of four children who included two sisters and a brother. Though some doubt exists, he was probably born in a wooden, thatched-roof house in Mereczówszczyźna, a small town in the province of Polesie. Located near Brześć-Litewski in the palatinate of Nowogródek, the rural village was situated in the great loop of the Niemen River north of the Pripet Marshes.[25]

In the long pantheon of Polish national history, the Kościuszko family was of relatively undistinguished minor *szlachta* status. Of Lithuanian-Ruthenian lineage, the first mention of the family in Polish annals was when Zygmunt I awarded Konstanty [Konstantine] a Polish coat-of-arms and the estate at Siechnowicze in 1509. At the time, Konstanty adopted "Kościuszko," the diminutive of Kost, the original Ruthenian spelling of his name, along with that of his estate, Siechnowicki, as his family name.[26] Most of the family's ancestors were minor landholders whom historian Mieczysław Haiman characterized as "not very active in public affairs, living in the sphere of their homes and immediate vicinity, but keeping strictly to old Polish virtues and customs."[27] Szymon Askenazy maintains the family was originally Orthodox in faith, with a Calvinist appearing during the Reformation, but by the mid-seventeenth century it had been thoroughly Polonized through marriage and cultural assimilation and counted none but Roman Catholics for more than a century. Only a few family members appear to have achieved political office, Tadeusz's great-grandfather holding appointment as a minor court official and his grandfather rising to district *skryba* [scribe] and *Podczaszy* [Cupbearer]. Titles of some importance during the Middle Ages, by the time they were bestowed on Kościuszko's ancestors the status of the former was reduced to a minor official and the latter had become largely an honorary appellation.[28]

By the time Kościuszko's father, Ludwik Tadeusz, became head of the family its financial status was greatly reduced. Regardless, he appears to have been popular and well-connected within the confines of the Słonim district, and was even known regionally within the Palatinate of Brześć as an active member of the district council and an honorable gentleman. A colonel of the Lithuanian Field Regiment, he held the title *Miecznik* [Swordbearer] of Brześć, once signifying a court official who carried the ceremonial sword before the king on important occasions but by the time it was bestowed on Ludwik it was largely an honorary title given to district-level officials. Given the poor circumstances of the family, no doubt much of Ludwik's local success resulted from his connection, however tenuous, to one of the most respected and powerful of the great magnate families. The lands Ludwik cultivated were part of the estates under the overlordship of Count Fleming, a relative of the Czartoryski family.[29]

Ludwik died in 1758, leaving behind a widow and four children. At the time, Tadeusz was twelve years old and had been, as was the custom of the day, kept at home to be educated for the first nine years of his life.[30] Generally regarded, according to George H. Bushnell, as "a woman of character, energy, and some education," Tekla Ratomska Kościuszko oversaw the education of the family's children, inculcating in them both a respect for the history and culture of the nation and for education itself. In this she was ably assisted by an elderly uncle who introduced the young boy to drawing, mathematics, and French.[31]

In 1755, at the age of nine, Tekla sent young Tadeusz to continue his formal education at the college operated by the Piarist Fathers at Lubieszów, near Pińsk. It was an institution to which, according to Bogdan Grzeloński, "few of the reforms and advances of the Enlightenment had as yet filtered down."[32] There he studied Polish, French, Latin, natural philosophy, history, mathematics, Geometry, trigonometry, drawing, and possibly German. As a student, he is said to have displayed little talent, and possibly been forced to repeat a year. Regardless, in addition to a sound fundamental education, Kościuszko gained from these years an historical context for the values he learned from his mother and his family while growing up. Evidence of this can be seen in his childhood attachment to an historical hero whom he used as a role model for the rest of his life. The figure was Timoleon the Corinthian. From a biography by Cornelius Nepos, Kościuszko learned that Timoleon had freed his native land from tyrannical oppression and then fought for the freedom of Syracuse, scenarios the young Pole could not help but equate with the plight of Poland during his formative years.[33]

Kościuszko returned home at the age of fourteen in 1760. There he remained for the next five years, engaging in further study and helping his mother operate the family estate. During that time, important events were taking place in Poland. Even before the death of King August III in 1763, political maneuvering was rampant to influence the choice of a successor. Russia, on the pretext of concern for Poland's Orthodox minority, claimed the right to a voice in the selection. Likewise, France sought to place August's son on the throne lest the solidification of Russian influence in Poland upset French foreign policy aspirations in Eastern Europe. In Prussia, Frederick II, chafed about Polish rule over the Germans in West Prussia, feared any reform that might lead to strengthening of the Polish state. His military and political power greatly reduced by the costs of the recently completed Seven Years War, he sought alliance with Catherine II and was willing to support the Russian nominee in return for her favor. In 1764 he negotiated a secret treaty with Russia in which the two nations agreed to cooperate in opposing any changes in the Polish constitution on the grounds that the *status quo* presented the best opportunity for them to control internal Polish politics. Any increase in the royal power might allow Poland to once again regain her past political and military stature as an East European power.[34]

Within Poland, the three most influential magnate families were the Radziwiłłs, Potockis, and Czartoryskis. Of the three, the Potockis and Radziwiłłs supported the *liberum veto* as a means of preventing development of a strong central government that might limit the gentry's powers and prerogatives. The Czartoryskis, related to the ancient Jagiełło family and the most powerful of the three, opposed the *liberum veto* on the grounds that its use made effective government impossible. To overcome Czartoryski opposition, and thus remove the most important internal Polish obstacle to Russo-Prussian influence, the Russian czarina promised to ease use of the *liberum veto* once political stability was restored and to nominate one of the magnate family's own as her choice for the Polish throne. To further insure success, Catherine II liberally distributed rubles to members of the Polish *Sejm* and, in the event this persuasion failed to have the desired effect, she moved a Russian army to within three miles of the building where the senators met to elect the new king. The methods were convincing. On September 7, 1764, the *Sejm* elected Stanisław August Poniatowski, nephew of the magnate Prince Michał Fryderyk Czartoryski, King of Poland.[35]

Although the new king and his supporters in the Czartoryski camp attempted to promote reforms, Russia proved unwilling to entertain any serious proposals that might strengthen the Polish state. Convinced that little progress could be made in rejuvenating the nation until its internal weaknesses were corrected, one of Poniatowski's first significant acts as king was to create a new Royal Military Academy which opened in Warsaw in 1765. Founded on the model of the *Collegium Nobilium* as "a boarding school for young noblemen," it marked the beginning of the reform of the Polish educational system.[36] One of the chief organizers of the venture was Prince Adam Kazimierz Czartoryski whose influence on the curriculum and subsequent appointment as the new school's commandant were ample evidence of the institution's patriotic intent. An advocate of educational reform, Czartoryski was a devotee of the Enlightenment and a patron of the arts who sought to implant the liberalism of each through the new courses of study. From its earliest years it became known as what Stephen Mizwa described as "a school of patriotism" that "offered a general liberal education."[37] Yet, its primary purposes, according to Bogdan Grzeloński were to educate "a new corps of officers" and "to produce enlightened public leaders."[38]

The first class of cadets entered the new academy, popularly known as the "Knight's School," in 1765. Among them was nineteen-year-old Tadeusz Kościuszko, admitted in 79th place of the 80-man initial class on December 18. No doubt the appointment of the otherwise undistinguished cadet was due to his family's association with the Czartoryskis, and the recommendation of a close family acquaintance, the prominent local magnate Józef Sosnowski.[39] Once enrolled, the cadet studied under the tutelage of Prince Czartoryski and the other founding faculty, excelling in geometry and drawing courses as part of his specialization in military engineering and fortification. Among the required courses of study was English, no doubt because of the king's lengthy visits to England and his affinity for that island nation. But, in keeping with the liberal curriculum, he also read widely in the fields of history, philosophy, ethics, and mathematics, including a Polish translation of Juvenel de Carlancas' influential history of the liberal arts and sciences. A foreword to this volume by Prince Czartoryski is very revealing of his intent for the cadets, and portrays a destiny not unlike that of Kościuszko's boyhood hero, Timoleon: "He, whom the chance of birth and fortune has chosen for active civic duties, should strive to perfect himself in such knowledge.... You, who now find your Homeland in the most lamentable state conceivable, should populate it with citizens ardent for its glory, for increasing its internal vigor and its international prestige, for improving its government, which is of the worst possible kind.... May you, the new generation, change the old form of your country."[40]

Kościuszko reportedly did well in his studies, graduating as one of the foremost scholars in his class and thus attracting the attention of both Prince Czartoryski and King Poniatowski. Commissioned a second lieutenant, he was assigned as an instructor on the faculty of the academy and remained in this position until 1768. In that year, the instructor's life was torn asunder by the death of his beloved mother. In keeping with the traditions of the day, the family estate went to Józef, Tadeusz's elder brother, while the young officer received a cash settlement as his portion of the inheritance.[41]

In the same year as his mother's death, political developments in Poland reached dangerous proportions. Although Poniatowski was recognized as king, Russian troops had to be stationed in Poland to guarantee his safety and allegiance to Catherine, and Frederick continued intriguing for Prussian influence and expansion by supporting retention of the *liberum veto*, opposing creation of a Polish national army, and trying to foment religious discord between Catholics and the religious minorities in Poland. In the face of this increasing pressure, Poland continued to be torn by internal factionalism with the Potockis promoting independence over reform and arguing for a strong nobility to restrict royal power while the Czartoryskis sought reform first in the belief that Poland was too weak to contend openly against Russia. Indeed, the Czartoryskis were soon proven correct. When religious differences became strained through Prussian intrigues, Protestants formed a confederacy at Toruń, while nobles opposed to political reforms that would limit the *liberum veto* did the same at Radom. Faced with these threats, Russia sent 80,000 troops to the Polish border and a smaller force to occupy Warsaw itself. The Russians arrested Catholic opposition leaders, including several bishops, and threatened further interventions if attempts at reform continued. As a result, in February the *Sejm* acquiesced to threats of war and signed a treaty that acknowledged Russia as Poland's protector. Thus Russia successfully foiled Prussia's attempt to force a partition and emerged as the dominant influence in Poland.[42]

Increasing dissatisfaction with Russian influence in Polish affairs resulted in the formation of a revolutionary group, supported by France, in the town of Bar on the Dniester River in the Podolia region of the Polish Ukraine. Led by Bishop Adam Krasiński and Count Józef Pułaski, the Confederation of Bar rose in open revolt against Russia, with Turkey and Austria covertly supplying the insurgents with arms and other support. Eventually, Russian troops drove the Confederates across the Turkish border, burning a Turkish village in the process. As a result of this incursion, Turkey declared war on Russia in 1768, demanding Russian evacuation of Poland. In February 1769 Frederick II, sensing in the conflict an opportunity to expand the influence of Prussia, proposed to Russia that the two powers partition the weakened Polish state. Russia agreed to give Frederick the Polish corridor if he would aid the Russians in their war against Turkey. Frederick, however, wanted more, and France, fearing the growth of Prussian influence in Eastern Europe, suggested to Austria that it should seize Polish territory along the Hungarian border. This the Austrians did in April 1769. The following year, the Turks, ostensibly at war to protect Poland, suggested to Austria that the two dismember the country between themselves. In the midst of all this international intrigue, the Confederates continued their unequal struggle for four long years.[43]

While the revolutionaries battled the forces of oppression, King Poniatowski offered Kościuszko one of four royal scholarships to continue his studies at the engineering schools in France. Though lacking funds for his travel and upkeep, this problem was solved by his long-time patron, Prince Czartoryski, who provided a stipend for Kościuszko's upkeep. Many writers have speculated why a person with such obvious concern for his country, a person who so admired Timoleon and his struggle for the freedom of his native land, a person with valuable military training and expertise, could leave his nation in the midst of a rebellion against foreign rule. Yet the answer appears simple. Because he gained office largely through Russian support, the king was as much a target of the revolution as were the Russians. Although Poniatowski considered joining the Confederates, radicals in the revolutionary movement called for his deposition or execution, precluding any chance for royal support. Because of this, Poniatowski's supporters in the Czartoryski family were not supportive of the revolt which they perceived as both a threat to their plans and a hopeless enterprise in any event. As a long-time beneficiary of the Czartoryskis and now indebted to the king for his patronage, Kościuszko could hardly be expected to suddenly change his allegiance in favor of a small movement with little chance of success.[44]

Promoted to captain of artillery, Kościuszko left for France in mid-1769, accompanied by Captain Józef Orłowski, another recipient of a king's scholarship. In Paris he enrolled in the famous Académie Royale de Peinture et de Sculpture where his studies are chronicled by dozens of surviving sketches, portraits, landscapes, and caricatures. As a foreigner, he could not enroll in the prestigious French military school at Méziéres or in the École Militaire in Paris, so he engaged faculty for private instruction in mathematics, military engineering, and artillery, studies that greatly advanced the elementary knowledge he gained at the Knights' School in Warsaw.[45] In addition to these practical military arts, he studied French literature, philosophy, history, and physiocratic economics. "During the five years of my life spent in foreign countries," the Pole later wrote, "I have endeavored to master those arts which pertain to a solid government, aiming at the happiness of all, also economics and military art; I earnestly tried to learn this inasmuch as I had a natural passion for these things."[46]

From Paris, Kościuszko visited Switzerland, and perhaps Italy as well, while taking advantage of the vibrant atmosphere of the Parisian Enlightenment to broaden both his circle of acquaintances and his intellect. Influenced by the famous engineer Perronet and the economist Turgot, he also found in Rousseau a liberalism that, tempered by the experiences of his youth in Poland, appealed to his own intellectual philosophy.[47] Already imbued with ideals of patriotism and loyalty, Józef Żuraw has shown that in Paris Kościuszko came under the influence of Deism and the thoughts of F. Quesnay that greatly effected his personal philosophy and world view.[48]

According to Żuraw, the underlying philosophy of the Enlightenment was Deism, an attempt to reconcile religious belief with the emerging rationalism of modern scientific and political thought. "According to deism," Żuraw explains, "God's interference is limited to the creation of the world and equipping it with the ability of autonomous development," a natural religious philosophy that "put emphasis on man's self-dependent effort to define the contents of faith."[49] Under this concept, the political philosophy of the Enlightenment envisioned a nation state including nobility, burghers, and peasantry living in harmony and justice. This fit well with Quesnay's theories of economics, which were in great vogue during the five years Kościuszko spent in Paris and in time formed "the basis of physiocratism in Poland."[50] Indeed, the coalescence of Deism and

Quesnay's economics reinforced in Kościuszko the egalitarian idea that the peasantry should be treated with the same respect accorded other human beings, a belief that would come to fruition later in his life.

Kościuszko also retained a strong belief in God. In a memorandum to Prince Adam Kazimierz Czartoryski he later wrote: "This immense universe—filled with an infinite number of stars and our hearts seeking refuge in unhappiness speak for the existence of the Supreme Being. We do not understand it but we feel it everywhere and we all have to worship it."[51] Thus, unlike the rationalism of Voltaire, Kościuszko relied upon emotion to prove the existence of God. Kościuszko, adopting the Deistic view, "claimed that God did not interfere in the life of *homo sapiens*. ... In his opinion the will of God is identical with character, justice and the humanistic conduct of man."[52]

Further, the liberal ideals of the Enlightenment fostered within Kościuszko his own sense that it was not sufficient to engage in philosophical debates, one must act upon one's beliefs. "Philosophy leads to a good understanding of politics, economics and ethics," the Pole later wrote, and philosophers should actively fight "against ignorance, injustice and the inequality of societies and nations."[53]

While his ideas developed and matured in the intellectual world of Paris, his homeland continued to suffer under the influence of its stronger neighbors. Following a series of Russian victories against the Turks, the growing concern of other European powers that Russia might become too powerful engendered fears of a general European war. To prevent this, the major Central European powers—Austria, Prussia and Russia—combined to partition Poland in 1772. Under this agreement, Poland lost about one third of its territory and almost half of its population. The Austrians received 27,000 square miles of land and 2,700,000 people in Galicia and the surrounding areas, Russia took 36,000 square miles and 1,800,000 people up to the Dniva and Dnieper Rivers, and Prussia claimed 13,000 square miles and 416,000 people along the Baltic coast. Each of the partitioning nations sent troops to occupy its portion of the spoils. Too weak to oppose the partition itself, Poniatowski's government appealed to England and France for assistance, but they declined to intervene seeing the partition as the only realistic alternative to Russian hegemony over all of Poland.[54]

With the consummation of the partition, Poniatowski was placed in a position of choosing between Russia and Prussia as a protector for the remnant of the dismembered nation. He chose Russia, which was only too eager to offer guarantees to preclude further Prussian acquisitions. As part of the arrangement, a new constitution, eventually ratified in 1775, provided for an elective monarchy, retention of the *liberum veto*, an increase in royal power, the creation of an executive council, and the establishment of a small national army of 18,000.[55]

For Kościuszko, as for many, the partition brought great financial difficulties. His portion of the family's inheritance had been small, and with the partition the king's stipend ceased. With the continued support of the Czartoryski's however, he managed to continue his education for another two years, including the study of fortifications in the French seacoast city of Brest. Not until the summer of 1774 did he leave Paris for home. There the young man found conditions in his homeland worst than he imagined.[56]

At home, his brother Józef proved to be a poor manager of the family estates, some Polish historians suggesting malfeasance that cost Kościuszko part of his rightful inheritance. Whatever the truth, by 1774 the family estate was on the verge of bankruptcy and the reduction in the Polish military and civil hierarchies occasioned by the new constitution left Kościuszko with little prospect of advancement. Under the circumstances, the homecoming was probably tense and Bushnell suggests the two brothers quarreled over the estate's finances.[57] Consequently, Kościuszko resided with his relatives, spending most of his time with his sister Anna and her husband, Piotr Estko, on their estate near Kobryń. "He wanted to serve his country and plunge into the work of reform which was to safeguard the state against total catastrophe," explained Grzeloński. "But opportunities for employment in government service were few and far between. There were no commissions to be had in the Corps of Cadets, nor in the army. He was forced to return to the family estate of Siechnowicze which his brother had encumbered with debts, and in fact to live with his sisters or friends."[58]

To support himself during this period of national prostration and personal turmoil, Kościuszko took a position teaching drawing and mathematics to the daughters of Józef Sosnowski. A future Field Hetman of the Grand Duchy of Lithuania, Sosnowski was then a powerful provincial governor and the scion of a magnate family that resided at a magnificent estate in Sosnowica. It is uncertain just how long Kościuszko spent at Sosnowski's estate, but it was long enough for him to fall in love with the magnate's youngest daughter, eighteen-year-old Ludwika. The feelings of attraction were apparently mutual, but the governor refused permission for his daughter to be betrothed to someone of Kościuszko's lowly stature. "Ringdoves are not for sparrows," he is supposed to have quipped, "and the daughters of magnates are not for sons of the *szlachta*." Lacking the sanction of Ludwika's father, the two lovers apparently planned to elope, but were discovered before it could be effected, the unwanted suitor attacked, wounded, and driven from the estate. To be sure that nothing further would come of the attraction, Sosnowski sent his daughter away to reside beyond the reach of the young captain. She would later marry one of Poland's great magnates, Prince Józef Lubomirski, thereby fulfilling her father's wish for socially and politically prominent connections.[59]

Stung and depressed by the loss of his love, his personal finances greatly distressed, his relationship with his brother strained, and with little prospect of advancement in a nation held hostage by its stronger neighbors, Kościuszko made the difficult decision to once again leave his homeland. On October 9, 1775, he signed a document giving Piotr Estko power of attorney to act in his stead in all matters, and the following day, using his portion of the estate at Siechnowicze as collateral, he borrowed 8,820 *złotys* from his brothers-in-law Piotr Estko and Karol _ólkowski, and another relative named Faustyn Kościuszko. The document acknowledging the debt is signed "Tadeusz Kościuszko Siechnowicki, Kapitan Kor[pus] Kad[etów]." With this, the disaffected young man was free to journey abroad.

Chapter 2

"Colonel of Engineers, Continental Army"

By the time Kościuszko left Poland he was no doubt already familiar with the dispute between England and her American colonies because news of the conflict appeared regularly in the newspaper *Gazeta Warszawska* which was widely read, even beyond the confines of the city. Some authors maintain that Kościuszko traveled by boat down the Vistula River to Gdańsk, taking ship from there to Hamburg. Grzeloński shows that he headed southwest, passing through Dukla in southern Poland, Kraków, and thence on to Dresden. In a letter dated October 19, 1777, Kościuszko requested the support of Jerzy Mniszech, Kastellan of Kraków, in obtaining an appointment in the army of the King of Saxony, but it is clear that whatever his immediate plans he expected to return home and be of service to his fatherland in the future.[1] In the same letter to Mniszech he concludes by expressing his purpose thusly: "My entrance into the Saxon Court has the special aim to be useful sometime in the future to our country and to repay her for the benefits of my citizenship."[2]

Kościuszko apparently spent some time in Dresden, Saxony, where he met Nicolas Dietrich, Baron von Ottendorf, a Saxon noble and veteran of the Seven Years War. Whether Kościuszko made his decision to go to America at this point is unknown, but he and the baron traveled together to France where they apparently met Charles Noël Romand, Sieur de Lisle, a captain in the French artillery, who was to journey with Kościuszko and Ottendorf to the New World.[3] Whether the meeting was accidental, circumstantial, or planned is not known.

Some authors maintain that while in Paris Kościuszko met Benjamin Franklin who convinced him to cast his lot with the North American revolutionaries. There is little likelihood, however, that the Pole met either Franklin or Silas Deane, the American minister to France. Franklin was not in Paris at the same time as Kościuszko, and Deane only arrived in France in mid-June, 1776, and in Paris on July 6. It appears Kościuszko left Paris for America in June. While there is no mention of Kościuszko in either the Franklin or Deane papers, nor is there evidence that the Pole carried any letters of introduction from either of the American emissaries, this cannot be taken as conclusive given the necessary secrecy involved in sending support to the revolutionaries. In fact, while he alluded to sending people to North America, Deane never mentioned *any* specific names.[4] Given the French and Saxon associates whose company Kościuszko enjoyed during his journey west, however, and the fact that France began systematic covert aid to the American revolutionaries the very month he appears to have left for America, it is probable that he was at least surreptitiously aided, if not indeed recruited, by the French to assist the Americans against France's old enemy.

Circumstantial evidence suggests Kościuszko received assistance, and no doubt encouragement, from Pierre Augustin Caron de Beaumarchais. A complex mixture of playwright, composer, merchant, diplomat, and spy, Beaumarchais took an early and sympathetic interest in the American Revolution, becoming increasingly an advocate of the revolutionaries and a conspirator in the clandestine French effort to provide support to their cause. On April 26, 1776, he wrote to Charles Gravier, Comte de Vergennes, the French Foreign Minister, counseling that above all the Americans needed gunpowder and engineers. "Without gunpowder and engineers," he asked, "how can they be victorious, or even defend themselves?"[5] Taking a leading part in developing "private" aid, Beaumarchais pledged in a letter dated May 8 "to make any sum" available to the Americans "through intermediaries by way of Holland." In the same letter, however, he again emphasized the great need of finding a way to get engineers and gunpowder to the revolutionaries.[6]

Kościuszko apparently arrived in Paris soon after Beaumarchais's second letter. As an engineer, and one familiar with the French capitol and language, Kościuszko would have been a prime candidate for the Frenchman's interest and assistance. Further, Kościuszko was a close friend of the Polish Princess Sanguska, wife of the German-French Prince of Nassau-Sieghen. Through the princess, Prince Nassau became a friend of the Czartoryski family, and through him she became a frequent guest of Beaumarchais and an acquaintance of another French supporter of America, the Marquis de Lafayette. Thus it is entirely possible that the prince and princess introduced Kościuszko, either directly or indirectly, to Beaumarchais at exactly the time he was seeking engineers to aid the struggling colonies in North America.[7]

On June 10, 1776, Beaumarchais received a one million livres loan from the French government which he used to found Roderigue Hortalez & Cie, a bogus trading firm designed to serve as a front for his efforts to aid America. Bolstered by a contribution from Spain matching the French loan, and contributions from private sources, two days later Beaumarchais wrote that he planned to send ammunition and powder to "Cap Français." The latter was the primary seaport on the French West Indies island of Saint Dominique (present day Haiti). The first ship left from the French port of Bordeaux. Beaumarchais himself left Paris for that port city on June 16, arriving on the 20th. If indeed Kościuszko was among the first of Beaumarchais's volunteers to sail for America, he may well have met Silas Deane in Bordeaux, the port city where the American emissary landed and spent some time before continuing on to Paris.[8]

Whatever the circumstances, Julian Ursyn Niemciewicz, a sometime travelling companion in later years, paints a stirring, if no doubt greatly romanticized portrait of Kościuszko's departure from Europe.

> New skies, all nature in a different form and the altered fruits of the earth and sea could not hold back a youth yearning to find himself on the field of glory as soon as possible. Heedless of the danger involved, he boarded a tiny fishing boat and sailed out across bottomless seas, but Providence had the noble knight in her care. It was she who calmed the rolling ocean waves and tamed gales so that he, who was to fight for the rights of peoples on both the world's axes, might be preserved for those peoples.[9]

Uncertainty exists about the route Kościuszko took to America and his circumstances when he arrived. Haiman believes the British minister in Paris, Lord Stormont, may have been referring to Ottendorf, and hence to his traveling companions Kościuszko and de Lisle, when he confided the following to the British Secretary of State on March 13, 1776: "I am sorry to say, My Lord, that I have now good Reason to believe that several foreign officers are gone to join the

Rebel army. They go under various Pretences to St. Domingo and from thence find their way to North America. I am almost certain that one officer of Cavalry, a German by Birth, who served in the last war under General Seidlitz, and who is reckoned a Man of distinguished Military Talents went to St. Domingo some Months ago with particular Recommendations to Monsieur d'Ennery."[10] The Comte d'Ennery was at that time the French governor of Saint Dominique, further evidence of the usual route taken by men and supplies destined from France to America, as well as evidence that the British themselves confused Saint Dominique with Santo Domingo. Although the time frame of this letter does not appear to coincide with the Kościuszko group, it is obvious the British took great interest in the movement of trained European soldiers to aid the revolutionaries.

The exact time and place of embarkation remain unknown, but the route through Saint Dominique would allow the men to travel in relative security between then-neutral French-controlled ports to within a short distance of the American coast. This is verified by an account published in a Polish newspaper in 1777 which related that Kościuszko's ship sank in a storm, but all aboard escaped and made it safely to shore from where they continued their journey to America.[11] Regardless of the precise details, when the creaking sailing ship that brought him to America approached its shores for the first time, the vessel brought with it a man whose historical traditions, cultural values, education, and personal experience forged a personality rich in patriotism, support for national self-government, advocacy of political liberty and personal freedom, tolerance for divergent religious and cultural traditions, and a general humanitarianism spanning all classes and varieties of people. He had a strong sense of patriotism forged over centuries of historical tradition and reinforced by the unfortunate situation of Poland he witnessed as he grew to adulthood in a nation that had lost its own political liberty, fostering in him a strong appreciation for the American quest for independence. Further, the Poland of Kościuszko's youth was a multi-cultural state, a nation comprising great cultural, national, and religious diversity. It was in this society of various groups living together under allegiance to a single central government that Kościuszko grew to manhood. This familiarity with the concept of unity in diversity—"E Pluribus Unum" the Americans would call it—was yet another personal experience he could relate to the American determination to preserve a harmonious society tolerant of diversity. Possessing these traits, as well as valuable training as a military engineer, he was well-suited to his imminent role in support of American independence and democracy.

The earliest evidence we have of Kościuszko's arrival in America is his application for a commission read in Congress on August 30, 1776. Neilson, in his history of Burgoyne's campaign in 1777, states that the Pole arrived "utterly unprovided with letters of recommendation or introduction and nearly penniless and offered himself as a volunteer in the American cause and solicited an interview with Washington."[12] If he began his journey with only the money borrowed from his brother-in-law, it is plausible that he reached America's shore with little left to sustain himself. But this is unlikely. It is less likely, given the prevailing conventions of the day, that he came absolutely without references. Another account from Gen. John Armstrong, who served with the Pole during the Revolution and became a close friend, testified: "That he came to this country penniless, cannot be true—as in that case he would have drawn his monthly pay like others; yet to my knowledge, he declined taking more than a ration of bread and meat for himself and provender for his horse during the two campaigns I served with him. All other expenses therefore, to which he was, in common with other officers exposed, [were] paid from his own funds." Armstrong asks "what can be more incredible, than the story of his coming, not only without money, but without a single professional credential or letter of even personal introduction?" Rather, Armstrong maintained, Kościuszko "arrived in this country late in the summer of 1776" and "presented himself and his credentials to the board of war."[13] Polish historian Władysław M. Kozłowski suggests that Kościuszko probably brought with him a recommendation from Prince Czartoryski addressed to Gen. Charles Lee, then second in rank among American generals only to Washington. Lee had journeyed to Poland in 1765 to enter its military forces and had become a close friend and house guest of Prince Czartoryski. After serving as the prince's aide-de-camp, he was eventually appointed major general. Given this connection between the Czartoryski family and both Kościuszko and Lee the possibility of a letter of introduction from the prince looms likely.[14]

Regardless, Kościuszko arrived at a time of great anxiety in North America. Though widely heralded today as the year in which Americans proclaimed their independence in an epoch-making document, 1776 was viewed by contemporaries as a year of disappointment and frustration. The thirteen colonies stood alone against the might of the British Empire. A few colonials lacking finances, industry, equipment, and manpower were daring to challenge one of the world's greatest military and naval powers, a power that only a dozen years before had defeated France, its primary world challenger, and virtually excluded the *fleur-de-lis* from North America. As the year wore on the seeming futility of resistance to English might had begun to become apparent to many colonials. Although a British attempt to capture Charleston, South Carolina, was defeated by a determined defense of Ft. Moultrie, the news elsewhere was hardly heartening. An American invasion of Canada ended in utter disaster with the death of Gen. Richard Montgomery and the decimation of the retreating troops by disease. On the high seas the powerful Royal Navy severely limited the ability of American merchants to trade overseas, placing great strain on the economy and forcing some into bankruptcy. American diplomacy produced not one nation willing to risk an American alliance, or openly extend credit for the purchase of sorely-needed military equipment and supplies. Funds and war materials were running out. Finally, and worst of all, British regulars landed on Long Island, easily swept aside Washington's American army, and established a headquarters in New York City.

Into this atmosphere of defeat and despair stepped, unheralded, the thirty-year-old Polish volunteer who came to Philadelphia to offer his services to the Continental Congress. In spite of his background, and in spite of the fact that America was alone and in desperate need of help, Kościuszko's arrival in Philadelphia did not create any outpouring of gratitude. Indeed, the Continental Congress was not at all anxious to advance a commission to the Polish volunteer. During 1776 a seemingly endless stream of foreign adventurers paraded themselves before Congress in attempts to extricate important military commissions. Accompanied by pompous personalities, lengthy credentials, and flattering letters of reference, most of these early arrivals sought nothing more, nor less, than fame and fortune. They demanded huge sums of money, generalships, independent commands, and several even proffered claims to the office of commanding general. Stung by often resplendent foreigners who proved to be incompetent nuisances, it is no wonder Congress showed no particular interest in an unknown Polish captain of artillery.

Kościuszko's credentials were presented to the Continental Congress on August 30, 1776, only three days after disaster overtook General Washington's troops when they faced a powerful British invasion force under Sir William Howe at the Battle of Long Island. Suffering complete defeat, Washington nevertheless managed to extricate his beaten army from almost certain annihilation by evacuating his men in boats to Manhattan Island under the cover of darkness. The British followed, defeating Washington again at Harlem Heights and White Plains and capturing Fort Washington and Fort Lee which had been designed to guard against British passage up the Hudson River. With these disasters occupying its time, Congress referred Kościuszko's papers to the Board of War. Though he had no inclination toward the selfish motivations of the masses of adventurers who came to American shores, Kościuszko's application for an appointment was filed among the myriad of credentials presented to Congress. The Pole waited patiently, but no offer materialized. It was only through dire necessity that he began his American career.[15]

In the fall of 1776, in the face of military reverses, there was a desperate need to fortify the city of Philadelphia against an anticipated British assault. Engineers were in great demand as General Washington could spare none of the trained personnel serving with his army. With the aid of an American friend, Kościuszko, along with his traveling companion de Lisle, gained employment with the Pennsylvania Committee of Defense to develop plans for fortifying the Delaware River. In this, his first capacity as a professional in America, Kościuszko acted swiftly and skillfully. In a short time he presented his plans for a sprawling fortress on the island of Billingsport in the Delaware River. Though a formidable structure on paper, the plans drew criticism for being too extensive to be manned by the troops assigned to the island. Other officers later scaled the plans down to a size that could be manned by the available troops. On October 24 Kościuszko received £50 for his services in fortifying the Delaware River. Regardless of the controversy over the relative merit of his plans, the works actually constructed under the eyes of the Polish engineer were resilient enough to last well into the twentieth century. Far more important for both Kościuszko and the cause of American independence, the skills exhibited by the engineer at last won him an appointment as colonel of engineers in the Continental Army with a pay of $60 per month dating from October 18, 1776.[16]

While Kościuszko was occupied near Philadelphia, Lord Howe

moved south from New York, forcing Washington's battered army to retreat across New Jersey, closely pursued by the British. The American army crossed the Delaware River into Pennsylvania on December 7, causing sufficient fear in Philadelphia for the Continental Congress to abandon the city and head farther south. In this crisis, Kościuszko worked ceaselessly to complete the defensive works along the river, while Gen. John Armstrong solicited the engineer's expertise to strengthen the overland defenses of the city.[17]

Word of Kościuszko's skill spread quickly, a tribute to the impression the Pole must have made on those around him. By December, 1776, General Washington, complaining bitterly to Congress about the lack of skilled engineers in his army and the ineptitude displayed by many of the French officers who had recently presented themselves as experts in the field of military engineering, sought the assignment of Kościuszko to his command. The general explained that while he had not met Colonel Kościuszko personally, he understood the engineer was a very capable professional and implored Congress to send him north from Philadelphia as soon as possible.[18] On December 3, with his army in retreat before the victorious British forces, Washington, fearing for the safety of Philadelphia, wrote to Gen. Israel Putnam about the need to fortify that city and suggested Kościuszko, whom he mistakenly identified as French, as the "most proper" engineer for the assignment. "Under the Circumstances, the Security of Philadelphia should be our next object. From my own remembrance, but more from Information (for I never viewed the Ground) I should think that a Communication of Lines and Redoubts might soon be formed from the Delaware to Schuylkill on the North entrance of the City. ... If something of this kind is not done, the Enemy might, in case any Misfortune should befall us; march directly in and take possession. ... If the measure of fortifying the city should be adopted, some skillful person should immediately view the grounds, and begin to trace out the lines and works. I am informed there is a French engineer of eminence in Philadelphia at this time; if so, he will be the most proper."[19] To John Hancock, then president of the Continental Congress, Washington wrote on December 20: "none of the French Gentlemen whom I have seen with appointments ... appear to me to know anything of the Matter. There is one in Philadelphia who I am told is clever, but him I have never seen."[20]

Congress, however, was reluctant to part with Kościuszko and Gen. Israel Putnam, then in charge of the defense of Philadelphia, employed the Pole in completing the construction of Ft. Mercer at Red Bank on the New Jersey side of the Delaware River.[21] In their final form, the works at Billingsport and Red Bank were described by Christopher Ward as "a double line of *chevaux-de-frise* that extended from the Jersey shore across the channel to Billings Island. These were crate-like structures made of heavy timbers, loaded with stones and sunk in the water. They were mounted with wooden beams, shod at the upper end with iron points, slanting upwards to within four feet of the surface of the river at low tides and pointing downstream. They were capable of ripping open the bottom of any ship that tried to pass over them. This line was protected by a small redoubt on the Jersey shore. That redoubt, however, was a slight affair, unfinished and lightly held. ... The next obstacle was thirty *chevaux* strung in a triple line from Mud Island, a little below the mouth of the Schuylkill, across the channel to Red Bank on the Jersey side. This line was guarded by a fort at either end."[22]

On December 5 the Continental Congress advanced Kościuszko and his friend de Lisle, who had been appointed major of artillery, two months salary for their work on the fortifications. When the crisis finally subsided with Howe's decision to suspend the campaign due to the onset of winter, Kościuszko continued to work steadily on the various projects under his supervision around Philadelphia. When Putnam left to rejoin Washington's army in February, 1777, his successor, Gen. Horatio Gates, quickly appreciated Kościuszko's talents and became a genuine and close friend of the engineer, factors that were soon to change the Pole's life forever.[23]

Chapter 3

"The Gibraltar of America"

The year 1777 was to be the culmination of British plans for victory in North America. The key to the British plan was the state of New York where many military officers in England believed the colonies could be divided into two parts, separating what they considered to be the seat of the rebellion in New England from the rest of the North American colonies. Governor-General Guy Carleton, the senior British official in Canada, tried to accomplish the first stages of this divide-and-conquer strategy by moving south along the Lake Champlain-Lake George route in 1776, but he found Fort Ticonderoga, at the confluence of these two bodies of water, too strongly held and the autumn season too far advanced to permit a lengthy siege operation. Instead, he returned to Canada to regroup for further action the following year.[1]

Over the winter, Carleton's second-in-command, Gen. John Burgoyne, returned to London. Beginning life in the military by purchasing a commission in the Royal Dragoons, "Gentleman Johnny," as he was known, solidified his financial and political connections by marrying the daughter of the Earl of Derby. By the beginning of the Seven Years' War he was a captain, serving with apparent ability in the campaigns in Portugal. A one-time member of Parliament who was well-known in London's social and gambling circles, by the time the American Revolution began he had risen to the rank of major general. In that capacity he was ordered to America when the crisis arose in Massachusetts.[2]

In his earlier service in Boston, Burgoyne spent much of his time writing reports to friends in England criticizing the moves of his superior officers, Gens. Thomas Gage, William Howe, and Henry

43

Clinton. Following the evacuation of Boston, Burgoyne returned to England, only to be assigned to Canada as a subordinate to Carleton in the spring of 1776. Once back in London after Carleton's abortive campaign, Burgoyne continued his habit of undercutting his superiors, suggesting to the Colonial Secretary, Lord George Germain, the person responsible for the conduct of the war in North America, a move south from Montréal similar to that attempted by Carleton would stand a good chance of success under "a more enterprising commander."[3] The suggestion fell on receptive ears. Lord Germain harbored a bitter hatred of Carleton who had once testified against his lordship when, as an army officer earlier in his career, Germain suffered through a court martial. Sensing an opportunity for revenge, Germain asked Burgoyne to commit his plan to writing with the promise that the Colonial Secretary would submit it to the king for consideration. Himself a frequent riding companion of the monarch that winter, it is little wonder that Burgoyne's plan, submitted on February 28, 1777, in his "Thoughts for Conducting the War from the Side of Canada," gained approval. Promoted to the rank of lieutenant general, Burgoyne received orders to return to Canada to head the movement that promised to vanquish the colonial rebellion.[4] Before leaving for his new assignment, a confident Burgoyne entered a wager in the new betting book at London's exclusive Brooks's Club: "John Burgoyne wagers Charles (James) Fox one pony that he will be home victorious from America by Christmas Day, 1777."[5]

Burgoyne's strategic design called for the movement of two forces into New York, aiming for a juncture at Albany and supported by Gen. William Howe's army in New York City. The plan assumed the Americans would attempt to hold Fort Ticonderoga, located at the strategic confluence of Lake Champlain and Lake George, in force. To cope with this eventuality, Burgoyne's invading army would be strong. In his memorandum composed in London, Burgoyne described his needs as follows: "I humbly conceive the operating army ... ought not to consist of less than 8000 regulars, rank and file. The artillery required in the memorandums of General Carleton, a corps of watermen, 2000 Canadians, including hatchet-men and other workmen, and 1000 or more savages."[6] Another 3,000 troops would be left to hold Canada. Once on the move, the army would establish a base of operations at Crown Point, move south to capture Fort Ticonderoga by mid-summer, then continue south via Lake George and the Hudson River to occupy Albany. From there, Burgoyne would establish contact with Gen. Howe in New York City and determine the best course of action for future cooperation. To support his invasion, mislead the Americans as to his intentions, and force the defenders to divide their forces, Burgoyne proposed to send Lt. Col. Barry St. Leger with 675 troops and a supporting force of Canadians and Indians across Lake Ontario to Oswego, from whence he would invest Fort Stanwix on the Mohawk River, then move east along the waterway to Albany.[7]

Burgoyne arrived in Quebec May 6, 1777, carrying with him a letter from Lord Germain to Governor-General Carleton dated March 26, 1777, announcing Burgoyne's appointment to command the new invasion and, in rather uncharacteristically insulting language for the time, blaming the governor-general for the failure of the British effort to subdue the colonies in 1776. Germain ordered Carleton to hold Canada with 3,770 troops and to provide 7,173 for Burgoyne's expedition. Justifiably angered by Germain's insulting letter and his relegation to a secondary role in the upcoming campaign, Carleton defended himself vigorously in a letter to Germain, but, to his credit, also cooperated fully with Burgoyne's effort to get his force ready for the march south.[8]

The heart of Burgoyne's army included 3,724 red-coated British regulars from combat-tested regiments whose names were to be found on the muster rolls of centuries of European battlefields. Rigidly trained and disciplined, these men were supremely confident of their ability to add new laurels to their long list of achievements. Most of these were organized into a division commanded by Major General William Phillips of the Royal Artillery. The 1st Brigade under Brigadier General Henry Powell included the 9th, 47th and 53rd Regiments of Foot, while the 2nd Brigade under Brigadier General John Hamilton contained the 20th, 21st and 62nd Regiments of Foot. This division would form the right wing of the army as it moved south along the lakes. The army's advanced guard under Brigadier General Simon Fraser included the 24th Regiment of Foot and the light infantry, grenadier, and flank companies of the 29th, 31st, and 34th Regiments of Foot, whose battalion companies were left behind under Carleton's command in Canada.[9]

Marching with the British were King George's mercenary allies, 3,016 blue and green-clad experienced German regulars from the states of Brunswick and Hesse Hanau. Obtained under the terms of a treaty signed with the Duke of Brunswick in January, 1776, the duke was to receive £7.4s:4 1/2d per soldier, an annual payment of £11,500, and a final payment of £46,000 upon completion of service. The duke was also to be compensated for any men killed or wounded. The troops, of course, received nothing save their normal pay, when that was available. Under the overall command of Gen. Baron Friedrich Adolph Freiherr von Riedesel, a very competent European professional commanding the troops from the Duchy of Brunswick, the Germans were also divided into two brigades and an advanced corps. The 1st Brigade comprised the von Riedesel, Specht and Rhetz Regiments of Brunswickers under Brigadier General Johann Friederich Specht. The 2nd Brigade included the Prince Frederick and Hesse Hanau Regiments under Brigadier General W. R. von Gall. The German advance corps commanded by Lt. Col. Heinrich Christoph Breymann included the grenadiers and light infantry, along with forty *jägers* and about an equal number of marksmen "selected from the different British regiments."[10]

Supporting the regulars were 42 field guns divided equally between the British and German divisions and served by 245 British artillerymen, 150 men transferred from the British infantry units, and 78 men of the Hesse Hanau artillery company under Capt. Georg Pausch. The expedition's naval support included nine ships, 28 gunboats, and a large quantity of bateaux. Including field pieces, ships guns, mortars, and siege cannons, the total artillery support included 138 guns. Altogether, the British and German regulars were well-trained, experienced soldiers led by capable field officers.[11]

To complement his professional force Burgoyne proposed to raise 2,000 Canadians and another 1,000 Indians, a project that proved overly optimistic. As Ward explained, the Canadians "were French; and, however willing they had been in Montcalm's time to fight for their flag, this war meant little or nothing to them."[12] Only 150 enlisted to help King George subdue his rebellious colonies. Another 100 Tories joined, largely in hopes of returning to New York in the wake of the British army to reclaim property now in the hands of the revolutionaries. The Indians responded with more enthusiasm, but still not in the numbers Burgoyne envisioned. About 400 came forward under Louis de la Corne St. Luc and Charles Michel de Langlade.[13]

Due in part to an unusually mild winter, the troops were in relatively good condition, but their clothing suffered from the wear and tear of the previous year's service and no new uniforms arrived to replace the old. Instead, British units were authorized to cut off the long tails of their great coats to patch holes in other places. The Germans, too, were poorly clad and lacked new shoes as well. Even when new, the uniforms of each group were not well suited to the North American climate, geography, or military tactics. "While the British uniforms ... were too heavy, too awkward, too tight, and too elaborate for rough campaigning in America," Ward explained, "those of these Brunswickers were far worse in all of these respects. Their dragoons, who had come without horses and were to serve dismounted to the end of the campaign, were most preposterously equipped for such service. Their great cocked hats, ornamented with a long plume, their hair worn in a long, stiff queue, their tight, thick coats, their stiff leather breeches, their huge leather gauntlets almost elbow-length, their great jack boots reaching to mid-thigh, weighing twelve pounds a pair without the long brass spurs always worn even on the march, made up as unsuitable an outfit for marching and fighting in a forested wilderness in an American midsummer as could have been devised by the most ingenious. Add to that a long, straight broadsword to trail at the thigh and a short heavy carbine, and one could have no feeling but pity for a Brunswick dragoon."[14]

Despite the ill-adapted uniforms and the failure of the Canadians and Indians to appear in the desired numbers, the force Burgoyne led south from his rendezvous at St. Johns on June 16, 1777, was formidable. "It was not a large army," Ward concluded, "but it was, for its size, a strong fighting force composed of trained, disciplined, and experienced men, under capable officers."[15] With it came an unknown number of servants, sutlers, laborers, women, and children. Among the non-combattants were the Baroness von Riedesel, her three young daughters, and Gen. Burgoyne's mistress. To carry the provisions and supplies for this vast array, Burgoyne brought along some 500 two-wheeled carts, thirty of which were assigned to convey his personal provisions, clothing, and champagne for his table.[16]

Lacking sufficient boats for the troops and the large train of supplies, Burgoyne consigned the artillery and baggage to the available water transport and had his troops march overland along the Richelieu River until they reached Lake Champlain where they boarded the British fleet and accompanying bateaux for the trip south to Crown Point. Loaded down by more than sixty pounds of equipment and supplies apiece, the foot soldiers made an average speed of eighteen miles per day over the rugged terrain of the Adirondack foothills surrounding the picturesque river.[17] Ward described the movement south along Lake Champlain thusly:

> Twenty or more great canoes, each holding twenty Indians, with another fleet bearing the Canadians and Tories dressed—or undressed—like Indians, formed the vanguard. Then came the gunboats and the bateaux of the British advance, the 24th regiment, the light infantry, and the grenadiers. The fleet was next in line, the tall-masted, square-sailed *Inflexible* and *Royal George*; the two schooners *Carleton* and *Maria*; the gundola *Loyal Covert*; the huge, unwieldy, absurd radeau *Thunderer*, that would "neither row nor sail" but had to be got along somehow; the captives of last year's encounter, the galley *Washington*, the cutter *Lee*, and the gundola *Jersey*; and the gunboats, twenty-four of them.
>
> After the fleet came the bateaux of the 1st British brigade "in the greatest order and regularity," and then Burgoyne and his two major generals, Riedesel and Phillips, each in his own pinnace. The British 2nd brigade was followed by the two German brigades. Ignominiously, the tail of the procession was a motley fleet of boats of all kinds carrying the sutlers, the women, and all the raggle-taggle of camp followers that hung on the rear of the armies of that day.
>
> Against a setting of the blue waters of the lake and the dark green background of its forested shores, the painted faces and bodies of hundreds of Indians and their make-believe savage companions, the masses of British scarlet and of German blue, the green of the jägers and the light blue of the dragoons, with their regimental facings of every hue, the shining brass of the tall hats of the Hessian grenadiers, the glinting of the sunlight upon polished musket barrels and bayonets, the flashing of thousands of wet paddles and oars made up a spectacular pageant, brilliant in its color, light and motion, thrilling in its purpose and intention.[18]

The advance force began arriving at Crown Point on June 25, only to find the colonials had abandoned the position in haste and retired south to Fort Ticonderoga, the main American position guarding the lakes.

Originally constructed as Fort Carillon by the Marquis de Lotbiniére, a French army engineer, in 1755, the stone fortress, situated at the confluence of Lake Champlain and Lake George on the strategically crucial route between Montréal and Albany, was regarded by many as the "Gibraltar of North America." Ward described the site as a bold, squarish, blunt-nosed promontory a mile long and three-quarters of a mile wide, that juts out from the western side of Lake Champlain, whose waters wash its base to the north, east, and south. At the foot of its southwest shoulder a very narrow gorge extends westward a mile or more, through which the waters of Lake George are poured into Lake Champlain. The highest elevation on the promontory is about seventy feet above the lake. From the east side of Champlain, another headland, a rocky bluff thirty to fifty feet high called Mount Independence, is thrust out towards the southeast corner of Ticonderoga. The points of the two narrow the lake to a width of about a quarter of a mile. This is the gateway from the upper lake to the lower, also to Lake George. Having passed through it one may go on by water directly south into the narrow, upper end of Champlain, and from its extremity up Wood Creek to within a few miles of the upper reaches of the Hudson. Or one may turn aside at Ticonderoga into Lake George and follow it to a point as near the Hudson. About two miles to the northwest of the nose of Ticonderoga, Mount Hope commands the road to Lake George. A mile to the southwest, another hill, called Sugar Loaf from its conical appearance as seen from the east—but renamed Mount Defiance by the British after its capture—rises 750 feet above the water. At this time both shores of the lake and all the mentioned heights, except where Ticonderoga had been cleared for its fortification, were densely forested.[19]

In July, 1776, the Americans began strengthening Ticonderoga's defenses, which had fallen into disrepair in the years following the conclusion of the French and Indian War in 1763, but their efforts were hampered by internal discord. In the second half of 1776 the colonial forces in northern New York were under the command of Major General Philip Schuyler. Born in Albany in 1733, Schuyler was a member of one of the oldest and most prestigious families in New York Dutch society. As a captain, he had fought at Lake George and in other campaigns during the French and Indian War. The owner of thousands of acres in the Mohawk and Hudson Valleys, he maintained a homestead in West Troy near Albany and a summer residence in the Saratoga Patent. Elected to the New York assembly in 1768, he proved an ardent patriot. An experienced logistics expert who insisted on rigid discipline, at the outbreak of the revolution he was named a general officer, outranked only by George Washington, Artemas Ward, and Charles Lee. Despite his prominence and success, Schuyler was roundly disliked by New Englanders for his activities on the boundary commission appointed to settle the dispute between

New Hampshire and New York over the "Hampshire Grants"—what is today Vermont. Probably exacerbated by this latent antagonism, Schuyler's brusque personality proved a constant source of irritation to New Englanders who resented what they perceived as the arrogant aristocratic demeanor of the "Yorker."[20]

Schuyler's subordinate in the Northern Department was Horatio Gates. Born in 1728, Gates served in the British army that Gen. Braddock led to defeat in the American wilderness in western Pennsylvania, participated in the defense of Ft. Herkimer in the Mohawk Valley, and served under Monkton in Martinique. Said to have greatly resented not moving beyond his servant-class social origins in England, in 1765 he sold his commission as major in the 60th Regiment of Foot and, with George Washington's encouragement and assistance, settled in Virginia in 1772. Most historians believe Gates cast his lot with the revolutionaries because of his hatred of the English social system rather than through any serious attachment to the ideals of freedom and liberty. Perhaps because of his friendship with Washington, Congress appointed him brigadier general and assigned him as Washington's adjutant general on June 17, 1775. Eleven months later he was promoted to the rank of major general and assigned to the Northern Department.[21]

Described by some as a "snob" with "an unctuously pious way with him," Gates clearly coveted the northern command. When he was ordered south with troops to reinforce Washington's army in November, 1776, he took advantage of the opportunity to lobby with Congress for appointment as Commander-in-Chief of the Northern Department to replace Schuyler. Meanwhile, New Englanders in Congress, seeking to embarrass Schuyler, arranged a vote calling for the relief of Dr. Samuel Stringer, Director of Hospitals of the Northern Department. Schuyler, taking offense at what he felt was interference in the internal affairs of his department without consultation, couched his protest in such an arrogant manner as to offend many in Congress. Taking advantage of the growing anti-Schuyler sentiment, Gates lobbied extensively with the Board of War until Congress dispatched him to take over command of Fort Ticonderoga on March 25, 1777.[22]

While in Philadelphia in February, 1777, Gates met Kościuszko and was immediately impressed by the thirty-one-year-old Polish engineer. What began as professional respect soon blossomed into a genuine friendship. So close did the two become that Samuel White

Patterson, Gates's biographer, concluded that "Until he left America for the last time to fight for his beloved homeland, more than a score of years later, Kościuszko was one of Gates's sincerest and most devoted friends."[23]

So impressed was Gates with Kościuszko's skill in fortifying the Delaware River that he asked the colonel to accompany him north when he received the appointment to Ticonderoga. Gates began his journey northward from Philadelphia on April 2. A few days later Kościuszko set out for the Northern Department in the company of Col. James Wilkinson and Dr. Jonathan Potts. Wilkinson was to be Gates's adjutant general of the Northern Department, while Potts would be his chief medical officer. The group arrived in Albany toward the end of the month, whereupon Wilkinson and Kościuszko were dispatched to Fort Edward and Ticonderoga with instructions to pay particular attention to lines of communication along the way.[24] This inspection of the area would be put to good use by the engineer in the coming months. Once at their destination, Kościuszko was to "examine and report the condition of that fortress; the extension (if any) to be given to Fort Independence, and lastly, whether Sugar loaf hill could be made practicable to the ascent of guns of large calibre?"[25]

On May 8, Gates wrote to Gen. John Paterson, then in command at Fort Ticonderoga, to inform him that Kościuszko, whom he described as "an able Engineer, and one of the best and neatest draughtsman I ever saw," would be arriving. "I desire he may have a Quarter assigned him," Gates continued, "and when he has thoroughly made himself acquainted with the works, [I] have ordered him to point out to you, where and in what manner the best improvements and additions can be made thereto; I expect Col. Baldwin will [offer] his countenance and protection to this Gentleman, for he is meant to serve not supersede him."[26] The reference to Baldwin was to Col. Jeduthan Baldwin, the engineering officer at Fort Ticonderoga, whom Gates wanted to reassure lest he fear his position in jeopardy. In fact, Baldwin's commission predated Kościuszko's by some six weeks, making the American the ranking engineering officer at the post.

Four days after Gates penned the above letter, Col. Baldwin acknowledged the group's arrival in his diary, commenting that "Dr. Potts, Col. Kosiosko & Col. Wilkinson came in."[27] In a letter a few days later he referred to Kościuszko as "an assistant Engineer" from

Poland who "is a beautiful limner."[28] Apparently Baldwin and Kościuszko cooperated because the Pole lodged with his counterpart, the two frequently dined together, and they spent several days jointly examining the fortress and the surrounding outworks.[29] Lynn Montross, in his history of the Continental Army, believed the two officers complemented each other well: "Colonel Baldwin could always do a good job of practical engineering, and the Polish volunteer supplied the technical theory."[30] That is, Baldwin could build the necessary works, but Kościuszko possessed the knowledge of *where* they should be built for the best military result. Whatever their relationship, Kościuszko's letter to Gates of May 1777, forwarding his recommendations for improvements in the defenses, reveals both an appreciation that the size of the garrison was an important consideration in forming the defenses and a concern that his work might provoke discord:

In consequence of your Orders I have visited every part or place, & from My remarks I send you the plan; what appears in black is what actually remains, what you see in red is my Scheme. As I perceived my Genl. that the trench lines are not properly defended, & that they are in a situation to be repaired, I think necessary to make some alterations at the same time, in some places vizt in g.

If we have a large Garrison, & as those three Redoubts are really made as expressed by 1; a communication will be necessary, by the lines expressed in Red, that a greater resistance may be made ag[ains]t the Enemy. & cover the Troops sent as a reinforcement in case of an Attack on this side, otherwise they cannot pass to sustain the Atack without being perceived by the Enemy, therefore the Entrenchment AAA will answer that end.

If the Garrison should be small, which appears likely. I think that the Entrenchments AABB will answer better, because we shall be near at hand to give one another assistance in Case of an Attack, also because we shall have no difficulty in saving the Cannon of the redoubts 111 from their distance, particularly if heavy Cannon should be mounted in that near or towards the Lake, which was made to annoy the shipping. Should they force us which I cannot believe making the Entrenchment week; we can make another which will not cost much Labour expressed by CCB.

I also observed, My Genl., that the Old Redoubt E is very bad for stopping the passage of shipping, more particularly as heavy Cannon cannot be mounted on it; only small & not more than 2 pieces, for the building inside. For which reason, it appears to me necessary to make the Redoubt D. My opinion & advice is asked. I cannot help giving my sentiments in regard to the Entrenchments. My General, I request the favour you would not give me Orders to proceed, before your arrival. I will give you the reason. I love peace & to be on good terms with all the world if possible; if my opinion or Ideas are adopted, which may be better I should the more so being a stranger[,] I am convinced how much I ought to be on my Guard, as also have regard to nationality[,] but our work would not be better.

I declare sincerely that I am susceptible, & love peace[.] I would chuse rather to leave all, return home & plant Cabbages; as yet my Genl. I have no reason of complaint of any one. I was well received by Genl. Paterson who overcome me with politeness, all the Officers are extremely Friendly.[31]

Although Kościuszko's original sketch has apparently been lost, Col. Wilkinson reported that the engineer "promptly and carefully discharged" Gates's orders. Of primary concern was Sugar Loaf Hill, an undefended summit Kościuszko believed could dominate the other works surrounding Ticonderoga. "The hitherto doubtful and highly interesting question with regard to Sugar Loaf Hill," Wilkinson wrote, "was fully discussed and the following conclusions arrived at: '1st—That the sides of the hill though steep, may, by the labor of strong fatigue parties, be so shaped as to permit the ascent of the heaviest cannon. 2d—That the summit, now sharp and pointed, may by similar means, be quickly reduced to table ground and furnish a good site for a battery, and 3d—that a battery so placed, from elevation and proximity, would completely cover the two forts, the bridge of communication and the adjoining boat-harbor.'"[32]

Apparently Baldwin, while outwardly friendly and accommodating, did not share Kościuszko's ideas for improving the defenses. For his part, though he disagreed with Col. Baldwin's preparations, Kościuszko, fearing that he might cause conflict, was reluctant to press his case. A modest man in an era often afflicted by pompous pretension, Kościuszko shunned controversy and political maneuverings at a time when political connections often counted for more than ability as a criteria for promotion. Further, as a foreigner, unlike many from abroad who made pretentious claims to expertise based on European service in their own countries, Kościuszko was acutely aware of the sensitivities involved in his assignment, as a "foreign" officer, to Ticonderoga. Regardless, he felt sufficient concern over the planning and progress of the work at Ticonderoga that only a few days later, on May 18, the Polish colonel informed Gates that "My Opinion may be dangerous. I say if we have time to make an Entrenchment like what I had the honour to send you a Model of; with the addition of a trifling thing towards the Lake to prevent passage of shipping, I say the Enemy cannot hurt us; we have an excellent place not only to resist the Enemy, but beat them, but Courage & more artillery men will be neccessary, for we have only one Company & that is not enough; we ought to have three."[33]

Kościuszko also expressed concern that a floating bridge planned to connect Fort Ticonderoga with Mount Independence had not yet been completed, and that much energy was being expended on blockhouses and other outworks of little value. Closing his letter with an expression of loyalty to Gates and confidence in their cause, he no doubt hoped the general would intercede to support his plan. "The Bridge is not yet finished nevertheless it must be; I say nothing of what unnecessary works have been carried on you will be a Judge yourself my Genl. we are very fond here of making Block houses & they are all erected in the most improper places. Nevertheless Genl. we'll conquer headed by your Excellency, our steady attachment to you, will be a great inducement added to the Sacred Duty which has engaged us to Defend this Country. If we cannot have more artillery men it will be necessary to Draft some soldiers & exercise them having great occasion."[34]

Frustrated by Kościuszko's lack of assertiveness with the officers at the fort, Colonel Wilkinson, adjutant general of the Northern Department, wrote to Gates on May 22 expressing his concern that the Pole's suggestions were being ignored and imploring the commanding general to resolve the situation. "I wish to Heaven," he pleaded, "either yourself or General St. Clair was here for a few days. Colonel Kosiusko is timidly modest; Baldwin is inclosing the lines on a plan of his own."[35]

The following day, probably in response to Kościuszko's letter of May 18, Gates wrote to Gen. Paterson, then commanding at Fort Ticonderoga, calling on him to make haste with the construction and to implement Kościuszko's plan. "I entreat, my Dear General, that You will keep every Soul at Work to Strengthen Our posts; perhaps the Enemy may give us two Months, before they come again to look at Ticonderoga; let us regard those two Months, as the most precious Time we have to Live; they may be worth an Age of Droning peace, and, well employ'd may give happiness, and peace to Millions. I

54

earnestly recommend it to You, to order Lieut. Colonel Kosciuszko's plan, to be immediately put in Execution; doing the most defensible parts first. Colonel Baldwin will gain my Affection, and Esteem, by cultivating the Friendship of that Capable Young Man; and he may be assured he can in nothing serve his Country more, than in going hand in hand, with him, in improving the Fortifications of Ticonderoga."[36]

Before Gates's letter reached Ticonderoga, Wilkinson, becoming increasingly concerned, arranged for Kościuszko to travel to Albany to present his plan to the commanding general in person. "Thinking that Col. Kusiusco would be of more Service by Personally representing to you the Situation of this Place," Wilkinson explained to Gates, "I have obtained leave for His Return."[37] Baldwin commented in his diary only that "Gen. Paterson & Col. Kosiosko went to Skeensboro [sic]."[38] From there the Pole continued on to Albany while Wilkinson, becoming more desperate by the day, wrote to Gates on May 31: "The works are now pushed on Baldwin's unmeaning plan. For God's sake, let Kościuszko come back as soon as possible, with proper authority."[39]

Whatever Kościuszko said, it was apparently convincing because the Pole arrived back at Fort Ticonderoga on June 6 ready to resume work. But, although Gates accepted Kościuszko's recommendations regarding the necessity of occupying Sugar Loaf Hill, petty jealousies and political maneuvers again interceded to disrupt implementation of his plan.[40]

Following his reprimand by Congress, Schuyler rushed off in April to plead his case at Washington's headquarters, then continued on to appeal directly to Congress, demanding a full inquiry into his conduct and insisting that he be given "an absolute command ... over every part of the army in the Northern department."[41] Eventually exonerated of any wrongdoing, Congress voted by a count of 5-4, with two abstentions, to reinstate Schuyler on May 15. To assuage Gates, Congress offered him the option "either to continue in command in the Northern Department, under Maj. Gen. Schuyler, or to take upon him the office of Adjutant General in the Grand Army immediately under the Commander in Chief."[42] The directive apparently arrived at Gates's headquarters in Albany during Kościuszko's visit. Refusing to serve again under the Dutch patroon, Gates rode off to Philadelphia to try and recoup his position.[43] Soon after he left, Kościuszko penned an effusive letter to Gates expressing his confidence in the general and asking to accompany him to his next assignment:

> An opportunity now presents [itself] to lay before you the real sentiments of my heart Also my present Ideas. If your love for your Country and your easy manner of communicating yourself to every one has attached me to you, among other things, your Great Military knowledge and true merit has so much inspired my confidence in you that I should be happy to be with you every where. Be persuaded General, that I am not actuated by Interest, otherwise than the ambition of signalizing myself in this War. And I seek an opportunity, which I am of opinion can never be better, than under your Auspices. If the Works at Ticonderoga, should be any hindrance to my going with you, that will be but triffling, because I can in very short time, do what is necessary for this Campaign. Inform me Genl. if I may prepare to go with you. You know well, that the change of a Commander esteemed by the Troops has considerable effect on their minds.
>
> I flatter myself, General, that you will grant me my request, which cannot but increase my Attachment to you, and encourage my utmost endeavors to gain your Esteem.[44]

All of this intrigue greatly detracted from efforts to fortify the defenses of Fort Ticonderoga. Major General Arthur St. Clair, a Pennsylvanian of Scottish birth, arrived at the fort to take command of the installation on June 12. Under his command were about 2,500 infantry in ten Continental and two militia regiments, 250 artillery-men, 124 artificers, and some scouts. As subordinates St. Clair had three brigadiers—Fermoy, Paterson, and Poor. Born on the tropical island of Martinique, Matthias Alexis de Roche Fermoy came to America in 1776 claiming to be a French colonel of engineers. Commissioned a brigadier general on November 5, 1776, he commanded a brigade in the attack on Trenton before being sent north. John Paterson, born the son of a colonial officer in 1744, graduated from Yale College in 1762 and taught school briefly in Connecticut before beginning a law practice. In 1774 he moved to Lenox, Massachusetts, where he was elected to the Provincial Congress as a revolutionary in 1774 and 1775. When war broke out he raised a militia regiment, organized the 15th Continental Regiment, worked on the defenses of Mount Independence, and fought with Washington at Trenton and Princeton before being promoted brigadier. Born in 1736, Enoch Poor enjoyed little opportunity for education. A cabinetmaker by trade, he moved from Massachusetts to New Hampshire where he became a trader and ship builder. After holding several elective offices, including two terms in the New Hampshire Provincial Congress, he became colonel of the 2nd New Hampshire Regiment.[45] An average lot, none of the brigadiers had attained great notoriety, nor would they rise to the occasion in the future.

Schuyler arrived at Ticonderoga on June 19 to consult with St. Clair about the defenses. Both Schuyler and St. Clair did not believe the British would make a serious effort to force the issue at Ticonderoga, the Dutch general suggesting they would make their major invasion along the Mohawk River route. Others also felt it unlikely the British would move in strength toward Ticonderoga. In March, no less a figure than Gen. Washington wrote to Schuyler informing him the commanding general believed it most likely British troops then in Canada would be sent by water down the St. Lawrence into the Atlantic and thence to New York to reinforce the main British army under Sir William Howe. Nor did the Continental Congress believe Ticonderoga would be the object of a major British push in 1777; rather, the politicians felt inclined to support Washington's interpretation. Because of the uncertainty, troops originally designated for the defense of Ticonderoga were instead diverted to strengthen the lower Hudson Valley and Washington's army, for, if Washington were right, troops sent to garrison Ticonderoga would be "useless" for other purposes. As late as June 16, when the British were beginning their march south, Washington was still writing Schuyler assurances that the enemy troops in Canada would be sent to New York by water.[46]

Although formidable in reputation, Ticonderoga was not a strong fortress in the summer of 1777. A star-shaped fort with five attached bastions, the stone fortress fell into decay after the Peace of Paris ended the French and Indian War in 1763. Under Baldwin's direction, valuable time and resources had been wasted building inconsequential works that did not add to the defensive strength in any appreciable way. Further, because of the uncertainty about British intentions, when Schuyler regained command Ticonderoga's garrison included only 2,546 Continentals. About 900 ill-trained and poorly disciplined militia arrived to bolster the defence before the arrival of the British force, but aside from these troops Schulyer could call on only one Continental regiment in garrison at Fort Stanwix on the Mohawk River and an assortment of small militia units at Skenesboro (modern Whitehall), Fort Ann, Fort Edward, and Albany. Altogether, St.

Clair's force at Ticonderoga was only about one-quarter the size necessary to completely man the fortress and its outworks.[47]

Because of the shortage of men, Schuyler preferred to abandon the stone fortress and concentrate his defenses on Mount Independence. But, a log and chain boom stretched across the water to impede the passage of enemy ships toward Lake George had to be protected at both ends, which meant that Ticonderoga had to be held. Yet, both Mount Independence and Fort Ticonderoga held a weakness that Kościuszko recognized earlier. Sugar Loaf Hill, a sharp hill with steep sides, rose 600 feet higher than Fort Ticonderoga and 550 feet higher than Fort Independence. Although it rested some 1,400 yards from Fort Ticonderoga and 1,500 yards from Fort Independence, fairly long distances for the time, because of its height Sugar Loaf Hill could command both of the colonial posts if sufficient artillery could be posted on its crest.[48]

Kościuszko arrived back at Ticonderoga on June 6. Apparently he immediately suggested to St. Clair that the general fortify Sugar Loaf Hill, but St. Clair deferred making any decision until Schuyler arrived. In the interim, Kościuszko busied himself constructing the works that had already been approved. According to Col. Baldwin's diary, on June 8 he accompanied Kościuszko, Gen. Paterson, Major Armstrong, and a small group of men on a reconnaissance to Crown Point, while on the 14th he and Kościuszko went to Mount Independence to determine the best plan for the defenses being constructed there.[49] Major Isaac B. Dunn, an aide-de-camp to Gen. St. Clair, reported that while inspecting the American lines "on Mount Independence he found a party of about one hundred men, under the direction of Colonel Kosciuszko, erecting three redoubts in the rear of the Mount, and forming an abbatis."[50]

When the commanding general finally appeared, Kósciuszko presented his assessment of the situation and his recommendations for strengthening the defenses, including the plan for Sugar Loaf Hill. Much to the colonel's surprise, Schuyler was not at all interested in fortifying the nearby hill. Noting that none of the previous French, British, or American engineers had suggested such a necessity, Schuyler, according to Armstrong, replied that he was "not disposed to embarrass himself or his means of defence, by making the experiment; and the less so, as he was 'fully convinced, that between two and three thousand men, could effectually maintain Fort Independence and secure the pass.' To this point therefore the General's attention was principally given; no doubt very conscientiously, but very erroneously, as the event proved."[51] Surprised by Schuyler's peremptory rejection of his plan, Kościuszko apparently maintained a calm exterior and did not press the issue, but Col. Wilkinson, who witnessed the conversation, reported he "detected, under his [Kosci-uszko's] placid silence, more than a little anguish and mortifica-tion."[52]

In spite of the rebuff, Kościuszko continued to do his best to prepare Ticonderoga's defenses. The fortress having been somewhat repaired and blockhouses constructed to strengthen the outworks guarding the approaches to the stone fort, he helped plan and construct additional breastworks and small redoubts to protect out-lying positions and designed the emplacement for a battery on Mount Hope that was to guard the road leading south along the shore of Lake George. Given between 500 and 600 men, Schuyler sent him to construct batteries on Mount Independence and strengthen the redoubt with fascines. Despite the stones and rocky soil that made it almost impossible to dig ditches in much of the area, Kościuszko built a large star-shaped redoubt and supporting works so strong they were later praised by both British and German professionals as first-class works. In addition, the engineer also constructed new works from the west end of the French lines on down to the lake. According to Lt. Col. Henry B. Livingston, Schuyler's aide-de-camp, "no measures were neglected to strengthen the works on both sides of the Lake. Fatigue parties were daily employed in this duty, and the direction of them generally committed to Colonel Kosciuszko, an active officer, who acted as an assistant engineer in the northern department."[53]

The British advance reached Crown Point, a few miles north of Ticonderoga, on June 25 with the rest of the army coming up during the next two days. Abandoned by the Americans, Burgoyne estab-lished his headquarters and supply depot there for the support of his movement south.[54] "We are now within sight of the enemy," wrote Thomas Anburey, an officer in the 24th Regiment of Foot, "and their watch boats are continually rowing about, but beyond the reach of cannon shot."[55] Aware now of the British approach, Schuyler still believed the force might be a diversionary move to take attention away from the primary invasion route down the Mohawk Valley. His illusions would soon be shattered.

Brig. Gen. Simon Fraser's advanced corps left Crown Point on

June 30 for Ticonderoga. His troops debarked on the western shore about three miles above Ticonderoga, observed with amazement by American sentinels on Mount Independence. In his wake came the rest of the British troops, while the Germans rowed across the lake to land on its eastern shore. The Canadians and Tories covered the British right wing, while the Indians protected the German left. The Brunswick dragoons formed the reserve. In all, the invaders numbered 7,213 rank and file, more than twice the number of defenders.[56] According to a muster prepared by Col. Wilkinson on June 28, the garrison at Ticonderoga included 2,066 Continentals, 450 militia, 229 artillerists, and 183 rangers and engineers.[57]

Fraser approached Ticonderoga on June 30, but the full extent of British intentions were not divined until he moved against Mount Hope in strength on July 2. In the face of this danger, the American troops manning the works set fire to the post and retired in haste about 9:00 a.m. Moving cautiously, Fraser occupied the remains of the fortifications that afternoon, cutting the colonial overland escape route to Lake George.[58] The British found the American positions, due in large part to Kościuszko's skill and effort, well situated. Lt. Anburey described them thusly, reserving his greatest praise for the works on Mount Independence constructed under the personal supervision of the Polish colonel:

By the scouting parties just returned we learn that there is a brigade which occupies the old French lines on a height to the north of the fort of Ticonderoga; the lines are in good repair with several entrenchments behind them, supported by a blockhouse; they have another post at the sawmills, the foot of the carrying-place to Lake George, and a blockhouse upon an eminence above the mills, together with a blockhouse and hospital at the entrance of the lake.

Upon the right of the lines, between them and the old fort, are two new blockhouses, and a considerable battery close to the water's edge. But it seems the Americans have employed their utmost industry where they are in the greatest force, upon Mount Independence, which is extremely lofty and circular. On the summit of the mount they have a star fort made of pickets, well supplied with artillery, and a large square of barracks within it; that side of the hill which projects into the lake is well intrenched, and has a strong abatis close to the water, which is lined with heavy artillery pointing down the lake, flanking the water battery, and sustained by another about half way up the hill. Fortified as the enemy are, nothing but a regular siege can dispossess them.[59]

Because of the strength of the American fortifications, the British finally approached the defences warily about 3:00 p.m. Gen. St. Clair ordered his men to hold fire as the English moved forward very carefully and with some hesitancy. When one of their skirmishers came within about forty paces of the American lines, Col. Wilkinson ordered one of his sharpshooters to pick him off. His shot sparked a general discharge from the American lines that Mark Boatner described as "3,000 rounds from 1,000 muskets at less than 100 yards" that "hit two Indians and a British lieutenant," the "only fatality was one of the Indians." The skirmisher who began the exchange escaped unscathed, but was taken prisoner providing the first reliable information on Burgoyne's force and intentions.[60]

Though surprised by the extent of the British invasion, the American position was not necessarily untenable. Supply and communication lines to Skenesboro remained open, the German left wing was bogged down in the swamps along East Creek, artillery fire during the day did little damage, and the colonial fortifications generally provided clear fields of fire along the probable main lines of British attack.[61]

Yet, Burgoyne was determined. On July 3 he ordered von Gall's Brigade shifted to strengthen the British right wing, replacing it with the Canadians and Fraser's light infantry. At the same time, he ordered von Riedesel to turn Mount Independence on the east and cut the colonial line of communication to Skenesboro. The following day he sent his chief engineer, Lt. William Twiss, a native of Switzerland, to reconnoiter Sugar Loaf Hill to see whether it might be practical to place a battery atop the peak. The engineer soon reported what Kościusko had warned about as early as May. Sugar Loaf was within range of Fort Ticonderoga and Mount Independence and a passageway for artillery could be cut to the top in about twenty-four hours. Gen. William Phillips, placed in command of the 700 men detailed for the operation, is said to have silenced doubters with the comment that "Where a goat can go a man can go, and where a man can go he can drag a gun."[62]

Work on the rough passage began late on July 4 so the darkness would disguise the proceedings. The rough roadway could be carved only part way up the steep slopes, the dismembered guns being dragged the rest of the way by block and tackle and reassembled on top of the hill. By noon on July 5, six 12-pounders were in position to open fire. Although their fire was not very accurate and the steepness of the hill made it difficult if not impossible to resupply the guns with ammunition fast enough to keep up a "sustained fire," the battery atop Sugar Loaf nevertheless posed a serious threat to the bridge connecting Ticonderoga to Mount Independence and to the boats beyond the boom in South Bay, both of which were essential to any successful evacuation. "[A]nother very great advantage," according to Lt. Anburey, was that "the enemy, during the day, could not make any material movement or preparation without being discovered, and even their numbers counted."[63] Still another serious threat was to colonial morale.[64] The sight of British guns above them, firing shot into their works, was, regardless of any physical effects, seriously damaging to American morale.

Faced with this threat, and the growing German threat to his line of communication with Skenesboro, St. Clair called an emergency council of war for 3:00 p.m. on the afternoon of the 5th. The situation was rapidly becoming critical, with the British guns already in position atop Sugar Loaf and the German column slowly moving through the woods toward the one secure overland escape route, the Military Road carved through the wilderness from Mount Independence to Castleton, Vermont. Faced at last with the realities of the situation, the council voted for withdrawal.[65]

Gen. St. Clair issued orders for the retreat about 10:00 p.m., the withdrawal to be accomplished during the night to place as much distance between the escaping army and Burgoyne's forces as possible. Behind them, the Americans left several tons of supplies and provisions, eighty pieces of artillery, a large cache of paper currency, and other useful materials.[66] The loss of Ticonderoga was a shock to most Americans, causing great depression in Schuyler's army and corresponding elation among Burgoyne's legions. St. Clair explained the decision to abandon the fortress by citing his inferior numbers, the fact that many of the fortifications remained incomplete, the lack of provisions, and the fact that "our whole camp on the Ticonderoga side was exposed to fire."[67] In a letter to John Jay, the general explained that the retreat "was done in consequence of a consultation with the other general officers ... and had their opinion been contrary to what it was, it would have nevertheless taken place, because I knew it would be impossible to defend the post with our numbers.... I may have the satisfaction to experience that although I have lost a post I have eventually saved a state."[68] But the explanation would not save him from a court martial later that fall.

History has been somewhat kinder to the general. Although Boatner concluded backhandedly that "Not even a good major general could have done more," St. Clair did as much as could have been expected with what he had. Placed in a poor position without adequate troops, St. Clair managed to save his army from complete surrender, thus making the ultimate victory at Saratoga possible. Indeed, if either commander could be faulted it was Burgoyne. By detaching von Gall's troops to cooperate with the British he weakened von Riedesel enough so the German was unable to push through as quickly as hoped to cut the Military Road before St. Clair escaped. Similarly, his premature disclosure of the British battery on Sugar Loaf gave the Americans time to execute their withdrawal before suffering serious casualties.[69]

Kościuszko felt St. Clair performed well under the circumstances. In a letter to the general from Fort Edward later that month he assured St. Clair of his support and his willingness to continue under his command:

> My General—Be well persuaded that I am wholly attached to you for your peculiar merit and the knowledge of the Military art which you most assuredly possess. If the retreat from Ticonderoga has drawn upon you many Talkers and to some Jealous persons has furnished the occasion of under-mining you, even to the point of saying yesterday at dinner, that it is necessary that someone be sacrificed for the public good, it seems to me rather for their own. Therefore my General it is necessary to take care and to try to shut their mouths. I offer you my services, to reply to give reasons the most convincing with the plan. My General I shall be in despair if we are going to lose you, so I have already Begun to say to Our Generals and Colonels that in losing you we should draw upon ourselves the greatest dishonor; they are convinced of the truth and they will rather quit the service.
>
> I am well persuaded my General that you are in a position yourself to Give Reasons for the retreat but as it is a matter which touches rather my condition I shall wish to be useful to you here in some way, therefore make use of me.[70]

As for himself, Kościuszko's contributions to the defense of Ticonderoga were substantial, regardless of the eventual outcome. While some historians have dismissed his advice to fortify Sugar Loaf as impractical given the limited troops at St. Clair's disposal, Kościuszko's recommendations for improvements in the defenses sent to Gates in May 1777, clearly indicate his cognizance of the importance of the garrison size in formulating alternative plans. Further, the fact remains that his assessment of the hill as a decisive liability for the defense of the fortress below was completely vindicated. Faced with his recommendation and the lack of troops, a prudent commander should have recognized the impossibility of defending Ticonderoga and withdrawn before being compelled to abandon precious supplies and equipment in order to barely escape with the army intact. Yet, the politics of the situation—public opinion and the Continental Congress—demanded a defense.

Aside from the Sugar Loaf episode, Kościuszko's military engineering skills gained praise from many quarters. Historians of the stature of Sir George Otto Trevelyan, author of the classic *The American Revolution*, and Hoffman Nickerson who analyzed the same events in *The Turning Point of the Revolution*, praised in highly favorable terms Kościuszko's work at Ticonderoga. Among the colonel's contemporaries, Lt. William Digby, who examined the fortifications of Mount Defiance as a member of the British 53rd Regiment of Foot, believed them to be "of great strength."[71] The famous Du Roi the Elder, who marched with von Riedesel's force, was favorably impressed by Kościuszko's skill in preparing the American positions he observed following their capture. "Not only the old fortifications of Fort Ticonderoga and the socalled French lines, had been renewed and increased during this time," he wrote, "but the hill just opposite the fort had been cleared of the wood, and a wooden fort been erected there, strengthening the whole with trenches and batteries. They had called this mountain on account of its location and their intentions 'Mount Independence.' The whole was well done and showed no lack of clever engineers among the rebels." Du Roi felt the bridge between Ticonderoga and Mount Independence did "honor to human mind and power" and "may be compared to the work of Colossus in the fables of the heathen."[72]

Clearly, at Ticonderoga Kościuszko amply repaid Gates's confidence in his ability with clear thinking, a realistic assessment of the situation, and skillful placement and construction of the works entrusted to his care. He would soon have opportunity to prove anew his skill and devotion to the cause of American independence.

Chapter 4

"A Labyrinthine Hell"

*T*he American retreat began after dark on July 5. As the sun set on that fateful day, St. Clair's guns opened a lively fire to mask the preparations for withdrawal. Strangely, Burgoyne appears not to have divined the significance of the American aggressiveness, remaining generally inactive and taking no precautions against such an eventuality. St. Clair's plan called for two separate evacuation routes. As many of the guns and as much of the accumulated gunpowder and provisions as could be carried were to withdraw first. Under the command of Col. Pierce Long, and guarded by upwards of 600 infantry, this important column, which was also to include the ill and wounded fit to travel, would move over South Bay in five armed galleys and more than 200 smaller boats, heading for presumed safety at Skenesboro. The second column, including the bulk of St. Clair's forces, some 2,500 troops, was to move across Kościuszko's bridge to Mount Independence. From there the column would take the Military Road, the only major avenue of escape open to it, a circuitous route that meandered east through Castleton, Vermont, before heading back to the southwest to join Long's force at Skenesboro, some forty-five miles as the road wandered.[1]

Long's men began their departure a little after midnight, rowing as silently as possible into the early morning darkness of July 6. About 2:00 a.m. the rest of the troops began traversing the bridge of boats across the narrow strait to Mount Independence. Inexplicably, Gen. Fermoy, whose troops were to form the American rear-guard, apparently went to sleep on the evening of July 5 without informing his men on Mount Independence of the impending withdrawal. Thus unprepared, confusion set in when the order finally arrived and much equipment and supplies were left to the enemy during the hastily organized evacuation. Worse still, when Fermoy, whom Col. Wilkinson later characterized as "a worthless drunk," finally moved out about 3:00 a.m. he set fire to the buildings in direct contravention of St. Clair's orders, lighting up the area like a theater stage and uncovering the American movement to von Riedesel's pickets.[2]

To make matters even worse, a rear-guard force left with four guns to cover the bridge and prevent an immediate British pursuit apparently used the opportunity to raid the abandoned supply of spirits, becoming completely inebriated and falling into enemy hands without offering the slightest resistance. Thus, the head start St. Clair had hoped for was lost and the Americans were unable to put a safe distance between themselves and their pursuers.[3] Worse still, the haphazard evacuation, whether through faulty planning or incompetent execution, failed to destroy vast quantities of supplies and military equipment. Among the captured items enumerated in Burgoyne's report were 349,760 pounds of flour, 143,830 pounds of salted meat, "five of their armed vessels taken and blown up ... and a very great quantity of Ammunition, Provisions and stores of all sorts, and the greater part of their baggage."[4] The retreating army had not even taken the precaution of spiking the guns that had to be left behind, most of which fell into British hands in serviceable condition. The extent of the disaster was almost incomprehensible.

Once alerted, Gen. von Riedesel immediately dispatched a force to harass the American withdrawal. Gen. Burgoyne learned of the American evacuation about dawn on July 6. Moving quickly once informed, he ordered Fraser, supported by von Riedesel, to lead a vigorous pursuit of St. Clair's main force while Burgoyne followed Long's retreat south by water. Burgoyne's force overtook the Americans at Skenesboro after Col. Long proceeded at a much too leisurely pace down the lake. Further, Long made no attempt to mount a delaying action at the places along the waterway where the channel narrowed and was overlooked by bluffs where guns could have been placed to interdict the passage.[5]

Arriving at Skenesboro only about two hours after the retreating Americans, Burgoyne's advance routed Long's defenders, but not before the colonel burned the small stockade, the shipyards, most of the boats, and much of the supplies. His men scattered in every direction, Long, with whatever force he could rally, fell back to Fort Ann, pursued by the British advanced guard. Reinforced by 400 New York militia under Col. van Renssalear at Fort Ann, Long mauled the British advance in a brief but fierce action on July 7, giving him time to retire in relative security into the fort. Soon, however, Schuyler ordered the indefensible stockade burned and the Americans retired further south to Fort Edward.[6]

Meanwhile, von Riedesel and Fraser pushed forward after St. Clair's main column of between 2,400 and 2,600 somewhat disorganized troops heading toward Castleton along a narrow, winding road carved through the woods only the previous year. Once the sun rose, the weather turned intensely hot and humid. "We marched till one o'clock in a very hot and sultry day," wrote Lt. Anburey, "over a continued succession of steep and woody hills; the distance I cannot ascertain, but we were marching very expeditiously from four in the morning to that time."[7] Ebenezer Fletcher, a sixteen-year-old fifer in St. Clair's column, recalled that the British "pursued us so closely as to fire on our rear."[8]

The British and Germans caught up with the Americans at Hubbardton, about fifteen miles from Mount Independence, on July 7. There, Col. Seth Warner commanded an American force with orders to await the arrival of the rear-guard and then fall back on the main American force at Castleton. With about 1,000 men including his own Vermont regiment, Col. Turbott Francis's Massachusetts Regiment and Col. Nathan Hale's New Hampshire Regiment, Warner halted rather than retreat and his force was surprised by Fraser's advance in the early morning mists. Forming under fire, Warner's men fought valiantly in what became a very determined two-hour struggle before von Riedesel arrived with German reinforcements that proved decisive. His lines crumbling under the weight of von Riedesel's attack, Warner ordered his men to scatter and reform at Manchester, effectively taking the entire force out of action. American losses were about 300, while the British and Germans lost approximately half that number.[9]

With his rear-guard routed and Burgoyne in possession of Skenesboro, Gen. St. Clair marched his battered troops south, taking a lengthy detour around Skenesboro, to rendezvous with Long's survivors at Fort Edward, which he reached on July 12.[10] It was a defeated and demoralized march. Major John Armstrong reported being "severely pressed by the enemy," the retreat being "made with great disorder and its usual accompaniment, frequent desertion."[11] Col. Wilkinson, another witness, wrote that "both men and officers [were] half naked, sickly, and destitute of comforts.... Our troops ... lost spirit."[12]

In less than two weeks, the patriot cause in the Northern Department seemed to degenerate into complete disarray. Col. Udney Hay, who had been St. Clair's deputy quartermaster at Ticonderoga and suffered through the debilitating retreat to Castleton and Fort Edward, observed that "misfortunes and fatigue have broken down the discipline and spirits of the troops and converted them in a great degree into a rabble. They seem to have lost all confidence in themselves and their leaders. The militia seem to be infected with the same spirit. Such as are with us are good for nothing but to eat and waste and grumble, and those at home think home safest."[13] Kościuszko formed the same impression. "I met some of the militia on retreat," the Pole wrote, "and having expressed my surprise at their not staying to fight for their country, they answered, they were willing to stay, but the officers would not."[14]

The loss of supposedly Gibraltar-like Ticonderoga with tons of supplies and scores of intact artillery pieces, the routs at Skenesboro and Hubbardton, and the disorganized retreats to Fort Edward all shocked the Americans. Clearly, there were several factors that contributed to the disastrous campaign including the failure of Schuyler and Gates to follow Kościuszko's advice to fortify Sugar Loaf Hill, the lack of sufficient troops to man Ticonderoga's extended defenses, Fermoy's incompetent performance during the withdrawal, the bridge guard's dereliction of duty, Long's poor performance at Skenesboro, and Warner's disobedience of orders at Hubbardton. But in the wake of the disastrous campaign, Congress and the general public demanded a scapegoat. St. Clair received most of the criticism, and by extension Schuyler's enemies renewed their demands for his removal. Schuyler, for his part, did much to fan factional antagonisms by blaming the loss of Ticonderoga on the failure of the New England states to supply sufficient troops.[15]

The finger-pointing aside, Schuyler rushed to meet his battered forces at Fort Edward and take command of them in person. What he found was most discouraging. On his arrival he described the situation thusly: "I am here at the head of a ... handful of men, not above fifteen hundred, without provisions, little ammunition, not above five rounds to a man, having neither ball, nor lead to make any; the country in the deepest consternation; no carriages to move the stores from Fort George, which I expect every moment to learn is attacked."[16] To Gen. Washington, Schuyler appealed for help, confiding that "Desertion prevails and disease gains ground; nor is it to be wondered at, for we have neither tents, houses, barns, boards or any other shelter except a little brush.... We are in want of every kind of necessities, provisions excepted."[17]

Washington wanted to send reinforcements but was reluctant to weaken his army significantly because of his uncertainty about the intentions of Howe's large army operating out of New York City. He sent the unit he felt would be most helpful in the wooded hills of northern New York, Col. Daniel Morgan's Virginia riflemen, along with ten fieldpieces. He also sent Gen. Benedict Arnold north without a command to assist Schuyler and dispatched Nixon's and Glover's brigades from his army to reinforce Gen. Benjamin Lincoln's command at Peekskill in the lower Hudson Valley in an attempt to prevent Howe from sending a force north to assist Burgoyne. Nixon and Glover were soon ordered north to reinforce Schuyler directly, as was Lincoln. Nixon arrived at Fort Edward on July 12 with some 600 effectives, the same day St. Clair arrived with the survivors of the Ticonderoga evacuation and Hubbardton, thus reuniting Schuyler's forces. Altogether, the Dutchman had under his command about 4,400 men including 2,800 Continentals and 1,600 militia.[18]

Desperate as the situation was for the colonials, Burgoyne also faced a major decision that could effect the outcome of the campaign. Once his army was reunited with the arrival of von Riedesel and Fraser at Skenesboro, the British commander had to decide whether to push on toward his ultimate goal of Albany via the overland route, or whether to move by water down Lake George and from there overland to the Hudson River before turning southward. Both options offered opportunities, but contained inherent weaknesses as well. The overland route would require only a 23 mile march from Skenesboro to the Hudson River which would allow Burgoyne to keep pressure on Schuyler, threaten Vermont and western Massachusetts, and probably force the latter states to keep their militia units close to home for their own defense. On the other hand, the overland route covered very difficult wooded hills and swampy areas that Burgoyne himself characterized as "impassible." Moving by water the British could move safely down Lake George where a good ten mile road would lead them to the Hudson, but this would require retiring some 25 miles back to Ticonderoga before his men could board boats for the 36 mile voyage down Lake George, a movement Burgoyne feared would give the appearance of a retreat and thus encourage the colonials. Further, the British commander lacked sufficient bateaux to move his entire force at once; rather, he would have to move it in relays.[19]

Weighing his options, Burgoyne decided to move his supplies and heavy artillery via Lake George while marching his troops and field artillery overland. It was a fateful decision that he later explained by noting that all of his boats were required to move his supplies, which meant that it would take just as long for his army to reach Ft. Edward, and that such a movement would be construed as a retreat and a sign of weakness by both "enemies and friends."[20]

Burgoyne's decision provided an opportunity for Schuyler to buy valuable time to regroup and reinforce his badly shattered army. While the British commander put his Canadian auxiliaries to work clearing a decent roadway for his advance, he bided his time awaiting the arrival of sufficient horses and wagons to drag his army's artillery and supplies via the overland route. While he waited, Schuyler was already at work. Although he soon retired farther south to Stillwater, a small town on the Hudson River 25 miles south of Fort Edward and only a few miles north of Albany, the arrival of Nixon's and Glover's Continentals raised his effective force to about 4,500 and he took positive steps to retard the British advance as best he could. Ordering that all sustenance and other supplies within range of the British be either carried away or destroyed so as not to sustain their march, he dispatched his engineering officer to take command of the rear-guard delaying actions.[21]

On July 16, the general wrote to Kościuszko: "I have sent one of the Quartermasters to Saratoga and the post below to bring up all the Axes which can be collected, and to deliver them to you. Col. Lewis has my orders to send you a horse immediately. I will give the orders for moving General Fermoy's and General Paterson's Brigade[s] to-morrow and dispose of them in the manner you wish."[22] Altogether, the Polish colonel would have about 1,000 men under his command.

Kościuszko went forward immediately to survey the land, not waiting for the troops Schuyler promised to place under his command. His first task was to retard Burgoyne's march south from his temporary base, a task he apparently achieved by felling trees and destroying bridges on the narrow roadways leading from the British camps. "We were obliged to wait some time in our present position," Lt. Anburey explained, till the roads are cleared of the trees which the Americans felled after their retreat. [One] would think it almost impossible, but every ten or twelve yards great trees are laid across the road, exclusive of smaller ones, especially when it is considered what a hasty retreat they made of it. Repairing the bridges is a work of some labour, added to which a stock of provisions must be brought up previous to our marching for Fort Edward. We lie under many disadvantages in prosecuting this war, from the impediments I have stated, and we cannot follow this great military maxim, "in good success push the advantage as far as you can."[23]

The overall task was to retard the British as long as possible along a 23-mile stretch of road that Hoffman Nickerson rightly noted was "only a single long day's walk for a healthy man."[24] Yet, in the hands of a capable engineer, the narrow, winding road from Skenesboro to Fort Edward was ideally suited for delaying action. Little more than what Edgar termed "an unfinished cart path, barely wider than an axle," a traveller through the region the previous year described it as "the meanest, worst and most desolate road I ever saw."[25] Criss-crossed by small streams, cloaked in the dense foliage of pine and hemlock forests, and sprinkled with boggy swamps, the terrain offered many opportunities for man to improve on the work of nature. Further, the weather that summer appeared to favor the colonials with heavy rains filling the bogs and softening normally firm terrain.[26]

To complement these natural obstructions, Kościuszko used every engineering trick he could devise. First, he put axemen to work felling trees along the narrow winding roadway to obstruct the British march. Lest they be too easily removed, he issued orders for the trees to be felled in such a way that their branches became intertwined preventing the British from simply dragging them aside.[27] Sgt. Roger Lamb, a musician in the 21st Regiment of Foot, characterized the nightly crashing of trees in the surrounding forest as the "leit-motif of the resistance."[28] So successful was this tactic that another British soldier described the felled trees as being "as plenty as lampposts upon a highway about London."[29]

While the noise of falling trees echoed through the woods, other troops moved in front of the British column destroying every bridge within miles, forcing the enemy column to halt and construct new overpasses at every stream of any size. English Lieutenant Thomas Anburey described the ordeal thusly:

"The country between our late encampment at Skenesborough and this place [Fort Edward] was a continuation of woods and creeks, interspersed with deep morasses; and to add to these natural impediments, the enemy had very industriously augmented them by felling immense trees, and various other modes, that it was with the utmost pains and fatigue we could work our way through them. Exclusive of these, the watery grounds and marshes were so numerous that we were under the necessity of constructing no less than forty bridges to pass them, and over one morass there was a bridge of near two miles in length. ... [The Americans] sometimes, when our people were removing the obstructions we had continually to encounter, would attack them."[30]

Meanwhile, Kościuszko moved about the terrain seeking with his trained eye any opportunity to further impede the invasion. Trees strategically felled into Wood Creek flooded the surrounding countryside creating an enormous impassible quagmire. The Polish colonel had his men roll boulders into the larger waterways, making it at once difficult for the British to navigate the waters and causing overflows that further immersed the surrounding area. Hurriedly dug ditches lowered water levels in otherwise navigable streams, while diverting water to create additional flooding in the surrounding lowlands.[31]

Livestock were driven away and grain fields burned, forcing the invaders to subsist on the monotonous, diminishing supplies they carried with them. To make matters worse, the intense heat and humidity, unlike the weather the British and German troops were familiar with in Euorpe, took a constant toll in sickness, debilitation, and falling morale. The obstructions, the bogs, the heat and humidity, constant sniping by patriot marksmen, and swarms of vicious mosquitoes created "a labyrinthine hell" through which Burgoyne's men struggled hour after hour, mile after mile, day after day.[32] When marching on its trip south along the Richelieu River, Burgoyne's army covered an average of eighteen miles per day. Faced with Kościuszko's delaying tactics, they made only an average of slightly over one mile per day from Skenesboro to Fort Edward. It took them a full twenty days to cover the 23 miles between the two locations. But seven of these miles were by water, leaving an average of less than one mile per day for the land portion of the journey.[33]

Ragged, hungry, ill, and exhausted, Burgoyne's advance arrived at Fort Edward on July 29, only to find Schuyler's army had vanished into the surrounding forests. The balance of the army arrived on the banks of the Hudson on July 30 in such weakened condition from its ordeal that Burgoyne felt compelled to remain at Fort Edward for two full weeks resting, gathering supplies, and preparing for his next move.[34] But the ordeal caused by Kościuszko's delaying action was still not over. Even here, the scorched earth policy implemented under the Pole's direction further delayed the invader. A German lieutenant in Burgoyne's Brunswick contingent wrote in astonishment that "Pains were taken, and unfortunately with too great success, to sweep its few cultivated spots of all articles likely to benefit the invaders. In doing this the enemy showed no decency either to friend or foe. All the fields of standing corn were laid waste, the cattle were driven away, and every particle carefully removed; so that we could depend for subsistence, both for men and horses, only upon the magazines which we might ourselves establish."[35]

To solve his critical supply problem, Burgoyne approved a plan proposed by Baron von Riedesel to send a column marching east through Vermont into the Connecticut Valley to procure badly needed horses and provisions said to be in that area. Burgoyne, however, still contemptuous of the fighting abilities of the Americans despite his experiences at Bunker Hill and on the road from Skenesboro to Fort Edward, modified the German's plan into a much larger penetration that would go further south. Von Riedesel felt the revisions too risky, but Burgoyne insisted. Consequently, Lt. Col. Friedrich Baum led some 800 German and Tory troops off on the expanded raid. The raiders marched steadily, if slowly, eventually making contact with Col. John Stark's Vermont militia near Sancoick's Mill on the Hoosic River in eastern New York, just west across the border from Bennington, Vermont, on the morning of August 14. After a brief skirmish, Baum sent back for reinforcements and Burgoyne sent forward Lt. Col. Heinrich Breymann with 642 men and two 6-pounder field pieces. Before they could arrive, Stark's militia overwhelmed Baum's force, completing the victory by smashing Breymann's relief column when it approached the field. Only a well-conducted rear-guard action by Breymann allowed the escape of most of his command from imminent disaster. In all, the Americans lost only about 60-70 killed and wounded against 207 German dead, including Lt. Col. Baum, and about 700 taken prisoner. Further, Stark took four cannon, four ammunition wagons, and several hundred muskets and rifles, all of which were badly needed by the American cause.[36]

This disaster, caused by Burgoyne's desperate need for horses and provisions, greatly shaped the course of the remaining campaign. When he finally moved south on August 13, Burgoyne made it only as far as Fort Miller where he again halted the next day to collect supplies and provisions, remaining there until September 11, almost another full month that gave the American army further respite to recover from the trials of their recent defeats.[37] As the delay increased, it became apparent to some that the invasion was proceeding much too slowly. "We still remain in this encampment," wrote Lt. Anburey, "till provisions are brought up to enable us to move forward, and notwithstanding these delays in our convoys and stores, it will certainly be thought we remain too long for an army whose business is to act offensively, and whose first motion, according to the maxims of war, should contribute, as soon as possible, to the execution of the intended expedition."[38]

On the long retreat from Ticonderoga it was Kościuszko's responsibility to choose the camps, posts, and fortifications, as well as conduct the rear-guard activities. At a time when the colonial army was in full retreat—beaten, disheartened, and disorganized—with the victorious British and German professionals pressing relentlessly forward, it was the Polish engineer's responsibility to protect the remnants of the Northern Army and buy the time necessary for Schuyler to reorganize that army and for reinforcements to arrive. While historians have long agreed that the difficult British advance south from Ticonderoga was a major cause of Burgoyne's eventual defeat, few have given Kościuszko the credit due him as the mastermind behind the colonial activities at this time. Edgar pronounced his work "invaluable to Schuyler in his attempts to first delay, and then stop Burgoyne on the way to Albany."[39] Contemporary accounts of his service point to his tireless activity and personal courage during this dark hour. Col. Wilkinson, for example, notes in his memoirs that it was Kościuszko who directed "placing obstructions in the route, breaking down bridges, [and] rendering Wood Creek unnavigable." A memorial preserved in Thomas Jefferson's papers notes that during "the retreat of the American army Kosciuszko was distinguished for activity and courage."[40] Because of his skill and persistence, the Americans gained an entire month of extremely critical time that they put to good use in rebuilding their shattered

army, stockpiling ammunition and provisions, and obtaining reinforcements from Washington's army and the New York and New
England militias. Kościuszko's Fabian tactics thus created both
distress for the invader and succor for the defending Americans. In
a very real sense this made possible the culminating events about to
unfold.

Chapter 5

"The Fortune of War"

*F*ollowing the successful delaying action in the wilderness between Skenesboro and Fort Edward, Schuyler retired before the British advance about four miles below Fort Edward to a position along Moses Creek that Kościuszko selected and fortified. But Schuyler tarried there only briefly, his army in no shape to face the British. One American officer described the troops as a "rag[g]ed, starved, lousey, thievish, pockey army," while the general himself commented that many of his officers had "so little sense of honor that cashiering them seems no punishment. They have stood by, and suffered the most scandalous depradations to be committed on the poor, distressed, ruined and flying inhabitants."[1] Morale and discipline had clearly fallen to new depths with the precipitate evacuation of Ticonderoga, the defeats at Hubbardton and Skenesboro, and the long, painful retreats with rumor and recrimination far more plentiful than sustenance or hope.

Continuing his retreat south on July 30, Schuyler marched first to Fort Miller, then Saratoga (modern Schuylerville) where his own mansion stood. On August 2 the retreat continued some twelve miles further south to Stillwater where Kościuszko began constructing defensive works with the intent of finally making a stand. No sooner had the work begun, however, than word arrived of St. Leger's expedition against the Mohawk Valley. This left Schuyler with a serious problem. Faced with a major British army only one or two days march to the north, the Americans were now in danger of being cut off from Albany and caught between two hostile forces should St. Leger succeed in reducing Fort Stanwix and advancing eastward along the Mohawk. To meet the new threat, Schuyler called a council of war at which he proposed the extraordinarily dangerous move of dividing his force and sending a relief expedition to assist the defenders of Fort Stanwix. Despite considerable dissent, Schuyler dispatched Gen. Benedict Arnold with about 900 Continentals to march up the Mohawk Valley to the relief of Fort Stanwix.[2]

As Arnold's expedition prepared to leave, Schuyler determined to continue the American retreat further south so as to place as much terrain between himself and Burgoyne as possible. Thus, the army continued south another twelve miles, finally halting at Van Schaick's Island near the junction of the Hudson and Mohawk Rivers only nine miles north of Albany. There Kościuszko once again went to work to fortify the natural strength of the position, creating at least some sense of security for the beleaguered army to rally upon.[3]

While Kościuszko labored on the new defenses, action took place on other fields of conflict. When Gates rushed south after Schuyler's reappointment to command of the Northern Department, he managed to get a hearing before Congress but made such an emotional defense of himself that many were put off and he was thereafter precluded from attending its sessions. Congress avoided any decision by remanding the matter to Washington, who was disposed toward giving Gates command of Lincoln's Division but did not take any immediate action. Regardless, Gates and his supporters, aided by Schuyler's New England detractors, kept his cause alive. The fall of Ticonderoga and the continued retreat of Schuyler's forces toward Albany strengthened their hand. Soon they were able to bring the matter before Congress once again, the politicians eventually voting on August 4 to relieve the New Yorker in favor of Gates.[4]

Gates arrived at Stillwater on August 19, by which time Schuyler had largely reorganized the army and stabilized the situation. Burgoyne's Germans had been defeated at Bennington, St. Leger's force was retreating back to Canada from the gates of Fort Stanwix, and Burgoyne, finding himself in a tenuous supply situation, continued to remain stationery. The earlier delaying actions, coupled with the Bennington defeat, would cost the British another three weeks, giving Gates time to assume command, assess the situation, and gather badly needed troops from the surrounding states.[5]

The situation for the Americans improved rapidly. The day Gates arrived, Louis de la Corne St. Luc, angered by Burgoyne's refusal to allow his Indians to plunder the local settlements, led all but about fifty of their number off to Canada, greatly impairing Burgoyne's ability to gain information and protect his flanks from inquiring colonial eyes. The next day, news came of the victory at Bennington, followed soon after by the intelligence that St. Leger was retreating. On August 28 Benedict Arnold returned with 1,200 troops from the relief expedition sent to Fort Stanwix, including the 2nd and 4th New York Continental Regiments under Cols. Philip van Cortlandt and James Livingston respectively. The same day reinforcements arrived from Washington's army—Col. Daniel Morgan's 367 riflemen and Major Henry Dearborn's 250 light infantry.[6] Though small in numbers, they were well trained and equipped for use in the wooded hills of northern New York where they would render excellent service. The riflemen, in particular, were an excellent addition to the Northern Department. Recruited from among the rugged, independent frontiersmen in western Pennsylvania, Virginia and the Carolinas, they were used to the life of privation and self-reliance of the frontier and carried with them the famed Pennsylvania rifle, a much more accurate weapon with a greater range than the Brown Bess smoothbores carried by the British infantry. It was said the average rifleman could with ease hit a two-inch target at 150 yards. Their arrival brought new hope to the army. "From this miserable state of despondency and terror," Col. Udney Hay marveled, "Gates' arrival raised us, as if by magic. We began to hope and then to act."[7] According to George Clinton, "things began to wear a new face."[8]

The addition of some Connecticut infantry brought Gates's force to about 6,300 troops by September 6. With the army's morale and physical condition improving, Gates decided the time was right to move. Calling Kościuszko to his side, he sent the Pole and Col. Hay ahead to reconnoiter and select a position farther north that could be fortified to block Burgoyne's march on Albany. During the conference, Kościuszko suggested that morale might improve appreciably if the troops sensed a positive move. Taking this advice, while the two colonels rode off on their mission, Gates placed the army in motion, the advance covered by Morgan's riflemen and Dearborn's light infantry.[9] "[H]aving no confidence in the means employed by his predecessor for restoring the morale of his troops," Major Armstrong reported, "he promptly withdrew them from their insular fortress, and put them in motion, apparently for the camp of their enemy."[10]

Kościuszko rode north, his trained eye scouring every hill and ridge for a place to anchor the American position. At Stillwater he stopped to outline a system of defensive works, and digging had actually begun before he determined that the lengthy meadows between the Hudson and the hills to the west could not successfully be manned by the available troops. Another, less ambitious position had to be found. Riding further north, the engineer found one about six miles above Stillwater where the river turned westward causing the distance between it and the nearby hills to narrow appreciably near a small tavern owned by Jotham Bemis. There, guns placed on the crest of a wooded hill named Bemis Heights could command the road following the Hudson south to Albany.[11] It was, according to Lynn Montross, "a strategic bottleneck which could neither be forced nor avoided without difficulty," a naturally strong position that a "brilliant but shy engineer" made even more imposing with "a system of mutually supporting redoubts and entrenchments planned for defense in depth."[12] Major Dearborn pronounced it "a very advantageous Post."[13]

Kościuszko selected the position, according to Major Armstrong, "without loss of time."[14] Gates rushed 1,000 men forward to construct defensive works under Kościuszko's direction. Edgar describes the resulting entrenchments as "made of earth, logs and fence rails and fronted by an abatis, [that] stretched nearly a mile, starting at the narrow riverbank near Bemis's tavern, then moving up the slope and across the plateau some 200 feet above."[15] When completed, the Hudson River guarded the American right against any attempt to turn that flank, while redoubts guarded the lowlands on the right of the position running from beneath Bemis Heights to the river. An advanced line along Mill Creek was prepared to disrupt any attempt by the British to use their favorite tactic, the bayonet charge. Behind the first line Kościuszko constructed a second, more formidable line fronting a road junction just south of Bemis Heights. Along the heights the Pole constructed defensive works laced with gun emplacements to cover the lowlands below. The effect was to create somewhat of a pocket into which troops pushing through the Mill Creek line would be funnelled, facing a trap fronted by substantial fieldworks while artillery ripped into their flank and rear.

Stretching generally west along the heights, Kościuszko used the woods to screen the American works and placed the defense lines behind four deep ravines that formed a natural barrier making a successful frontal assault all but impossible. Placing fieldworks along the winding military crest of the hill, he concentrated the largest portion of the artillery here where it could cover both the lowlands to the right and the ravines at the center of the American line. With the front covered by log entrenchments, felled trees, fence rails, and earth, so as to strengthen the natural terrain with redoubts and interlacing fields of fire, Kościuszko used the natural contours of the earth and the woods to establish strongpoints that would channel any attacks into the few relatively open clearings where the colonial troops could be massed for best effect. Once fitted with gun emplacements, the works and their approaches were well-situated to punish any force attempting to move along the road to Albany or to assault the northern face of Bemis Heights.

The left, the most obvious point for a potential turning movement, was similarly covered by woods and hills improved by fieldworks. Kościuszko converted the Neilson barn into a fortified strongpoint supported by a well-entrenched battery. Turning south at the Neilson farm, the fieldworks continued to follow the natural line of the ridges. To the left of the Neilson farmhouse, fieldworks adorned a small knoll outside the main line. Additionally, Kościuszko ordered all the bridges in the area destroyed to retard the British advance, placed pickets at various points along the several ravines and winding roads that might be used to gain the American front or turn their left flank, and detached riflemen to create a screen fronting the only large cleared area near the center at Freeman's Farm.[16] Given the relatively short time available, the preparations were remarkably thorough, presenting a formidable obstacle to any further southward movement by Burgoyne's legions.

"Throwing into the duties of a military engineer his fiery energy, and something of his national tendency towards the grandiouse," wrote George Otto Trevelyan, "he had crowned Bemis Heights with a stronghold which resembled a citadel rather than a temporary field work."[17] Later in the war François Jean Marquis de Chastellux, one of Europe's most prominent military experts, visited Bemis Heights and left this description of the defenses:

> The eminencies, called Breams [sic] Heights, from whence this famous camp is named, are only a part of those high grounds which extend along the right bank of the Hudson, from the river Mohawk to that of Saratoga. At the spot chosen by General Gates for his position, they form, on the side of the river, two different slopes, or terraces. In mounting the first slope, are three redoubts placed in parallel directions. In front of the last, on the north side, is a little hollow, beyond which the ground rises again, on which are three more redoubts, placed nearly in the same direction as the former. In front

of them is a deep ravine which runs from the west, in which is a small creek. The ravine takes its rise in the woods; and all the ground on the right of it is extremely thick set with wood. If you will now return upon your steps, place yourself near the first redoubts you spoke of, and mount to the second slope proceeding to the westward, you will find, on the most elevated platform, a large entrenchment which was parallel with the river, and then turns towards the north-west, where it terminates in some pretty steep summits, which were likewise fortified by small redoubts. To the left of these heights, and at a place where the declivity becomes more gentle, begins another entrench-ment which turns towards the west, and makes two or three angles, always carried over the tops of the heights to the south-west. Towards the north-west, you come out of the lines to descend another platform, which presents a position the more favourable, as it commands the surrounding woods, and resists every thing which might turn the left flank of the army.[18]

Burgoyne, having finally acquired thirty days' provisions for his army, resumed his march on September 13. Since Albany lay on the western bank of the Hudson, and the farther south he went the wider and deeper the river became, his first move was to cross his troops to the west bank, which he accomplished by constructing a temporary bridge of boats at Saratoga. Once across the river, the British commander set up his headquarters in Gen. Schuyler's summer home,[19] which Lt. Anburey described as including "a handsome and commodious dwelling-house, with outhouses, an exceedingly fine saw-and grist-mill, and at a small distance a very neat church, with several houses round it.... This beautiful spot was quite deserted, not a living creature on it. On the grounds were great quantities of fine wheat, as also indian corn; the former was instantly cut down, threshed, carried to the mill to be ground, and delivered to the men to save our provisions; the latter was cut for forage for the horses."[20] This abundance was surprising in light of the American policy of denying sustenance to the enemy. "Evidently," Edgar writes with obvious sarcasm, "the scorched earth policy that Philip Schuyler had had his army enforce upon the settlers in the region had not been applied to his own fields."[21]

Freeman's Farm

Since he could not afford to detach troops to guard his supply and communication lines, Burgoyne dismantled the boat bridge across the river, freeing his force from contact with the lakes to the north. Breaking camp on September 17, the British veterans followed the river road south making steady if ponderous progress under the weight of thirty days' supplies. They marched in three columns, the British in the meadows and hills to the right of the roadway, the artillery and wagons on the road itself, and the Germans to the left of the road in the lowlands between it and the river. Supplies, baggage, and whatever else that could not be carried on the men's backs or in the rickety two-wheeled carts was consigned to some 200 bateaux that followed along in the river itself, guarded by six companies of the 47th Regiment of Foot. Without his Indian allies, however, Burgoyne was largely blind, unlike Gates who used Morgan's riflemen and some of the militia irregulars to hover about the British flanks obtaining information. On the 18th the lack of sufficient Indian allies to cover his right flank exposed the British to American sniping. One party sent forward to repair a bridge had to retreat hastily when attacked, while another sent out to dig potatoes suffered thirty casualties when caught in the open by colonial marksmen.[22] Angered that the Americans fired upon the potato-digging party before offering them an opportunity to surrender, Lt. Anburey wrote that "Such cruel and unjustifiable conduct can have no great tendency while it serves greatly to increase hatred and a thirst for revenge."[23] Despite the losses, the invaders pushed on until they reached a point about two miles north of the American defenses on Bemis Heights, still not entirely aware of the exact location or intent of Gates's army.

With the river road blocked so an attack would be a costly affair, and an assault through the heavy pine woods on the unknown American earthworks, so skillfully masked by Kościuszko's preparations, equally risky, Burgoyne determined, as Kościuszko had foreseen, to turn the American left. To accomplish this, the British commander divided his forces into three attacking columns numbering about 4,000 troops and several fieldpieces. Von Riedesel's Germans would move along the river road, pressuring the colonial defenses enough to keep the troops there from reenforcing any other portion of the line. Von Riedesel's force included the Specht, Rhetz, and von Riedesel Regiments and Pausch's Hesse Hanau artillery company with eight field pieces—about 1,100 men in all.[24]

The center column, commanded by Gen. Hamilton but accompanied by Burgoyne, was to march westward uphill, then turn south along the Great Ravine, then west to Freeman's Farm. Located about a mile north of Gates's headquarters on Bemis Heights, Freeman's Farm was the largest clearing along the center of the American line. Hamilton's force included the battalion companies of the 20th, 21st, and 62nd Regiments of Foot, with the 9th Regiment of Foot held back as a reserve in case of emergency. Six light fieldpieces provided additional firepower. Like the Germans to his left, Hamilton had at his disposal about 1,100 troops.[25]

To the right of Hamilton, Gen. Fraser would lead the final column two miles to the west before turning south to gain the high ground west of Freeman's Farm. Because mobility was important to his mission, his force included the British light infantry under Major the Earl of Balcarres, the grenadier companies under Major John Dyke Acland, the battalion companies of the 24th Regiment of Foot, Lt. Col. Breymann's Brunswick riflemen, and about 75 Canadians, 150 Tories, 50 British marksmen and the remaining 50 or so Indians. Also present were eight artillery pieces divided evenly between six-pounders and three-pounders. Fraser's total force, designed as the main striking force to turn the American left flank, was about 2,000 men.[26]

The six battalion companies of the 47th Regiment of Foot served as guard for the bateau, while the Hesse Hanau Infantry Regiment guarded the baggage and supply wagons. The surviving fifty or so Brunswick dragoons acted as Burgoyne's personal guard. The entire British-German force numbered by this time only some 6,000 men. When all was in readiness, Burgoyne would fire three guns as the signal for advance. Then, while von Riedesel held the Americans in place along the river, Hamilton would attack the center at Freeman's Farm and Fraser would turn the American left, gaining their flank and rear. Victory would be complete.[27]

Burgoyne planned the advance for the early morning of September 19, but the night had been cold, with hoarfrost on the ground, and a resulting dense early morning fog prevented the troops from getting underway until about 10:00 a.m. When the movement finally began, von Riedesel advanced behind a screen of light infantry against the Continental brigades of Brig. Gens. John Glover and John Paterson, and Col. John Nixon. The Americans held positions on Bemis Heights and in the lowlands leading to the river under the direct command of Gates, but they made little move to advance and engage the enemy. In conformity with Gates's intention to force Burgoyne to expend his forces in costly attacks on the American positions, the defenders were content to hold their positions and force the Germans to do the attacking. Von Riedesel, however, found it necessary to stop frequently to repair bridges and clear felled trees, obstructions ordered by Kościuszko that slowed the attackers' progress considerably. "The march was excedingly tedious," noted a German staff officer, "as every moment new bridges had to be made, and trees cut down and removed out of the way." Not until nearly 1:00 p.m. did the Germans penetrate beyond Wilbur's Basin to a position from which they could launch an attack on the American lines.[28]

To the west of the Germans, the distances, hills, and woods all made it nearly impossible to coordinate the movements and attacks of Hamilton's and Fraser's columns. Almost as soon as they began, the movement of each column came under colonial scrutiny and reports were sent back to Gates at regular intervals to inform him of the British movements and progress. Hamilton's column began arriving at a position slightly west of Freeman's Farm about noon. There it halted for the better part of an hour to give the left and right wings time to move into position. Roughly opposite Hamilton's position, about a mile away, was the American center held by Continental troops under Brig. Gen. Ebenezer Learned and Cols. John Bailey, Henry Jackson, James Wesson, and James Livingston. To the left of the American center, and within reach of Hamilton's column, lay Major Gen. Benedict Arnold's force including Morgan's riflemen, Dearborn's light infantry, three New Hampshire Continental regiments, two New York Continental regiments, and some Connecticut militia units.[29]

About 1:00 p.m. the signal guns echoed through the woods and the British began their final movements. Faced with increasing reports of enemy activity, Gen. Arnold appealed to Gates for permission to lead the American left forward to meet the British at Freeman's Farm, but permission was denied, Gates preferring that the British should come to him rather than he to them, thus forcing them to absorb more punishment attacking the American defenses. These defensive tactics were not universally popular, and Arnold persisted in his entreaties until Gates finally relented and allowed him to push forward Morgan's riflemen and Dearborn's light infantry to protect the left flank with orders to call upon Arnold's command for support if necessary.[30]

Morgan's riflemen, spread out in a thin skirmish line, soon met Fraser's advance, consisting of his Canadians, Tories and Indians, south of Freeman's Farm. In a very sharp action lasting only about fifteen minutes, Morgan's and Dearborn's men proved their reputation as marksmen by devastating the British advance, downing every officer and many of its men. The rest turned and ran in precipitate flight, pursued, unwisely, by Morgan's men. Rushing across an open field, Morgan's men met a withering volley from a force of Tories under Major Forbes sent out to support the shattered advance guard. It was now the Americans' turn to run.[31]

Arnold sent forward two of his New Hampshire Continental regiments which he placed on the left of Morgan's reformed line so as to overlap Fraser's right flank. The Americans advanced on the British flank, but met "a tremendous fire" from the grenadiers and light infantry Fraser rushed forward to meet the threat. About this time, Hamilton arrived at Freeman's Farm and deployed his men in the thin pine woods along the clearing, the guns placed on the northern edge of the field. From the right, the British units included the 21st, 62nd, and 20th Regiments of Foot, with the 9th held in reserve. The American fortifications lay about a mile away, concealed by the woods and the intervening hills and ridges. Yet, on the American left Arnold learned of Hamilton's advance and thought he saw an opportunity to place a strong force between Fraser and Hamilton, thereby cutting the two forces off from one another. To accomplish this he left Morgan and Dearborn to hold Fraser in check while leading his two New Hampshire regiments off to battle Hamilton and ordering forward Hale's, Van Cortlandt's, James Livingston's, Bailey's, Wesson's, Jackson's, Marshall's, Cook's, and Lattimer's regiments—virtually his whole force. This quick shifting of units was possible largely because of Kościuszko's expertise in designing the American defensive works. By channeling the British attack to the left, away from the open riverside meadows, the Pole allowed Gates to concentrate his best troops in larger number to oppose the only serious avenue for British attack. Further, his placement of the redoubts, abatis, and other field obstacles offered strong defense but also provided interior lines and sally ports for quick egress to facilitate a counterattack such as the one Gates launched on Burgoyne's flanking column.[32]

Arnold's attack on Hamilton's force provoked a brutal battle of charge and countercharge across the Freeman's Farm clearing. The British guns fell into American hands, but were then retaken in a spirited counterattack. Outflanked on the right, the 21st Regiment fell back, leaving the 62nd in a very exposed salient at the British center, but Fraser dispatched Breymann's riflemen and the battalion companies of the 24th Regiment of Foot to support Hamilton's right. What started out with promise for the Americans, ended up as a slugfest in the forest clearing. Time and again one side, then the other, would charge, gain control of the guns, then be forced to retire. Morgan sent his riflemen up into the trees to pick off the British officers and artillerymen, and so effective was the American fire that every artillery officer save one was hit, as well as 36 of the 48 gunners. One Briton later recalled "Senior officers who had witnessed the hardest fighting of the Seven Years' War declared that they had never experienced so long and hot a fire."[33]

With the British center under severe pressure, but his entire division already committed, Arnold appealed to Gates for more reinforcements, sensing that a forceful attack might break the British lines and shatter their army. Gates, however, was concerned that Arnold's advance had left the defensive works assigned to him virtually empty. If Fraser succeeded in turning the flank, or if Arnold suffered a reverse, there would be no effective force to man the entrenchments and prevent a major disaster from overtaking Gates's army. With this in mind, he initially refused Arnold's request for reinforcements. Later he did send forward Gen. Ebenezer Learned's brigade of Continentals from New York and Massachusetts, but this attack went too far to the left, hitting Fraser instead of Hamilton.[34]

While Arnold sought reinforcements, Gen. Phillips, riding over from von Riedesel's column to find out what was happening, was appalled at the conditions he found when he reached Hamilton's position. He immediately sent word to the German to rush forward some guns and infantry to support the British center. Von Riedesel led two companies of the Rhetz Regiment off through almost two miles of woods to assist his allies, ordering his own regiment to follow as soon as it formed. Reaching Hamilton's position, von Riedesel found "The three brave English regiments had been, by the steady fire of fresh relays of the enemy, thinned down to one-half and now formed a small band surrounded by heaps of dead and wounded." Clearly a crisis had been reached. Without waiting for the Von Riedesel Regiment to arrive, the German general led the two Rhetz companies forward at the double-quick, "drums beating and his men shouting 'Hurrah!',", against the advancing Americans. His daring momentarily stunned the colonials, driving them back until

Capt. Pausch brought up two fieldpieces and the Von Reidesel Regiment arrived to save the British from a potentially serious defeat.[35]

Although the British held the field that night, allowing them to claim a victory, they had clearly been mauled, and badly. "We have gained little more by our victory than honour," Lt. Anburey lamented. Ward estimated British losses for the day at 600 killed, wounded, and captured, including 350 in the three regiments that held Hamilton's position in the center. Burgoyne's official report listed 245 killed and 444 wounded—a total of 689. The 62nd Regiment of Foot, which went into the fight with about 350 men and held the exposed salient in the middle of the line, could count only about 60 present and fit for duty at the end of the day. American losses were recorded as eight officers and 57 enlisted men killed, 21 officers and 197 enlisted men wounded, 38 missing; a total of 321, or slightly less than half the number lost by the British. For all the severe fighting and the heavy losses, Burgoyne gained nothing. Gates, playing a waiting game to garner his strength and force Burgoyne into a less advantageous attacking position, gained both time and position.[36]

Bemis Heights

Despite his losses, Burgoyne planned to resume the attack the following morning, but Gen. Fraser argued that his grenadiers and light infantry, who were scheduled to lead the attack, needed a day to recover and Gen. Phillips convinced Burgoyne to wait until the troops were better rested and resupplied before undertaking a further advance. When the 21st dawned, however, the British general received a message from Sir Henry Clinton in New York City informing him that Clinton planned to make a move against the American positions in the Highlands along the Hudson to divert American troops from opposing Burgoyne's movement south. With this intelligence Burgoyne again postponed the attack to await the results of Clinton's move. In doing so, he lost any opportunity he had to attack the American positions when they were still somewhat disorganized from the fight at Freeman's Farm and continued disagreements between Gates and Arnold over battlefield tactics.[37]

Once he decided to await events further south, Burgoyne determined to entrench his position to discourage any American attack. The Germans, reinforced by the survivors of Hamilton's battered 9th, 20th, 21st, and 62nd Regiments of Foot, remained in position along the lowlands between the Hudson River and the North Branch of Mill Creek. To the west, the British right flank under Gen. Fraser was held, from east to west, by the grenadiers, the 24th Regiment of Foot, and the light infantry. The latter, under Major Alexander Leslie, Earl of Balcarres, held the salient at Freeman's Farm, fortified with a redoubt bearing the major's name. Lt. Col. Breymann's command was entrenched in another smaller redoubt about 500 yards to the north, the intervening space covered by the Canadians and Tories who occupied two reinforced log cabins located there. The front was covered by picket outposts a few hundred yards in advance, and behind the front the British built three more redoubts on the high ground above Wilbur's Basin where their supplies, wagons, and bateaux were gathered.[38]

On the American side, conditions were not well disposed to meet a renewed British attack had one been made the morning of September 20. Considerable disorganization existed among the American units that had seen combat at Freeman's Farm, while the rudimentary commissary system produced little in the way of food or ammunition to relieve those who had borne the brunt of the battle. Indeed, Gates's entire reserve ammunition amounted to no more than forty rounds per man and virtually none of this reached the American left by the morning after the battle. Had Burgoyne continued his advance, he would have encountered a disorganized American army, its combat units seriously short of ammunition to continue the fight. With Burgoyne's decision against renewing the attack the next morning, Gates, following the recommendation of Kościuszko, continued to improve his defensive positions on Bemis Heights. He also sent troops to occupy the high ground to the west of the American position, the area that had been the objective of Fraser's flanking column on September 19. Once in possession, Kościuszko supervised the fortification of the high ground west of the Neilson House, about one-half mile beyond the main works on Bemis Heights. The activity did not go unnoticed by the British.[39] "[T]he Americans [are] working with incessant labour to strengthen their left," reported Lt. Anburey, "their right is already unattackable."[40]

During this time, Col. Robert Troup, an aide-de-camp to Gen. Gates, was at headquarters where he observed Kościuszko's activities. According to the colonel, during the entire campaign the Pole was "constantly about General Gates' person," dining with him, advising him, and working on the defenses. To Troup, the engineer appeared a "rather young man—of unassuming manners—of grave temper."[41] Grave he should have been. These were trying days, there was no time for anything but hard work if the invaders were to be vanquished.

While the front line remained quiet after the fracus at Freeman's Farm, considerable fighting occurred behind the American entrenchments. Angered that Arnold had left his defensive works virtually unguarded on the 19th, risking, in the commanding general's estimation, the safety of the entire army, Gates's anger grew when he learned his enemies were crediting Schuyler's preparations and Arnold's leadership for the British repulse at Freeman's Farm. Subsequently, and possibly because of the pro-Arnold lobbying by Schuyler loyalists Capt. Richard Varick and Major Henry Brockholst Livingston, Gates omitted any mention of Arnold's contribution, or the brigades of Learned and Poor from Arnold's division, when the commanding general penned his official report. At the same time, he attributed the victory to the gallantry of Morgan's riflemen and Dearborn's light infantry, mentioning the former general by name.[42] Not to be overlooked, Col. Livingston, a Schuyler loyalist now allied with Arnold, wrote to Schuyler to tell him that "Arnold is the Life & Soul of the Troops. Believe me, Sir, to him, and to him alone is due the Honor of our late Victory. Whatever since his Superiors may claim, they are entitled to None."[43]

Seething with anger at his treatment by Gates, Arnold rushed to the commanding general's headquarters where a loud confrontation took place, Arnold accusing Gates of purposely besmirching his contributions and character. Gaining no satisfaction, Arnold penned a formal letter of protest to Gates, requesting permission for himself and his aides to travel to Philadelphia to present his own views to the Continental Congress. Much to Arnold's surprise, Gates agreed, calling Arnold's bluff. When Arnold continued his protests in person, Gates openly ridiculed him, telling Arnold he no longer had a command in the army and his position was being taken by Gen. Lincoln. Angry declarations and vituperative letters were exchanged, one observer commenting that "Gates was irritating, arrogant and vulgar; Arnold indiscreet, haughty and passionate." The result was that Gates banned Arnold, now without a command, from visiting army headquarters.[44]

While the Americans fought amongst themselves, the British waited. His strength now reduced to some 5,000 effectives, Burgoyne must have begun to feel the strain of mounting difficulties. Swarms of militia now hung about his army preventing reconnaissance activities and sniping at anyone who ventured away from camp. Some bold riflemen climbed trees to fire directly into the British lines. "From the 20th of September to the 7th of October, the armies were so near, that not a night passed without firing, and sometimes concerted attacks, on our advanced picquets; no foraging party could be made without great detachments to cover it; it was the plan of the enemy to harrass the army by constant alarms and their superiority of numbers enabled them to attempt it without fatigue to themselves," Burgoyne later wrote. "I do not believe that either officer or soldier ever slept during that interval without his cloaths, or that any general officer, or commander of a regiment, passed a single night without being upon his legs occasionally at different hours and constantly an hour before daylight." Unable to forage, its supplies dwindling, the army had to subsist largely on a bland and monotonous diet of salt pork and flour. By October 3, daily rations had to be reduced by one-third. Horses began to die from starvation and desertions increased almost daily.[45]

Unlike the British, the Americans, aside from their internal squabbling, seemed to grow stronger each day. Gen. Benjamin Lincoln arrived on September 29 with militia from Vermont, while other units came in from New York and New England almost daily. By October 4 Gates had over 7,000 troops, a number that swelled to 11,000 within the next three days as militia continued to rally to his army. Further, Gates's ammunition was replenished from stores Schuyler accumulated at Albany, and food was not only abundant but in great variety.[46] Additionally, Kościuszko kept busy strengthening the American lines wherever he could, including the erection of some field abatis. In the British lines, Lt. Anburey, assigned to Fraser's command on the British right near where Kościuszko labored on the works at the Neilson farm, commented that "The enemy, in front of our quarter-guard, within hearing, are cutting trees and making works, and when I have had this guard, I have been visited by most of the field-officers, to listen to them."[47] Clearly, each day that went by increased Gates's advantage.

Given the deteriorating situation, Burgoyne called a council of war on October 4 to discuss the alternatives available to the army. Present in addition to the commanding general were Fraser, Phillips and von Riedesel. The high hopes of the early campaign had by now given way to a more depressing view. Rations were running seriously low, the warm weather of the summer was fading into memory as the cool September nights began giving way to colder October weather, and the road to Albany was blocked by a well-intrenched enemy who apparently also outnumbered the invaders. Further, the activity of the American riflemen, coupled with Kościuszko's skillful placement of the American lines, left the British with virtually no intelligence on the positions facing them or the best way to approach them for attack. The British situation was not yet desperate, but it was certainly difficult and deserved a full discussion of the various options.[48]

Burgoyne opened the meeting by proposing a general assault on the American position. His plan called for leaving about 800 troops to guard the supplies while the balance of the army attempted to turn the American left, much the same plan as earlier except that the army would march together rather than in separated columns. The others immediately voiced objections. No one knew exactly where the American left was or how it might be fortified. Moving virtually the entire army on a wide circuitous march would leave the camp and supplies open to attack by the Americans, and leaving the redoubts lightly held would invite their loss as well. Faced with overwhelming opposition, Burgoyne did not push his plan any further. When asked for their opinions, von Riedesel advocated retreating north immediately to Fort Edward to reestablish contact with the lakes, obtain supplies, and await the outcome of Clinton's efforts on the lower Hudson. Fraser agreed, but Phillips offered no opinion one way or the other. Yet, Burgoyne was loath to retreat without one more try. Since lack of adequate information appeared to be a large stumbling block, he proposed a reconnaissance in force to develop the American position and possibly seize the heights west of the American line. The plan revealed the paucity of Burgoyne's information for, while he knew the Americans were working on their defenses, he did not yet know that Kościuszko had already fortified that position, which Gates occupied after the action at Freeman's Farm.[49]

The reconnaissance in force began early on October 7 when 1,500 infantry moved about three-quarters of a mile southwest from Freeman's Farm, halting in a large clearing to allow a group of workers who accompanied them to harvest the grain in the field to feed the army's dwindling supply of horses. The force consisted of some of the best troops in Burgoyne's army: the British light infantry under the Earl of Balcarres on the right, the British grenadiers on the left under Major Acland, and in the center under von Riedesel the 24th Regiment of Foot, Col. Breymann's jägers, and a select group of Brunswick infantry chosen from each of the German regiments. The attacking force was supported by six 6-pounders, two 12-pounders, and two howitzers. While the troops sat in their ranks, officers with field glasses peered intently for a glimpse of the American lines.[50]

The move did not come as any surprise to the Americans because Kościuszko's engineering skills made the American right and center nearly impregnable to attack, leaving the left as the only feasible place for Burgoyne to again cast the dice. Warning of the British movement came to Gates early. He sent Wilkinson to reconnoiter the enemy march and when the major reported the British halted in a thin line on open ground Gates ordered Morgan forward "to begin the game."[51] With him, in addition to his own riflemen and Dearborn's light infantry, Morgan brought the veteran Continental brigades of Enoch Poor and Ebenezer Learned. Across the field separating the two armies, under cover of the surrounding woods, the troops moved forward quickly but quietly, Poor forming opposite the British left and Learned opposite the enemy center. Morgan sent the riflemen and light infantry to cover the British right flank. Once again, thanks to Kościuszko's preparations, Gates was able to deploy about 2,100 men against Burgoyne's 1,500, and to add a steady stream of 3,000 reinforcements.[52]

Suddenly a shot rang out from the woods, then another and another. The work party dropped their tools and ran for the protection of the battle line. Learned's brigade was the first to come into action, making contact with the Germans under von Riedesel in mid-afternoon. Within minutes, Poor's New Hampshire brigade moved to the attack against Acland's grenadiers, who met them with a flurry of volleys and artillery. The British, holding the top of a rising hill, apparently aimed too high, a common problem when troops fire on attackers coming at them from lower ground, and their fire failed to stop the American assault. With Acland wounded, the British line wavered, reformed, then broke.[53]

In the center, the Germans fared better. For nearly an hour the small force of 300 Brunswick infantry, supported by Pausch's artillery, beat back repeated attacks by Learned's Massachusetts regiments. Firing furiously, the guns became so hot they could not be touched with the naked hand. Yet, the Germans suffered heavy losses in maintaining their position.[54]

On the American left, Morgan and Dearborn pressed home their attack on the British light infantry and the 24th Regiment of Foot. Extending beyond the British right, the Americans outflanked the attackers, forcing them to halt and refuse their flank to avoid being turned. This, in turn, opened the Germans holding the center to further flanking fire. With the British right beginning to waver, Gen. Simon Fraser spurred his horse forward to rally his troops. But Morgan's marksmen soon shot him from his saddle and the British right began to break, exposing the Brunswickers in the center.[55]

About this time, Gen. Abraham Ten Broeck arrived on the field with his brigade of several Albany County militia regiments. Some 3,000 strong, they numbered twice the size of the original British reconnaissance force and, thought not as well trained or experienced, their weight of numbers was overwhelming. By now the German position was desperate. With both of the flanks collapsed, the Brunswick infantry was virtually surrounded and Pausch's guns, all but a handful of gunners by now killed or wounded, dangerously exposed. In the face of Ten Broeck's attack, the captain managed to save one gun, but the rest were lost as the retreat became general under increasing American pressure.[56]

In the face of disaster, Burgoyne ordered a retreat to Freeman's Farm where he planned to rally on the Breymann and Balcarres redoubts. As the British and Germans retired, American pursuit began to slow, the various regiments having been greatly disorganized in the attacks. At this juncture, however, Arnold, unable to restrain himself in camp, arrived on the field. Without any formal command, Arnold raced about rallying Learned's Massachusetts troops, then led them forward against the Balcarres redoubt, but stiff British resistance drove the attackers back. Moving to the left, he next gathered up some of Morgan's riflemen and light infantry, leading them in a spirited attack that broke the Canadians and Tories posted in the two stockaded log cabins in the area between the two redoubts.[57]

Once his men penetrated the defensive line, Arnold wheeled toward the Breymann redoubt, taking it in flank and rear. Breymann, his position now exposed to fire from nearly every side and his troops reduced to only about 200 effectives, fell mortally wounded defending the redoubt. Arnold, too, fell, shot through the same leg that had been wounded at Quebec the previous year, but the attack carried the day leaving Burgoyne in an untenable position with no alternative but further retreat to the Great Redoubt guarding his camp and supplies. Behind him the British general left 198 killed, 232 wounded, 443 prisoners and missing—a total of 873 men—and ten guns. American losses were about 150 killed and wounded.[58]

By the end of the fight on October 7 Burgoyne found himself in serious trouble. His army of more than 7,000 effectives stood reduced to only about 4,100 troops present and fit for duty. Further, loss of the line anchored by the Breymann and Balcarres redoubts exposed his position to assault from flank and rear, concerns that could not be overlooked given his diminishing strength and his precarious position with the Hudson River at his back.[59]

The next day, October 8, Gates moved his troops forward to take firm possession of the British works captured the previous day. At the same time, he sent Brig. Gen. John Fellows with 1,300 Massachusetts militia to cut off Burgoyne's line of retreat. Marching up the east side of the river, Fellows forded the stream considerably north of Burgoyne's camp and went into position west of Saratoga. Gates also ordered Brig. Gen. Jacob Bayley with 2,000 New Hampshire militia to occupy Fort Edward, but he made no offensive move with his main army, preferring to remain on the defensive and force Burgoyne into action. While both Fellows and Bayley were strong forces on paper, they could have offered only modest resistance to a determined British attack if Burgoyne had acted decisively in withdrawing his army.[60]

Under cover of a heavy rain on the evening of October 8, Burgoyne began to withdraw his army northward along the Hudson River toward the village of Saratoga [modern Schuylerville], leaving 300 sick and wounded in his hospital and a large quantity of baggage for the Americans to take possession of the next day. Led by Lt. Col. Sutherland with the 9th and 47th Regiments of Foot, Burgoyne moved slowly, keeping his camp fires burning to deceive Gates about his intentions. Soon Sutherland discovered Fellows's camp, which he reported as largely unguarded, but Burgoyne refused permission for an attack, preferring instead to avoid contact and go into camp with his main force about three miles away. With excruciatingly slow progress, the British did not reach Saratoga at the mouth of the Fish Kill until late on the evening of October 9.[61]

His troops exhausted by the march in heavy rain over hopelessly muddy roads, Burgoyne decided to halt at Saratoga for a rest, but dispatched Lt. Col. Sutherland with the 9th and 47th Regiments of Foot, a force of Canadians, and some engineers and sappers to build a bridge near Fort Edward to transfer the army to the east bank of the Hudson. While the bridge was a necessary move, the decision to halt for rest at Saratoga proved a fatal mistake.[62]

Gates gave Burgoyne every opportunity to escape, not beginning his pursuit in earnest until the afternoon of October 10. When his advance finally approached Fish Kill late that afternoon, Gen. Hamilton, commanding the rear guard consisting of the 20th, 21st, and 62nd Regiments, burned the Schuyler mansion and withdrew across the creek.[63]

The following day, the Americans captured most of the British bateaux carrying their supplies and bridging equipment, a serious loss that at once brought a serious supply problem and made withdrawal all the more difficult.[64]

By October 12, Burgoyne's army was virtually surrounded with only a small opening to the north available for possible retreat. Faced with an increasingly precarious position, Burgoyne called a council of war—including von Riedesel, Phillips, von Gall, and Hamilton—at which he presented five possible options[65]:

1. The army could hold its ground and await developments in the Highlands above New York City where Sir Henry Clinton had promised a demonstration against the American positions that might force Gates to send troops south, thereby decreasing the pressure on Burgoyne.

2. The army could attack, hoping to inflict a reverse on Gates and thus reduce American pressure.

3. The army could fight its way northward to Fort Edward, carrying its remaining guns and supplies with it.

4. The army could abandon its baggage and wagons and move north that night under cover of dark.

5. If Gates should move west to flank the British, the army could march quickly south for Albany.

In the discussion that followed, Phillips and Hamilton generally debated the last option, while von Riedesel argued that only a precipitate withdrawal such as envisioned in option four could possibly save the army. He proposed retiring rapidly up the west bank of the Hudson, crossing north of Fort Edward, and from there proceeding immediately to the relative succor of Fort George where resupply and reinforcement could be effected via the lakes.[66]

In the end, the decision was to retreat. The movement was to begin that night, the troops taking six days' provisions and all the supplies they could carry. The artillery, baggage, and anything else that could not be carried was to be abandoned. Von Riedesel notified Burgoyne that he was ready to move at 10:00 p.m., but instead of the anticipated marching orders he was told the movement had been postponed. "Every hour the position of the army grew more critical," von Riedesel worried, "and the prospect of salvation grew less and less. There was no place of safety for the baggage; and the ground was covered with dead horses that had either been killed by the enemy's bullets or by exhaustion, as there had been no forage for several days.... Even for the wounded, no spot could be found which could afford them a safe shelter—not even, indeed, for so long a time as might suffice for a surgeon to bind up their ghastly wounds. The whole camp was now a scene of constant fighting. The soldier could not lay down his arms day or night, except to exchange his gun for the spade when new entrenchments were thrown up. The sick and wounded would drag themselves along into a quiet corner of the woods and lie down to die on the damp ground. Nor even here were they longer safe, since every little while a ball would come crashing down among the trees."[67]

By the next day, John Stark arrived with 1,100 New Hampshire militia to close the northern escape route and Burgoyne was completely surrounded. Burgoyne responded by convening another council of war, this time including field officers and captains. He proposed the same five alternatives he had previously, but with an explanation of the difficult position the army was in and the comment that he would consider surrender only if those in the council so advised. In this regard, he posed three questions[68]:

1. Could an army of 3,500 effective combatants enter into an agreement with the enemy without detriment to the national honor?

2. Was this now the case for this army?

3. Was this army's situation such as to make an honorable capitulation really detrimental?[69]

The consensus was that, under the circumstances, surrender would not be dishonorable.

Burgoyne sent Major Kingston to the American lines under a flag of truce to suggest a cease fire while terms could be discussed. Disregarding the military propriety of the day, which called for the vanquished to first propose terms, Gates presented the major with a written set of terms calling for the surrender of Burgoyne's army as prisoners of war and the grounding of arms prior to the troops marching out of their camp. Greatly offended, Burgoyne refused the terms, proposing instead that the troops march out to the full honors of war and that they be allowed free passage on British ships to Great Britain in return for a pledge not to serve again in North America during the conflict. Burgoyne apparently never thought Gates would agree to the terms in their entirety, since they contained many very liberal provisions, but the American commander surprised him by agreeing to every provision. Because of Gates's haste in accepting Burgoyne's terms, and the American's insistence that the formalities take place the next day, Burgoyne became convinced that Clinton's forces had been successful north of New York and Gates found it necessary to conclude events quickly because of some other threat, possibly a British army marching to Burgoyne's rescue. Consequently, the British general asked for a postponement of the actual ceremony as a means of gaining time.[70]

Gates agreed to a brief postponement, and when Burgoyne further suggested that the official agreement be called a "convention" rather than a "capitulation," Gates also agreed, heightening Burgoyne's suspicion that Gates was operating under some time constraint. In his mind, that could only be Clinton coming to his rescue. Only after yet another council of war affirmed the need to surrender did Burgoyne finally relent.[71]

War being what it was in the eighteenth century, Burgoyne, von Riedesel, Phillips, and their staffs rode to Gates's headquarters resplendent in their dress uniforms. "The fortune of war," Burgoyne told Gates, "has made me your prisoner." Gates graciously assured Burgoyne that "I shall ever be ready to testify that it has not been through any fault of your Excellency," whereupon the British accepted an invitation to dine at the American headquarters.[72]

The formal ceremonies took place on October 17, the British and their German allies marching out of their encampment under arms, musicians playing "The Grenadiers' March," and flags flying as was the custom for honorable capitulation. The vanquished strode through the American camp between two lines of troops drawn up at attention, marched on to a large meadow along the banks of the Hudson, and there placed their arms and accoutrements in piles to be gathered up later by the victors. The grounding of arms complete, Burgoyne formally tendered his sword to Gates, becoming the first British general in history to surrender a major army to an adversary in the field.[73]

Burgoyne's surrender at Saratoga proved to be a significant turning point of the war. Indeed, the battle is usually numbered among the ten most important in history. As Ward enumerated it, the captured men and material included "Two lieutenant generals, two major generals, three brigadiers, with their staffs and aides, 299 other officers ranging from colonels to ensigns, chaplains and surgeons, 389 noncommissioned officers, 197 musicians, and 4,836 privates passed out of the armed forces of Great Britain in America. The materiel captured was of vast importance, including 27 guns of various calibers, 5,000 stand of small arms, great quantities of ammunition, and military stores and equipment of all kinds," a total of more than 5,700 captives.[74] Further, the American military situation improved materially when, as a result of the Saratoga disaster, the British were compelled to abandon both Fort Ticonderoga and Crown Point, to recall Clinton's force from its march up the Hudson River from New York, and to abandon Fort Clinton in the Hudson Highlands.[75]

Equally important were the psychological and political results. The victory at Saratoga restored to a great deal the wavering confidence of both the patriots and their foreign supporters. At home, the victory offset to a large extent the disastrous Philadelphia Campaign which ended with General Washington's defeats at Brandywine and Germantown and the subsequent occupation of the fledgling nation's first capital. Abroad, Saratoga brought new hope to America's friends on the continent. Within days, the French agreed to open recognition and support for the American cause, resulting, on February 6, 1778, in a formal treaty bringing France and Spain into the war on the side of the Americans, which brought arms, ammunition, and ultimately the French army and navy to North America. In this, Saratoga made Yorktown possible.[76]

To a significant extent, it was Tadeusz Kościuszko who made Saratoga possible. Kościuszko worked long, and with great skill, to improve the defenses of Fort Ticonderoga, Mount Independence, and the surrounding positions. His advice to fortify Sugar Loaf Hill, though never acted upon, proved exactly correct. Following the loss of that post the Pole participated in the tenuous American retreat from Ticonderoga and directed the successful delaying operations along the upper tributaries of the Hudson River. Likewise, it was

Tadeusz Kościuszko who selected and fortified the American positions at Bemis Heights and the surrounding area, as well as sighting the American lines of defense that allowed rapid offensive sorties while at the same time defying British attempts to approach near enough to assault. Proof of this comes from several sources, including Gates's official report in which he stated without qualification that "Colonel Kosciuszko chose and entrenched the position."[77] No doubt it was largely Gates's report and letters, supplemented with the reports of others, that led Washington to report to Congress on November 10, 1777, that he had "been well informed that the engineer in the Northern Army, Kościuszko I think his name is, is a gentleman of science and merit. From the character I have had of him he is deserving of notice."[78]

General John Glover who was present at Saratoga penned words of praise for Kościuszko when he wrote his memoirs. In describing the campaign against Burgoyne, Glover noted that it was indeed on the advice of Kościuszko that Gates moved his army up-river prior to the battles at Saratoga. In his *History of the United States* the famous American historian Edward Channing wrote of Saratoga: "whatever credit there may be would seem to belong to Gates and to his Engineer, Kosciuszko, the Polander." In a similar vein Woodrow Wilson wrote in his *History of the American People* that: "It was the gallant Polish patriot, Tadeusz Kosciuszko, who had shown General Gates how to intrench himself upon Bemis Heights." Lynn Montross, historian of the Continental Army, credits Kościuszko, along with Gates, Schuyler, and Morgan, as the four men most responsible for the victory.[79]

These recurring words of praise were well-deserved. But it remained for Kościuszko's superior at Saratoga to write the final chapter in the story of the Pole's contribution. What did Gates himself think of Kościuszko's aid? Shortly after the battle, when a friend, Dr. Benjamin Rush of Philadelphia, visited Gates's headquarters and began to lavish praise upon the general, Gates called a halt to the adulation: "Stop, Doctor, stop, let us be honest. In war, as in medicine, natural causes not under our control, do much. In the present case, the great tacticians of the campaign, were hills and forests, which a young Polish Engineer was skilful enough to select for my encampment."[80] Who else should know where credit was due but the man who received the plaudits for victory?

Chapter 6

The Conway Cabal

*F*ollowing Burgoyne's defeat, Kościuszko continued his service in the Northern Department, operating out of its headquarters in Albany to plan and direct a number of projects aimed at strengthening the defenses and communications in northern and eastern New York. Although still nominally under the command of Baldwin, the chief engineer, Kościuszko appears to have operated with much autonomy and to have been the engineer of choice for the important projects in the department.[1]

Although the immediate threat to the Northern Department had ended, the regional, factional and personal disputes that marred the northern campaigns in 1777 continued throughout the war. In the wake of the signal victory at Saratoga, many began to compare the success of the army under Gates with the long series of failures of the main army under Washington. Throughout the late fall of 1777 and early spring of 1778 many raised the possibility, some openly, of replacing Washington with Gates. New Englanders, in particular, saw in Gates, who was on friendly terms with many of New England's leaders, an opportunity to wrest back their waning political and military influence.[2]

Chief among the leaders of the anti-Washington faction were Samuel Adams, John Adams, Richard Henry Lee, Thomas Mifflin, and Dr. Benjamin Rush. Together and separately they labored mostly behind the scenes to undermine Washington's popularity and promote within Congress doubts about the general's competence. Their circulation of a pamphlet titled "Thoughts of a Freeman," ostensibly written by Rush but more probably of at least dual authorship despite the physician's signature, was a more blatant and open criticism of Washington's leadership. Addressed to Henry Laurens, then president of the Continental Congress, its addressee lost little time forwarding the damning document to Washington's attention. "My enemies take an ungenerous advantage of me," the general responded with incredible self-restraint. "They know the delicacy of my situation, and that motives of policy deprive me of the defense I might otherwise make against their insidious attacks."[3]

At the same time, rumors of an anti-Washington conspiracy became so rife as to find their way into the pages of a Tory newspaper published in New York City. On December 19, one of its articles informed readers that "a junto is formed ... and said to consist of Generals Mifflin, Thompson, Arnold and Sinclair [St. Clair]; their object is the removal of General Washington from the chief command of the rebel army. The Generals Lee and Gates, with all the Yankees who have resolution enough to declare themselves of a party, wish well to the enterprise."[4]

The whole cabal, if indeed there ever was one, become more public, and more believable, when Major James Wilkinson, Gates's aide-de-camp, met Major William McWilliams, Lord Stirling's aide-de-camp, at Reading, Pennsylvania, while enroute to Philadelphia. The two engaged in conversation and Wilkinson shared the information that Gen. Thomas Conway, an Irish-born officer who had served in the French Army and the least senior of the twenty-four brigadier generals then on duty, had sent a letter to Gates in which he commented on Gates's victory in the battles about Saratoga in the following words: "Heaven had determined to save our country, or a weak general and bad counsellors would have ruined it."[5] To McWilliams, the statement was clearly designed to impune Washington's good name and ability. McWilliams passed the information along to Lord Stirling who wrote to Washington on November 3 informing him of the "wicked duplicity of conduct."[6]

Once aware of the correspondence, Washington, uncertain as to whether Gates was involved in the gossip or whether he had merely arranged for Wilkinson to pass the information along to him, wrote to Conway, citing the specific offending passage, and asking for a clarification of the meaning and intent. Conway replied that the letter was only an expression of congratulations to Gates on his victory and was not intended to reflect negatively on Washington. As proof, he offered to have the original sent for Washington's inspection, but never did. Instead, he hurried to Washington's headquarters to assure the general he meant no harm or disrespect. Gates, for his part, unaware of how Washington came by the personal letter, assumed that someone had stolen it from his private papers and professed great umbrage about the theft. Perhaps assuming a Washington partisan was at fault, or perhaps sensing the old Schuyler clique at work, Gates wrote both Congress and Washington expressing his anger that someone had stolen a copy of his private correspondence from Conway and demanding to be informed of the identity of the culprit on the pretext that the whole incident was designed to undermine Gates.[7] Both of the addressees appear to have initially ignored Gates's demand.

Meanwhile, as confidence in Washington began to waver among some, Congress reestablished the Board of War on October 17, 1777, to oversee the conduct of the war. The anti-Washington forces soon managed to have Gates appointed president, a serious blow to Washington's prestige and influence. The other members of the Board included Quartermaster General Thomas Mifflin, Adjutant General Timothy Pickering, Col. Joseph Trumbull, and Richard Peters as secretary.[8] Given the presence of Gates and Mifflin on the Board, and Richard Henry Lee's prominence in securing some of the appointments, some writers have used this as evidence that an organized cabal existed and that it was aimed at embarrassing and eventually replacing Washington as commanding general.

At the same time, angry at the promotion of Baron Johann de Kalb over him, Gen. Conway submitted his resignation to Congress on November 14. Congress referred the matter to the Board of War and Gates, rather than accept the resignation, tried to convince Conway to remain in the service. "I firmly believe," he wrote,

> there would be more greatness in continuing to serve the States notwithstanding the provocation you think you have received—than in resigning the commission you hold. Caprisious or disgraced warriors so often leave the army, that I do not wish to see the name of Conway on the list of officers who have withdrawn from the service of our republic.[9]

Thus entreated, Conway decided to stay. Prior to Gates's nomination to the Board of War, Conway, no doubt through the influence of the anti-Washington faction, was assigned to develop a recommendation for reform of the army. His final report, submitted in December, called for the creation of an Inspector General reporting to Congress, through the Board of War, rather than to the general-in-chief. Since the Inspector General would be the primary investigative and disciplinary official, removing the post from Washington's jurisdiction would be a serious blow to his authority and might even pose a threat to him as commanding general. Needless to say, the Virginian was not at all pleased with the turn of events.[10] He became even more disgruntled when Gates, after mollifying Conway, appointed him to the new post of Inspector General, a move that also brought protests from many of the other brigadier generals who coveted the position and the promotion to major general that accompanied it.

When Conway traveled to visit Washington's headquarters, then at Schuylkill, in his new capacity as Inspector General, the general-in-chief received him with great formality, but also understandable reserve. The irritable Irishman, sensing some slight in the precise etiquette and formality observed during his stay, complained to Henry Laurens, President of the Continental Congress, about the lack of warmth in Washington's reception. When questioned by Laurens, Washington replied: "If General Conway means, by cool reception, that I did not receive him in the language of a warm and cordial friend, I readily confess the charge. I did not, nor shall I ever ... make progessions of friendship to the man I deem my enemy and whose ... conduct forbids it."[11]

In the end, Washington wrote a personal letter to Gates informing him of how he obtained the information in the Conway letter indirectly through Wilkinson. Congress eventually supported Washington, reassigning Gates, Mifflin, and Conway to the army. Gates was dispatched back to the Northern Department as commander, then, in 1779, transferred to the Eastern Department based in Boston.[12] Whether or not there was actually a formal "cabal" against Washington has long been the source of debate among historians. Gates's biographer, Samuel White Patterson, concluded, not surprisingly, that "To say that the greatly disliked Conway was at the head and front of an organized movement to put Gates in Washington's place is not a myth, but nonsense. It is equally nonsensical to think, on the other hand, that Gates would have declined to hold the reins if the Continental Congress had decided to entrust them to him."[13] Regardless, Washington *believed* there was an organized conspiracy and that belief certainly influenced some of his future actions.

Following Gates's appointment to the Board of War, Kościuszko, who had become not only a loyal subordinate of Gates but a close personal friend of the general and his wife, did not wait long to reiterate what he surely must have conveyed personally to the general before his departure—that he wished to accompany Gates to whatever new assignment he might receive. On January 17 he wrote to Mrs. Gates: "I rely upon your good Heart that you will not refuse me the favor to remember me to General Gates to whom I write a letter asking his protection and his recommendation before Congress."[14]

The letter Kościuszko wrote to Gates has apparently been lost, so it is unclear whether Kościuszko sought some appointment with Gates at the Board of War or a reassignment to a more active command. About that time a plan began to be considered for an American invasion of Canada to destroy British boats and supplies on Lake Champlain and seize Montréal. Haiman speculates that Kościuszko, concluding that Gates would be designated leader of the new expedition, wanted to accompany him as part of the enterprise. Yet, if this were the case such a campaign would have been launched from the Northern Department, thus there would have been no reason for Kościuszko to go south or to ask Gates for his assistance. The Pole was already in the Northern Department and would surely be involved in any such effort.[15]

More likely, the reference to the "recommendation before Congress" alluded to Kościuszko's nomination for promotion to brigadier general which was then being considered by some in view of his performance during Burgoyne's invasion. In fact, in a letter dated November 10, 1777, to Henry Laurens, then President of the Continental Congress, no less a figure than George Washington, commenting on the application of Col. du Portail for promotions for himself and the other French engineers accompanying him, recommended Kościuszko for consideration. "While I am on this subject," he wrote, "I would take the liberty to mention, that I have been well informed, that the Engineer in the Northern Army (Cosieski, I think his name is) is a Gentleman of science and merit. From the character I have had of him he is deserving of notice too."[16] While he no doubt would have relished advancement, Kościuszko's timidity probably hurt his own cause. Unlike many other European offices whose unabashed self-promotion repelled most of their erstwhile American colleagues, Kościuszko sought tranquility rather than create any stir through his application for advancement. In a letter dated January 17, 1778, to Col. Troup, Kościuszko cautioned "if you see that my promotion will make a great many Jealous, tell the General [Gates] that I will not accept of one because I prefer peace more than the greatest Rank in the World."[17]

In any event, Kościuszko's promotion never materialized, probably because it would have conflicted with the appointment of the French engineer du Portail to brigadier general and commander of engineers. Command of the proposed Canadian operation went instead to the Marquis de Lafayette, who arrived in Albany on February 17. Appalled by the lack of troops, supplies, and planning for the venture, Lafayette wrote to Henry Laurens soon after his arrival in Albany, complaining vehemently about the state of affairs. "I'd loose rather the honor of twenty Gateses and twenty boards of wars, than to let my own reputation be hurted in the least thing," the Marquis confided.[18] He entrusted the letter to Kościuszko for delivery when the Pole left Albany for York, Pennsylvania, on February 19. Kościuszko arrived in York, where the Continental Congress was then meeting, the British having captured Philadelphia, on the 26th where Gates introduced him to Laurens and the letter was safely delivered.[19]

When Kościuszko arrived in York he found the atmosphere charged because of the ongoing recriminations of the Conway Cabal.[20] When it finally became known that Wilkinson, a member of his own staff, had leaked the information, Gates felt at once betrayed and enraged. Gates had befriended Wilkinson during the Northern Campaign and arranged for his promotion to brigadier general at great personal political cost to himself. Now Gates felt Wilkinson had turned on him by leaking the contents of Conway's letter. In his anger, he publicly berated Wilkinson, who then sought to assuage his honor by challenging Gates to a duel on February 23, just three days before Kościuszko's arrival. Gates declined the invitation to settle the matter on the field of honor, but Gen. John Cadwallader challenged Conway and wounded him so severely it was thought he would not survive. He did, sent a letter of apology to Washington, and returned to France.[21]

While Kościuszko was known as a Gates loyalist, there is no evidence he participated in any way in the supposed cabal. He did, however, take advantage of the opportunity afforded by his presence in York to lobby Gates for a transfer to a more active post. Gates, still the titular commander of the Northern Department, agreed to his friend's wishes and on March 5 the Board of War determined that Kościuszko "be directed to repair to the Army under General Putnam, to be employed as shall be thought proper in his Capacity of an Engineer."[22]

Despite the new assignment, recriminations from the Conway Cabal continued to plague Gates and his Polish friend through much of 1778. Though not directly involved in the particulars of the "cabal," Kościuszko became associated with it through his friendship with Gates and an unfortunate series of incidents that pitted him against John Carter, a son-in-law of Gen. Schuyler whom Gates's biographer characterized as "a bankrupt Englishman, who had come to America to fatten himself at the public crib."[23] It began in September, 1778, when Wilkinson exchanged angry words with Gates and once again challenged the general to a duel. Gates agreed and asked Kościuszko to act as his second. Carter served as second for Wilkinson. When the duel finally took place, Gates's pistol misfired, Wilkinson fired his into the air. On a second try, Wilkinson fired but Gates would not. A third attempt also yielded no blood, at which time the seconds interceded. The demands of honor seemingly fulfilled, both parties agree that each other had "behaved as gentlemen" and Carter, being more fluent in English than Kościuszko, was delegated to draw up the appropriate documents to verify everyone's honorable behavior.[24]

With the document completed, Carter asked Kościuszko to sign to verify the events, which the Pole did. Only later when he returned to headquarters did it become apparent to him that the document, while detailing Wilkinson's honorable behavior, said nothing of Gates's good conduct. Whether from subterfuge or Kościuszko's poor command of English, a grievous wrong had been perpetrated on Gates. Kościuszko immediately rode over the Schuyler's headquarters and confronted Carter, demanding that the damage be repaired. According to Major John Lansing, a witness to Kościuszko's arrival late that evening, the Pole

> told Mr. Carter that he proposed to leave camp early next morning, and that he wanted a copy of the paper Mr. Carter and he had signed. Mr. Carter immediately took a paper out of his pocket, and presented it to the Colonel, saying "their it is, copy and I will sign it." After having received the paper, he folded it and pocketed it; and upon Mr. Carter's questioning him, respecting his intentions in putting it in his pocket, he answered, that that paper contained a declaration, relative to the propriety of Gen. Wilkenson's conduct; but not a word respecting that of General Gates at their interview at York-Town that

his unacquaintance with the English language, had caused him to misapprehend the terms in which it was conceived—That in being appointed Gen. Gates's second, he looked upon himself, as interested in supporting his honour, and that he would rather loose the last drop of his blood than consent to a measure which would tend to its prejudice or words to that effect; and unless Mr. Carter would agree to certify, that General Gates's conduct, had been unexceptionable, on the occasion of his and General Wilkenson's meeting at York Town, he must keep the paper. Mr. Carter observed, that the paper was delivered confidentially; urged to him the inconsistency of certifying to a fact, with which he was entirely unacquainted, and requested him to restore the paper—This the Colonel absolutely refused, repeating his former objections; Mr. Carter asked him whether he had not signed the paper, which he had then taken, and whether Gen. Gates had not previously assented to it; to this he applied affirmatively, and upon Mr. Carter's observing that it was in his power to publish it, and that the Colonel could not pretend to deny his Signature; he answered, that though he knew it to be true, that he had signed it, he would deny it—that he was unacquainted with the cause of the duel, and unapprised of General Gates's intentions respecting it, till within an hour before it happened; that the shortness of that time had prevented him from receiving the necessary information—that that was another reason of his omitting to require a similar certificate, respecting Gen. Gates's behaviour; that he had since had an opportunity of being undeceived; that Col. Troup had removed his deception; Mr. Carter then requested a copy of the paper contended for, which Col. Kosciusko refused to give—much altercations passed, and after a variety of repetitions of the discourse above related: Mr. Carter proposed that Col. Kosciusko should declare upon his honour, that he would on the morrow at Ten o'clock in the morning, with General Gates, meet General Wilkenson and Mr. Carter at General St. Clair's quarters, and bring with him the paper alluded to—that he would there produce it to Generals Gates and Wilkenson, and that if the former refused to deliver it, the matter was to be on the Same footing as before they fought; that if General Gates refused, to appear at the time and place appointed he would himself attend, and return the paper to Mr. Carter; this declaration the Colonel made, without the least hesitation, and then went off with the paper.

General Schuyler was present at the time the above conversation passed and overheard it.[25]

When the principles met the following day, Gates refused to return the document unless Wilkinson was willing to supply a similar testimonial to the general's conduct and honor. According to Carter's account of the meeting, "Gen. Wilkenson told him he could not prostitute his honour, and that he would not, and proposed to Gen. Gates to fight again and desired him to fix a time, which Gen. Gates refused. On Gen. Gates's refusal either to give up the paper or fight, Gen. Wilkenson told him in the presence of Gen. St. Clair, Col. De Hart and Major Dunn, that he was a rascal and a coward, and that he only wanted to shift the quarrel from his own shoulders on those of Col. Kosciuszko; when Major Armstrong, aide-de-camp to General Gates, who was with him, immediately said that was not the case, for that to his knowledge Col. Kosciuszko had offered General Gates to fight for him the day before, but that the General would not suffer him." Armstrong's view of the exchange, contained in a letter to Kościuszko, differed somewhat. According to him, it was Col. Troup whom Wilkinson spoke of and not Kościuszko. "I perfectly remember my answer to Gen. Wilkenson," Armstrong wrote, "when he alleged that Gen. Gates wished to draw, not YOU, but Col. TROUP into the dispute: It was thus 'so far from that, Sir, I heard the General lay the strongest injunction upon Col. Troup not to challenge you, as he, suspecting what has happened, was in that case, determined to fight you."[26]

Regardless of the particulars, the meeting solved nothing and only inflamed passions all the more. After the meeting broke up, Carter intimated to those who remained at St. Clair's headquarters that he intended to prosecute Kościuszko as a thief and report him to headquarters for taking the document in question. News of these comments soon reached Kościuszko, who felt greatly aggrieved by the accusation. On September 6 he responded by addressing a letter to Lt. Col. Lewis Morris, who was present when Carter made the comments in question. "Sir," he began,

As I learn from undoubted authority, that you have spoken in a very disrespectful and ungentlemanly manner of me, by calling me in a public company, a thief, and seriously determining to prosecute me as such, or report me, to Head Quarters: I make no doubt but that you will meet me precisely at six o'clock this evening, at the smith's shop, upon the hill between Schuyler's and Col. Baldwin's quarters, with your second and arms.—I expect a receipt for this by the bearer—if no other answer—a letter sent any time before five o'clock will find me at Gen. Gates's quarters.[27]

Carter refused to face Kościuszko, choosing instead to answer him with the following note:

> Until the paper is returned to me of which you requested a copy, and which I delivered to you for that purpose last Friday night, in the presence of Major-Gen. Schuyler, Major Lansing, and Mr. Morris and which in the presence of those gentlemen you not only refused to return to me, but even refused me a copy; I shall not consider myself, either in point of honour or justice bound to make any apologies or to meet you at the time you request.[28]

Not to be put off, Kościuszko sent a second letter via Major Armstrong in which he explained that possession of the document was an entirely separate issue from Carter's vile and insulting comments, and called upon Carter to accept his challenge.

> As in your note of today by Mr. Morris you consider my retaining the certificate an injury to you; I now wait at Col. Baldwin's quarters prepared to redress it with my sword. The injury you wished to do my reputation by the assertion mentioned in my letter this morning, is posterior and entirely distinct from this—Therefore, Sir, I insist upon your meeting at the hour and place appointed, should you refuse I shall take proper steps to get satisfaction.[29]

Other notes were passed, but Carter still refused Kościuszko's challenges, on one occasion insisting to Lt. Jedidiah Rogers that he "tell Col. Kosciuszko, that he had been much misinformed; that he had never called him a thief, nor ever said he would report him to Head Quarters, or prosecute him as such." The Pole, of course, was not fooled, but threatened to publish a letter portraying Carter "as a villain" and treating him thusly whenever they might meet. Carter "retorted with a new contemptuous remark on Kosciuszko and added that he would defend himself if attacked and publish the particulars of the affair in newspapers."[30] But Carter did not wait to defend himself, instead, he published a lengthy, selfserving description of the affair in the Fishkill, New York, *Packet*, closing with the following comments:

> From what passed on Friday night, it is very apparent that Col. Kosciusko forfeited all pretentions to honour by obtaining the certificate of what passed at the duel, from me under false pretences, and openly vowing that on account of Gen. Gates's reputation he would

deny what he knew to be true, which undoubtedly puts it out of the power of any gentleman to put himself upon a level with him. The Colonel offers in his letter to redress the injury with his sword,—a midnight robber, who steals a purse, or an assassin, who attempts a gentleman's life might with equal propriety offer to make amends with his sword but every man of common sense would look upon the person who met him on such terms, as a mad-man.

Kościuszko responded in kind in a letter that appeared in the newspaper on September 24, defending his honor and providing his version of the events:

The general voice of the army hath already pronounced you a scoundrel and coward—You are sensible that in Camp, or where your transaction with me is known, you are not considered as a gentleman, if that is the character you are apprehensive that I will take liberty with you are mistaken.—Your pusillanimous behaviour in the course of our late dispute, even according to your state of facts, will convince the public as well as me, that you are destitute thereof.

But it seems you thought it was necesary to fight me some way or other; and wisely judged that types were safe weapons; in this you discover a degree of cowardice, not indeed so great as when you drew your pistol upon me at the Court-Martial, when I was unarmed, and when the appearance of guard (by order of the Court) to apprehend you as an assassin, and the indignant shouts of the spectators, put you to an ignominious flight. I should have treated your publication with contempt, if you had not basely misrepresented my behaviour respecting the certificate. I think it my duty to correct that part of your state of facts, in a public manner, and to convince you Sir, that I can defend my reputation with my pen, as well as my sword;—I shall not add to your disgrace by a tedious detail of circumstances, in your own account of the matter you acknowledge yourself a coward.—Late in the evening after Gen. Gates and Gen. Wilkenson had fought, you produced a paper, which you read, and with much importunity requested me to sign,—and being in haste and so dark that I could not read it, I very inadvertently did so. But I soon discovered that you had ungenerously, taken advantage of my inattention, and obtained a certificate in favour of your principal only, and relating to a former affair at York-Town, with which I was totally unacquainted. I therefore came immediately to your quarters, demanded a copy of the paper, and observing that Gen. Gates was not named, and—that it only related to Gen. Wilkenson's behaviour on a former occasion; I expostulated with you,—told you that you had taken the advantage of my ignorance of the language and inattention,—that as a second to Gen. Gates I was bound in honour to support his reputation, on this occasion, which I would with my blood,—and that unless you would give me a similar certificate on his Part I would retain yours,—this you refused, assigning as a reason that I had not demanded it on the spot. You then said you would publish the paper,—I answered I would deny, not my signature, as you have maliciously intimated, but the intention and design of the certificate; and I am persuaded the gentlemen who were present understood me in that sense.

You also say that Gen. Gates refused to fix a time for a second duel with Gen. Wilkenson,—I am pretty sure that when the altercation on that subject happened, that you was at such a distance in warm conversation with me, as to make it impossible, for you to hear what passed between Gen. Gates and Gen. Wilkenson, — but supposing it to be true, the General certainly did right, I had told him that the affair was become mine and not his,—and that if retaining the certificate was a prejudice either to you or Gen. Wilkenson, I—only was answerable, and would not permit him to fight for me, and that I would consider myself injured by his interference.

I have now done with you Sir, unless you intrude among gentlemen where I may happen to be, on such occasions, I shall think myself at liberty to treat you as a scoundrel.[31]

Hoping that his response would meet with positive response from Gates, Kościuszko wrote to the general on September 28 to inform him that "I have answer to Carter in York Paper if you find good in your part I am very happy[,] if not I will publish more in the next as you Judge proper to add. Believe me Sir that I have real attachment for you, and I have nothing so in view as your reputation which is dearest at present for me than mine."[32]

But Carter, apparently determined to have the last word, would not let the matter end. On September 26 he published yet another letter in the *New York Packet*:

In what other light than that of a mercenary bravo can that man be considered, who (by his own confession unacquainted with the circumstances of a quarrel) can offer to fight a person (with whom he has not even the shadow of a dispute) for another man? and his subsequent conduct proves him the needy desperate adventurer, who having nothing to lose, but with a view of pleasing his patron and in hopes of advancing his fortune, is ready to undertake any dirty action, or fight any man for him, and failing in his schemes and detected in his villainy, falsely imagines, that by fighting or sending a challenge, he shall wipe every odium from his character, and re-establish his shattered reputation; and chagrined at being disappointed by a gentleman's refusal to put himself on a level with him has recourse to scurrility, abuse and falsehood.—Such is his representation of what passed at the Court-Martial a few days after, when meeting me (not unarmed, as he declares, but with his sword on) he became abusive, and kept his hand in his pocket as I supposed handling a pistol: I immediately drew one from my holsters and told him that if he made any attack upon me I would blow his brains out; the Court-Martial was disturbed and ordered out a guard, and as I did not belong to the army preferred riding off rather than be taken into custody by the guard: —- this he calls an ignominious flight.

I shall not trouble the public or you, Sir, any more with this dispute, as I will not be provoked to answer any future publications of so contemptible a being as Col. Kościuszko.[33]

Kościuszko replied on October 13, enclosing two letters from witnesses to support his version of the events and castigating Carter for his shabby treatment of Gen. Gates.

TO THE PUBLIC

Reduced by Mr. Carters illiberal attack upon my reputation, in the Fish-Kill paper of the 17th of September last, to the necessity of defending myself with TYPES; I declared in my letter to him, published the following week, and in the same paper, that I had done with him &c.—His publication of last Thursday cannot provoke me to honour him with a continuation of such hostilities; and his cowardice as well as my pride perfectly Secure him against those of that nature he is most afraid of. But I believe it is my duty to submit to the judgment of the public: sufficient information for preventing Mr. Carter's character from being considered as equivocal.

For this reason a certificate from Gen. Morris is now published, with another from Mr. Rogers, a Liut. in Col. Sheldon's regiment of light dragoon's. It will plainly appear from them that my altercation with Mr. Carter, was occasioned by his invectives and threatnings, thundered against me, in my absence; and that, when he accidentally met Mr. Rogers, by whom I had sent him the letter he published in his first sally against me, and in which I demanded satisfaction for those invectives, he then denied the fact.

To these certificates is joined a letter from Major Armstrong, which demonstrates the baseness of my contemptible antagonist, in representing me "as a bravo," &c.

He has abused Gen. Gates under the cover of a narrative of fictitious facts, which, he pretends, have happened between Gen. Gates and Gen. Wilkenson.

Whether the wretch be a mercenary calumniator, in the pay of the understrappers to the principal tools of our enemies, for injuring our cause, by abusing our Generals, I shall not determine; but I firmly believe, with many others, that, should he return to Boston, and visit the Convention troops, they THEMSELVES, would tar and feather him, for having presumed to mention so irreverently the character of Gen. Gates.

The affair eventually sputtered out, with Kościuszko's reputation emerging generally intact. Among those in the army, most apparently sided with him against Carter. Major Samuel Shaw of Massachusetts opined that "Full credit is due to what [Kościuszko] says, so that you cannot be at a loss to form an opinion of the matter." Lt. Col. Morris, who should have been in a position to know the particulars since he was a participant in some of the events at St. Clair's headquarters, penned a letter to his father on December 7 in which he enclosed his own account of the affair and stated: "You will there observe, the parts Mr. Carter made use of to screen himself from the Resentment of Col. Kosciuszko. Under the influence of Fear and at the expence of his own Veracity he has impeached your's in that publick Manner. The character of the Coward and Lyar is frequently connected in the same Person, and I think it is conspicuously so in him—A Coward for refusing to give a Gentleman satisfaction for the Injury he had done to his Reputation, and a Lyar for denying such injury when called upon to answer it." Morris explained to his father that he had written to Carter directly, but had received no answer and consequently sent a second letter. "If that does not produce an answer," Morris concluded, "I shall take the Liberty of caning him whenever I meet him, and will publish him as a Coward and a Lyar."[34]

The Conway Cabal and the resulting affair with Carter reflected on Kościuszko in two ways. First, though closely associated with Gates, there is no evidence that Kościuszko was ever linked to the "plot" or suffered any ill consequences as a result of his friendship with Gates. Lafayette, a close associate of Washington, trusted Kościuszko to carry letters for him, while Washington spoke well of the Pole on many occasions. The assertion by some historians that because Washington linked Kościuszko with Gates the commander-in-chief took an aloof attitude toward the Pole and kept him at a distance is not supported by the evidence. Rather, Washington commented favorably on the engineer's talents and contributions several times during the rest of the war, going so far as to seek his appointment to the main army on one occasion, supporting Kościuszko's application for promotion in 1783, bestowing personal gifts upon the Pole, and inviting him to visit Mount Vernon upon his return to America in 1797. Clearly, though a well-known friend of Gates, Kościuszko conducted himself so as to remain on friendly and trusting terms with both sides in the controversy.

Secondly, the affair with John Carter provides an insight into the integrity of Kościuszko's loyalty to his friends. Having erred in signing a document unflattering to Gates, he put his own reputation, and in fact his life, in jeopardy to repair the potential damage his mistake caused to his friend Gates. Rather than leave Gates to the mercy of his enemies, or find some reason for inaction, Kościuszko took positive steps, at considerable personal risk, to correct the error and redeem Gates's reputation. In this, according to the weight of contemporary evidence, he acquitted himself with honor.

Chapter 7

The "Key to America"

*T*he unqualified success of the Saratoga Campaign sent a thrill of excitement through the colonies, reassuring many and encouraging others who had previously been lukewarm patriots to join the cause more openly. Nevertheless, most people realized that no matter how sweeping the victory had been, much remained to be done before independence could be secured. Despite Burgoyne's failure, the threats of invasion from Canada or a northward movement by the British from New York City were not entirely removed. In the event that Sir William Howe decided to march north along the Hudson, he might well be able to reach Albany unaided. The vulnerability of the crucial Highlands above New York City became all too apparent during the movement of Sir Henry Clinton's force north to support Burgoyne. Although too small to carry out the task implicit in Howe's orders, it did succeed in capturing all of the forts guarding the route north to Albany. American losses in these actions were heavy, and had the British successes been followed up quickly with a push on Albany by a larger force history might well have been different.

Situated only forty-five miles north of New York City, the Hudson Highlands rose to heights as much as 500 feet, the highest barrier between the port city and Albany. Rugged hills with sometimes sharp peaks characterized the terrain, along with deep ravines and high cliffs overlooking the Hudson River within easy cannon shot of the waterway. These Highlands, if properly fortified, could present a formidable barrier to any British attempt to move north. The Continental Congress recognized the importance of the area as early as 1775, but attempts to fortify various positions proceeded slowly and proved ineffectual when Clinton's force easily captured the area in the fall of 1777.[1] In view of this vulnerability, American military planners recognized the necessity of improving the fortifications as early as possible. It was important to contain British forces in New York City if the colonials were to have uninterrupted passage of the Hudson River for troops and supplies. Gen. Washington detailed the significance of this area in a letter to Gen. Israel Putnam dated December 2, 1777:

> The importance of the Hudson River in the present contest, and the necessity of defending it, are subjects which have been so frequently and fully discussed, and are so well understood, that it is unnecessary to enlarge upon them. These facts at once appear, when it is considered that it runs through a whole State; that it is the only passage by which the enemy from New York, or any part of our coast, can ever hope to co-operate with an army from Canada; that the possession of it is indispensably essential to preserve the communication between the Eastern, Middle and Southern States; and further, that upon its security, in a great measure, depend our chief supplies of flour for the subsistence of such forces as we may have occasion for, in the course of the war.... These facts are familiar to all; they are familiar to you. I therefore request you, in the most urgent terms, to turn your most serious and active attention to this infinitely important object. Seize the present opportunity and employ your whole force and all the means in your power for erecting and completing, as far as it shall be possible, such works and constructions as may be necessary to defend and secure the river against any future attempts of the enemy.[2]

With this purpose in mind, the French Lt. Col. Louis de la Radière received orders to proceed to a rocky point of land where the Hudson River narrows north of New York, a site known as West Point, to act as chief engineer for the construction of major defensive works. The place selected was along a portion of the river that narrowed as it passed through a gorge surrounded by heights on both sides of the river. There the southerly course turned abruptly eastward for about a quarter of a mile before turning once more southward. To east and west, plentiful hills provided ample opportunity for defense from the landward sides, the whole geography providing the potential for a significant blockage of both river and land traffic.[3]

Much had to be done to prepare the site, but the climate and rocky soil were not very hospitable to major construction during the winter months and there was a general lack of building materials, tools, labor, and shelter. Under these conditions, de la Radière became increasingly frustrated with both the progress of the project and his assignment to the remote post. First the French colonel spent considerable time lobbying Congress for promotion, then he argued openly with Governor Clinton, Gen. Putnam, and others about the site selected for construction of the fortress, preferring instead to merely rebuild and expand the existing Fort Clinton. When West Point was confirmed as the construction site in early January, 1778, de la Radière began the works but complained incessantly about the location and extent of the plans, provoking another dispute with Putnam who derisively labeled the Frenchman a "paper Engineer."[4] According to Edward Boynton, the engineer's personality was largely responsible for many of the difficulties. "[A]n impatient, petulant officer," Boynton wrote, de la Radière "planned the work at the outset, on a scale entirely too large. He required means altogether beyond the resources at command, and projected curtains, banquettes, and terrepleins sufficient to enclose the greater portion of the north and east crest of the river's bank."[5] To Governor George Clinton, Radière appeared "deficient in point of practical knowledge" and "unfit ... for the present task."[6]

Throughout January and February, de la Radière continued to grouse about the plans, the location, his assignment, the lack of promotion, and anything else he could find to criticize. Meanwhile, the important work of building defenses strong enough to prevent the British Army from moving north languished. On February 18, 1778, Brig. Gen. Samuel Parsons, temporary commander of the post at West Point, wrote in exasperation that "almost every obstacle within the circle of possibility has happened to retard their progress."[7] Finally the cantankerous engineer gave up altogether. On March 7, Parsons wrote to Washington to inform him that the lieutenant colonel, "finding it impossible to complete the Fort and other defenses intended at this post, in such manner as to render them effectual early in the spring, and not choosing to hazard his reputation on works erected on a different scale ... has desired leave to wait on Your Excellency and Congress, which I have granted him."[8]

De la Radière left West Point in early March, heading south to Valley Forge to plead his case for promotion directly to Gen. Washington. His departure left the important post without a chief engineer to prosecute the construction. To fill the void, the Board of War, now led by Kościuszko's close friend and benefactor Horatio Gates, named the Pole to the position on March 5, 1778. His appointment was occasion for sad goodbyes in the Northern Department where the engineer made many strong friendships forged during the months of hardship the previous summer and fall. Among his colleagues in Albany, he would be missed. "Kosiuszko left this, for West-Point, on Monday," Col. Robert Troup wrote to Gates on March 26. "When I cease to love this young Man, I must cease to love those Qualities which form the brightest & completest of characters."[9]

Journeying south almost immediately, Kościuszko stopped briefly in Poughkeepsie where New York Gov. George Clinton provided him with a letter of introduction. "Colo. Kuziazke who by a Resolve of Congress is directed to act as an Ingeneer at the Works for the Security of the River will deliver you this," he wrote. "I believe you will find him an Ingenous Young Man and disposed to do every thing he can in the most agreeable Manner."[10]

Kościuszko probably reached West Point on March 26, shortly before Gen. Alexander McDougall who had been named to succeed Gen. Putnam in command of the Hudson Highlands.[11] In making the appointment of McDougall, Washington emphasized the particular importance of West Point to the war effort. "I need not observe to you that West Point is to be considered as the first and principal object of your attention," the commanding general wrote. "I am persuaded you will neglect nothing conducive to its security, and will have the works directed for its defense prosecuted with all the vigour and expedition in your power. You are fully sensible of their importance and how much their completion will ease and disembarrass our future general operations."[12] With Kościuszko now at West Point, McDougall had little to worry about. Almost immediately change became evident to those accustomed to the carping excuses of de la Radière. Capt. Boynton attested that "operations were at once resumed, and pushed forward with great vigor."[13]

Unfortunately, however, these changes did not end the difficulties that beset construction of the fortifications. When Col. de la Radière arrived at Valley Forge, about the same time Kościuszko arrived at West Point, Washington, unaware as yet of Kościuszko's assignment to West Point, immediately ordered the French engineer to return to his post. This created a situation not unlike that which obtained on Kościuszko's arrival at Ticonderoga where he found his ideas and plans stifled by divided command. In this instance, however, unlike at Ticonderoga, the Pole ranked as senior engineering officer with de la Radière his junior. Despite this, the Frenchman refused to obey orders the Pole issued, considering himself subject only to commands issued by the Continental Army's chief engineer, his countryman

Brig. Gen. Louis le Bègue de Presle du Portail. Du Portail led a contingent of four French engineering officers who arrived in North America in February, 1777. On July 8 he received a commission as colonel of engineers, made retroactive to February 13. As was the case with many of the early foreign arrivals, du Portail and his associates spent more time lobbying for higher rank and more privileges than they did attending to their duties. Through a multitude of machinations du Portail managed to induce Congress into appointing him senior engineer, with the rank of brigadier general and title of Chief of Engineers forthcoming on November 17, 1777. This promotion over the heads of senior officers angered many, as did the tendency of the other French engineers to refuse orders from anyone save du Portail. Given de la Radière's disposition, and the prevailing atmosphere, it is little wonder he and Kościuszko did not agree on how best to proceed with construction, or anything else.[14]

In an effort to solve the growing problem that saw construction begun on two separate plans, Gen. Parsons wrote to MacDougall on March 28 to endorse Kościuszko and ask the general to put an end to the continued engineering conflict. "Inclosed are the Resolutions of Congress and Board of War respecting this Post and the conduct of the Engineer employed. Col. Kościuszko sent to this Place is particularly agreable to the Gentlemen of this State and all others concerned at this Post. ... As we are desirous of having Col. Kościuszko continue here and both cannot live upon the Point, I wish your Honor to adopt such Measures as will answer the wishes of the People and Garrison; and best serve the public Good."[15] Before McDougall could act, however, he received a letter from Washington in which the commanding general, now aware there were two engineering officers in the Hudson Highlands, sought to remedy the situation by transferring Kościuszko to his own command. "The presence of Colonel de la Radière rendering the Services of Mr. Kościuszko, as Engineer at Fishkill, unnecessary," Washington wrote, "you are to give him orders to join this Army without loss of time." Yet, still apparently uncertain about the Pole's appointment, Washington also noted he did not wish to interfere with any orders of the Board of War contrary to his own. "However desirous I am that Mr. Kosciousko should repair to this Army," he concluded, "if he is specially employed by order of Congress or the Board of War, I would not wish to contravene their Commands."[16]

Faced with the possible loss of his best engineer, McDougall responded quickly to Washington's letter on April 13, providing the general with information he hoped would lead the Virginian to retract his earlier order:

> Mr. Kościuszko is esteemed by those who have attended the works at West Point, to have more practice than Col. DeLaradiere, and his manner of treating the people more acceptable, than that of the latter; which induced Genl. Parsons and Governor Clinton to desire the former may be continued at West Point. The first has a Commission as Engineer with the rank of Colonel in October 1776. Colonel Delaradiere's Commission I think is dated in November last, and disputes rank with the former, which obliges me to keep them apart; and avail the services of their assistance in the best manner I can devise. This seems to be the Idea recommended by the Board of War in consequence to a reference of Congress to them, on the subject of Disputes relative to the Construction of the works. If your Excellency should think proper in this State of those Gentlemen, to order Mr. Kosciusko to join your army, whenever I am honored with your Commands on this head, I shall despatch him.[17]

This and other evidence, including his own experience with the French position-seeker, quickly decided Washington in favor of the Pole. "As Colo. La Radière and Colo. Kościuszko will never agree," the general replied to McDougall on April 22, "I think it will be best to order La Radière to return, especially as you say Kościuszko is better adopted to the genius and temper of the people."[18]

The command squabble finally resolved, Kościuszko could now pursue construction on his own plan, without obstruction. The situation, however, remained difficult for other reasons. Hardly anything substantial had been achieved in months, the project now being almost hopelessly behind schedule, with de la Radière admitting in a letter to Washington before his removal that "little or nothing" had been accomplished under his direction. While the Frenchman had developed some general plans, traced the outlines of a proposed fort along the Hudson River, and begun construction on some small outworks, there was little of consequence to show for his months in charge and his one major project, a fortification to be constructed on a turn in the river bank, had to be abandoned as impractical.[19]

Much work remained to be done. The highlands overlooking the fort had to be secured lest the position become as untenable as

Ticonderoga had, various outposts had to be completed to assure adequate warning and defense-in-depth, and obstructions had to be placed to interdict river travel. Only then could work begin on the massive fortifications to render the position permanent. In this, the ground which provided excellent potential for defensive positions also posed great difficulties for construction. The thin rocky soil covered solid rock that impeded construction, while the bitter cold of the winter made laboring in the frozen soil all the more difficult. Lack of sufficient equipment and teams of draft animals were a constant irritation, as was the periodic departure of militia units when their terms of service expired. The latter often left Kościuszko short of manpower for lengthy periods of time until replacements arrived. A return of artificers at West Point prepared by John Bacon and dated April 27, 1778, included, in addition to Col. Kościuszko, one major of engineers, 45 carpenters under Capt. Thayer, 21 carpenters under Capt. Blake, 28 carpenters under Capt. Pendleton, 29 carpenters under Lt. Thorp, 24 carpenters under Sergt. Colling, 23 carpenters under Sergt. Whiteman, and 7 masons under Capt. Stagg—a total of only 177 men.[20] The resulting manpower shortage was often exacerbated by officers in the regiments supplying work details who granted leaves or furloughs to their men. To solve this problem, the engineer tried to put a stop to this practice. An entry in the orderly books for Col. Henry Sherburne's Continental Regiment, for example, commands that officers are not to grant leave to their men without Kościuszko's express permission.[21]

Despite the difficulties involved, Kościuszko appears to have plunged into the work with great energy, gaining the respect of those about him as he had earlier in the Northern Department. Whereas the French engineer made virtually no provision for resisting a land attack, concentrating instead on opposing British vessels moving up river, Kościuszko immediately laid out "a chain of Forts and redoubts ... on the high ground bordering the plain" to protect West Point from land assault until more extensive works could be erected.[22] The focus of these new defenses was Fort Putnam, erected on a rocky hill that commanded the plain below and the West Point prominence. Among Kościuszko's priorities were the completion of Fort Arnold where the river narrowed somewhat and turned abruptly southward from its easterly course, construction of obstructions to interdict river traffic, completing a water battery, erecting permanent barracks, and finishing outworks, abatis, and *chevaux-de-frise* to support Fort Putnam.

In addition, when these priorities were completed he would have to plan and execute additional batteries, redoubts, barracks, and magazines, as well as strengthen the works already finished so that the whole formed an interlocking defense-in-depth.[23]

Once able to devote his full energies, and those of his men, to pursuit of a single plan, Kościuszko's progress in improving the defenses was immediately noticeable. After scaling down the plans for Fort Arnold, the waterside battery was soon completed and on April 30 a large chain barrier emplaced across the Hudson to prohibit British ships from moving north of the growing fortifications. The chain actually consisted of a separate chain and boom which, with their accompanying apparatus, contained 136 tons of wrought iron and a large number of logs, each about eighteen feet in length and fifteen inches in diameter. "It will be observed," Boynton explained, "that the Boom combined great strength with practicability. It was indeed the main obstruction, and placed below the Chain to receive the first shock of approaching vessels."[24] The shock would be greatly lessened by the placing of the chain and boom, adroitly located beyond the sharp bend in the river so as to force any ships to slow before encountering the obstruction, thereby lessening their impact on the barriers and increasing the chances the obstructions would withstand the shock. Gen. William Heath described it thusly:

This chain was as long as the width of the river between West Point and Constitution Island, where it was fixed to great blocks on each side, and under the fire of batteries on both sides of the river. The links of this chain were probably 12 inches wide, and 18 inches long; the iron about 2 inches square. This heavy chain was bouyed up by very large logs, of perhaps 16 or more feet long, a little pointed at the ends, to lessen their opposition to the force of the water on flood and ebb. The logs are placed at short distances from each other, the chain carried over them, and made fast to each by staples, to prevent their shifting; and there were a number of anchors dropped at distances, with cables made fast to the chain, to give it a greater stability. The short bend of the river at this place was much in favour of the chain's proving effectual; for a vessel coming up the river with the fairest wind and strongest way must lose them on changing her course to turn the Point; and before she could get under any considerable way again, even if the wind was fair, she would be on the chain, and at the same time under a heavy shower of shot and shells.[25]

Col. Troup, writing from Albany, reported to Gates on April 18:

"I have not seen the Works erecting at West Point, but it is said, They are in great Forwardness. Kościuszko has made many Alterations, which are universally approved of; & I am happy to find he is esteemed as an able Engineer."[26] Those closer to the scene felt the same way. "[T]he works are now carried on with a Degree of Spirit that promises their speedy Completion," an obviously reassured Gov. Clinton soon informed Washington.[27] This opinion was echoed by Gen. McDougall who shortly informed the commanding general that "the Fort is by this time so enclosed as to resist a sudden assault of the Enemy."[28] By June 12, when Dr. James Thatcher climbed to the top of a neighboring mountain, he was able to report laid out before him "a picturesque scenery of peculiar interest. ... Fort Putnam, on its most elevated part, the several redoubts beneath, and the barracks on the plain below, with numerous armed soldiers in active motion, all defended by the most formidable machinery of war."[29]

While the immediate exposure of the post was soon alleviated, much still remained to be done. The chain and boom across the river had to be reinforced and the wood repaired and treated with tar as a preservative. The initial works constructed on land had to be woven into an intricate defensive system by the creation of supporting blockhouses, redoubts, and *chevaux-de-frise*. To house troops and supplies, barracks, magazines, and bombproofs had to be constructed within the primary works.

Late spring brought a pleasant relief from the tedium of work. In April Congress reassigned Gen. Gates from the Board of War to command of the Northern Department. Gates established his headquarters a short distance from West Point. Overjoyed, Kościuszko rushed to resume in person his friendship with the general and his wife. "Yours not forgiting of me shall be always in my memory," he wrote to Gates later that summer, "and attach me so much that no time not any Circumstance can't ever change my sentiments, my obligation and altirat [alter] my real Frindship."[30] The friendship was genuine and would last throughout the two men's lives. Now, while they were again within a short distance of one another Kościuszko was apparently a frequent visitor to the Gates household, taking advantage of any opportunity to visit for dinner or just an evening conversation.

As the summer of 1778 began to appear, the campaigning season opened again, and with it came fears the British might try to repeat their move north from New York City of the previous year. Kościuszko rushed ahead with his construction activities against the time when the enemy would pay them more attention. "I must beg you," Gates cautioned Gen. John Glover, temporarily in command at West Point, "to give your whole Attention to the compleating of, First the Out Works at West Point, and then the Body of the Place; Col. Kusciuzsco cannot be too vigilant in this important Service."[31] Clearly, Gates expected an eventual British move and wanted to force the construction forward against that eventuality. Commanding several companies of artificers, carpenters, and fatigue parties detailed from the various garrison regiments, Kościuszko rose early and usually worked late into the evening. By early June, work had advanced far enough on Fort Arnold so that it could be garrisoned, while outworks, redoubts, and other defenses began to take shape in an intricate system of mutually supporting positions.[32] Reports to headquarters were positive about the progress of the work, so much so that in July Washington wrote to Gen. William Malcolm, temporarily in command at West Point, to express his belief that Kościuszko was "fully competent to the Business."[33]

While Kościuszko labored constructing West Point, news arrived that a treaty of friendship and alliance had been signed between the United States and France, the first foreign alliance in the history of the infant American republic. Made possible by the victory at Saratoga, the alliance was perhaps unique in the annals of diplomacy. In it, an older, established nation, arguably the strongest land power in Western Europe, openly pledged its support for a revolutionary movement whose purpose was to gain independence from its bitter rival for continental supremacy. Actually two treaties, the first recognized American independence and concluded commercial agreements, while the second provided for a military alliance. Together, the treaties extended the first official recognition of America abroad, brought significant military aid from France, and eventually brought Spain into the war against England as France's, and thus America's, ally.[34]

As a result of the treaty, a French fleet arrived off American shores in June under the command of Admiral Charles Hector Théodat Comte d'Estaing. Faced with this new threat, and fearing for the safety of New York, the British decided to abandon Philadelphia and concentrate their forces in New York. This movement resulted in the Battle of Monmouth, New Jersey, that July, thus precluding any enemy movement north along the Hudson. On July 16, having moved his main army northward after Monmouth, Washington visited West Point to inspect Kościuszko's work on the fortifications. Numerous myths and legends notwithstanding, it is probable that this was the first face-to-face meeting between the two officers. Though no official report is known to exist, the general's correspondence following the visit betrays his satisfaction with the progress of construction.[35]

Another effect of the French treaties was to greatly strengthen the high esteem for France, and things French, in America. Already in good graces because of covert aid provided by King Louis XVI since May, 1776, and because of the positive effect of the Marquis de Lafayette in America, the prestige of French officers in America increased greatly, and this soon brought new challenges to Kościuszko's authority at West Point. Less congenial than Washington's visit was the arrival, soon after, of Brig. Gen. du Portail and Col. de la Radière who, with the army now encamped in the vicinity, took advantage of the proximity to visit West Point, ostensibly on an inspection. Their real purpose was no doubt to cast aspersions on Kościuszko in the hope of having de la Radière reappointed to the post. Perhaps unaware of the Pole's close relationship with Gates, de la Radière had already written to the reappointed commander of the Northern Department to warn the general "not to risque his reputation for a gentleman who does not know his duty."[36] Not content with this, however, du Portail soon raised anew the question of de la Radière's supposed seniority of rank over Kościuszko, basing the claim on the bogus assertion that assurances had been given him that the French officers who accompanied him to America would enjoy seniority over all engineering officers previously appointed. On August 27 the French general took up the matter in a letter to Congress complaining that Kościuszko "would not acknowledge Mr. de la Radière, Col. of the Engineers, for his Superior. It is a matter of importance, Sir, that these things should be determined, and I beg you do your endeavors to have them as soon as possible."[37]

A similar letter went to Washington, who wrote to Henry Laurens, then President of Congress, to inquire whether any such arrangement existed and to express his support for Kościuszko.

> General Du Portail lately delivered me a Memorial, in which among other things he represents that he had made an agreement with Congress, at his first appointment, that neither himself nor the other Gentlemen with him, should ever be commanded by any of the

Engineers who had preceded them in our Army. I could not but answer, that the Commissions of Officers were the only rule of precedency & command I had to judge by: ... It will be for the good & tranquility of the service that the claim be determined as speedily as possible one way or the other. At the same time I think it right to observe, that it cannot be expected that Colo. Cosdusko, who had been a good while in this line and conducted himself with reputation and satisfaction will consent to act in a subordinate capacity to any of the French Gentlemen, except Gen. Portail.[38]

Eventually Congress denied du Portail's claims, and in this climate of antagonism he and de la Radière journeyed north to inspect the fortifications being prepared by a rival who had the effrontery to deny de la Radière's claims to superior rank.

On September 7 Washington wrote to the commanding officer at West Point to advise him of the inspection visit and solicit Kościuszko's cooperation. "Sir," Washington began, "Brigadier General Du Portail Chief Engineer is by my orders on a visit to the posts in the Highlands, to examine into the state of the fortifications carrying on there. It is my wish that Colo. Koshiosko may communicate every thing to this Gentleman, who is at the Head of the department, which he may find requisite for the purpose he is sent upon. I am persuaded you will show him every proper attention."[39]

Whether by coincidence or design, the Pole was not present at West Point during the inspection, having been summoned to appear on September 7 and 8 as a witness before the court martial of Gen. Arthur St. Clair over the loss of Fort Ticonderoga. Convened at White Plains with Gen. Lincoln presiding, the court met throughout most of August and September. When called, the colonel of engineers, true to his earlier professions of support, provided testimony in favor of St. Clair's decision to withdraw from the fortress. Others provided similar testimony, and in the end the court acquitted St. Clair "with honor."[40] This duty, however, led to Kościuszko's absence during the inspection and one can only imagine that he probably found the court martial appearance eminently less distasteful than facing the two French inquisitors. Yet, the visit to White Plains was not without its own moment of uneasiness. While there the engineer was approached by John Carter, his nemesis from the fallout of the Conway Cabal. Although the exact details of the confrontation are not known, Col. Jeduthan Baldwin who was also attending the court martial and witnessed the meeting wrote in his diary on September 8 that "Colo. Kosiusko [was] insulted by Mr[.] Carter."[41]

Du Portail, for his part, took pains to note in his official report of September 13 that Kościuszko had not been on hand to meet with him.[42] Yet, despite his predilection to find fault, and whatever offence he may have taken at Kościuszko's absence, du Portail could find little to complain about in his lengthy report. Fort Putnam, the main fortification designed to provide security for the rest of the works, he found "almost impregnable," lacking only a bomb-proof and the extension of one wall. Fort Arnold he found "pretty well situated and traced," while a battery placed to interdict the river appeared "extremely well placed for battering the Vessels which should approach the Chain." Although offering a few proposals for changes or additions, his only serious criticism was leveled at Fort Wyllys which he considered too poorly laid out and too extensive in its present state, suggesting instead that it might be "best perhaps to rebuild this fort altogether." With these changes, he believed "the Works which are in hand at West Point and some inconsiderable ones, which it is necessary to add to them, will, with the help of [the] chain, perfectly fulfill the object which is proposed,—that of hindering the enemy's remounting the North River."[43] Given du Portail's temperament, the general approval of the West Point fortifications with such minor alterations must stand, in itself, as a favorable comment on Kościuszko's work.

In the aftermath of the inspection, and with the approaching winter bringing to a conclusion the normal campaigning season, Washington soon moved his headquarters to West Point. Once there he conducted a second personal inspection of the works, looking specifically at the points noted in du Portail's report. His findings confirm even more the quality of the Polish engineer's work. Washington overruled any changes in Fort Wyllys, where du Portail suggested the most serious reconstruction, and allowed only some of the minor alterations the chief engineer advocated. In a letter to du Portail dated September 19, Washington explained:

> I have perused the memorial, which you delivered relative to the defence of the North River at this place, and upon a view of them highly approve what you have offered upon the Subject, Colo. Kosciousko who was charged by Congress with the direction of the forts and batteries, has already made such a progress in the construction of them as would render any alteration in the general plan a work

of too much time, and the favorable testimony which you have given of Colo. Kosciousko's abilities prevents uneasiness on this head; but whatever amendments subordinate to the general disposition shall occur as proper to be made, you will be pleased to point out to Col. Kosciousko that they may be carried into execution.[44]

Haiman believes that Washington probably expressed his verbal satisfaction to Col. William Malcolm, then temporarily in command at West Point, because upon his return Kościuszko penned a letter to Gates on October 6 in which he expressed satisfaction that the inspection had turned out well and his judgement been vindicated. The letter read, in part:

> His exellency was here with General Portail to see the works after all Conclusion was made that I am not the worst of Inginier. General Washington told him that he should give me direction about the works, but he givet me any what was not lay before and aprouved all some time against his will. I see planly that was the ven to show me that I have superior and abowe me and indeed Sir I discover in Conversation that this Gentlemen wanted little practice because he believe that is the same thing upon the paper as upon the Ground we most always have the works according to the Ground and Circumstance but not as the paper is level and make the works accordingly. That is between us.[45]

Despite the commanding general's approval, Kościuszko longed for a change of scenery in the fall of 1778. Having been on duty at West Point for several months of constant hard work, under pressure from various commanders including Washington to push the construction as quickly as possible, and now with the increasing interference of generally unfriendly French newcomers, it is easy to understand why Kościuszko longed for a field command and a return to the friendly headquarters of Horatio Gates. Early that fall a seeming opportunity presented itself which, if realized, would allow Kościuszko to resume a more active role in the field. Seeking to take advantage of the elimination of Burgoyne's army, the Board of War proposed to launch an invasion of Canada scheduled for the spring of 1779. Because of the growing anti-Washington sentiment in the wake of Saratoga, the commander-in-chief was not told of the plan until late January when, on January 22, the Board selected the Marquis de Lafayette to command the expedition.[46] When he found out about the proposed invasion of Canada, Kościuszko, no doubt assuming Gates would be the logical leader for such an expedition, and sensing an opportunity for active service, wholeheartedly approved of the idea. "You most think Sir to Expedition for Canada which will be Your Consquet not doubt and will add to your Honour, your Reputation and your Habilities of Surrender Borgon," he wrote to Gates. "Believe me Sir, if we have not Canada the Bretain will be you verry Trubbelsom. You must not suffer not only them, but any puissance [power] whatsoever in yours North part of America. Every Preest preach for his Parishoners, and soch interest will never give you Good, but divide your Opinions and unannity and deslike your o[w]n Country, add to this the Gold soch power that hihave upon mind of many Men."[47]

When Lafayette arrived in Albany, however, he found a serious lack of preparation and supplies for the planned expedition. Less than half of the proposed 2,500 troops were on hand, and John Stark's militia, which was to join the movement, had yet to be called out. Given the lack of preparations, a disgusted Lafayette recommended to Congress that the idea be abandoned. Congress agreed. Washington, for his part, contemptuously referred to the abortive plan proposed by his rivals as "the child of folly."[48] To Kościuszko, its demise meant the end of an opportunity for active field service.

Yet, another chance for change presented itself during this same period. With Washington's army encamped along the Hudson River north of New York, the general sent a portion of his forces east into the Connecticut River valley where they would be in a position to either defend against a British move up the Hudson or cooperate with the French forces operating out of New England. Command of this portion of the army went to Gates.[49] To assist him in his new command, Gates sought Washington's approval for the transfer of Kościuszko to his new command. "I earnestly entreat your Ex[cellency]," he wrote to Washington on September 11, "will be pleased to permit Col. Kusiusco to be the engineer to serve with the troops marching under my command if I had not an affectionate regard for this amiable foreighner, I should upon no account have made this my request. The out works at West Point are in a manner finished & the body of the place in such forwardness as to put it in the power of the two Engineers now there to complete the whole with the utmost facility."[50]

Much to Kościuszko's great disappointment, Washington denied the request. "Colo. Kosciusko has had the chief direction and superintendence of the Works at West Point, and it is my desire, that he should remain to carry them on. New plans and alterations at this time, would be attended with many inconveniences, and protract the defences of the River. This possibly in some degree, might take place in case of his absence, under the management of Another Engineer."[51] Kościuszko's great distress at this disappointment can be seen in his letter to Gates on learning of Washington's decision. In it he laments not being able to join Gates and, still holding out hope of a Canadian invasion, indicates his willingness to serve with Gates as a volunteer if necessary. "You cannot Concive in what passion I am having not plaisure to be under your Command my hapiness is lost, but I hope that you will help me to recover it soon as possible. You most remember Sir to have me with you and if you will forget that I beg the faveur of your Lady to have me in her memory. Because I have determin tu go with you Sir if not in the other Caracter I must go as Volenter for the next expedition tu Canada."[52]

Two days later, in a letter to John Taylor, an Albany merchant, Kościuszko continued his lament, stressing his unhappiness that all of his friends had left either with the main army to White Plains or with Gates's command eastward into Connecticut. "I am the most enhappy man in the World," he wrote, "because all my Jankees the best Frinds is gone to Whit Plains or to Eastern and left me with the Skoches or Irishes [who are] impolites as the Saviges. The satisfaction that I have at present only is this to go all day upon the Works and the Ni[g]ht to go to bed with the Cross Idea of lost of good Compani. I should go to the Eastern with General Gates but Gl. Washington was obstacle of going me ther and I am verry sorry of it."[53] Even two week later, though his temper mollified, his disappointment was still evident in another letter to Gates: "You should not forget your Good Frind I have not news from you since I lefted Whit Plain. Believe me Sir you Cannot find better frind and more attach to you this Confession I will prouve in every Circumstance whatsoever[.] Will you remember Sir that I want to be with the Army under your Comand.... I look after happy delivrance from her[e] for northern Expedition."[54]

But the hoped-for reunion was not to be. On October 20 Washington ordered Gates to repair to Hartford, Connecticut, and two days later Congress assigned him to command the Eastern Department with headquarters in Boston. Regardless, the gloomy autumn did present some occasions for camaraderie amongst the many hours of hard labor. Now and then an opportunity presented itself to renew friendships. Col. Baldwin passed through West Point in mid-October, late November, and again in early December, lodging with Kościuszko each time. On December 4, Baldwin, Gen. McDougall, Gen. Paterson, and several other visitors dined with Kościuszko.[55]

By the end of 1778, Kościuszko had made considerable progress on the defenses, supplementing them with *chevaux-de-frise*, fireboats, gunboats, chains, redoubts, and, according to Montross, "every imaginable obstacle to discourage attacks by land or water. After the summer of 1778 a strong garrison always occupied the fort, however urgently troops might be needed elsewhere."[56] Nevertheless, given its importance, some amount of understandable nervousness continued among the high command. On December 17, McDougall ordered Major Jean Baptiste Obrey de Gouvion to travel to West Point to inspect the works with an eye to how he would attack them if he were the enemy. Gouvion was to report the results of his observations to McDougall at his earliest convenience. "[I]t is necessary the state of the works at this post should be ascertained, as much Expense and Labour have been bestowed upon them," McDougall confided to Gouvion. "Colonel Kusciosko will shew you the Ground and the works."[57]

As a result of the inspection, Gouvion reassured McDougall that the works were in good condition. So far advanced were they that Lynn Montross, historian of the Continental Army, concluded that by the end of the year "Clinton could no more dream of attacking this stronghold than Washington could hope to storm the works of New York."[58] Despite these expressions of satisfaction, however, work remained to be done and Kościuszko's efforts continued to be plagued by the lack of reliable manpower. On December 28, the Pole wrote to McDougall from Fort Arnold to apprise him of existing conditions, indicate that supplies of tar would be needed to treat the logs used for the chain and boom in the river, and ask the general's assistance in obtaining a reliable source of workmen.

> As Confusion has taken place Respecting the artificers since Col. Malcom took the Command at the Post, I should be glad your Honor would regulate those Matters that each one may [know] what [to] depend on in prosecuting the Business carrying on here, I should be very glad if I might have a daily report made me that I may know how many I can have to employ on the Works. I think the Q. M. [quartermaster] of the Place or Captain Furloughing the men is

attended with bad Consequences that they ought to be given by the Commander of the Garrison with my consent. That the Q. M. should not have Liberty to take the Artificers from other works but by thro proper application. There is one Company of Carpenters here whose pay is 12. per Day consisting only of Nine men Capt. Black has resigned his Liut. is here if we can keep him and his sergant (what I believe) and put those who are Drafted from the Masons are of but little use at this Time in this sivere Season. The Drafts four men from the Garrison in my opinion would be Sufficient to Compleat the necessary chimnies when the Weather moderates. The Chain is safe and can be easy taken up when the Cold abates. The boom lies where it was and will be taken up. We shall want I think about fifty barrels of Tarr for the use of the Logs of the Chain Boom and Bumprowes [i.e., bombproofs]. Capt. Clow is of Opinion that he can raise a good Company of Masons for the Summer if he can have permissison. Those Matters you can Judge better than my self you will excuse me in giving my Opinion that shall perfectly acquess in and execute your Commands.[59]

Two days later McDougall, determined to press the construction as vigorously as possible, ordered Kościuszko to give special attention to cutting logs and timber for various purposes.

You will give all possible attention to cause timber to be cut for compleating the works at West Point. The season is now favourable to draw it to the water—you will get as much chevaux de frize as you can with all possible despatch made till further orders. They should be fitted for the axis, all of one size and Iron chains made to be fastened them to each other. Your first attention must be to cutting the Timber for the Works. What Artificers can be spared from this will be employed on the chevaux de frize. Take to your assistance every officer and man of B. G. Patterson's Brigade Qualified to aid and further those services.[60]

Regardless of McDougall's orders and Kościuszko's efforts, by January 1 the number of artificers under the engineer's command at West Point shrank to five officers and 105 men.[61] The following day Kościuszko wrote to Gen. McDougall to inform him of arrangements the engineer made to obtain a supply of tar and lime from Col. Hay and to apprise him of further progress and the state of troops at his disposal. "Capt. Black's Company was discharged by Col. Hay before my return," he wrote

I therefore drafted twenty men from the Garrison and put them at work on the Chevaux defrise, from the other two Companies I have send Eighteen cuting timber for the Bumbe [bomb] proofs agreable to your orders. I find many of the Logs at the Chain that are rotten, should think it best to send up the River to Cut white Pine to replace them, which are much better for that Purpose, but shall want more Carpenters to prosecute the Plan. We have taken up and got on Shore three Hundred links of the Chain with about one hundred of the small one where it was fastened to the Skid block. I send you two big and two small Boles could not find knots for more.[62]

Throughout the depths of the winter months and on into spring he kept continually busy repairing the log boom and chain, placing new *chevaux-de-frise*, constructing bombproofs and magazines, and erecting additional barracks and redoubts.[63] Having virtually denuded the immediate area of usable timber in the construction of the works already completed, one of the recurring difficulties was the procurement of sufficient logs of the requisite quality to repair the river boom and chain and push work on the land fortifications. On February 6 Kościuszko wrote to McDougall to inform him of the condition of the chain and indicate his need for lumber and logs. "I should be happy to know your determination respecting the Chain," he asked the general, "it is certain that not much more than half the Logs will be fit for Service again next Summer and we Cannot get those that are good short of Coeymans, if you should think this advisable it ought to be begun immediately as the Season approaches fast." Then, referring to a plan he enclosed for a proposed redoubt, he continued: "As it is very difficult to procure good Fascines near that Place, I think that the Parapet can easily be done with Timber up to the Frise E and the rest with Fascines. If you approve of this Plan it will be time to begin cutting the Timber for the Bombproof immediate. I am in great Want of a Whip saw and Cannot get it from Fishkill. Should beg the Favour of having one from Maj. Campbell. I send you by the Bearer four Tin Plates and one for Sugar."[64]

Gen. McDougall responded as best he could, sending what tools he could locate and asking Gen. Paterson to assign trusty axemen to assist with the felling of trees. "[T]he Engineer informs me twenty white pine Logs are necessary to replace the like number unfit to Float the Chain," he informed Paterson. "I wish you to send eight good axe men of the line with a sufficient number of carpinders [carpenters] to cut those Logs and trim the Barks. To encourage those men to expedite this service, engage to give them, half a Gallon of Rum for every approved piece they shall deliver at West Point, over and above the daily allowance. The Engineer thinks it necessary, a good officer should be sent with this party. You will please to send one; & cause every other preparation to be made to extend the chain across in its place."[65]

During this time a French engineer, Lt. Col. Jean Baptiste Gouvion, arrived to serve as Kościuszko's assistant. "It seems that he was more accessible than his colleagues," Haiman writes, "as there is no record of any misunderstanding between them, though both together spent a long time at West Point." Apparently this relationship, though it appeared to work well, caused some confusion at army headquarters. On February 9 Washington wrote to McDougall to express his concern that Gouvion may have replaced Kościuszko in the sensitive position at West Point. "I am in doubt whether Col. Koshiosko still remains at West Point, or not. As he has not been removed by my order or permission, I should imagine he is still there. If he is, he will inform you of the plan agreed upon between General Du Portail & myself, which he was instructed in the first place to carry into execution, as might be found necessary to render the plan more perfect. I have spoken to General Du Portail, on your request concerning Col. De la Radière or Gouvion. Whether the former will be sent or the latter continued will depend on circumstances which are not now decided. But if Koshiosko be still at West Point, as he is a senior officer he must of necessity have the chief direction."[66] To this, McDougall replied reassuringly that "Colo. Kusiasco has been undisturbed in his Line at West Point."[67]

By the end of February, Kościuszko still struggled to advance the defenses despite inadequate tools and labor. On February 24 he informed McDougall he had "no more Intrinching Tools but twenty spades and twenty five Pickakes. Som is in the Regiments but very fews. About the Timber that was upon the Ground when General Paterson took Command is forty five sticks Good for the Bum proof [bombproof]; and small timber for the Barack of 200 foot. The men was sent today for the Logs of the Chain."[68] Patterson, too, complained to Major Richard Platt, adjutant general and aide-de-camp to Gen. McDougall, of the small number of men available to form labor battalions. By the beginning of March there were only about 400 men left, and so many of these were detailed to other duties that the remaining number was "so small that we can make no progress in the Works which want to be Done immediately to be in any State of Defence should the Enemy" appear.[69]

Kościuszko continued working long hours with the available manpower to finish as much of the new construction as possible. With the weather inhibiting communication, a despairing Kościuszko lamented in a letter to Gates on March 3 that "West Point is as barren of news as the mountains that surround it." In the same letter the lonely engineer professed his friendship and chided the general for not writing. He wrote, he said, "without any self interest not expecting an Answer having received none in return for four sent you. I will Continue to write and if I cannot give you any satisfaction or Pleasure, I shall gratify my own Vanity in expressing my sentiment as an Old woman, who by age expects not a reciprocity of affection or interest to her." Then, after passing along some news, Kościuszko closed by observing that "I suppose to be my self at this time more than half a Yankee."[70]

To fight his growing feeling of isolation, Kościuszko kept up a lively correspondence with several of his friends, including Major Armstrong who was now serving once again under Gates's command. "I do not tax you with want of Friendships in not writing to me knowing that you have a good reason to give that the handsome Girls ingross the whole of your Time and attention and realy If I was in your place I should of Choise do the same." Then, in asides to other friends in Armstrong's company he chided "But you Col. Clairjon can give me no Reason but your Laxiness. I have ben told you are about Marying a Young girl and mean to exert yourself that the name of Clairjons may not be extinguished. You Col. Troop as a good officer of Artillery will make use of your Activity and prove the Goodness of your Cannon on the wedding Day of Col. Clairjon. Your help Doctor Brown will be wanted with all your Surgical Faculties to promote so laudauble a design for the interest of Mr. Clairjon and administere such Medicine as will make him Strong and Fameus as Priapus."[71]

While the Pole longed for word from his friends, he had to devote most of his time to the work at hand. Under the circumstances, with a shortage of logs, tools, and manpower, some portions of the defenses lagged behind schedule. In mid-March McDougall, concerned that the chain had not yet been returned to its place in the river, asked Kościuszko for an explanation. "I am Sorry to hear the chain is not yet extended," he wrote. "I wish to know the impediments which have prevented it." Noting that boards enroute from Albany should arrive soon, he instructed the engineer "to take the utmost care of them and not suffer one to be cut up for any purpose but public buildings." The general also requested a map of West Point and the surrounding area be sent to him on which was to be noted the current progress of the defenses.[72]

On April 25 Kościuszko sent a map of the defenses to McDougall, along with a request for more bread for the carpenters. By that time, however, McDougall was becoming increasingly concerned that the spring weather would bring with it a British attempt on West Point. On April 17 he committed these fears to a letter addressed to Kościuszko, including the admonition to make sure the engineer was ready for any eventuality.[73]

But while Kościuszko labored to push the construction forward that spring, other events occurred that would once again interfere with his command. In keeping with a reorganization of the engineering department, Congress changed Brig. Gen. du Portail's title to "Commandant of the Corps of Engineers and Sappers and Miners," clearly giving him control over all engineering activities and personnel. When some delay intervened before formal approval, du Portail lobbied the Continental Congress to formally approve his new appointment, arguing that despite the critical importance of West Point, and his "Directions to the officer entrusted with the fortifications of that Place" notwithstanding, the general reported that "unhappily, I have lately heard, that almost nothing has been done." Despite the obvious falsity of this claim, knowing of the importance of the position along the Hudson, du Portail pressed for his confirmation lest the worse befall West Point before he could correct the situation. "If the Enemies happen to take possesion of West Point, ... Congress or the Commander-in-Chief will betake themselves to me, and ask of me, why I did not take care that the works at West Point should not be carried on with regularity and dispatch.... My answer will be this; 'I had no right to demand the necessary informations from the Engineer entrusted with the fortifications of the Place: When I went there in September by the Commander-in-Chief's order, I requested him to render me an account every month of the Condition of the Works, of the difficulties of every kind that might arise in the Execution:—He has not done it. But that officer is not in any manner to be blamed for he had no orders in writing for that purpose from Congress or the Commander-in-Chief.'" Unless he were given complete control, du Portail argued, he would not be responsible "for the neglects or interruptions which may happen in the Works of the Fort."[74]

Whether this plea was effective or not is uncertain, but Congress approved du Portail's new position effective May 17. On the 28th Washington wrote to McDougall to reiterate the importance of fortifying West Point and assure him the commander-in-chief was "persuaded every thing has been done by you for this purpose."[75] Five days later Washington again assured McDougall that "It gives me pleasure that the forts at this critical moment are in hands where they may be safely trusted."[76] Nevertheless, despite these reassurances on the same day the French engineer arrived at West Point under orders from Washington to conduct a second inspection of the works. On the 8th the commander-in-chief himself arrived for a personal tour, stressing the significance of what Washington regarded as "the most important Post in America."[77]

By the end of May warmer weather heralded the beginning of the campaigning season for 1779. With its arrival, the British in New York did indeed became more active, with Sir Henry Clinton moving north to capture Verplanck's Point and Stoney Point, a dozen miles south of West Point, on June 1. In the face of this threat, work on the fortifications of West Point was pushed forward with renewed vigor, concentrated particularly on the defenses surrounding Fort Putnam.[78] But manpower continued to be a limiting factor. On June 30 Col. Alexander Scammell, Adjutant General, conveyed an order from Washington's headquarters to Gen. William Heath to the effect that "All those Soldiers who are masons by trade in the line, are immediately to be drawn out, and sent to the Fort, for special service. They are to take their orders from Col. Kosciuszko."[79] Regardless, on the next day Kościuszko again complained to McDougall about the need for more men. "Thes[e] works want at less six hundret men[,] one hundred & sixty Carpenters[,] twenty Massons, and twelve Miners, ten teams for two months."[80] In a similar complaint addressed directly to Washington, Kościuszko explained that

> I have only two Masons as yet come from the Main Army, and do not expect any more, the Officers being unwilling to part with them. I applyed to the Detachements here who had a number of them, wrote to the Officers in the most pressing terms shewing the necessity of it but got none. I am out of the lime, it is true I have a promise of having some more but when I cannot tell.

One of the Justice wrote to Mr. Whiting, G.Q.M., that General Green[e] had excused the Inhabitants from sending more Teams than Ten, I suppose he has in view to imploy the Teams of the Brigades, as they do nothing at Present to ease the Burthen of the Inhabitants.

I have Twenty Carpenters Sick by raison of drinking Water in this hot Weather they suppose that one Half Gill added to their daily allowance would remedy the Evil.

Col. Stewart was so good as to let me have a Stone Cutter from his Regiment for One Week. I wish to have him for a Month having much to do and know not where to find another.[81]

Additional assistance eventually came after Washington transferred his headquarters to New Windsor, near West Point, on July 25, remaining in the area until November 28.[82] At the same time the Virginian ordered that "all those soldiers who are Masons by trade in the line are immediately to be drawn out & sent to the Fort for a special & temporary service. They are to take their orders from Colonel Kosciuszko."[83] With this support, both material and moral, the defenses of Fort Putnam were completed and the remaining positions greatly advanced.

To rush the construction, an average of 2,500 men per day were employed on fatigue duties under Kościuszko's direction. With a greatly enlarged labor force, however, came new problems. Kościuszko now had to deal with increased responsibility unrelated to his actual engineering duties. Overseeing the workforce, the engineer continually had to solve those aggravating problems which occur from day to day such as provisions, pay, clothing, illness, and insubordination. In treating with these aggravations, Kościuszko has been described as displaying great sympathy and human understanding. He continually attempted to look out for the welfare of his men, going so far as to share his own rations with British prisoners confined in the post's stockades. He wrote to General Heath about the lack of supplies and especially the irregularity in the distribution of his men's pay. He supported these complaints by noting that from a practical standpoint it would be difficult to reenlist men whose pay was constantly months in arrears.[84]

To Philip Schuyler, then a member of the Continental Congress, Kościuszko addressed the following letter seeking proper clothing for his engineers.

As you are the only Person in Congress with whom I have the

Honor to be acquainted, that knows the System of the whole Army and it's several departments; you will forgive me the trouble I am about to give you in favour of the Corps of Engineers. We beg that the Honorable Congress would grant us Clothing in Apointed maner as for the Army. Why should all Departments receive and we be excluded? Justice speek for it's self without any farther request from us. If Cloathing could be purchased very easy, in this Country and without injuring the Public service, in the Time which most be necessarily employed for that purpose we should not solicit, but you know how difficult it is to get it, and what inconsistancies it would be, for us to be absent often from Camp. Your remonstrating to Congress in our behalf will I am sure bare great weight, which favour will always be greatfully acknowledged, with the greatest Sincerity from us.[85]

Samuel Richards, who observed Kościuszko during his long stay at West Point, later left a revealing personality portrait of the engineer. "I quartered a considerable time with Kosciuszko," he wrote, "in the same log hut, and soon discovered in him an elevation of mind which gave fair promise of those high achievements to which he attained. His manners were soft and conciliating and, at the same time, elevated. I used to take much pleasure in accompanying him with his theodolite, measuring the heights of the surrounding mountains. He was very ready in mathematics."[86] With the possible exception of the French engineers who continually jockeyed with Kościuszko for rank and command, Richards's opinion about the Pole's character was almost universally held among those who knew the soft-spoken engineer.

By August, despite the many problems, progress was noticeable. Later that fall, Col. Israel Angell of the Second Rhode Island Regiment described the scene as consisting of "a fort on Every Emminence Some Distance round."[87] Fortunately for the patriot cause, the British were equally impressed with the fortifications, deeming them too strong to successfully assault. Instead, Clinton's army contented itself with occupying Verplanck's Point and Stony Point until November 1 when it finally gave up any hope of moving on West Point that year. Thereafter, the direct threat to West Point ceased, but not the American concern for continuing to improve its fortifications.

Throughout the fall of 1779 work continued on the fortifications. With Washington's army in the vicinity until November 28, Kościuszko enjoyed meeting some of his friends. On November 1 Major Armstrong paid a visit enroute to Philadelphia. Even more enjoyable was a brief visit by Gates and his family who arrived on November 23, providing an opportunity to renew in person one of Kościuszko's closest friendships of the Revolutionary period. During the same month, however, he received information that another friend from the Northern Department, Col. Richard Varick, would be unable to visit. "I am very sorry that your business will not per mit to pass winter Quarters with me," he told Varick. "I send you your Pictor which when you will give to you Sister pray not forget to pay my best respects to her and tell her that I promise to make her pictor; I suppose will be very good resemblance if I make the Handsommest feature of Fear [fair] Creature that I am only able with my Genius mind."[88]

The winter of 1779-1780 was, according to Boynton, "one of unexampled severity at West Point. ... So intense was the cold, that for a period of forty days, no water dripped from the roofs which sheltered them. The snow was four feet deep on a level, requiring a heavy force to be constantly engaged in keeping open the communication with the six or seven redoubts built and building. Twice during the winter the North Redoubt barely escaped total destruction by fire. The parapet, built of logs, covered with earth, and difficult of access, burned nearly three days before the fire could be extinguished. The South Barrack in Fort Arnold was entirely consumed, with a large quantity of stores; but the adjacent buildings were saved by the indefatigable labor of the garrison."[89]

Despite the bitter cold and the thick blanket of snow, Kościuszko could not afford to be idle. Constantly at work, he reconstructed the burned portions of the post, added outworks, and completed work on barracks, magazines, and other necessities as the weather permitted. Work continued on into the spring of 1780, increasing in pace as the weather became more mild, but the old nemesis of diminished labor returned to frustrate progress. On March 23 Kościuszko wrote to Col. Richard K. Meade, assistant adjutant-general to Washington, detailing his problems finding men and supplies.

> I wrote also to his Excellency respecting teams which I Cannot get by the great scarcity of Forrage and you know I can do nothing without them.
>
> I beg you would inform him I have but Eighty fatigue men for all the works at West Point and I expect less and less every day; this ill

be the Cause, that the works will not be Compleated and not to be imputed to my neglect. I wrote to Governor Clinton two days agoe, that he would send some teams with the Fourage of the opulent and rich inhabitants, I have not yet received an answer. I ... have three masons from the Virginia Line. They the best Masons of few number that I have I should beg to keep them, but as they are in Great want of shoes, I will thank you to procure an order for three pairs of shoes on the Commissary of Cloathing at Newburgh.[90]

To break up the monotonous daily routine of work, Kościuszko often spent his off-duty hours in a secluded spot among the rocks that jutted form the sides of the cliffs fronting the Hudson River. There the Pole began constructing a small garden. With his own hands he carried baskets of earth to this nearly inaccessible spot. Working in his spare time Kościuszko planted flowers in his new garden, creating an enchantingly serene spot among the preparations for war. It was a spot he visited often not only as a diversion, but to meditate on his daily problems. As early as July, 1778, Dr. James Thatcher, visiting West Point, wrote in his journal of having "the pleasure of being introduced to Col. Thaddeus Kosciuszko, a gentleman of distinction, from Poland. He has amused himself, while stationed at this point, in laying out a curious garden in a deep valley, abounding more in rocks than in soil. I was gratified in viewing his curious water fountain with spouting jets and cascades."[91] It is a spot which long ago became part of the lore of West Point. In his *Tales of the Garden of Kosciuszko*, published in 1834, Samuel L. Knapp described it in these words:

> It was here, when in its rude state, that the Polish soldier and patriot sat in deep contemplation on the loves of his youth, and the ills his country had to suffer. It would be a grateful sight to him if he could visit it now, and find that a band of youthful soldiers had, as it were, consecrated the whole military grounds to his fame. His martial spirit would take fire in beholding such exact military maneuvers, as are exhibited by the scientific corps; and in the pride of his soul he would declare that a country who gave her sons such an education could never be conquered or enslaved.

Boynton's *History of West Point*, published a generation later in 1863, speaks of "The marble fountain, the shrubbery and the secluded seats, with an occasional bit of ribbon or a glove, suggest that it is yet a resort for some who, it is hoped, are as patriotic and quite as sincere as the unfortunate Pole."[92] The spot is maintained to this day by the Corps of Cadets as "Kościuszko's Garden."

By the end of July, 1780, Kościuszko's work at West Point was nearly complete. Passing through the area in late 1780, the Marquis de Chastellux described the Pole's achievement thusly:

> Fort West Point and the mighty fortifications that defend it draw the eye to the western shore of the river; but looking up one can see on all sides towering heights bristling with redoubts and batteries. I dismounted from my horse and had a good look through my field-glass since this is the only way to view at once all the fortifications which surround this important point. Two towering elevations, each of which has its own large redoubt, guard the eastern shore. They have no names other than the Northern and Southern redoubts. However, starting from the fort of West Point itself, which is situated on the river bank, and proceeding to the top of the height at the foot of which the fort was built, I counted six various fortifications rising in tiers after the manner of an amphitheater, each of which shielded the previous one ... up to the highest peak there are three mighty redoubts equipped with cannon; each of the redoubts would call for a separate siege. As dusk was approaching I contented myself with a quick glance which sufficed to enable me to appreciate the soundness of conception owing to which they can protect one another.[93]

"West Point was a fortress far ahead of its time," concluded Dave R. Palmer, author of *The River and the Rock: The History of Fortress West Point, 1775-1783*. "The practical Pole shaped each stronghold to conform best to its nearby terrain, using whenever he could nature's sheer walls and rocky obstacles. ... All in all, the separate works constituting fortress West Point displayed a remarkable level of engineering sophistication. Observers were invariably impressed."[94] The system of naturally supporting strong points arrayed in a defense in depth would not come into general use for another century. The extent of Kościuszko's skill in constructing the fortress was probably best expressed by the distinguished American historian George Bancroft who concluded that "Until 1778 West Point was a solitude, nearly inaccessible; now it was covered by fortresses with numerous redoubts, constructed chiefly under the direction of Kości-uszko as engineer, and so connected as to form one system of defense, which was believed to be impregnable." These defenses effectively denied the British use of the Hudson, while protecting the valuable grain of the Mohawk and Schoharie Valleys that fed Washington's army. West Point effectively bottled the British forces up in New York City, making a movement southward their only viable option and allowing Washington to concentrate his meager forces against such an eventuality. "Strategically," Hoffman Nickerson concluded, "West Point neutralized New York. From the moment when its works came into existence the army of Sir Henry Clinton on Manhattan Island was held in a vise."[95] In the words of General John Armstrong, "Kościuszko's merit lies in this that he gave the fortifications such strength that they frightened the very enemy from all temptations of even trying to take the Highlands." Washington agreed. "To his care and sedulous appreciation," the general wrote of Kościuszko, "the American people are indebted for the defense of West Point."[96]

Chapter 8

"The Safety and Support of the Army"

Following the victory at Saratoga, while Kościuszko busied himself with preparing the works at West Point, the fortunes of war turned against the revolutionaries in the Southern colonies. With the failure of Burgoyne's campaign in New York, British military planners determined to make some move to restore allegiance in the Southern colonies where Tory sympathies were strong among much of the upper class gentry. On December 29, 1778, a British force of 3,500 troops from New York under Lt. Col. Archibald Campbell captured the port of Savannah, Georgia, as a staging point for further operations in the South.[1]

The British offensive began in January, 1779, with the capture of Augusta, Georgia. Following this movement the armies fought a series of inconclusive engagements along the Savannah River, highlighted by a threatening move on Charleston by British General Augustine Prevost, an experienced officer who had been gravely wounded while serving with Wolfe at Quebec in 1759. Although Charleston was saved by the timely arrival of Gen. Benjamin Lincoln with 6,500 troops, Prevost inflicted a sharp defeat on the colonial forces at Stono Ferry on June 20, 1779, before retreating back to Savannah.[2]

The next colonial attempt to defeat the British campaign in the South took the form of a Franco-American movement against Savannah. About September 3, 1779, a French fleet of 33 ships under Admiral d'Estaing arrived off the Savannah River with some 4,000 French troops. On September 16 d'Estaing demanded that Prevost surrender the city of Savannah. Prevost asked for 24 hours to consider the proposal. It was granted and the unwise delay allowed 800 British reinforcements to reach Prevost's undermanned garrison.[3]

Joined by the American army under Lincoln, d'Estaing planned to carry the city by storm. This ill-advised and poorly executed attack resulted in complete defeat for the allied effort, despite heroic individual efforts to avert the disaster. Numbered among the mortally wounded in this operation was one of Kościuszko's countrymen, Brig. Gen. Kazimierz Pułaski. The defeat at Savannah led d'Estaing to remove his forces to the West Indies. Saddened by this turn of events, many Americans began to doubt the advantages of a French alliance which had failed to bring any relief to New York, Rhode Island, or Savannah. Conversely, the British success in holding Savannah heartened Loyalists in the area and insured the South would be the scene of serious campaigning in 1780.

Beginning in December, 1779, Sir Henry Clinton left New York by sea for Savannah with some 8,700 troops. Moving north from Savannah in the early spring, Clinton soon approached Charleston, defended by 3,600 men under Gen. Benjamin Lincoln. Throughout the latter part of March and all of April the two armies jockeyed for position, with the British clearly getting the upper hand. The end came on May 12, 1780, when Lincoln surrendered both the city and his entire army, thus providing the British with their greatest conquest to that time. With the extinction of the Southern Army, Clinton left for New York on June 5 with about one-third of the troops, leaving Lord Cornwallis with 8,345 men to extend British control over the South. Cornwallis kept his main force at Charleston, with strong outposts at Savannah, Augusta, and Ninety-Six. He also established a forward base at Camden and outposts at Rocky Mount, Hanging Rock, and Cheraw, with another post located at Gerogetown at the mouth of the Pee Dee River. Civil war ensued with patriot forces under Cols. Andrew Pickens, Francis Marion, and Thomas Sumter jousting for control of the Backcountry area against Loyalists under Lt. Col. Banastre Tarleton and Capt. Patrick Ferguson.[4]

The repulse at Savannah and the capitulation of Charleston, coupled with dashing victories by Tarleton at Monck's Corner, Lenud's Ferry, and the Waxhaws, were serious blows to the patriot cause. Loyalists rallied to the British cause and patriots lay low or joined the British for self-protection. With both South Carolina and Georgia virtually pacified, the Patriot cause was indeed gloomy, prompting the Continental Congress to action. Fearing that unless a new Southern Army was established the revolution in the South would surely expire, Congress authorized the creation of a new army and sought an officer to command the effort. Having already sent, at the suggestion of Gen. Gates, a force of 1,400 Delaware and Maryland Continentals south under the command of Major General the Baron Johann de Kalb to reinforce Lincoln, upon the surrender of Charleston this force became the nucleus about which the new army would be created. Hoping to capitalize on his popularity after the Saratoga campaign, and hoping as well for another such success, Congress appointed Horatio Gates to this new Southern command. Significantly, the appointment was made without consulting Washington who preferred General Nathaniel Greene over Gates.[5] Nor was Washington the only person to hold reservations about Gates. Several officers felt he received too much credit for Saratoga, refusing as he did to acknowledge the contributions of Arnold and others. John R. Alden concluded that Gates "had gone so far, however, because of a pleasing personality, powerful friends, and good fortune rather than superlative abilities. He had displayed no more than good sense on the Hudson in 1777, digging in and letting Burgoyne rashly advance to his destruction."[6]

De Kalb left Morristown on April 16. His force included the 1st Brigade under Brigadier General William Smallwood with the 1st, 3rd, 5th, and 7th Maryland Regiments, and the 2nd Brigade under General Mordecai Gist with the 2nd, 4th, and 6th Maryland Regiments and the Delaware Regiment. With the infantry went the eighteen guns of Col. Charles Harrison's 1st Continental Artillery Regiment. De Kalb marched through Philadelphia to Head of Elk where the troops boarded ships for Petersburg, Virginia. The guns went by land. De Kalb moved south from Petersburg at an average of 15 to 18 miles per day, learning of the surrender of Charleston on June 20 when he was at Parson's Plantation, North Carolina, about 35 miles northeast of Hillsboro. Despite the news, he decided to push south even though little militia support materialized. He reached Hillsboro June 22 and continued on to Deep River, about 50 miles from Cheraw, where he met 120 survivors of the Pulaski Legion under the Marquis de la Rouerie, better known as Col. Armand. Unable to locate the Virginia units of Brig. Gen. Edward Stevens and Lt. Col. Charles Porterfield, and with Maj. Gen. Richard Caswell's North Carolina militia refusing to join him, de Kalb camped for two weeks at Buffalo Ford where word finally reached him of Gates's appointment. With this, de Kalb halted his southerly march, moving instead to Hollingsworth's Farm (known also as Coxe's Mill) where he awaited the new commander's arrival.[7]

Gates received his appointment to the Southern command on June 13. Preparing for his new assignment, the general's thoughts immediately turned to the necessity of engaging a qualified, reliable engineering officer. On June 21, 1780, he wrote the following lines in a letter to Washington: "Congress have doubtless acquainted Your Excellency with Their having sent me Orders to take Command of the Southern Department, and to proceed immediately to Petersburg. As all appearances from that Quarter are exceedingly Gloomy, I could wish Your Excellency would somewhat Brighten the Scene by indulging me in my request to Obtain Colonel Kuscuiusco for my Chief Engineer. His services with me in the Campaign of 77 and the High Opinion I entertain of His Talents, and His Honour, induce me to be thus importunate with Your Excellency, to let me have the Colonel for my Chief Engineer."[8] About the same time, Gates wrote to another companion of the Saratoga campaign expressing his concern that others might prevent the Pole from joining him. To Major John Armstrong he wrote: "I am destined by the Congress to command in the South. In entering on this new and (as Lee says) most difficult theatre of war, my first thoughts have been turned to the selection of an Engineer, an Adjutant-General and a Quarter-Master-General. Kosciuszko, Hay and yourself if I can prevail upon you all, are to fill these offices, and fill them well. The excellent qualities of the Pole, which no one knows better than yourself, are acknowledged at head-quarters, and may induce others to prevent his joining us. But his promise once given, we are sure of him."[9]

Gates was particularly interested in having Kościuszko accompany him south, not just because of his obvious friendship and professional skill, but because of his philosophical principles. He was "a pure republican" Gates believed, "without any dross." Gates's biographer, Samuel White Patterson, explained it thusly: "Gates felt that, like himself, Kościuszko knew what the fight was all about. The goal was not merely a victory on the field of battle, but the realization of a political ideal."[10]

Apparently Gates's letter was not delivered for some time because by the end of July, restive at the relative lack of work at West Point because of the detachment of the artificers from that post to assist Lt. Col. Gouvion with construction of some smaller works along the lower Highlands, Kościuszko wrote to Washington requesting reassignment to a combat position in the general's army. "To this day," he wrote, "I have not received your Excellencys order respecting my destination, having nothing to do at present as all the artifficers are directed to receive Liut. Colo: Gouvions orders, I beg your Excellency to give me permision to leave the Engeneer Department and direct me a Command in the light Infantry in the Army under your immediate Command or the Army at the Southward agreable to my ranck I now hold. Your Excellency may be certain that I am acquiented with the Tactic & discipline and my Conduct joind with a small share of ambition to distinguish myself, I hope will prove not the Contrary."[11]

Washington replied promptly, informing Kościuszko that the detachment of the artificers was only temporary, but that another assignment could be arranged if he preferred. "The Artificers are drawn from the post at West Point for a particular and temporary service only," he explained, "and as there is a necessity for a Gentleman in the Engineering department to remain constantly at that post, and as you from your long residence there are particularly well acquainted with the nature of the Works and the plans for their completion, it was my intent that you should continue. The Infantry Corps was arranged before the receipt of your letter. The southern Army, by the captivity of Genl. du portail and the other Gentlemen in that branch, is without an Engineer, and as you seem to express a wish of going there rather than remaining at West Point, I shall, if you prefer it to your present appointment, have no objection to your going."[12]

Kościuszko was apparently quite happy with Washington's response because he immediately replied to the general's letter, indicating his desire to head south. "The Choice your Excellency was pleased to give me in the letter of yesterday is very kind and as the Complition of the works at this place this Campaign as Circumstance are, will be impossible in my opinion, I prefer going to the Southward to Continuing here. I beg you to favor me with your orders, and Letter of recommendation to the Board of War, as I shall pass throw Philadelphia. Shall wait on your Excellency to pay due respects within a few days, but lest the movements of the Army should prevent, beg my request may be granted and sent me at this place."[13]

Only after the issue of Kościuszko's transfer was resolved does it appear that Gates's letter of June 21, requesting the Pole's assignment to the Southern army, finally arrived at Washington's headquarters. On August 8 Washington penned a letter to Gates which appears to respond to the June 21 letter. In it, Washington explains that "A few days since upon Col. Kosciuisco's application for leave to serve to the Southward, he obtained my permission, and I suppose designs setting out immediately."[14] Four days later he penned another letter to Gates expressing his approval of the Pole's work in the Northern Department: "I have taken oppurtunity of writign by Colonel Kosciuszko with whom I part reluctantly as I have experienced great satisfaction from his general conduct and particularly from the attention and zeal which with he has prosecuted the works commited to his charge at West Point."[15]

Kościuszko left West Point around August 7, arriving at Washington's headquarters at Orange Town on the 12th to extend his regards and express his appreciation to the commanding general. His business at headquarters complete, Kościuszko continued his journey south to Philadelphia where he stayed for about one week. While there he learned of the illness of Robert Gates, the general's son, and determined to make a detour from his route to visit Gates's family. On August 20, William Clajon wrote to Gates informing him of the intended visit and the resulting delay in joining the Southern army. "The exhausted State of the Treasury prevents my joining you as yet," he related, "or I would set out with Col. Kosciusko" who "intends to visit Traveller's Rest [Gates's home] before he joins you, so that you will have by him a more circumstantial Account than you can otherwise have from your Family."[17]

Once at the Gates estate, Kościuszko apparently stayed longer than he initially anticipated. During the extended visit he was struck by the relatively common appearance of the Gates home and determined to turn it into a place of grandeur befitting the rank and importance of its master. The result was a detailed set of plans in Kościuszko's hand that, had they been implemented, would have added greatly to the elegance and ambiance of the buildings and grounds. While not working on the plans, the Pole offered his assistance to Mrs. Gates, but while he hoped to be able to bring good news to General Gates on his arrival in the Southern Department, it was not to be. Young Robert Gates soon died and Kościuszko continued his journey south under the terrible burden of unbearable news.[18]

While Kościuszko was in Philadelphia and at Traveller's Rest, Gates, hurrying south to his new command, caught up with de Kalb on July 25 and assumed command of what was to become the nucleus of the Southern army. De Kalb had planned to move south toward Camden along a circuitous route through Salisbury and Charlotte, areas abundant in provisions and populated by people generally favorable toward the revolution. Gates scrapped that plan, insisting instead on a movement by the most direct route despite the relative lack of both provisions and population. The advance began July 27, crossing the Pee Dee River on August 3. Three days later General Richard Caswell arrived with 2,100 North Carolina militia to bolster Gates's small force.[19]

Gates pushed forward despite intense heat and scanty provisions, arriving at Little Lynch's Creek on August 11 to find a British force under Lord Francis Rawdon firmly entrenched on a commanding height along the opposite bank. Wisely avoiding an attack on Rawdon's strong position, Gates marched westward to turn the British flank, forcing Rawdon to retire back toward Camden. At Rugeley's Mill, north of Camden, Gen. Edward Stevens joined Gates, bringing with him 700 Virginia militia on August 14. This increased Gates's army to 1,100 Continentals and 2,350 North Carolina and Virginia militia, but he soon dispatched 100 Continentals and 300 North Carolina militia to cooperate with Col. Thomas Sumter operating against British and Loyalist forces in South Carolina.[20]

On August 16 Gates advanced, his force soon making contact with Lord Cornwallis, lately arrived to command the 2,200 British troops opposing the American move. Included in his force were the 33rd Regiment of Foot, three companies of the 23rd Regiment of Foot, five companies of the 71st Regiment of Foot, four companies of light infantry, Col. Banastre Tarleton's British Legion, the Royal North Carolina Regiment, the Volunteers of Ireland, more than 300 North Carolina Tory volunteers, and several dozen artillerymen and auxiliaries. The advanced guards of the two armies exchanged fire during the night, but both sides awaited daylight before making serious efforts.[21]

The next morning, Gates deployed his army with the mounted troops of Armand's Legion in the lead, flanked on either side by Lt. Col. Charles Porterfield's Virginia militia and Gen. John Armstrong's North Carolina militia. The Continentals marched next, followed by Gen. Richard Caswell's North Carolina militia, Gen. Edward Stevens's Virginia militia, and the baggage train guarded by mounted troops. Lord Cornwallis, who hoped to attack Gates, brought his army onto the field along the same road as the Americans, with the British Legion in the advance. The two columns came together unexpectedly near Gum Swamp, triggering a meeting engagement in a place neither side expected to fight.[22]

Cornwallis deployed with the light infantry on the right near the swamp, then three companies of the 23rd Regiment and the 33rd Regiment filling the gap leftward to the roadway. Across the road the Volunteers of Ireland deployed, followed by the British Legion's infantry and the Royal North Carolina Tories extending to the swampy area on the left flank. The five companies of the 71st Regiment and Tarleton's cavalry formed behind the center, astride the road, as a reserve. Opposite the British, Gates formed with his militia on the left, an unfortunate move because it placed them directly opposite the British regulars. The American right, commanded by de Kalb, included the 2nd Brigade of Maryland and Delaware Continentals. The reserve, placed across the road behind the first line, was comprised of the 1st Maryland Continental Brigade.[23]

Cornwallis advanced shortly after dawn, sending his regulars forward against the American left. The Virginia militia and much of the North Carolina militia fled early in the fight, leaving the Continentals unsupported. DeKalb valiantly held his position in the face of the British assaults on his front and his left flank, exposed by the precipitate flight of the militia. When the British attack faltered, de Kalb counterattacked with the bayonet. After some disorder, the British reformed and attacked repeatedly, de Kalb and his Continentals holding on stubbornly despite being outflanked and facing greatly superior numbers. Their position became particularly precarious when Tarleton's British Legion gained their rear, but de Kalb continued to fight until mortally wounded. Still the Continentals fought on, but the odds were too great and the position too exposed. Eventually, the Americans were driven from field with heavy losses, about 650 Continentals killed, wounded, or captured, and an unknown number of militia. Estimates of the latter are generally stated as about 100 killed and 300 captured. British losses were about 68 killed and 256 wounded.[24]

Camden left the American army routed, its survivors fleeing for their very lives. Most of the militia fled, never to reform. The Continentals, who bore the brunt of the fighting and suffered grievous losses, retired as best they could, but were confused as to where to go because no rallying point had been established before the engagement. Cornwallis quickly reformed his ranks, sending Tarleton's cavalry on a vigorous pursuit that lasted more than twenty miles. Gathering up prisoners and supplies all along the way, Tarleton captured Gates's entire baggage and ammunition trains while preventing the American survivors from reforming to offer any serious resistance. Some of the fugitives pushed on to Charlotte, where a few of the militia and the remains of Armand's Legion also halted. Once assembled, the group continued the retreat to Salisbury, North Carolina. Gen. Otho Williams described this "wretched remnant" of the Southern Army as a disorderly march of "Compound wretchedness, care, anxiety, pain, poverty, hurry, confusion, humiliation and dejection" that formed a "mortifying picture."[25]

His army shattered, Gates made little attempt to rally his troops. Instead, he fled in haste to Hillsboro, North Carolina, a distance of some 160 miles, which he reached three days after the defeat with apparently little idea where his scattered army was or what it was doing. At Hillsboro he was eventually rejoined by about 700 Continentals and a few of the militia. In his defense Gates claimed that Hillsboro was the logical place to rally the defeated army, call out the Virginia militia, and meet Continental reinforcements arriving from the north. Not everyone agreed. "Was there ever an instance of a general running away as Gates has done from his whole army?" Alexander Hamilton asked. "And was there ever so precipitous a flight?"[26]

Whatever the circumstances and motivations, Gates was finished as commander of the Southern Department. Following the disaster at Camden, Congress consulted General Washington on the selection of a new commanding officer. Washington's immediate choice was Nathaniel Greene. Born in Rhode Island in 1742, Greene was descended from a family that arrived in Massachusetts in 1635 to escape religious persecution. As a boy he is reported to have been a good student, excelling in mathematics. As soon as he was able, he went to work in his father's iron foundry in Potowomut (modern Warwick), Rhode Island, until 1770 when he took over management of the family's foundry in Coventry. He served in the Rhode Island General Assembly in 1770-1772 and again in 1775. In October 1774 he enlisted as a private in the Kentish Guards, a militia unit he apparently helped to recruit, but his application for a commission as an officer was rejected because of a stiff leg that accompanied Greene

from childhood. By May of the following year, however, his prominence led to his selection to lead Rhode Island's three regiments as
a brigadier general. Greene arrived at Long Island on June 3, and on
the 22nd of the same month was appointed brigadier general in the
Continental Army, the youngest of the initial group of brigadiers
appointed. Long a favorite of Washington, Greene displayed more
talent than most colonial officers and was rather adept at getting
along with people in the atmosphere of personal and inter-colony
jealousies that prevailed in many circles.[27]

While the army awaited Greene's arrival, units began to drift into
Hillsboro where Gates plunged into the work of reforming the
survivors and trying to get the Virginia and North Carolina militias
to turn out. The Continentals who retreated to Salisbury arrived at
Hillsboro on September 6 under the command of Gen. William
Smallwood. Others arrived singly, or in small groups, almost daily.
Eventually, less than one-quarter of the men from the army of 4,000
that fought at Camden made it safely to the rendezvous at Hillsboro.
With the militia largely failing to respond, Gates reorganized the
remaining Maryland Continentals into two battalions, survivors of
the 1st, 3rd, 5th, and 7th Regiments forming the 1st Battalion under
Major Archibald Anderson and those of the 2nd, 4th, and 6th
Maryland and the Delaware Regiment, the latter now down to two
companies, being designated the 2nd Battalion under Major Henry
Hardman. The regiment thus formed fell under the command of Col.
Otho Williams. Only enough cavalry remained for a single troop
under Lt. Col. William Washington. To this small force was added
some 200 new Virginia recruits, a few Virginia Continentals under
Col. Abraham Buford who survived the defeat at the Waxhaws, and
about 50 of Porterfield's light infantry. Another who arrived was
Daniel Morgan. Having resigned and retired to his home in Virginia
over a dispute involving his promotion and seniority, when Morgan
received news of the disaster at Camden he rushed to Hillsboro,
arriving on October 2.[28] Yet, by the time of Morgan's arrival, the
army remained in poor condition. According to Delaware Lieutenant
Caleb Bennett, "We found ourselves in a most deplorable situation,
without arms, ammunition, baggage and [with] very little sustenance
and for some time our situation was unenviable."[29] Clearly, the army
was in no condition to take to the field again without serious
reinforcement, arms, provisions, clothing, and virtually every necessity of service including discipline.

While Gates tried to reform his army, Cornwallis resumed the offensive on September 8, but a month later, on October 7, patriot militia defeated a force of Tories at King's Mountain under Major Patrick Ferguson. With the defeat of his Loyalist allies, Cornwallis, who had advanced as far as Charlotte, retired to Winnsboro which he reached in late October. There he eschewed any further movement while trying to pacify the local partisans. Despite his best efforts, however, the partisans under Cols. Francis Marion and Thomas Sumter were able to disrupt Cornwallis's communications and supply lines with relative impunity. In late November, Major General Alexander Leslie arrived in Charleston with 2,200 British reinforcements from New York including the 82nd and 84th Regiments of Foot, the Bose Regiment of Hessian infantry, and loyalist units under Edmund Fanning and John Watson. Cornwallis deployed Fanning to Georgetown while leaving the 82nd and 84th Regiments in Charleston. About 1,500 troops under Leslie marched inland, arriving at Camden on January 4, 1781. This addition raised Cornwallis's field strength to about 4,000 men, allowing him to contemplate further offensive action.[30]

Upon learning of the disaster that befell Gates, Kościuszko determined to continue south and do whatever he could to aid the patriot cause. By the third week in September the engineer was in Richmond where he lingered briefly to conduct some business with Thomas Jefferson, then serving as governor of Virginia.[31] This was apparently the first meeting between the Pole and the illustrious Virginian. Although their exact exchange is unknown, they were apparently impressed with one another because this brief meeting led to a firm lifetime friendship between the two.

Kościuszko probably reached Hillsboro during the first part of October. The first definite reference to him there came in the form of a letter from Gen. Smallwood to Gates asking that he be sent to assist in constructing some defensive works to cover his camps. By the 30th Kościuszko was back in camp to participate in a council of war called by Gates to discuss the situation and options available to the army, and to decide if a movement further westward would be advantageous. The result was a decision to remain at Hillsboro until further reliable information could be obtained.[32]

In Hillsboro, Kościuszko bunked with Gen. Isaac Huger and Dr. William Read, the army's chief physician, but their quarters and supplies were so poor the three had to share the general's cloak in place of blankets. The weather turned cold, provisions were scarce, and morale remained low. The Pole attended another council-of-war held at New Providence on November 25 to determine if the army should move to Charlotte or to the Waxhaws where the countryside would be better able to provide provisions. With only Smallwood dissenting, the group declared for Charlotte.[33]

The army arrived in Charlotte at the end of November. On its heels came Nathaniel Greene who arrived on December 2, 1780. The change of command officially took place the following day. Though pained by Gates's departure, Kościuszko nevertheless enjoyed the company of several other friends from the Northern Department, now assigned to the Southern Army. Among them were Daniel Morgan who served conspicuously at Saratoga, his close friend Major John Armstrong from Ticonderoga and Saratoga, Lewis Morris, and Dr. James Brown. Armstrong, Morris and Brown had supported Kościuszko in the Carter affair, and no doubt the Pole was glad for the continued support and camaraderie of these old friends in his new surroundings.[34]

Greene inherited an army that numbered 2,457 on paper, but with only about 1,500 men present and fit for duty and even fewer, approximately 800, actually equipped and outfitted for service. Morale remained poor, and the lack of discipline was evident in the complaints of local farmers being terrorized by roaming bands of men in search of food, clothing, and whatever else they could find. "The appearance of the troops was wretched beyond description," Greene wrote, "and their distress, on account of [lack of] provisions was little less than their suffering for want of clothing and other necessaries." Clearly, he needed more time to rebuild the army before he could hope to have an effective fighting force. To gain the time necessary, on December 21 Greene dispatched Gen. Morgan with 320 Maryland and Delaware Continentals and 200 Virginia riflemen under Gen. John Howard and some 80 light dragoons under Col. William Washington to circle southwest around Cornwallis's force and work against his supply and communication lines in cooperation with the local militia in the area between the Broad and Pacolet Rivers.[35]

Greene was also concerned that the area around Charlotte was not sufficiently productive to support his army for any appreciable time. To gain further intelligence, he dispatched Brig. Gen. Edward Stevens to reconnoiter the Yadkin River area, Col. Edward Carrington, his quartermaster, to survey the Dan River, and Kościuszko to "explore the navigation of the Catawba river from mill creek below the forks up to Oliphant mill." The engineer was to "Report to me its particular situation as to the depth of water, the rapidity of the stream, the rocks, shoals or falls you may meet with and every other information necessary to enable me to form an accurate opinion of the transportation which may be made on the river in the different seasons of the year. It is of the utmost importance that your report to me should be very particular and as early as possible."[36] Travelling the river in a canoe with Capt. William Thompson of South Carolina as his only guide and companion, Kościuszko exposed himself to grave danger in an area torn by civil war between Loyalists and Rebels. The Tories were, according to Greene, "as thick as the trees," but the two travellers succeeded in avoiding capture to complete the first detailed survey of the western reaches of the waterway.[37]

Another of Kościuszko's tasks was to survey the local area to determine whether it could support Greene's army. The reconnaissance found that the area surrounding Charlotte would not be sufficient to sustain the army, causing Greene to give Kościuszko the additional responsibility of finding a suitable place for a new American encampment. "You will ... examine the country from the mouth of Little River," Greene instructed the engineer, "and search for a good position for the Army. You will report the make of the Country, the nature of the soil, the quality of the water, the quantity of produce, number of mills, and the water transportation that may be had up and down the River. You will also enquire respecting the creeks in the Rear, the fords and the difficulty of passing them; all [of] which you will report as soon as possible."[38]

Accompanied by Major William Polk of North Carolina, the Pole traversed the Pee Dee River from the mouth of the Little River downstream some twenty miles. Until he found a suitable location, Greene could not begin to move his small army. On December 16 the engineer returned to camp with news he had identified a spot at Cheraw Hills near where Hick's Creek flows into the Pee Dee.[39] The admirable choice of Cheraw Hills offered an abundance of food, as well as certain distinct military advantages. Not only was the position a strong one for defensive purposes, but its location threatened Camden, disrupted British communications from Charleston, and placed Greene within supporting distance of the very active guerilla force led by Francis Marion. As Green explained in a letter to

Washington on December 29: "I was apprehensive, on my first arrival, that the Country around Charlotte was too much exhausted to afford subsistence for the Army at that place for any considerable time. Upon a little further enquiry I was fully convinced; and immediately despatched Col. Kosciuszko to look out [for] a position on the Pedee that would afford a healthy camp and provisions in plenty. His report was favorable, and I immediately put the army under marching orders."[40]

To Kościuszko, Greene assigned the task of fortifying the new camp near Cheraw, South Carolina. Greene left Charlotte on December 20 and arrived at Cheraw six days later. With him he brought Gen. Isaac Huger with 650 Continentals, 303 Virginia militia, and 157 Maryland militia. A few days later some 400 Virginia militia arrived under Col. John Greene and Henry Lee arrived with Lee's Legion, some 300 strong, on January 13, 1781. Greene sent the latter to support Francis Marion in his attacks on Cornwallis's supply and communication lines.[41]

Once at Cheraw, Greene placed Cornwallis in a strategic quandary. If the British general moved against Morgan, Greene could march on Charleston. If Cornwallis moved on Greene at Cheraw, Morgan could attack the British posts at Ninety-Six or Augusta. If the British ignored the Americans entirely and moved north, Greene, Morgan, and the other partisans could threaten their flanks and cut their supply and communication lines.[42] To take advantage of his strategic position and provide his army with some transportation, on New Year's Day, 1781, Greene ordered Kościuszko to construct a sufficient number of boats to transport his army, the whole to be constructed so they could be moved from place to place on land. "You are desired to go to Cross Creek," Greene ordered, "and apply to all staff officers either in the Continental or State service to assist you in procuring a number of tools suitable for constructing a number of boats and the quantity and kind that will be wanted, you are perfectly acquainted and will point them out to the officers. ... If you obtain tools you will engage all the carpenters you can find that you may think necessary to dispatch to the construction of the boats. Confiding in your zeal and activity I persuade myself you will make all the despatch the business will admit as the safety and support of the Army depend upon your accomplishing this business."[43] Kościuszko immediately set out to search the countryside for carpenters and tools to build the required boats.

Once the boats were completed, Kościuszko traveled sixty miles south from Cheraw Hills to Rocky River, where he constructed a defensive stockade for General John Lillington's camp. This done, he developed a system of rapid transport at Irwin's Ferry on the Dan River.[44]

While Kościuszko proceeded with these important duties, the contending armies sought to improve their strategic positions by using guerilla actions and hit-and-run tactics to keep each other off-balance and unaware of each other's intentions. By the beginning of 1781 Cornwallis had at his disposal about 4,000 troops with his main army at Winnsboro, South Carolina, including the 7th, 23rd, and 33rd Regiments of Foot, three companies of the 16th Regiment of Foot, the 2nd Battalion of the 71st Regiment of Foot, the von Bose Regiment of Hessians, 600 Hessian jägers, Tarleton's Legion, and about 700 Tories. According to Christopher Ward, "It was a force so much greater in numbers, so much better trained, armed and equipped than Greene's whole army of 3,000 tatterdemalions that one would have supposed Cornwallis secure in his position and confident of the future."[45] As if this were not enough, Cornwallis could call upon the services of another 4,000 troops deployed among the various British outposts throughout the Carolinas. On the evening of January 1 he received information that Morgan was moving toward the post at Ninety-Six. On the 3rd, word came that Col. Washington's dragoons were raiding the area near Hammond's Store, even closer to Ninety-Six. Fearing an American attack on that outpost, Cornwallis sent Col. Banastre Tarleton with a force to secure the area. Not finding Morgan in the vicinity, Tarleton suggested to Cornwallis that the two move by separate routes toward King's Mountain in the hope of trapping Morgan between them. Cornwallis agreed, moving out of Winnsboro on January 7 and ordering Leslie to lead his 1,500 men to Cornwallis's support from Camden on January 9.[46]

On January 13 Greene sent a message to Morgan warning him that "Col. Tarleton is said to be on his way to pay you a visit. I doubt not but he will have a decent reception and a proper dismission."[47] Before Tarleton and Cornwallis could spring their trap, Morgan formed his troops at Cowpens to do battle with Tarleton's pursuing force. With his back to the Broad River, Morgan placed 150 picked riflemen in a skirmish line in front of his position, with 300 militia under Andrew Pickens 150 yards behind. Another 150 yards behind the militia, on the crest of a hill, he placed his main line consisting of 400

Continentals. Behind the hill he located 100 dragoons under William Washington. Morgan ordered his riflemen not to fire until the enemy were within 50 yards, to aim at the officers, and to fire at least twice before retiring around the left of the main line to reform as a reserve. Including the North Carolina, South Carolina, and Georgia militia that had recently joined him, Morgan had about 1,040 men. Tarleton's force included his Legion, one battalion each of the 7th and 71st Regiments of Foot, the 17th Light Dragoons, a detachment of the Royal Artillery, and a number of Tories, some 1,100 in all.[48]

When Tarleton's horse attacked to begin the battle the colonial riflemen decimated their ranks, forcing them from the field. Tarleton then sent forward his main line. Morgan's militia fired twice, then retired as planned. Thinking the Americans were retreating, the British rushed forward into the muzzles of the Continentals who fired steady volleys into the disorganized British ranks. Washington's dragoons, previously unseen behind the small hill, then drove into the British flank and rear and Tarleton's force disintegrated. Although Tarleton managed to ride to safety, 90% of his force became casualties. The British lost 39 officers and 61 enlisted men killed, 229 wounded and captured, and about 600 unwounded prisoners. Lost also in Morgan's crushing victory were two field pieces of the Royal Artillery, 800 muskets, 35 baggage wagons, 100 horses, the colors of the 7th Regiment, and a vast quantity of ammunition. American losses were only 12 killed and 60 wounded.[49]

Following his victory, Morgan marched quickly through Ramseur's Mill, crossing the Catawba River at Sherrald's Ford and placing that river between himself and Cornwallis to prevent the British from mounting an immediate attack on him. Cornwallis did not move until the 19th, but when he did he led a powerful force of 3,000 troops off toward King's Mountain in the apparent belief Morgan was still in the area. Recognizing his mistake at last, Cornwallis turned toward Ramseur's Mill, reaching that location on January 25. There he destroyed any unnecessary baggage and equipment to lighten his troops and speed their pursuit of Morgan.[50]

When Greene learned of Morgan's victory and Cornwallis's pursuit he feared for Morgan's safety. Seeking to reunite his army, he ordered preparations made for a march to Salisbury, North Carolina, a city on Morgan's likely line of retreat. His troops moved out of Cheraw on January 28 under the command of Gen. Huger, while Greene, with a small escort, rode to meet with Morgan. The two met in Morgan's camp near the Catawba River on January 30. Morgan counseled Greene to move west into the mountains with his whole force, but the commander of the Southern Army had other plans. Greene decided on a difficult course of action he hoped would allow him to repeat Gates's earlier successes in New York. Greene proposed to retreat directly northward in the path of Cornwallis's advancing troops, luring the British aristocrat deep into North Carolina, all the time moving farther from his base of supply. Once Cornwallis was into North Carolina, his supplies exhausted and cut off from his bases by guerilla actions, Greene hoped enough militia would turn out to allow him to turn on Cornwallis and crush him as Gates had beaten Burgoyne under similar circumstances.[51]

To succeed, Greene's plan called for excellent timing, hard marching, and diligence. Moving too fast might discourage Cornwallis from following. Moving too slow, or being unable to cross a river, would mean destruction at the hands of Cornwallis's well-trained regulars. Probably the greatest post of responsibility on this hectic race against time and redcoats was that of Greene's director of transportation. On the shoulders of this man lay the responsibility for selecting routes of march, providing the appropriate transport at the correct time and place, and insuring that measures were taken so the various rivers along the route of march would be passable. A mistake on any one of these and disaster could overwhelm Greene's army. The man chosen for this manifestly important task was Tadeusz Kościuszko. On February 1, Greene's aide-de-camp wrote to Kościuszko ordering him to join Greene on the Catawba "or where ever he may be as soon as possible. You will pass by the way of Salisbury where you will probably hear of him. I think you had better come up on the east side of the Pedee and cross at Closton's Ferry. You will order such of the boats as are finished to follow the Army immediately.... The artificers you will order to join the army as soon as possible, they are much wanted."[52]

Greene's plan was almost defeated before it began. On February 1 Cornwallis crossed the Catawba, scattering the North Carolina militia on guard at the fords and nearly capturing Greene who was nearby. Heading north to coordinate his troops, Greene reached Salisbury early on the morning of February 2. With Cornwallis now in hot pursuit, time was extremely critical. Greene sent Gen. Huger an order to rendezvous at Salisbury within twenty-four hours, or march directly to Guilford Courthouse if unable to make the Salisbury rendezvous on time. Meanwhile, Morgan marched as quickly as he could for the Yadkin River, arriving on February 2. Because of Kościuszko's previous work, he found boats waiting and crossed at Trading Ford during night. Cornwallis arrived too late to interfere.[53]

But Cornwallis still hoped to catch Greene despite his failure at the Catawba and the Yadkin. When he reached Salisbury on February 3, Cornwallis was only about ten miles behind Morgan. Greene realized he was in no position, either geographically or militarily, to meet Cornwallis's army in the field. Instead, his primary objective was to save his scattered force by continuing his retreat across the Dan River. But the Dan lay more than 100 miles away and Greene had to get his army there in time to cross unmolested if it were to be saved. Soon the chase was on with both forces racing for the Dan River; Greene to cross and save his army, Cornwallis to capture the fords and trap the colonials against the river. Greene moved toward the lower Dan on February 4, momentarily tricking Cornwallis who believed Greene would move toward the more easily fordable upper Dan. Meanwhile, abandoning his pursuit of Morgan, Cornwallis crossed the Yadkin River, heading toward the upper Dan in an effort to occupy the fords and trap Greene against the wider, deeper waters of the lower Dan where his army could be pinned against the river and destroyed.[54]

Rushing northeast barely ahead of Cornwallis's pace, Kościuszko appeared to be everywhere, handling the myriads of details necessary for success, planning lines of march, gathering and dispatching crucial boats, and seeking out little-known shortcuts. After keeping to his original line of march to fool Cornwallis, Greene turned east just short of Salem. A forced march of 47 miles in 48 hours brought him into camp near Guilford Court House on February 7 where he was joined the same day by Huger and Lee. Although he briefly considered making a stand at Guilford, only 200 local militia turned out, persuading him against the idea. With less than 1,500 Continentals to oppose Cornwallis's 2,500 regulars, Greene headed for Irwin's Ferry, 70 miles away. Speed was still essential, but so were boats. Without boats in sufficient number to ferry the army across the Dan, Greene would find himself trapped by Cornwallis's larger force with his back to the river. To mask the move, a force of 360 light infantry and about 340 mounted troops were to screen the movement, acting so as to make Cornwallis believe Greene was making for Dix's Ferry some twenty miles above Irwin's Ferry. Kościuszko was to plan the movement, make sure adequate boats were on hand once the army arrived at the river, and prepare Irwin's Ferry for the crossing.[55]

The rear guard under Gen. Otho Williams led Cornwallis off in the wrong direction for two valuable days before the British determined Greene's main line of retreat and turned to pursue. Intermittent rain and snow turned the red clay roads into a slippery muddy slime making marching difficult and tiresome. Temperatures dropped so that by night the wet roads froze, adding yet another hardship to the march. Cornwallis pushed his men on throughout the night, stopping only briefly for rest. Ahead of him, Greene did the same. Kościuszko kept constantly busy seeing to the safety of the supplies, planning routes, and galloping ahead to see whether the marshy roadways needed bridging, then rushing to the Dan himself to lay out defensive works to protect the crossing. When the army finally began reaching the Dan late on the evening of February 13, the enemy only a few hours march behind, they found the boats they so desperately needed.[56]

With William's rear guard slowing the British advance, Green hurried his main body across the Dan to the safety of the far bank. The British had pushed rapidly forward, covering the last forty miles in only twenty-four hours, but the Americans made the same march in sixteen. By the evening of the 14th Greene's rear guard was safely across the river, due in no small part to Kościuszko's tireless efforts. In a movement fraught with danger where one error by the engineer could well doom the army, he made none. "Every measure of the Americans during their march from the Catawba to Virginia," concluded British Col. Tarleton, "was judiciously designed and vigorously executed."[57] Given the precarious American situation at the beginning of February, the strongest appraisal of Kościuszko's work is the fact that Greene's entire force escaped across the Dan without loss, preserving the Southern Army from destruction.

Chapter 9

"Blind Fortune"

*F*or Cornwallis the end of the "Race to the Dan" was one of bitter disappointment. Lacking the boats necessary to cross the river, 250 miles from Winnsboro and 375 miles from Charleston, without adequate supplies for an army the size of his force, he had no alternative other than retreat. He began moving his redcoats toward Hillsboro, North Carolina, on February 17. With Cornwallis in retreat, Greene sent Lee back across the Dan with his Legion and two companies of Maryland Continentals to operate against the British supply and communications lines in company with 700 newly arrived militia under Brig. Gen. Andrew Pickens. Two days later Gen. Williams crossed with the light infantry, followed shortly by Greene who had been reinforced by 600 Virginia riflemen under Gen. Edward Stevens. In recrossing the Dan, Greene hoped to keep pressure on Cornwallis while newly recruited militia and Continental reinforcements under Baron von Steuben marched to join him. The last two weeks in February and the first half of March saw continuous maneuvering as Greene attempted to harass Cornwallis and prevent Loyalists from joining the British, while still avoiding a potentially disastrous general engagement. After Lee won a victory over a Loyalist force at the Haw River on February 25 the Tories generally remained passive.[1]

Uncertain as to Cornwallis's exact intentions, Greene feared the British might make a sudden march against Halifax some eighty miles away on the Roanoke River in North Carolina. The capital of the local revolutionary government, Halifax stood amid a rich agricultural area important for its potential to support the Southern Army. To guard against this eventuality, Greene ordered Kościuszko to "repair immediately to Hallifax on the Roanoke in the State of North Carolina and see if it is practicable to fortify it in a short time and whether it may be garrisoned with a small force against any attempts by storm. If you find on your arrival the position and other circumstances favorable for the purpose of fortification you will immediately apply to the Legislature and Major General Caswell for men and other things necessary to execute the work as soon as possible."[2] Given the distance and the condition of the roads, the engineer did not arrive until the 18th when he wrote to Greene to advise the general of his arrival. "It seems I travaill very slow," he explained, "but as I Could not get Horses on the road, and was obliged to go [on] foot part of the way, you will be pleased to thing that I have don[e] what I Could."[3] After inspecting the area the following day in the company of Col. Nicholas Long, he estimated that minimum fortification would call for six redoubts while there was a serious lack of tools and labor for the project. Under the circumstances, he found it would be difficult to fortify the location to any extent in a short period of time. Instead, he proposed removing the stores and magazines to the other side of the Roanoke River where a force of militia could guard the ford against any attempt to capture them. "Nothing Could tempted the Enemys to come her[e] in my opinion but the Stores and Magasines of provision. Should the Enemy Come we will have always the advantage by the Brocking ground, and very thick Bushes" and a "Thousend of Good Militia ... could cover intirely Halifax and the adjacent Country."[4]

While Kościuszko completed his work around Halifax, Greene moved slowly south with the main force of about 4,500 men. The majority of these were militia from Virginia and North Carolina, with less than 1,000 being trained Continentals. Near Guilford Court House on March 15 he met Lord Cornwallis's force approaching from the southwest. Greene positioned his army in an area of rolling hills and woods in a formation of three lines. In the first he placed the North Carolina militia behind two open clearings, their flanks covered by veteran cavalry and light infantry under William Washington and Henry Lee. About 400 yards behind the militia he placed the Virginia militia, backed by riflemen with orders to shoot anyone who did not stand and fight. About 400 yards behind the Virginians Greene placed his final line manned by the Continentals in a position on the crest of a nearby hill. Much like Morgan at Cowpens, he asked the first line to fire twice, hoping the Virginia militia in the second line would inflict further casualties on the British attackers before falling back. Once the militia had delivered their volleys and retired, the Continentals would stand fast against the final assault and drive back the weakened British lines.[5]

Cornwallis aligned his troops, some 2,000 strong, with the fusiliers, Highlanders and the von Bose Regiment in the first line, backed by two battalions of foot, some light infantry and Tarleton's light dragoons. When his attack began, the Hessian regiment became entangled in a spirited battle with Lee's Legion while the militia, true to its orders, fired twice and then fled. The British suffered some loss from the first American line, but continued their attack against the Virginians, some of whom fled but enough held firm to actually halt the assault. The redcoats regrouped and came on a second time with the bayonet, putting the second line to flight and driving toward the Continentals. The third line held firm, counterattacked, and was only stopped by Cornwallis's desperate move of opening fire with three guns that hit some of his own men but finally halted the Continentals' attack. The British attacked again, but once more Greene's regulars held. Though holding his own, as losses mounted and the militia showed no sign of rallying, Greene eventually began an orderly withdrawal from the field, leaving it in control of the British.[6]

Cornwallis pursued only a short distance. Though he claimed victory by virtue of holding the field, his army was badly mauled, losing 532 killed and wounded, about 28% of his entire force. American losses were reported as 261 killed and wounded.[7]

The losses sustained in the hard-fought decision at Guilford Court House and increasing Patriot attacks on his communication and supply lines left Lord Cornwallis with but one tenable alternative—retreat. Rather than acknowledge failure by retiring back into South Carolina, Cornwallis left his wounded behind and headed for the coast to gain resupply by sea. He moved slowly, hoping Greene would follow rather than invade South Carolina because the nearer the seacoast Cornwallis's army moved the stronger it would become. Cornwallis arrived in Wilmington on April 7, but Greene did not take the bait. After following a short distance to the vicinity of present Fayetteville, North Carolina, the American general turned south, determined to eliminate the system of British outposts guarding central and western South Carolina. Rather than moving south to protect British interests in South Carolina, Cornwallis instead rested his men before heading north on April 24 with 1,500 men bound for the Chesapeake Bay.[8]

Completing his work at Halifax, Kościuszko returned to Greene's main army, but it is uncertain whether he arrived in time to take part in the engagement at Guilford Court House. While he traveled, another potential challenge to his authority arose from the French officers under Washington's command. When the Marquis de Lafayette joined Baron von Steuben's forces in Virginia he requested that Lt. Col. Gouvion be assigned to his command. Since Virginia was technically under Greene's command as part of the Southern Department, Washington, not wanting to interfere with either Greene's command or Kościuszko's authority, denied the request. Instead, Washington answered that Gouvion was needed in the north and that there was "another reason which operates against his going with you, it is, that he would interfere with Colo. Kosciusko who had been considered as the commanding Engineer with the southern Army."[9]

By April 20 Greene reached the vicinity of Camden where Kościuszko selected a site at Hobkirk's Hill for the American encampment. To oppose Greene, Lord Francis Rawdon-Hastings scraped together a force of some 900 men and moved north from Camden to launch a surprise assault on the American encampment at Hobkirk's Hill. Born in 1754 of Irish nobility, Lord Rawdon served from the beginning of the war at Bunker Hill, and in the New York and New Jersey campaigns. Promoted to lieutenant colonel in 1778, he raised the Volunteers of Ireland, a Loyalist regiment, and fought at Monmouth. A seasoned soldier despite his relatively young age, he came south with Clinton in 1780 and contributed to Cornwallis's defeat of Gates at Camden. Aggressive but not incautious, Cornwallis left him in command of nearly 8,000 troops spread out over Georgia and South Carolina. Among the troops in his field army, only the 63rd Regiment of Foot were British regulars, the balance consisting of loyalists of the King's Americans, New York Volunteers, and the Volunteers of Ireland. Though not regulars, the loyalists were mostly veterans whose training and morale were high. Thus, though smaller than Greene's army, Lord Rawdon's force was strong enough to cause a serious problem for the American.[10]

Alerted at the last moment by his pickets, Greene moved his army of about 1,200 men out of its camp to attack Rawdon on the morning of April 25. Greene's force included the 1st and 5th Maryland of the Continental Line, the 4th and 5th Virginia of the Continental Line, Capt. Robert Kirkwood's company of Delaware Continental light infantry, Lt. Col William Washington's light dragoons, about 250 North Carolina militia, and three small six-pounder field guns under Virginian Charles Harrison. He moved them forward to a sandy ridge in the pine forests with his flanks secured on the Wateree River and the swamps along Pine Tree Creek.[11]

Greene placed the 4th and 5th Virginia Continentals on the right of his line, with the 1st and 5th Maryland to his left. Washington's dragoons and the North Carolina militia formed the reserve, with Kirkwood's Delaware Continentals covering the front and left of the American line. Rawdon entered the field with the King's Americans on his left, the New York Volunteers in the center, and the 63rd Regiment of Foot on the right. He placed the convalescents behind the King's Americans, with the New York Dragoons behind them. The Volunteers of Ireland went into position behind the 63rd, with the South Carolina Tories behind and to the left of them. Rawdon placed Tory marksmen to guard each flank and to try and pick off the American officers, then ordered an advance on a narrow front aimed at the Maryland Brigade. Greene, seeing that his longer line outflanked Rawdon, decided to attack in an ambitious double-envelopment coupled with a wide sweeping move by American cavalry forces against the British rear. The plan began to unravel when Rawdon's troops quickly extended their flanks to counter the American maneuvers and held fast to their position, while Washington's dragoons failed to gain the enemy's rear as planned. Then, as the fighting raged, the two Maryland regiments mistook an order to reform as an order to retire, throwing Greene's army into a retreat that could not be stemmed. Although losses were nearly equal—the British admitted 38 killed and 220 wounded while Greene reported 18 killed and 248 wounded—the British won a tactical victory by driving the Americans from the field.[12]

Despite his victory, Lord Rawdon, much like Cornwallis in the previous campaign, found it necessary to retire due to insufficient forces, failing supplies, and broken communication lines. As a result, the British success at Hobkirk's Hill, like its predecessor at Camden, remained a hollow victory. On May 10, Lord Rawdon abandoned Camden, sending orders at the same time to the commanders of the British posts at Ninety-Six and Ft. Granby to evacuate their men and fall back toward the seacoast. The messengers, however, were intercepted and the garrisons remained unaware of Rawdon's retreat or his order for them to withdraw.[13]

Meanwhile, smaller forces of American irregulars began scoring successes against the British outposts. On April 23 Col. Francis Marion and Col. Henry Lee forced the surrender of the 120-man garrison at Ft. Watson, while on May 11 Col. Thomas Sumter captured the garrison of 85 men at Orangeburg. Ft. Motte fell the next day to the forces of Marion and Lee, and on the 15th the garrison at Ft. Granby capitulated to Lee. Moving into Georgia, Lee joined forces with Andrew Pickens and Elijah Clarke to capture Augusta. Thus, despite the British victory at Hobkirk's Hill, within two months of that confrontation British forces in South Carolina and Georgia were reduced to possession of only the post at Ninety-Six, so named because it was located ninety-six miles from Ft. George on the Keowee River, and enroute to the areas immediately surrounding Charleston and Savannah.[14] That Ninety-Six was deemed an important place can be seen in a letter from Lord Cornwallis to Col. Nisbet Balfour in which he cautioned the post "must be kept at all events & I think no reasonable expense should be spared" to maintain it.[15]

Under the circumstances, Greene, joined by Lee, Pickens, and several smaller Patriot forces, put his army in motion toward the next obvious objective, the strategic outpost at Ninety-Six. Commanded by Lt. Col. John Harris Cruger of New York, the scion of a prominent Tory family and son-in-law of Gen. Oliver DeLancey, the garrison numbered about 550 veteran loyalists: 150 men of Cruger's 3rd Battalion of DeLancey's New York Volunteers, 200 from the 2nd Battalion New Jersey Volunteers, and 200 of Col. Andrew Devaux's South Carolina militia recruited from the surrounding area. According to John R. Alden's *The South in the American Revolution*, this group of Tories was particularly fierce, having "indulged in devastation, looting, and rape, and they hated and feared the patriots."[16] With the defenders in Ninety-Six were about 100 Tory civilians and a labor battalion of slaves. Their defense was aided by a visit from Lt. Henry Haldane of the Royal Engineers who displayed excellent professional judgement in strengthening the small outpost with outworks and abatis. The village, enclosed by a wooden stockade, was further fortified on its eastern side with a strong star-shaped redoubt, the whole surrounded by eight-foot-deep ditches fronted by an abatis some thirty feet from the ditch. The dirt excavated from the ditch was used to create a corresponding line of parapets. Much of the labor was done by slaves impressed from local patriots or hired from area loyalists. Though small, the entrenched village posed a serious obstacle if defended resolutely against an army as small as Greene's that lacked formal siege trains. It appears to have had but one serious weakness. In a letter to Lord Cornwallis, Lt. Col. Isaac Allen, second-in-command at Ninety-Six, confessed it was "the want of water I should most fear." The only water supply came from Kate Fowler's Branch, a small stream located outside the west end of the village stockade. To cover this, Col. Cruger constructed a covered causeway leading across the stream to Ft. Holmes, a smaller, less formidable position than the Star Redoubt but one capable of guarding the approaches to the vital water supply.[17]

Greene reached the vicinity of Ninety-Six on May 22, 1781. With him came less than 1,000 troops, a force barely adequate for the task at hand, and no heavy artillery or formal siege equipment. His force included 427 Maryland and Delaware Continentals, 431 Virginia Continentals, 60 of Kirkwood's Delaware light infantry, and 66 North Carolina militia. Greene anticipated being reinforced by Lee and Pickens when they returned from Georgia, and counted on Marion and Sumter to arrest any British force moving to the aid of Ninety-Six from Charleston or Savannah, but could rely with certainty on none but the troops at hand.[18]

On his first evening at Ninety-Six, the general took advantage of a very dark, rainy night to reconnoiter close to the British works in the company of Kościuszko and Capt. Nathaniel Pendleton, the general's aide-de-camp. Their presence was discovered, bringing forth a flurry of musketry but resulting in no casualties. Despite the darkness and the enemy action, the party saw enough to realize the strength of the fortifications. Following the reconnaissance, the general wrote to the Marquis de Lafayette that "the fortifications are so strong and the garrison so large and so well furnished that our success is very doubtful."[19]

During the night Greene, Kościuszko, and the other senior officers met to discuss the best way to proceed. As chief engineer, the Polish colonel's opinions naturally held great importance to the gathering, not only because of his professional experience but because he would be responsible for constructing the siege approaches. It appeared, he wrote, that "the Star Redoubt upon our left was the Strongest post," not only because it was the most complete of the fortifications but because it commanded both the fortified village and Ft. Holmes. Being "not strong eno[u]gh to capture the trenches to our left and wright at the same time against the Garison of about 500 st[r]ong," the Pole wrote, "we thought proper to begin against the Star Redoubt."[20] The star-shaped redoubt was the strongest of the loyalist positions and it commanded the other works. Greene's reasoning in deciding to concentrate his efforts against this strong point was twofold. Since he lacked the strength to pursue multiple approaches, he would have to settle on a single major effort. Consequently, it made sense to assault the Star Redoubt because its fall would make the other positions untenable. Conversely, the fall of Ft. Holmes or the village stockade would not necessarily force the capitulation of the Star Redoubt.

Under Kościuszko's direction, workers began digging the siege approaches during the night of May 22-23 at a point only about 70 yards from the Star Redoubt. Aware that a passive defense would leave the patriot forces unimpeded and probably bring about a quicker assault on his position, Col. Cruger determined to make the siege operations as costly and time consuming as possible. Using a newly completed gun platform to surprise the laboring Americans with artillery and small arms fire, he took advantage of the confusion to send Lt. John Roney of New York with a picked force of thirty men to attack the rebel work party early the next morning. When the unprepared Greene was slow to react to the surprise attack, Roney's raiders chased off the construction party, captured its tools, and carried the equipment away. Before retreating back into the protection of the Star Redoubt, the accompanying loyalist militia and Black laborers filled in the completed section of the beginning approach. The entire party then retired with only one casualty, the mortally wounded commander, Lt. Roney.[21]

Clearly, Greene's forces were surprised by Cruger's aggressiveness, but faster work on the approaches during the first night would have allowed the rebels to bring up artillery and greatly strengthen the forward position before dawn, making Roney's sally either impractical or costly. Kościuszko ascribed the surprise to the fact "the troops were novice to the operation" and the lateness of the hour at which they began digging precluded finishing by morning. With the night's construction unfinished, the artillery could not be properly placed to guard the area, leaving it open to a sudden rush like that led by Lt. Roney.[22]

New approaches were begun on the night of May 23-24, this time at a respectable 300 yards distance. Kościuszko's plan called for three approach parallels to be dug, roughly in the shape of an elongated

"Z," with the final leg ending near the walls of the Star Redoubt. According to the engineer, the work was begun at a greater range to acquaint "the men of the proceeding and of the nature of [the] work with less danger."[23] In the morning the patriots brought artillery forward and opened fire on the Star Redoubt "with great effect" that "Alarmed the Enemy prodigious[ly]."[24]

Under the cover of their guns, the rebels worked round-the-clock digging the necessary approaches. According to their antagonist, Lt. Col. Cruger, the Americans worked "very industriously."[25] But, the hard ground and lack of sufficient tools made progress slow. According to Kościuszko, "As the Nature of the Ground was very hard and aproched very much to Soft Stone the Approches Could not be so fast advanced." When the first leg of the "Z" was completed, the engineer noted "the Workmen began to be exposed to the Continuel of the Enemy's fire all night and the suckiding [succeeding] but, more danger foreseen, was immediately conteracted by more Exertions of the Troops."[26]

Despite the difficulties, by May 27 the rebel guns moved up to within 250 yards of the Star Redoubt, with the approaches reaching to within 180 yards. On May 30 Kościuszko reported "the Parallel was half done at one Hundred and fifty yards."[27] With the enemy lines coming menacingly close, Cruger ordered another surprise attack to disrupt the work, but his Polish antagonist reported "the Second Sallies the Enemys made but with small effect—Three or four men of both side were killed."[28] Further, the arrival of various rebel militia companies gave the engineer enough men to begin a series of parallels aimed at Ft. Holmes, forcing Cruger to stretch his troops to make provisions for the defence of both areas. "The militia now began to come very fast from the adjacent Countys," Kościuszko wrote, "which gave opportunity to [open] the Trenches against the smal[l] Redoubt mention[ed] upon our right.—and the same day the Battery was made at 250 yards with the aproches of 70 yards more advanced."[29]

By June 3 work on the second leg toward the Star Redoubt advanced to a point approximately where Lt. Roney had attacked the initial work party. That day, Cruger wrote "Our neighbors continue industriously at Work, [and] they are within less than Sixty yards of our Star Redoubt."[30] At that point Greene paused briefly to call upon the garrison to surrender before the final assault, but Cruger rebuffed this overture.[31] Unbeknown to either Greene or Cruger, on the same day the siege entered its new phase three British ships docked in Charleston brings hundreds of badly needed Irish regulars of the 3rd, 19th and 30th Regiments of Foot to bolster Lord Rawdon's force. The British commander immediately made plans to march to the relief of Ninety-Six, a campaign he began on June 7.[32]

On June 4 the siege entered a new phase. "[U]pon our left," Kościuszko reported, "the parallel [was] Complited, [and] the Battery was made at 180 yards" from the Star Redoubt. The approaches reached another 30 yards in advance of the battery.[33] As the last leg of the "Z" approach neared the British abatis, the defending loyalist fire grew intense and more accurate. According to Kościuszko, they "were so industrious and great marksmen that no finger could be held up half second without been Cut off."[34] To counter the increased volume and accuracy of British fire, Kościuszko constructed a Maham Tower, essentially a protected gun platform, about forty feet high, only thirty-five yards from the outer British lines. Plunging fire from this position into the Star Redoubt temporarily silenced the Loyalist marksmen. "[N]ot a Man could show his Head but he was immediately shot down," Greene observed.[35]

In response, Col. Cruger ordered his men to pile sandbags on their parpets to increase their height, and with it the protection afforded against sharpshooters on the tower. He also tried firing heated solid shot into the tower to set it afire, but the wood was still green and the British lacked sufficient furnaces to make the shot hot enough to ignite the fire. Kościuszko's men replied by firing "African Arrows" tipped with burning pitch into the British lines in an attempt to set fire to the wooden roofs on the various buildings. Cruger reacted by ordering the shingle roofs torn off the buildings to prevent their burning. Further, with the patriots now within easy range, the loyalist commander renewed his surprise attacks in hopes of keeping the rebels off balance and disrupting further progress on the approaches.[36] The attacks, however, met with little success. According to Kościuszko: "the Enemys Trow down the roofs of the houses in the Town and in the Star Redoubt and made the Sallies suporting with Canon from the work upon our left with no other Sucess than to cut down the mantelet w[h]ich there was posted to Cover the workmen from Rifle shot and [quiet the British] if possible by ours."[37] Nevertheless, he complimented the loyalists "for their Vigilance, frequent judicious Sallies and proper means to counteract the assailant measures."[38]

The closer the patriots approached, the more intense the firing became. On June 5 the rebel artillery "desmount the Canon in the Star Redoubt from the Battery and killed a few men in it."[39] The following day Kościuszko increased the height of the battery by some twenty feet to further discomfort the defenders. This "oblig[ed] the Enemy to intrenche inside half way with the parapet of sixteen feet high.—we advanced the aproches but very little and Complit the paralell upon our left at 120 yards."[40]

Col. Henry Lee arrived with his Legion on June 8, "viktorious" from the recent operations in Georgia, and assumed command of the operations aimed at Ft. Holmes.[41] With him he brought a large number of captives from Augusta whom he marched outside the loyalist fortifications to intimidate those inside. But, according to British fusilier Roderick Mackenzie, this humiliation only convinced the defenders that "death was preferable to captivity with such an enemy."[42]

The same day, Greene learned of the arrival of the British reinforcements in Charleston, and two days later word reached him of the departure of Rawdon's relief force for Ninety-Six. To oppose Rawdon, Greene directed Thomas Sumter, then south of Orangeburg, to obstruct the relief column as much as possible, removing all provisions and transportation from its line of march. But Rawdon took a circuitous route, bypassing both Sumter and the cavalry forces of Col. Andrew Pickens and Lt. Col. William Washington. The route was somewhat longer, but allowed Rawdon a virtually unopposed march to Cruger's aid.[43]

News of Lord Rawdon's march forced Greene to rush preparations for the reduction of Ninety-Six. The defenders, however, remained alert and detected the increased activities. On the night of June 9-10 Cruger ordered two raiding parties sent out because of his "apprehension that something extraordinary was carrying on in the enemy's works."[44] One of the parties attacked Henry Lee's men, bayoneting some and capturing the officer in command before the raiders withdrew to the safety of their fortifications.[45] The second attack force overran a battery, but could not spike the guns because they lacked the requisite spikes and hammers. Neither did they have sufficient time and men to drag the artillery pieces away. They did, however, pour into the nearest siege approaches where they discovered the entrance to the mine Kościuszko had begun north of the Star Redoubt for the purpose of undermining the defenses and blowing them up. When Cruger's attack began, Kościuszko was examining the works in person and only barely escaped capture or death, being wounded during his escape in what fusilier Mackenzie referred to as "the seat of honour."[46]

When Greene received word on June 10 of Lord Rawdon's departure from Charleston, siege operations were pushed forward as quickly as possible. Despite Kościuszko's wound, Lynn Montross noted in *The Story of the Continental Army* that "neither the pain nor the customary ribald jests kept him from duty."[47] The second parallel was completed the same day and the engineer began anew work on the "subterranean gallery" to undermine the fortifications. The engineer estimated it would take only a few more days to complete operations at the Star Redoubt, including the mine to blast a passage for the assault column. Once again that night "The Enemys made Sallies with prodigous fury and killed 4 or 5 men," but the work continued.[48]

At 11:00 a.m. on June 12 covered by what Henry Lee called "a dark, violent storm ... from the west, without rain," a sergeant and nine privates from his Legion infantry snuck close to Ft. Holmes carrying incendiary materials in an attempt to set fire to the stockade. Before this could be accomplished they were discovered, a counter attack launched, and the sergeant and five of the privates killed.[49] This setback notwithstanding, by the 14th the approaches had been completed to within twenty yards of Ft. Holmes and forty of the Star Redoubt. On the 16th "the Battery was made upon our left" [Star Redoubt], the mine gallery nearing within four feet of [the] ditch surrounding the Star Redoubt and the approaches within six feet.[50]

By the 17th Lee's approaches were close enough to cut off Loyalist access to the fresh water supply provided by Kate Fowler's Branch. According to Marvin L. Cann's analysis of the siege in *The South Carolina Historical Magazine*, this "deprived the garrison of drinking water and, in the intense June heat, caused great suffering among soldiers and civilian refugees alike." The garrison tried digging a well, but could find no water. To alleviate the distress, naked slaves were sent to sneak down to the stream at night and bring back buckets of water for use during the day.[51]

That same day word arrived that Lord Rawdon was only thirty miles away. This intelligence meant Greene could no longer wait to complete the siege operations. He was left with three options. He could retreat, he could move to oppose Lord Rawdon's column, or he could attempt to take the fort by storm. Greene rejected the idea of retreat for fear of the negative effect on the troops' morale if the lengthy siege were abandoned without success. Similarly, since he had only half the number of regulars in Lord Rawdon's relief column, he felt the risk of a pitched battle too great. Greene did not want to launch a frontal assault as he believed it enjoyed "a poor Prospect of Success."[52] But, given the time constraints and the other considerations, storming the fort appeared to be the only viable alternative. In Kościuszko's words, Greene "Tho[u]ght prudent to try the ardor and enxiaty of the Troops by the attack upon both redoubts—[a] number of Officers and soldiers hearing the intention of the General present[ed] self as Wolunteers."[53]

Greene's plan called for a coordinated assault on both Ft. Holmes and the Star Redoubt, the two columns to be led by Cols. Henry Lee and Richard Campbell respectively. The assault forces moved forward about noon. Lee's Legion and Kirkwood's Delaware light infantry quickly reached the small redoubt, compelling its surrender with but little loss.[54] Col. Campbell enjoyed less success commanding the primary assault of the 1st Virginia, reinforced by Maryland and Delaware Continentals, against the Star Redoubt. Moving ahead of the main attack column, and covered by fire from the siege approaches, a "forlorn hope" cut a path through the abatis, threw fascines into the ditch to create a causeway for the main attack, and employed grappling hooks to pull down the sandbags the loyalists used to heighten their works. Reacting quickly to this threat, Col. Cruger sent out two raiding parties of thirty men each to attack the rebels at work in the trenches. The sudden attack succeeded in defeating the forlorn hope, killing or wounding forty Americans, about two-thirds of the advance force, and the entire assault stalled. After about forty-five minutes Greene called off the attack.[55]

Commenting on the repulse, Kościsuzko somberly philosophized that "blind fortune [did] not always keep pace with C[o]urage and [a] Good Cause." He lamented that "Capt Amstrong and 30 soldiers were killed of which Valor intrepidy left us Chearish their memory, regret the loss and bring the Example to posterity."[56]

Greene retreated on the 19th. Lord Rawdon reached Ninety-Six on the morning of the 21st with 2,000 troops. The twenty-eight-day siege cost the Americans 57 killed, 70 wounded, and 20 missing, a total of 147. British losses were 27 killed and 58 wounded, a total of 85.[57]

The British pursued Greene for about thirty miles before abandoning the chase because they had been unable to diminish Greene's two day head start. "I regret that we were not more successful in this enterprize," Greene wrote to Gen. Arthur St. Clair, "as the post is of great importance to the enemy, and our troops have been exposed to excessive labor and annoyance in the attempt."[58] To Col. Francis Marion he lamented that "the enemy have obliged us to raise the siege of Ninety-Six, when it was upon the eve of surrendering."[59] He apparently took little solace that Lord Rawdon soon felt compelled to abandon Ninety-Six and retreat on July 3 with his entire force to Charleston. Greene, having marched 950 miles, fought three battles and several smaller skirmishes, and captured almost 3,000 prisoners, withdrew into the Santee Hills to rest his weary men from the searing summer heat.[60]

But the retreat of the two armies from Ninety-Six did not end the fighting, it only changed the nature of the conflict. With the failure of the operation, explanations were in order. Kościuszko wrote that the siege "will afford the Example what Fortitude, persevirence, Courage, and exertions of the troops can perform." He found kind words for each side. The Americans, he observed, "exposed [themselves] Chearfuly to inavoided Denger." At the same time he praised the British for "their Vigilance, frequent judicious Sallies and proper means to counteract the assaliant measures." In the end, he blamed the failure of the siege on the unexpected hardness of the ground, the inexperience of the troops in siege warfare, and Col. Cruger's unexpectedly aggressive defense, all of which appear justified.[61] To his friend Horatio Gates, he likewise explained that "the Ground was so hard that our aproaches Could not go but very slow, had Lord Roudon gave us four days more we should blow up Theirs Works and take Six Hundred men in it—however by our Maneuvres we have oblidged the Enemys to evacuate Ninty six."[62]

One who agreed with the Polish engineer was Col. Otho Holland Williams of the 1st Maryland Regiment of the Continental Line, who observed the siege. In a letter to his brother he commented that "Coll Kosciuszko a young gentleman of distinction from Poland who left his native country to follow the banners of Liberty in America, superintended the operations, and by his Zeal, assiduity, perseverance and firmness promoted the business with ... expedition."[63]

Further support for the engineer came from General Greene. In his reports he did not point to any failure on the part of his subordinate or inadequacy in planning. Rather, he pointed to the failure of the Virginia militia to arrive and the failure of Sumter to impede the progress of the British relief force. The former left him with a force inadequate to more vigorously prosecute the siege, while the latter allowed Lord Rawdon's relief column to advance virtually unopposed before the final demise of Ninety-Six was accomplished. Both of these reasons support Kościuszko's conclusion that with more men or time Ninety-Six would have fallen. Gen. Greene's Order of the Day for June 20, 1781, stated: "The General presents his thanks to Colonel Kosciuszko chief Engineer for his Assiduity, preserverance and indefatigable exertions in planning and prosecuting the approaches which he is persuaded were judiciously design'd and would have infalliably gained Success if time had admitted of their being Compleated."[64]

Regardless of Greene's or Kościuszko's views, some sought to blame the failure to reduce Ninety-Six on the commanding general or his chief engineer. Kościuszko came under criticism because of the apparent slow progress of the siege. Chief among Kościuszko's accusers was Henry Lee who, though he acknowledged that Kościuszko "possess[es] skill in his profession" and was "much esteemed for his mildness of disposition and urbanity of manners,"[65] accused the engineer, in his published memoirs some thirty years after the event, of "Never regarding the importance which was attached to depriving the enemy of water, for which he entirely depended on the rivulet to his left" while he "applied his undivided attention to the demolition of the star, the strongest point of the enemy's defence" while the "enemy's left had been entirely neglected, although in that quarter was procured the whole supply of water."[66] Lee believed the initial objective should have been the weaker Ft. Holmes, claiming that as the siege wore on "We now began to deplore the early inattention of the chief engineer to the enemy's left; persuaded had he been deprived of the use of the rivulet in the beginning of the siege he must have been forced to surrender."[67] In conclusion, he stated:

> Kosciuszko was extremely amiable, and, I believe a truly good man, nor was he deficient in his professional knowledge; but he was very moderate in talent—not a spark of the ethereal in his composition. His blunders lost us Ninety-Six; and General Greene, much as he was beloved and respected, did not escape criticism, for permitting his engineer to direct the manner of approach. It was said, and with some

justice too, that the General ought certainly to have listened to his opinion, but never ought to have permitted the pursuit of error, although supported by professional authority.[68]

These criticisms were repeated by early historians of the Revolution including G. G. White who was very critical of Kościuszko in his *Life of Major General Henry Lee* and Edward Channing who claimed in his monumental six-volume work *A History of the United States* that Greene had no engineer "of the requisite ability."[69]

In the first instance, it is not entirely certain whether the garrison was without water. There were many people within the colonial forces who were familiar with the area about Ninety-Six. Water sources were common knowledge among the area's inhabitants, information which certainly would have been communicated to the engineer in command of the siege. Indeed, some evidence suggests Greene and Kościuszko had information there were wells within the works which could have supplied the garrison regardless of the outside water source. Kościuszko, in fact, says in his account of the siege that the decision to concentrate on the Star Redoubt came about "very much by the Inteligence broud [brought] that the Enemys had Waills [wells] in every work and Could not be distresed [by] been Cot of [i.e., cut off] From the spring which could be effectued by takin possession of the smal redoubt."[70] This, and other comments, leave the clear impression that the general feeling among the besiegers was the land was so low and flat that water could be easily obtained by digging wells almost anywhere.

On the other hand, the letter of Lt. Col. Allen, second-in-command at Ninety-Six, to Lord Cornwallis specifically stated his primary concern as "the want of water." Further, Col. Cruger's initial preoccupation with extending a covered causeway across Kate Fowler's Branch and constructing Ft. Holmes to guard the causeway indicates his concern for protecting that water supply. Then too, sources indicate the defenders attempted unsuccessfully to dig wells during the siege and were eventually reduced to sending naked slaves down to the spring in the dark of night to procure what water they could carry in buckets. These bits of information appear to indicate a lack of fresh water within the fortifications. How could the perceptions have been so different within and without the loyalist position?

There are three possible explanations to account for the discrepencies about whether or not there was water available in Ninety-Six.

First, there may well have been water within the village as stated by natives of the area, but it may not have been sufficient for the needs of the garrison. Second, if the spring weather had been dry and the June days as hot as contemporary accounts would lead us to believe, the wells within the village may have been dry or very much reduced. Or, third, as Mieczysław Haiman suggests in his *Kosciuszko in the American Revolution*, "It is possible, therefore, that Greene had wrong intelligence on this point, and that Lee was right. But it was much easier for Lee to decide the question *post factum*, than for Greene to weigh it accurately before the attack."[71] In fact, since the area surrounding Ninety-Six was known to be largely Loyalist in sentiment, reports of water in Ninety-Six may have been circulated to dissuade the patriots from interdicting Kate Fowler's Branch. In any case, it appears there was concern about the water supply within Ninety-Six and the Americans did little to deny the loyalists the use of the nearby stream until very late in the siege. Whether earlier action against the water would have been decisive is problematical; nevertheless, little was done to explore this tactic.

Regarding the second criticism, Kościuszko could well have chosen the easier Ft. Holmes redoubt as his first target, but it's capture would not have ensured the fall of the main position and, being dominated by the Star Redoubt, it would have been difficult and costly to maintain. The reverse course of action, the one adopted by Greene, no doubt on Kościuszko's recommendation, would have made the other positions untenable. This was, to a certain extent, proven when the combined assault of June 19 carried Ft. Holmes but did not successfully cause the fall of the Star Redoubt. Possession of the former did not lead inevitably to the capitulation of the village and the Star Redoubt. The siege failed not because of faulty engineering, but for lack of time. Wasting efforts building approaches to outworks of dubious significance would only have wasted more valuable time.

In the end, it was General Greene who was in charge of the American forces at Ninety-Six. If he wanted to shift responsibility for the failure of the siege it would have been very easy for him to have blamed his chief engineer. He did *not*.

Chapter 10

"Master of His Profession"

*T*hough he had yet to win a major engagement while in command of the Southern Army, Greene had virtually eliminated British control from all but a thin coastal strip in the Carolinas and Georgia. Following the setback at Ninety-Six, both armies bided their time. Greene rested his army in the High Hills of the Santee where his weary men could recuperate in comparatively cooler, healthier surroundings richer in provisions than the depleted regions the armies marched through during the spring campaigns. From there, Kościuszko wrote to Gates to inform him of the army's circumstances. "By our Maneuvers we have obliged the Enemy to Evacuate Ninety-Six," he reported, putting the best face possible on the recent action. "We took at present this position [which is] very healthy and expect to be reinforced by North Carolina and Pennsylvania Brigades who are in their march. If the circumstances would not change their course of affairs we will be able very soon to confine the Enemy to Charleston."[1]

While camped near the Santee, Kościuszko visited the hospital to procure some coffee, sparking a misunderstanding with one of the surgeons. After his visit Dr. Peter Fayssoux complained that the engineer "intruded himself" into the hospital to satisfy his needs when there was not enough coffee to distribute to the sick. Dr. William Read soon came forward to preserve Kościuszko's honor, explaining that in exchange for the coffee the Pole "gave up all his rations to the hospital, never touching a drop of ardent spirits, but contenting himself with the slops and soups of that establishment, which fare was no luxury, and that he had invited him, as a companion, to [likewise] do so."[2]

Gradually, the army's health improved and reinforcements arrived to bolster Greene's depleted force to nearly 2,100 effectives. The troops included about 910 Delaware, Maryland, North Carolina, and Virginia Continental infantry, Col. Washington's 80 Continental cavalry, and Lee's legion with about 60 cavalry and 100 infantry. Also joining his force were 150 South Carolina state troops and varying numbers of militia which, by the beginning of September, rose to 700. Supporting the army were about 100 artillerists serving four field guns.[3]

While Greene's army recuperated, Lord Cornwallis marched northward through North Carolina into Virginia with his reinforced army causing great consternation through those regions. Fearing for the safety of his state's military stores which were threatened by raids from British-held Wilmington, or from forces dispatched from Cornwallis's army, Governor Thomas Burke of North Carolina requested assistance from Greene to secure several strategic points. In response, Greene dispatched Kościuszko to protect the military stores by constructing a series of blockhouses and other fortifications at strategic locations around the state. "I will send to your assistance Colo Kosciuszko, our principal Engineer," Greene replied, "who is Master of his profession and will afford you every aid you can wish."[4] It is doubtful, however, that much of this work was ever actually completed given Cornwallis's movement into Virginia and his eventual entrapment at Yorktown. Indeed, Kościuszko's exact whereabouts from mid-August through early December cannot readily be ascertained. No doubt he spent some time in the Tarheel State, but the exact date of his return to Greene's army is uncertain.

Soon after Kościuszko headed north, Greene again moved south, but Lord Rawdon was ill and the American found himself opposed by Lt. Colonel Alexander Stewart. Born in 1741, Stewart came from a long line of British military officers. Promoted lieutenant colonel of the 3rd Regiment of Foot on July 7, 1775, he arrived in Charleston with his regiment on June 4, 1781, and assumed command at Orangeburg when Rawdon fell sick. Stewart, attempting to hold Orangeburg, encamped his force just south of the Congaree River, within sixteen miles of Greene's position, but the flooded river prevented any serious action between the contending armies. In an effort to force Stewart's retreat, Greene sent raiders to the very outskirts of Charleston, but the British colonel was not fooled and maintained his position.[5]

Greene resumed the offensive on August 22. Because the flooded Santee and Wateree Rivers prevented movement directly toward

Stewart, Greene marched by a circuitous route through Camden that threatened to turn the British flank from the northwest. Stewart responded by withdrawing to Eutaw Springs where he could be more easily supplied from Charleston. As the two armies neared each other, Col. Francis Marion joined Greene on September 7 bringing the American force to about 2,100 men including approximately 850 militia. The Continentals included two battalions of the Maryland Line under Col. Otho Williams, three North Carolina battalions under Gen. Jethro Sumner, two Virginia battalions under Lt. Col. Richard Campbell, Capt. Robert Kirkwood's Delaware company, Lee's Legion under Lt. Col. Henry Lee, and Lt. Col. William Washington's cavalry. The militia included 145 South Carolina State Troops, the South Carolina militia units of Brig. Gen. Francis Marion, Col. Andrew Pickens, and Col. Thomas Sumter, and the North Carolina militia of Col. Francis Malmedy. Also included were two 3-pounders and two 6-pounders of the Continental artillery.[6]

By dusk on September 7, Greene's army lay only some seven miles from Stuart's force. The British commander had about 2,300 troops, mostly British regulars of the 3rd, 63rd, and 64th Regiments of Foot, and the light infantry and grenadiers of the 3rd, 19th, and 30th Regiments of Foot which had recently arrived from Ireland under Major John Marjoriebanks. Also included in the British force were the following provincial troops: one battalion of De Lancey's New York Brigade under Lt. Col. John H. Cruger, one battalion of New Jersey volunteers, one battalion of New York volunteers, and one troop of South Carolina Loyalist cavalry.[7]

Because Greene's irregulars harassed the British so much, Stewart was apparently unaware of how near Greene was until early on the morning of September 8 when the American attack commenced. To meet the assault, Stewart moved his troops quickly into line with the 3rd Regiment of Foot anchoring his right against Eutaw Creek, the Loyalists holding the center, and the 63rd and 64th Regiments of Foot on the left. To protect his left flank, which was otherwise "in the air," he placed his mounted troops in rear of the flank in position to protect it from any column that came from that direction. Stewart placed two guns in the center of his line along the Charleston Road. The ground was somewhat wooded, providing some defensive cover as Stewart awaited the American attack.[8]

Greene advanced in a formation similar to that he used at Guilford Court House. In his first line he placed the North and South Carolina militia with the light troops and cavalry protecting their flanks. The second line contained the Maryland, Virginia, and North Carolina Continentals. Finally, the third line included Greene's reserve, Kirkwood's company of Delaware Continentals and Washington's Continental cavalry. Greene ordered the first line forward about mid-morning. Moving to the attack, the militia kept in line, driving home their attack and causing some losses in the British line before they began to falter. Seeing the attack grind to a halt, Greene sent forward the North Carolina Continentals under Gen. Sumner to close the widening gap in the American line. A desperate fight followed, but the Americans were forced back and the British line advanced. Sensing an opportunity, Greene ordered the remaining Continentals of the second line forward. The British attack halted, then broke, swept from the field by the American advance.[9]

On the verge of complete victory, the pursuing Continentals, famished from their long march on infrequent and repetitive rations, broke ranks to pillage the British camp. The momentary break in discipline gave the British an opportunity to rally. Major Marjoriebanks led a counterattack and the disorganized Americans fell back, the impetus of their victorious charge now vanished. But the Americans soon rallied and the fighting raged on for three full hours, the two sides trading volleys in what deteriorated into a bloody slugfest.[10]

When the firing finally stopped and the smoke cleared, the British controlled the field. Defeated once again, Greene's small army lost 139 killed, 375 wounded, and 8 missing—a total of 522. Yet, the British fared little better. Stewart's army lost 85 killed, 351 wounded, and 257 captured and missing—a total of 693. So badly mauled were the British that Stewart was unable to pursue the defeated Americans or interfere with Greene's retreat. Instead, the British retired to Monck's Corner, closer to Charleston. Greene followed warily at a safe distance hoping for another chance to defeat Stewart, but Col. Paston Gould arrived in Monck's Corner with the 30th Regiment of Foot, newly arrived from Charleston, on September 12, precluding any further opportunity for Greene to attack with hope of victory. As ranking officer, Gould assumed command until Lt. Gen. Alexander Leslie arrived in Charleston on November 6, 1781, to take command.[11]

Over the years since that fateful September day in 1781, legend has persisted that during the thick of the fighting at Eutaw Springs Kościuszko interceded just in time to save the lives of some fifty

British captives being threatened by American troops. Where this story began is difficult to determine, but it has been repeated by many authors. In fact, the circumstances may have been right for such an event to occur since shortly before the battle the British had summarily executed Col. Isaac Hayne on August 4, thereby inflaming many with passion for revenge. Further, at the beginning of the battle the British advanced party lost an officer and about 40 men captured, many, and perhaps most of whom were wounded. This scenario fits with the general number of British wounded, and because it happened before the general engagement began there may have been time for the incident to happen. The difficulties, however, are that no contemporaneous documentation of this event has yet surfaced and, in fact, it is generally believed that Kościuszko was still in North Carolina at the time of the battle. In fact, there is no known primary source that places him at Eutaw Springs. Though the story is entirely in keeping with Kościuszko's character, the veracity of the event remains to be conclusively proven or disproven.

Following the Battle of Eutaw Springs, the only significant British-held locations south of Virginia were the port cities of Wilmington, North Carolina, Charleston, South Carolina, and Savannah, Georgia. Greene could do little to molest them. Retreating back to the relative safety of the High Hills of the Santee, the army was further devastated by illness and the expiration of enlistments, shrinking the force to little more than 1,000 men fit for duty. Ill, lacking clothing, pay, and food, dispirited by yet another defeat, discontent and even threats of mutiny surfaced.[12]

By the end of October, however, came the exhilarating news that Cornwallis had surrendered his entire army of 7,157 men at Yorktown on October, 19, 1781. The defeat of Cornwallis in Virginia allowed reinforcements to be freed at last for service in the South. On November 1 Washington sent Gen. Anthony Wayne south with the Pennsylvania Line and a detachment of artillery, followed shortly afterward by 700 Maryland and Delaware recruits under Gen. Arthur St. Clair. Altogether, the reinforcements numbered about 2,000 men. Before they arrived on January 4, however, the British abandoned Wilmington on November 14 to concentrate their forces in Charleston. Greene moved his army out of the High Hills of the Santee on November 18. Though outnumbered by the British, now under Gen. Leslie, Greene held the initiative and the wary English commander slowly called in his outposts and retired upon Charleston where he began throwing up fortifications to withstand a siege.[13]

Not strong enough to assault the city, Greene nevertheless drove in most of the remaining British outposts and brought his army into proximity of the seaport. During the first week in December Greene sent Kościuszko ahead of his column to select the best location for his troops. The engineer found an area surrounding a small crossroads named Round O between the Pon Pon and Ashepoo Rivers that offered excellent defensive positions behind rivers and swamplands which formed shields against a quick enemy advance, while at the same time offering provisions sufficient to support the army. Fertile rice plantations in the area offered, according to Greene's biographer, not only rice but "poultry, wild game, vegetables and fruit." For troops accustomed to a limited, unvaried diet, the richness of the lowland area proved an immediate tonic to depression and disease.[14]

Greene arrived at Round O on December 7, establishing his headquarters at the plantation belonging to Roger Saunders within 35 miles of Charleston, while a portion of the troops encamped around nearby Skirving's plantation. With the British now confined to the environs of Charleston and Savannah, Loyalist activity abated in South Carolina and soon the General Assembly began meeting at Jacksonbourough near the Pon Pon River about ten miles south of Greene's headquarters. To protect the legislators, Greene assigned a military escort commanded by Col. Kościuszko, a certain confirmation of the confidence he placed in the Polish officer. At the same time, Greene sent Gen. Wayne with troops to invest Savannah, which the British eventually abandoned the following July, moving its garrison by water to Charleston.[15] The war had definitely turned against the British in the South.

As the army settled into new camps, Kościuszko apparently found accommodations along with Col. Otho Williams in the home of Mrs. Susan Hayne, whom the Pole found to be a "good Clever Sensible Woman."[16] There, with the slowdown in activity, the officers recuperated from their recent campaigns. Kościuszko, his clothing worn thin from use, applied for new supplies from the growing army quartermaster stores and took the opportunity provided by the respite from campaigning to renew his correspondence with his acquaintances to the north and develop new ones in the south.[17] Soon he received a letter from Gates, the first since their parting in 1780. Kościuszko was overjoyed. "Your kind letter I received by Major

Pineknee [Pinckney]," he replied, "you Cannot Conceive what Satisfaction I felt, as I had already given up all hope of ever happen to me such a favor." The purpose of Gates's letter was to support Kościuszko for a long-overdue promotion to brigadier general. In the wake of Cornwallis's surrender at Yorktown, Congress agreed to promote du Portail, Gouvion, and others, and Gates felt Kościuszko should no longer be overlooked. But once again the Pole's reluctance to have others lobby extensively for him probably hurt his chances for the well-deserved advancement. "Congress lately resolved to make no more Brigadier-generals," Kościuszko wrote to Gates, and "for my part neither confidence I have enough to think I deserve it nor resolution to ask, am extremely obliged to you for your kind offers and think them of great weight if importance should you use your influence, but as to the others recommendation in my favor am entirely against, [as] what I beg of you will always deny to the others." Thus dismissing the opportunity Gates offered, Kościuszko pledged to visit whenever next he might be in the vicinity of the Gates home. "I do not expect to go very soon to Philadelphia but if ever I should you may be sure that I will do me the honour to call on you, and would not Choose by no means to be depraved of the Satisfaction [to] see you both in good health at Travellers rest. My best respect to Mrs. Gates and I beg her to believe that not time or place will ever make me forgive her good heart and my Sentyments of gratitude."[18]

Aside from writing, there were other diversions to occupy time as the stalemate before Charleston dragged on through the spring and early summer of 1782. Many of the officers were attracted to the young ladies inhabiting the region, Kościuszko apparently being no exception. "[E]very body is in love," he wrote to Otho Williams, who had returned to his native Maryland. "Colo. Moris fancy himself to be with Miss Nancy Eliot in love" and "displayed upon the occasion [a] waste [vast] store not seen before of the humorous spritty disposition."[19] For his part, Kościuszko flirted, enjoyed the dinner company of several local ladies, and drew sketches of the damsals who frequented Mrs. Haynes's home. On one occasion, Kościuszko wrote, several young ladies "approached me with very smiling Countenaces, kissed me half dousen times each, and beged I would instantly draw them but hansome—Such unexpected Change put me almost to extasy, I drew my pencil, paper Coulours and in a half hour time made perfectly like them."[20]

On March 22 Greene moved his army to a plantation owned by John Waring near Bacon's Bridge on the Ashley River. The new campsite was not far from Dorchester, some fifteen miles from Charleston, allowing Greene to further restrict British land movement out of the seaport city. Theodore Thayer, Greene's biographer, called it a "strong position [where] the army built huts of logs and bark as the number of tents available was far from enough to cover the troops."[21] As spring turned into summer, however, the unremitting heat, insects, lack of meat and clothing, malaria and other diseases began to take their toll upon the troops. Hospitals filled to overflowing and death became an all too frequent visitor. By the end of April Greene reported the "army literally naked, badly fed, and altogether without spirits. Certainly this is pushing an army to desperation. Mutiny appears in many forms." At one point some of the soldiers hatched a plot to turn Greene and some of his officers over to the British if their grievances were not addressed, but the hanging of the ringleader appears to have quelled any potential uprising.[22]

By this time, however, the British were becoming increasingly uncomfortable themselves. Provisions were running dangerously low, prompting Gen. Leslie to ask for a truce on the grounds that peace talks were now being conducted in Europe and he wanted to avoid further unnecessary bloodshed. Since he had no information on the peace negotiations, and no approval from Congress to grant such a general truce, Greene declined. This forced Leslie to send out a large foraging expedition to gather in produce and other provisions from the plantations along the Combahee River. Greene responded by sending Gen. Mordecai Gist with a force to oppose the British. Gist was only partially successful, with Leslie's expedition bringing in some 300 barrels of rice and a quantity of cattle. More significant was the loss of Lt. Col. John Laurens, son of the one-time president of the Continental Congress, in an otherwise insignificant skirmish during the British raid. On August 27, he and a small party of dragoons from Lee's Legion were ambushed by 140 British troops who called upon the Americans to surrender. Instead, Laurens led the dragoons in a charge during which he was mortally wounded.[23]

In the wake of Laurens's death, his comrades-in-arms proceeded, as was the custom of the day, to divide his possessions among themselves. In a letter to Greene, Kościuszko expressed his contempt for such activity which he felt appealed to "mean, low thinking" people. "As to my part," he proclaimed, "I wanted to be clear of

Boleslaw Jan Czedekowski, (1885-1969) *Kosciuszko at West Point* oil on canvas, from The Kosciuszko Foundation, Inc. Permanent Collection of Polish Masters, New York.

Jan Styka, (1858-1925) *Kosciuszko at the Battle of Raclawice* oil on canvas, from The Kosciuszko Foundation, Inc. Permanent Collection of Polish Masters, New York.

Jan Styka, (1858-1925) *Peasants Capturing the Cannon at Raclawice* oil on canvas, from The Kosciuszko Foundation, Inc. Permanent Collection of Polish Masters, New York.

Hy. Hintermeister, *Washington bids Farewell to His Officers at Fraunces Tavern, 1783.* Kosciuszko is fifth from the right. Reproduction, from the Kosciuszko Foundation Inc. Archives, New York.

Frank Reilly, *Welcoming Return of Polish American General Kosciuszko, Philadelphia, 1797*. The horses from his carriage were unhitched and the carriage was drawn by the committee. Reproduction, from the Kosciuszko Foundation Inc. Archives, New York.

(Bottom Left) Tadeusz Kosciuszko (1746-1817), *Thomas Jefferson, a Philosopher, a Patriot and a Friend, Dessinee par son ami Tadee Kosciuszko*. (Drawn by his friend Thaddeus Kosciuszko), reproduction, from an original engraving from The Kosciuszko Foundation Inc, Archives, New York. (*Bottom Right*) H.D. Saunders (Dmochowski), ( ) *T. Kosciuszko* (1857). From the Architect of the Capitol, Library of Congress Prints and Photographs Collection.

Zygmunt Ajdukiewicz (1861-1917), *George Washington Congratulating Kosciuszko* from a portfolio of 12 lithographs depicting the life of Kosciuszko, from The Kosciuszko Foundation Inc. Archives, New York.

Zygmunt Ajdukiewicz (1861-1917), *Kosciuszko Falling Wounded at Maciejowice* from a portfolio of 12 lithographs depicting the life of Kosciuszko, from The Kosciuszko Foundation Inc. Archives, New York.

Zygmunt Ajdukiewicz (1861-1917), *Kosciuszko in Switzerland* from a portfolio of 12 lithographs depicting the life of Kosciuszko, from The Kosciuszko Foundation, Inc. Archives, New York.

(Below left) Portrait of Kosciuszko; (Below right) Young Thaddeus Kosciuszko and his Great Love Zygmunt Ajdukiewicz (1861-1917), both from a portfolio of 12 lithographs depicting the life of Kosciuszko, from The Kosciuszko Foundation, Inc. Archives, New York.

(Clockwise, starting upper left) Polish American News Exchange Co. *Monument to Kosciuszko in Yonkers, N.Y.* (1912); *Monument to Kosciuszko in Cleveland, Ohio* (1904); Washington Photo Studio, W. M. Rozanski, *Monument to Kosciuszko in Chicago, IL* (1904); *Monument to Kosciuszk in Fall River, MA* (1950). All from black & white photographs, The Kosciuszko Foundation, Inc. Archives, New York.

(Clockwise, starting upper left) Shaw Photo Service, Boston *Monument to Kosciuszko in Boston, MA* (1926); *Monument to Kosciuszko in the Saratoga Battlefield* (1936); *Monument to Kosciuszko in Milwaukee, WI* (1905). All from black & white photographs, The Kosciuszko Foundation Inc. Archives, New York.

A. Pawlikowski, photographer, *Professor Roman Dyboski accepts earth from American battlefields a[t] Kosciuszko Mound, Krakow, Poland July 4, 1926.* Black & white photograph, from The Kosciuszko Foundation Inc. Archives, New York.

, Wojniakowski, *Portrait of Kosciuszko* oil on board, collection of the National Museum in
znan.

Michal Stachowicz (1768-1835) *Kosciuszko's Oath in Krakow's Market Square, March 24th, 1794.* The artist was an eyewitness of this event. Collection of the Polish Army Museum, Warsaw, gouache on paper.

Pistol given to Kosciuszko by George Washington from the collection of the Czartoryski Museum, Krakow.

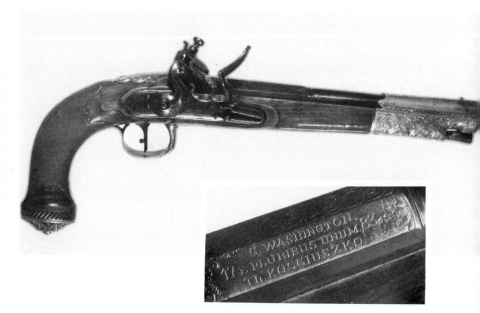

arol Schweikart, *General Tadeusz Kosciuszko* oil on canvas, ca 1802, collection of the National
Museum in Warsaw.

Mereczowszczyzna, birthplace of Kosciuszko, artist unknown. Photo archive of The Kosciuszko Foundation Inc., New York.

W.T. Benda (1873-1948) *The Kosciuszko Foundation House*, 15 East 65th Street, New York. Pencil on paper, from The Kosciuszko Foundation Inc. Archives, New York.

The Kosciuszko Foundation Medal of Recognition. "He is as pure a Son of Liberty as I have ever known"—Thomas Jefferson. Struck bronze, from The Kosciuszko Foundation Inc. Archives, New York.

. Falke *A. Czartoryski,* (19th c.). Engraving on paper, from The Kosciuszko Foundation Inc. rchives, New York.

From a print by A. Oleszczynski engraved by W. Hall, *Kosciuszko*, engraving on paper, from The Kosciuszko Foundation Inc. Archives, New York.

(Below) Bulhakowna, photographer, *Silver Engraved Gift from Bristol.*

n Matejko (1838-1893). *Stanislaw August Poniatowski,* reproduction, from The Kosciuszko
undation Inc. Archives, New York.

Bonneville, F. del. -J.B. Compagrue sculpt., *Kosciuszko General de L'Armee Revolutionaire Polonaise en 1792* ca 1830, engraving on paper, from The Kosciuszko Foundation Inc. Archives, New York.

Maurnier, *Kosciuszko* ca 1826, engraving on paper, from The Kosciuszko Foundation Inc. Archives, New York.

intierely and to have nothing to do with any article whatsoever [that] belong[ed] to L[t] Col Laurence."[24]

While desiring nothing for himself, Kościuszko did take the time to petition Greene on behalf of two other people. "I recomend to you two negroes belong[ing] to L[t] C[ol] Laurence," he explained, "that they may have part [of his clothing as] they are nacked they want shirts & jackets [and] Breeches and their skin can bear as well as ours good things."[25] A fervent philosophical democrat, Kościuszko was by this time well aware of the existence of slavery in America, a custom of which he thoroughly disapproved. While at West Point, Gen. John Paterson provided Kościuszko with one of his slaves, Agrippa Hull, to act as the engineer's servant. The Pole apparently became quite close to Hull, treating him as a free man would be treated and generally enjoying his company. When transferred south, he asked and received permission to take Hull with him. There the Pole came face to face with the worst situations of human bondage, conditions he was not averse to criticizing. In this he was not alone for there is reported to have been much anti-slavery sentiment in Greene's army and the general himself once advocated enlisting blacks into his army. "That they would make good soldiers I have no doubt," the general believed, provided they were treated "in all respects as other Soldiers." Lewis Morris, Kościuszko's friend and Greene's aide, spoke for many when he expressed sorrow for "the poor unhappy blacks who, to the disgrace of human nature, are subject to every species of oppression while we are contending for the rights and liberties of mankind."[26] On another occasion, Kościuszko explained his philosophy of human relations to Greene, explaining to the general that he prefered not to contract the sphere of his friends by limiting it only to those like himself: "Are we ought to like only our Compatriots, not allowance to be made for one sort of Strangers; from your Philosophical turn of mind I would expect of enlarging the limits of our affection contracted by prejudice and superstition towards the rest of mankind, and more so for whom we have a Sincier Esteem, let him be Turck or Polander, American or Japon."[27]

Another consequence of Laurens's untimely death was a change in Kościuszko's assignment. With little to do while the army was in camp, the engineer apparently lobbied for transfer to a more active post. His opportunity came when Greene assigned him to replace Laurens in command of the advanced post at Ashley Ferry, six miles closer to Charleston than Greene's latest encampment. There the commanding general entrusted the Pole with two squads of dragoons from Lee's Legion and a force of infantry from the Delaware and Pennsylvania Continental Line to conduct scouting activities, interdict contraband destined for the British in Charleston, develop any intelligence he could about the British forces and activities in Charleston, and hinder as much as possible any enemy detachments operating in the area.[28] This assignment as a line officer provided him for the first time with an opportunity to lead troops in battle.

For his intelligence activities, Kościuszko developed a number of contacts with patriots living in Charleston, frequently using as spies and intermediaries several blacks who shuttled back and forth between his post and the city. Particularly useful for this purpose was an intelligent messenger named Prince who made trips into the city to deliver communiques to patriot residents and gather intelligence for Greene's army. Among the contacts in the city, Edmund Petrie's name is known, but the others appear in the surviving documentation only by initials such as W., P. and X.[29]

While these people risked their lives for the cause of the revolution, and Greene's soldiers often went without even the basic necessities of life, others sought to profit from the hostilities by selling supplies and provisions to the British in Charleston. So pronounced was this that South Carolina Governor John Mathews described it as "infamous traffic carried on by persons who will contribute nothing for the army, because they can get an enormous price, and the cash, for what they send to town."[30] The interdiction of this illicit trade required intelligence, constant vigilance, and the proper use of force. On one occasion, after seizing a number of cattle owned by a man named Youngblood who was apparently engaged in smuggling the animals into the city, Kościuszko jokingly commented "Let be young or old Blood it is very bad one to furnish such quantity of Ca[t]tle for the Ennemys."[31]

Gen. Anthony Wayne, who returned to the army after the British evacuated Savannah on July 11, was appalled to find Greene's troops "experiencing every possible distress for want of provision, even of the meanest kind."[32] Yet Wayne proved to be part of the problem that resulted in the shortages afflicting the American army. The general's liberal dispensing of passes to the local inhabitants made it very difficult to interdict traffic conducted under this official sanction. In one incident reported by Kościuszko, two ladies journeyed into Charleston loaded with turkeys, geese, and "Fouls of every kind in great Plenty with 10 or 12 Buchel of rice with the pass from General Wayne and as you ordered to raport only I have let her pass."[33] To Kościuszko's mind, this made a "joke" of attempts to cut off the flow of supplies and provisions, and cast him in the role of overbearing military authority. Such a situation, he complained to Greene, would "serve only to expose me to the Hatred of the inhabitants, [because] if I stop according to your orders every provision Boat and General Waine will have exclusif power to gives passes. Every one will suppose that my ill natured disposition rather or interested wue [view] governe me and favorise one more than the other, the People will be apte to thinck so and I woute [would] of the other too in the same circumstance."[34]

In late September Kościuszko became aware of beef again being smuggled into Charleston. "I hope we can discover what persons are" involved, he wrote to Greene, but he also feared that members of the army might be involved which would create a negative "Reflection upon" the army.[35] Soon after, the colonel reprimanded a quartermaster officer, possibly for involvement in the same activity, telling him to "thing [your]self as in the arrest and I will ask the General for the Court Martial."[36] But the affair did not end there. Soon, information surfaced which appeared to implicate Gen. Wayne himself. While the general vigorously denied any involvement, his liberal dispensing of passes no doubt contributed to the difficulties.[37]

Yet, it appears Kościuszko himself was not above trading items for his own comfort. In early September he informed Greene that he would make every attempt to stop large-scale transactions, but would not interfere with those who sought to trade a "few small articles to buy sugar and coffee for the family use."[38] In this vein, the Pole wrote Dr. Read: "I Expected Supply of Coffee from Charlestown but Could not get, and this news was brod. Yesterday to my great mortification now you must return me to a sick because I cannot live without Coffee and I propose to trouble you with it and to begin I beg you to Send me Six pound of Coffee, with Sugar in proportion, that surprise you I see but when I have the pleasure of Seeing you at my Quarters I Convince you of the necessity that I Should be well. God bless you and your family."[39]

While some in Charleston attempted to purchase, barter, or smuggle supplies and provisions, the British garrison also staged various forays aimed a procuring what they needed from the countryside. To prevent this, Kościuszko undertook the third part of his mission as a field commander. He fought a successful skirmish near Quarter House in which his troops ambushed a force of Tory dragoons, killing several without loss to his own troops. Along with other pressure, this action may have led the British to evacuate that post on August 4. Four days later, Kościuszko wrote to Williams to acknowledge a letter and inform his friend of recent events. "I recv'd yours with great pleasure as you Could expect from the person who have re[c]all friendship not intervowing with the interested wue. The Ennemys will leave Charlestown in two month time at farthest they embark the Canon and the Bagage—the Quarter House is Evacuated four days ago, ho[w]ever they made advance post near Shubrick house three mill from the Town."[40]

In early September, Kościuszko's force was increased with the addition of the St. Andrew's Company of militia which Gov. Mathews ordered "to wait on Col. Kosciuszko for his particular orders."[41] On September 10, having observed a small party of the enemy approaching on the other side of the river to reconnoitre on three successive evenings, the colonel led a patrol across the river to try and capture the enemy, but there is no account of any contact on this occasion.[42]

Eight days later Kościuszko advised Greene that British troops were moving up the Cooper River, while on the 20th he asked Greene's permission to attack an enemy force on James Island. Again in early November he returned to James Island where he captured about sixty excellent horses, once again without loss to his own men, but sparking a controversy with state authorities. Since some of the horses were claimed by South Carolinians who said they had been carried off by the British, state authorities attempted to intervene and prevent the auction of the livestock as provided by Congressional law. Greene called a council of war, including Kościuszko, which affirmed his interpretation of the law, but recognizing that some people might have legitimate claims he instructed his quartermaster, Lt. Col. Edward Carrington, to "dispose of the horses taken by Colonel Kosciuszko and demanded by the Council of this State. In the sale you shall notify the purchasers that should any of the horses prove to be formerly the property of inhabitants of this state and they should lay claim to them, and Congress determines that their right of post limin[i]um shall extend to property under such circumstances they must be given up to them and the purchase money will be returned by the public Agents."[43]

The colonel led a detachment against a British force that landed at Dill's Bluff on James Island on October 23,[44] and in another skirmish on November 4.[45] Ten days later, Kościuszko, with Capt. William Wilmot, Lt. John Markland, and about 60 other men attempted to surprise a party of British cutting wood near Fort Johnson on James Island. Knowing from observing the British routine that they generally appeared around daylight, Kościuszko moved his men cautiously forward about 2:00 a.m. to take up positions before the enemy arrived. When the British dragoons appeared at the anticipated hour, the Americans received them with a volley from the cover of their positions that caused some loss and drove them back in disorder. Forming his men for the attack, Kościuszko led them forward in pursuit until he ran into the British infantry advance. After a sharp skirmish the redcoats retreated, but the closer to the fort they came the more reinforcements arrived until the Americans found themselves opposed by nearly 300 men and a field piece. Leading his men in the midst of the fray, a ball shattered a spontoon in Kosciuszko's hand, four more balls pierced his coat, and a British dragoon closed in on the colonel. As the redcoat raised his sword, William Fuller, a young civilian volunteer, shot the trooper from his saddle, possibly saving the Pole's life. Unable to advance any further, Kościuszko retired in good order, but lost Capt. Wilmot killed, Lt. Moore mortally wounded, and three other men.[46]

As the days turned into weeks, the British gradually contracted their lines closer to Charleston, leaving many local residents in fear of plunder by both armies should the British eventually evacuate. "The Inhabitants upon the Neck and in Charles Town," Kościuszko informed Greene, are "very much allarmed and affraid to be plundered by the Ennemys and by our people. I assured them of our Army that they will Loose not a pin but I cannot say of the militia if they go first. I mentioned that you will pay particular attention so far as will be in your power to prevent any desorder of any Troops."[47]

On December 6 the colonel expressed his own frustration to Greene, fearing that if the British did not evacuate Charleston soon they would probably not do so until the following spring, which would mean another difficult winter in the camps outside the city. "I wish I was mistaken in my opinion," he confided, "that if the Ennemys not goes today or tomorow they will not go till next Spring."

But as he wrote, information arrived that the enemy was preparing to evacuate. "Hura and again Hura," he excitedly concluded. "[J]ust now I recive inteligence from James Island that all are going tomorow but I will know more sure this day wich I will comunicat to [you] immediately."[48]

But another week of waiting remained. Finally, on December 14, Gen. Leslie withdrew his remaining outposts into Charleston, marched his men to Gadsden's wharf at the foot of Calhoun Street, and embarked the last British force in the South onto the waiting transports. With him went some 4,000 Loyalists and about 5,000 slaves forcibly removed by their Tory owners. At 11:00 a.m. Gen. Anthony Wayne occupied Charleston. Among the first to enter was Col. Kościuszko at the head of his small command.[49]

With the evacuation complete, Mrs. Greene suggested a grand ball to celebrate the occasion. A close friend of Kościuszko, she drafted the colonel to help her plan the event and decorate the building. Given the season, Kościuszko used the available magnolia leaves, complementing them with paper cut-outs resembling the summer flowers of the region. All reports indicate a merry time was had by all.[50]

Despite the British withdrawal, work remained. With his army desperate for provisions, Greene ordered Kościuszko to lead an armed force to bring in rice from the surrounding plantations. The colonel found what should have been a fairly easy task greatly complicated by the refusal of the local people or the state government to cooperate. Instead of being grateful to the army, they now considered it a nuisance and a potential threat to their liberties. "The former [are] not willing to go," he explained to Greene, while "the later [has] not taken proper measure.... The Public affaires seames to be not very much at heart, reluctance in spit[e] of many shows her impire."[51] Greatly deploring this attitude, Kościuszko lamented to Otho Williams that "hospitality in this Country was in alliance in many parishes with the interested wue [view] wich after the Evacuation of Charles Town by the Britysh, died and to wich was erected very pompeus Thomb with the butifull inscription Never rise again."[52]

To enforce discipline and keep the army together, Greene moved the troops to James Island, a location Kościuszko proclaimed a "butifull and healthy place." Comfortable quarters, a very mild winter, new clothing, and regular provisions greatly improved the health and morale of the men. The officers found it easy to obtain passes to go into town, many of them dining there with Gen. Greene and his wife. Kościuszko was a frequent visitor to the Greene household throughout the winter and spring.[53]

Despite the easier lifestyle, Kościuszko appears to have come down with a serious fever which kept him from duty for some time. Residing at the Scott home, he found the owners very solicitous of his health, treating him "wyth afection, friendship and nurs[ing]" him "like their [own] Child."[54] Although the illness soon passed, it apparently caused some concern to Gen. and Mrs. Greene, both of whom wrote and inquired about his health. "Your the lest uneasiness for my health would be to make me more sick," Kościuszko replied to Mrs. Greene.[55] "I am sorry that I was the object of uneasiness in your breast," he told the general, "your generous attention of your Friends health, make me more alarming of yours, of wich all care ought to be taken, I had fears of the fever but today I am prety well and expect to come over tomorow very early."[56]

During April another small crisis arose that presaged the states' rights controversy which would erupt in civil war some eighty years later. When a British officer and two Loyalists were allowed into Charleston under a flag of truce, the city sheriff, acting on orders of the state's governor, placed the three in jail. Greene, offended that men under his protection would thus be jailed, complained to Governor Benjamin Guerard that the Articles of Confederation "vests in Congress the sole power in all matters relating to War and Peace." The governor replied that since no enemy troops remained in South Carolina, such matters as flags of truce became internal concerns under the authority of the state. Greene convened a council of war to discuss the issue, including among its members, Gen. Wayne, Gen. Gist, Kościuszko, and several other officers. The council agreed entirely with Greene's interpetation. Eventually, under threat of military action, the South Carolina authorities backed down and released the three prisoners. Greene, however, sent all of the documents relating to the episode to Congress with the comment that South Carolina appeared to have little attachment to the United States and to be steering a course of separatism.[57]

On April 11 Kościuszko, jestingly refered to by his friends in the Southern Army as the "Count of Poland," accompanied Greene on an inspection of Fort Moultrie. Five days later news arrived that preliminary agreements had been reached to end the war on the basis of American independence. Celebrations, fireworks, and congratulations filled the next few days.[58]

Within a few short weeks, many of the officers began to return to civilian life, while those who remained wrote to friends, went for rides in the country, and dined with each other or with local families. Somewhere around the first of June, Kościuszko boarded a ship, accompanied by Mrs. Greene and Capt. William Pierce, for Philadelphia.[59] Behind him in the Southern Department he left a record of faithful service and achievement. Col. David Humphreys described him as "expert" in all of the various responsibilities of a military officer, "to change the front, retreat, advance, and judge of ground with military glance."[60] Kościuszko's close friend John Armstrong affirmed that the Pole "rendered the most important services to the last moment of the war" which elicited from Gen. Greene "the most lively, ardent, repeated acknowledgements."[61] The greatest accolade, however, came from the person in the best position to appraise Kościuszko's role in the Southern Campaigns, his commanding officer. In 1783 Greene wrote the following to General William Irvine:

Among the most useful and agreeable of my companions in arms, was Colonel Kosciuszko. Nothing could exceed his zeal for the public service, nor in the prosecution of various objects that presented themselves in our small but active warfare, could anything be more useful than his attention, vigilance and industry. In promoting my views to whatever department of the service directed, he was at all times, a ready and able assistant. One in a word whom no pleasure could seduce, no labor fatigue and no danger deter. What besides greatly distinguished him was an unparalleled modesty and entire unconsciousness of having done anything extraordinary. Never making a claim or pretension for himself and never omitting to distinguish and commend the merits of others. This able and gallant soldier has now left us for the North; intending to return directly to his own country, where he cannot fail to be soon and greatly distinguished.[62]

Chapter 11

"The Best Engineer of the Continental Army"

*T*he ship carrying Kościuszko and his travelling companions north arrived in Philadelphia during the first half of June, 1783. As he stepped from the wooden decks to the dock, the colonel had two items of business to conduct with Congress before he could pursue his desire to return to his native land. First, having foregone personal advancement during the war, he sought a long-overdue promotion, not wishing to await the inevitable brevet advances sure to be distributed before the army mustered out of service. To garner support for his claim he visited Gen. Benjamin Lincoln, then the Secretary of War. On August 18 the general wrote to Congress on the Pole's behalf:

> At the close of the Campaign of 1781, Congress, from a conviction of the services and merits of General Du Portail, and of the other Gentlemen, officers in the Engineering department, gave them promotions, in the army of the United States. At that time Colonel Kosciuszko, who is among the oldest Colonels in our service (his Commission is dated 18 October 1776) was with General Greene, who has made the most honorable mention of his services to Congress, they have been such from his first entering into our service, as to gain the notice and applause of all under whom he has served. I beg leave therefore to mention him to Congress as a highly deserving officer and hope that the same regard to merit which procured the promotion of the greatest part, if not all, of his brother officers in the Engineering department will operate in his favor so far that he may be promoted to the rank of Brigadier General.[1]

Once read, Congress referred the letter to the appropriate committee where it languished for weeks. Meanwhile, Kościuszko took up his second issue with Congress—his financial accounts. During the war pay was infrequent, leaving men and officers alike in often destitute circumstances. At the close of hostilities, cries arose for payment of past debts, leading some to propose a march on Congress if their demands were not met. Though not of this radical group, Kościuszko nevertheless sought payment of the accumulated debts owed him. Since he had not drawn his normal pay during the war, the amount owed him was substantial by the standards of the day. On March 22, 1783, Congress voted to pay the outstanding debts to military and naval officers by issuing certificates of indebtedness and grants of western lands. Eventually, his service would yield the Pole some 500 acres of land and $12,000. Future promises, however, were of little avail to Kościuszko who, planning to return to Europe, sought payment in cash to cover the expenses of his proposed journey and, no doubt, his debts in Poland.[2]

For assistance, Kościuszko turned to his friend Nathaniel Greene.

> The enxiety I have of going to my country, as I will be of no further service here by the Peace so happily obtained, induce me to request you the favor, wich will be per haps the last.
>
> In setling my accounts I forsee and aprehend will be tedious and difficult mater without your recomendation to the Financier and the President of Congress wich I would beg you was of such nature that they could setled with me the Pay what is due, and what Congress resolv'd for half pay wich is five years pay in ready money if possible.
>
> It gives me sensible pain that I am forced by unruly Chance of nature to write to you upon the subject, wich irrited even the disposition of thought of the thing.[3]

Greene agreed to contact Elias Boudinot, then President of the Continental Congress, on the Pole's behalf. At the same time, the general wrote to Kościuszko, counseling the shy colonel that his best opportunity for fast settlement of his claims would be, in effect, to make a pest of himself with Congress.

> [R]epeated application may obtain what no influence can effect. I know your modesty and feel your difficulty on this head; but unless you persist I am appre[he]nsive nothing will be done in the matter. For once you must force nature and get the better of that independent pride which is our best support in many Situations, and urge your suit from the necessity of the case which may accomplish the business;

and without which I have too much reason to apprehend a disappoint-ment. Political bodies act not from feeling so much as policy; but if they find there is no other way of getting rid of an application which has become troublesome they will grant the thing altho[ugh] against policy. I only offer these remarks to your consideration. Your own feeling must determine your conduct in the matter. In human life we are in a state of probation, and for the trial of our virtues mortification is sometimes necessary. Be not discouraged therefore because you dont succeed at once; nor drop your application from little obstacles.[4]

Though the advice was probably sound, the conduct called for was antithetical to Kościuszko's nature. While he decided to wait on Congress for their action, he did not push himself forward other than asking the intercession of Greene and other friends. Unable to put aside his natural modesty, without state authorities to push for his promotion or the politics of the French alliance acting in his favor, his only hope of support lay with the friends he had made in the army.

About this time a threatened mutiny of the Pennsylvania Line over the continued lack of pay forced Congress to abandon Philadelphia for Princeton. Kościuszko followed in the hope of securing his aims, but instead Congress assigned him to prepare the fireworks for its celebration of the anniversary of national independence on July 4. The Pole had planned to meet his friend Otho Williams in Elizabe-thtown on July 4, but felt compelled to accept the assignment. To Williams he wrote on July 2:

Congress having intention to make Illumination on the forth of July, they have made Choise of me as nobody is beter for the execution of it, it was in vain to say that I was ingaged to go to Elisabeth Town, to join my friend. They insisted upon, judge but favorably that is not my fault, that I will be not able to see you onles [unless] you Come her[e] and join to celebrate the festivity. I [am] afraid you condemn in your self my disposition or rather fickle temper, but you will do wrong if you think so, the witness is [Major William] Jackson that my write [right] foot was forward as to the left foot it is true she was behand [behind]. I do not know how Philosopher will argue upon the occasion and will decide wether the heart was with the write foot and the reason with the left, true it is that I was overpowered with Thousand stoffs [stuffs] and promised them to stay[.] ... [T]his morning the ... famous Heroe of Savana [Savannah] made his apearence and gon[e] to Philadelphia. Give my Compliments to all my acquientence at west point particularly to General Washington, Colo Nicolas, Colo Jackson, Colo Brooks and Mrs. Brooks, tell her that I come [to] see her when ever she will be able to receive me in a Silk Gown.[5]

The celebrations complete, Kościuszko continued to wait, hopeful that Greene's intervention would be helpful. The general, true to his word, wrote to Elias Boudinot, President of Congress, on the Pole's behalf. "Col. Kosciuszko," wrote Greene,

who has been our chief engineer in the Southern department and with the Northern army at the taking [of] Burgoyne; and whose zeal and activity have been equalled by few, and exceeded by none, has it in contemplation to return to Europe. To enable him to do this and bring his affairs with the Public to a close in this Country, he wishes to have such pay and emoluments, as be is entitled to from the rank he holds in the Army, and the service he has performed for the accomplishing [of] our independence, put on such a footing, as to enable him to reduce it all to ready money. From his peculiar situation, I beg leave to recommend his case to Congress, and, if the thing be practicable, that the financier be desired to settle and accomodate the matter with him.

My friendship for the Colonel must apologize for the singularity of this recomendation. My feelings are warmly interested in his favor, but I pressume not to judge of the difficulties attending the business.[6]

Expecting to visit Philadelphia himself in September, Greene promised Kościuszko he would pursue the matter in person then. Still believing, however, that the Pole intended to return to Europe at any time, Greene wished him the best and encouraged him to write whenever possible. He closed by thanking Kościuszko for the "zeal with which you served the public under my command and for your friendly disposition towards me. My warmest approbation is due to you as an officer and my particular acknowledgments as a friend."[7]

Unwilling to make any precedent-setting decisions, especially in view of the widespread clamor for payment of Revolutionary debts, Congress forwarded Greene's letter to Robert Morris, Superintendent of Finance, who answered Greene in glowing terms. "That young Gentleman's acknowledged Merit and Services joined to your warm Interposition in his favor excite my sincerest Wish to render the adjustment of his affairs equal to his most sanguine Expectations." Despite the warm endorsement, however, Morris feared "the Danger of excepting Individuals out of the general Rules," explaining to Greene that in any case the matter was really out of his hands. "This my Dear Sir, is a Thing which I cannot do but Congress may[.] Should they think proper to make a special Order on the Occasion I shall be very happy to carry it into Execution."[8] A law passed in 1781, Morris pointed out, stipulated that foreign officers were to be paid off with one-fifth of the amount due in cash and four-fifths on credit with interest. "That the merit of Col. Kosciuszko is great and acknowledged," Morris concluded, "application must be placed among those which are not to be declined unless for the most cogent Reasons and even insurmountable obstacles. But that if it be complied with other officers of Merit[,] Talents and Zeal will doubtless make similar applications."[9]

Congress agreed with Morris, placing Kościuszko's request with others subject to the law of 1781. Nor would it agree to pay immediately that portion due under the law's provisions, for the Treasury was in financial distress and could not accommodate even the reduced cash payment called for in the law. Given the situation, the treatment of Kościuszko's request might appear understandable if all were considered equally as Morris argued. Yet, in October when Gen. du Portail requested payment of the debts owed him and his French colleagues—Lt. Col. Jean Baptiste Obrey de Gouvion and Col. Jean Baptiste Joseph, Chevalier de Laumoy—Congress approved the complete balance in four days, and in six more days the three men had both their money and free passage to Europe at government expense. Clearly, the French were once more an exception to the rules that governed everyone else.[10]

With his planned departure thus delayed, Kościuszko returned to Philadelphia where he continued to write to his friends. In late September Greene arrived. Kościuszko accompanied him to Trenton where they met Washington, all three then continuing on to Princeton together. There the men dined with Boudinot, but this seemed to have little effect on Kościuszko's requests. His claims for payment placed on hold, he decided to leave once again for Philadelphia, but before doing so he determined to make a last attempt to secure his elusive promotion. During the war Kościuszko, unlike most of his fellow Continental officers, refrained from pushing himself forward for honor and promotion. Rather, to Otho Williams he shared his thoughts on the great reward he found in the success of their mutual cause: "O! how happy we think our Self when Conscious of our deeds, that were started from principle of rectitude, from conviction of the goodness of the thing itself, from motive of the good that will Come to Human Kind."[11] Now that the war was ending, Kościuszko's motivation in pushing for promotion was his desire to avoid the anonymity of being included in the general brevet promotions soon to be approved. To avoid this "oblivion," he penned a letter to Washington asking for the general's intercession on behalf of his promotion.

> General Lincoln was pleased to recommend me to Congress and requested them to promote me to the Ranck of Brygadier General, which by the date of the Commission I hold he thought I was intitled to long ago.
>
> Your Excellency will forgive me the Liberty I take in troubling you in this affair, Unacquiented as Congress may be out of my Services, but the different promotions already granted to many, Made me fearfull of puting me at last in the oblivion List of a General promotion.
>
> One word from your Excellency to Congress in my favor [if I can flater my self to obtain it] will Clear the doubt and rise my hope to certainty.[12]

"I heartily wish your application to meet with success," Washington replied.[13] To Congress, the commanding general recommended Kościuszko's promotion, noting that "from my knowledge of his merit and service and the concurrent testimony of all who knew him I cannot but recommend him as deserving the favor of Congress."[14] But even this small honor was to be denied. Before the endorsements of Lincoln and Washington could be acted upon, Congress passed a bill on September 20 granting a brevet promotion of one rank to all officers who had not been promoted since January 1, 1777. When Kościuszko's case finally came under review, the examining committee refused to take action since the bill on brevet promotions "has already effected the promotion of Col. Kosciosko to the Rank of Brigadier General; [therefore] nothing further on that subject can with propriety be done at this time." The only concessions Congress was willing to make were to acknowledge that the Committee was "deeply impressed with the great merit and beneficial services of that officer" and to propose a resolution "That the Secretary at War transmit to Colonel Kosciosko the brevet commission of brigadier general; and signify to that officer, that Congress entertain an high sense of his long, faithful and meritorious service."[15] But even this meaningless gesture was tempered by the concerns of some that recognition of one individual might open the door to such recognition of others. Where the original version of the resolution sought to commend Kościuszko for his "great merit," the final version deleted the word "great." Similarly, where the draft spoke of his "beneficial services," the resulting resolution spoke only of "service."[16]

Undoubtedly disappointed, the Pole appears, in his surviving letters, to have refrained from any comment. Instead, he remained on duty in the general vicinity of Washington's headquarters, apparently moving north with the general when he moved his headquarters to Newburg along the Hudson River in New York. At some point before his departure for Europe the commanding general bestowed upon him the personal gift of a sword and a set of pistols. The former, its blade inscribed "America cum Vashington suo Amico T. Kosciusconi," would eventually be preserved in the National Museum in Warsaw. The mahogany pistols, ornamented in gold and bronze, their barrels inscribed "G. Washington 17 E Pluribus Unum 83 Th. Kosciuszko," were preserved in the National Museum in Kraków.[17]

Another honor from his fellow-soldiers came with induction into the Society of the Cincinnati. Formed at Newburgh, New York, on May 10, 1783, at the suggestion of Gen. Henry Knox, the Society brought together officers who wished to promote remembrance of the Revolution and the comradeship of their wartime friends. It honored the spirit of the citizen soldier by deriving its name from Lucius Quintius Cincinnatus, a Roman who twice answered the call to leave his farm and save Rome, returning to his agrarian home once the crises had passed. Its philosophical ideals were expressed in the motto "Omnia reliquit servare Rempublicam" [He left all to serve the Republic]. Kościuszko's signature appears on the original roll of the society, to which he donated one month's pay as an initiation fee.[18]

When Washington made his triumphal entry into New York City on November 25, 1783, Kościuszko was with him. On December 4, the same day the last British ships departed from New York Harbor, Washington met his officers at Fraunces' Tavern on Broad Street to bid them farewell.[19] "With a heart full of love and gratitude," Washington began, his voice choking with emotion, "I now take leave of you. I most devotedly wish that your later days may be as prosperous and happy as your former ones have been glorious and honorable. I cannot come to each of you, but shall feel obliged if each of you will come and take me by the hand."[20] One by one they passed in silence, exchanging an embrace, the tears streaming down their sad faces. Among the many who gathered for this memorable occasion was Tadeusz Kościuszko. When his turn came to embrace his commanding general, the stately Virginian removed from his finger a cameo ring of the Society of the Cincinnati and placed it on Kościuszko's finger as a personal tribute to his services in the cause of American independence.

From New York, the Pole traveled to Newport, Rhode Island, for an extended visit with Nathaniel Greene and his family. While there, comrades-in-arms from the Southern Army and Greene's earlier service with Washington stopped to visit, giving Kościuszko an opportunity to bid farewell to many friends and meet others he may not to that point have known. According to one of Greene's earlier biographers, the Greene home was vibrant with some of the most famous personalities of the era. "Lafayette passed pleasant days, talking hopefully of the future of his France, ... Steuben told entertaining stories of the Great Frederick, ... Kosciusko painted in imperfect English the wrongs of Poland, and [Rev. William] Gordon questioned the actors in the scenes which his homely but honest pen was busily recording for posterity."[21]

From Rhode Island, Kościuszko journeyed south once again. Haiman believes he attended a national meeting of the Society of the Cincinnati in Philadelphia from May 1 through May 18, a meeting also attended by Greene whom the Pole probably accompanied south. While in Philadelphia Kościuszko no doubt pursued payment of his much overdue debts from Congress. When eventually settled, he received a certificate of indebtedness for $12,280.49, with interest payable at six per cent from January 1, 1784. In addition, he also received 500 acres of land located along the Scioto River in Ohio where the city of Columbus now stands.[22] Harboring no bitterness at the delay in receiving his due, Kościuszko offered his appreciation to Robert Morris: "Your generous behavior towards me, so intirely took hold of my heart that forgeting your uncommon delicat feelings, I am force, by a great uneasiness of my mind, to present my warmest thanks to you, before I quit this country; and to assure you that your kindness will be always fresh in my memory with the gratitude I owe you, and shall endeavour to put in practice what susceptibility now sugest the means to adopt."[23]

His finances at last secured, though not yet actually paid, Kościuszko left Philadelphia on July 9 for New York where he planned to
take ship for Europe. His remarkable military career in America
concluded, Kościuszko corresponded with his many friends. To John
Armstrong, anticipating a return to his suffering homeland and
satisfied with the new nation he helped create, the Pole wrote: "If
the state of my Country remains always the same I will say to my
countrymen, 'Come, pass over the seas, and insure your children
liberty and property.' If my countrymen do not listen to me I will
say to my family, 'Come.' If my family refuse, I will go by myself
and die free with you."[24]

"At last the necessity force me to quit this Country," he wrote to
Otho Williams the same day he left Philadelphia, "you may be sure
with great reluctance, as I have so many acquiantence amongst the
number, some are very valuable friends, for whom no boundary can
be afixed of my affection."[25] Taking the opportunity afforded by his
remaining few days in America, he continued to write to his American comrades-in-arms, thanking them for their friendship, wishing
them well, and asking them to write him in Europe. One of the last
missives went to Greene:

> The principal of propryety inculcated in my early age have so
> strong hold of my feelings, that, to act against inward conviction
> make[s] me very unhappy indeed.
>
> As I must part, give me Leave to present my Sinsier thanks to you
> both, for so generous hospitality I experienced in your house, for so
> much interesting your self in my favor, and for your friendship for
> me, your delicat feelings forbids me to express my Greatitude, and
> the wishes of my heart[.] I leave to the strogle of my inward emotion;
> and the practice, to time; whenever uportunity will presents its self
> without Knowledge to you.
>
> The Separation must be very sensible to a Person of susceptible
> mind and more so when the affection with Esteem links to the person
> of Merit. I expect ho[w]ever that you will do me the honor to write
> me, it will be the only satisfaction I may yet enjoy by absence, and
> sure you will not deny me that. Farewell my dear General once more
> farewell, be as happy as my bosoom will augur for you, Let me Shook
> here you by the hand by my delusive imagination as you should be
> present in Person and seal our friendship for each other for ever.[26]

During seven years of constant service from 1776 through 1783,
Kościuszko took only one leave of absence, the brief time he spent

at Traveler's Rest with Gen. Gates's dying son. He was always loyal to his commanding officers, speaking highly of St. Clair, Gates, and Greene both in private letters and, when occasion permitted, in public forums. Kościuszko was also a humane officer who readily gained the friendship of his colleagues, cared for the needs of his men, sought to relieve the suffering of British prisoners, and did what he could to better the plight of the slaves he encountered.[27]

Surrounded by some of his Revolutionary friends, Kościuszko departed from New York for Paris on July 15, 1784, aboard the *Courrier de l'Europe*.[28] Behind him he left many enduring friendships and a legacy of selfless service that insured his enduring fame as, according to historian Lynn Montross, author of *The Story of the Continental Army 1775-1783*, "the best engineer of the Continental Army."[29]

Chapter 12

"Faithful to the Polish Nation"

*D*uring Kościuszko's lengthy sojourn in America his family and friends in Poland received little information concerning his whereabouts and well-being. After receiving an initial letter from Kościuszko when he reached America in 1776, Prince Czartoryski heard nothing else for two years. Finally, despairing of his friend's safety, the prince asked his contacts in Paris to make inquiries with Benjamin Franklin. In 1781, Anna Estko enlisted the support of Princess Sapieha in an attempt to solicit information on her brother through the princess's family connections to the French court. By the end of the year the Chevalier de Luzerne was able to report that

> Some of our officers returned from America after the glorious York expedition, and they told me that they Saw him and that at present he is with General de Grasse in Virginia, that he performed functions of an engineer there, that he was occupied with building of a few small forts, and that, it seems, they are very well satisfied with him in the army, where he won recognition for his good conduct. I am very glad, Princess, to be able to give you much welcome news about a person in which you are evidently interested; in the near future he will return to his country with American laurels.[1]

This passage led some researchers to speculate that Kościuszko saw service at Yorktown. More probably, since there is a reference to constructing "a few small forts," some French officers met Kościuszko while he was engaged in this activity in North Carolina.

Early the following year the Estkos made additional inquiries to Franklin for information when Józef Kościuszko's creditors, aware of the rumors of his brother's death in far-off America, attempted to seize Tadeusz's portion of the family estate to satisfy his brother's accumulated debts. Under the circumstances, confirmation of Tadeusz's safety was essential. Again in October, 1783, Anna Estko contacted Benjamin Franklin in Paris with an urgent inquiry about her brother. Franklin wrote to America for news and Gen. Nathaniel Greene replied that Kościuszko was well, had left the Southern Army and was planning to return directly to Poland.[2] Although Greene's assurance that Kościsuzko would soon be leaving for Poland was somewhat premature, this word from America was a welcome reassurance to his relatives.

Meanwhile, the wandering patriot finally reached the shores of Europe in the summer of 1784. From Paris he wrote to Otho Williams, seemingly still rejoicing at the success of the American Revolution while at the same time already missing his North American friends and fearing for the future of his homeland. "Can you believe that I am very unhappy been [i.e., being] absent from your Country, it seems to me the other world here, in which every parson finds great pleasure in cheating himself out of Common sense. Time may have some power to preposses my mind in your Countrys favour, and adopt the opinion of greater number of men, bot Nature more, it is in every breast, here they take great pains to subside thos[e] Charmes which Constitute real happiness, but you fol[l]ow with full speed the marked road, and you find by experience that domestick life with liberty to be the best gift, that nature had to bestow for the human species. Tomorrow I am going to Poland and with some reluctance as I am informed by one of my Countryman that the affairs of the republick, as well as mine are in very horrid Situation, you shall know it in my next. I am prepared for the worst."[3]

When he finally returned to his native land that fall, Kościuszko resided on the family estate at Siechnowice which his relatives had somehow saved from his brother Józef's many creditors. There he settled into a routine of gardening, reading, and visiting with family, friends, and neighbors who came to renew their acquaintance. His greatest pleasures seem to have been trading visits with his sister Anna's family and tending his garden. But retirement was not an untroubled life. Though rich in honors from his American service, his financial situation remained difficult. Interest on the money owed him in America, which he counted on for his support, did not arrive and the modest yield of the Polish estate was not sufficient for its upkeep. In September, 1787, he wrote to Congress complaining that despite its promises he had not received any remittance in three years. Congress referred the letter to the Treasury, which sent him the interest for only a single year, something over $700. Though this helped to ease his financial situation somewhat, monetary problems continued.[4] To another friend he wrote:

> What is about your Congress do writ[e] me. It is not famous, that to this date according to the Certificates given to the officers dont chuse to pay, nether the interest nor the somme due to them. I do not speak for myself, but I heard great many complains, and ill languages of my beloved Country, her reputation is dear to me, and I suffer myself more than great many in Congress perhaps. For God sake writ[e] to your friends in Congress, I suppose you heard great deal in Paris yourself not to be convinced of the propriety in discharging the debt. My respecte to Mrs. Greene, Moris[s] of Charlestown, and my love to Williams, Armstrong and if is living to Gates.[5]

During this time he met Tekla Żurowska, the eighteen-year-old daughter of a member of the landed gentry, became enamored, but was once again thwarted in his quest for marriage by the young lady's father. The empty home, continuing financial problems, the lack of opportunities to serve his homeland because of Russian dominance, and infrequent word from his friends in America all plagued Kościuszko for several years after his homecoming.[6] His frustration is evident in letters to his sister Anna and his former commanding officer, Nathaniel Greene. "Be sure," he confided to the former, "that nothing keeps me here in Poland, but you."[7] To Greene he was equally blunt:

> It surprise me very much that to this time, I have not one line from you, I am alarmed and my friendship for you puts Thousands disagreables thoughts into my head. Who knows, you may be sick or dead, ... perhaps you have forgot me as I am no more in your Country.... Do write me, my dear General, of the Situation of your Country, because I heard many bad things; ho[w]ever when our King has asked me, I gave him the best description I could. Write me of yourself, of your family, and of my friends. As to myself am in good health, something richer, but very inhappy of the situation of my Country which I believe *nulla redemptio* as well as I am, so much am attached to your Country, that I would leave every thing behind, and would fly this very moment even in the Baloon to embrace you, Could I obtain

an honorable rank in your Country's Army. ... My respects to your Lady.[8]

Then, mellowing somewhat to the more playful nature that endeared him to his American colleagues, he asked Greene to convey a message to Mrs. Morris in Charleston. "[T]el[l] her I propose to mar[r]y her when her Husband dies and if he is in Life, which would be the most surprising thing to live so long in that Country, my best Compliments to him."[9]

Unfortunately, one of the first letters he received from his Revolutionary friends was a communication from Major Elnathan Haskell, a companion of the Northern Department, who wrote from Paris to inform the former engineer that Gen. Greene had died on June 19, 1786. The grieving Pole wrote to Haskell to thank him for the letter and complain about Congress's lack of action on paying its debts.

> My Dear - Dear Haskell, Happy I am that once in five years [I] can have at last the news of the country to which I am so much attached.
> Hearteli I thank you for the obliging letter, your person was alway dear to me, and am not disappointed in your character few—very few such exemples in the world, of the lasting friendship at such a Distance. ...
> He is gone, my good friend Green[e] rains begins to fall heavy from my eyes whenever I think of. You ought to make a Statue or a Mausolium for his memory.—I knew his merit perhaps better than anyone, and shall think always very ungreatful Country if she will not Crown him with a title of a great General and Citizen.[10]

Several years later when the author of a history of the Revolution asked for his opinion of Greene, Kościuszko was only too happy to oblige.

> I am delighted that the occasion is presented to render homage to the memory of one of the best generals of America upon whom you demand some information from me. ... In regard to his moral character, he had all the qualities requisite to a man of state, to a general, to a Republican, and to a man of society. He was sweet, compassionate, generous, a good citizen, a good friend. He had a profound penetration, a just judgment, firmness, energy, activity. His mind was ingenious in difficulties, his glance precise. Nevertheless, simple in his manners, affable and polite.[11]

Despite his meager resources, Kościuszko commissioned an engraving of Greene in Paris and sent copies to his American friends. David Humphreys, who assisted in arranging for the engravings, assured Kościuszko that "Your acquaintances and friends in America all remember you with great affection. And the more so from the honorable agency you had in assisting to establish the Independence of that Country, a Country, which now, in reality begins to enjoy the fruits of its Revolution."[12]

At the same time that Kościuszko grieved for the loss of Greene, he pained for the fate of his homeland. In his absence, Poland suffered under Russian rule which stifled economic and social development. In this atmosphere, the Natural Law philosophy of the Enlightenment attracted reformers who used it to support calls for a noble democracy. Though not as egalitarian as its American and French counterparts, the Polish adherents generally extended the principles to all levels of society, emphasizing the rule of law. This teaching was adopted by the National Education Commission in 1774 for use in all of the schools under its jurisdiction.[13]

By the end of the 1780s, debate raged within Poland about the political implications of this Natural Law philosophy. Though opinions differed on the most desirable form of government and the extent to which the political franchise should be made available, most political philosophers interpreted Natural Law to support the equality of all persons before the law. This philosophy found a ready supporter in Kościuszko who extended its precepts to all segments of society including the hitherto neglected peasantry. A philosophical democrat, his ideals of equality were shaped in the cauldron of revolution in America where his exposure to the institution of human slavery further cemented his beliefs.

At last, events would provide Kościuszko with his long-sought opportunity to place himself in the service of his homeland while pursuing his ideals of societal equity. When the Russo-Turkish War broke out in 1788, the Polish *Sejm* took advantage of the resulting Russian preoccupation to exert its independence from foreign domination. The Russo-Prussian treaty of alliance having expired in the same year, the *Sejm* took advantage of the situation to sign an alliance with Prussia in March, 1790, under which the two nations pledged assistance to one another in the event either were invaded. The treaty, the Poles hoped, would give them some assurance of assistance in the event Russia attempted to reassert its control over the nation.[14]

Ignoring efforts by the Russian ambassador to maintain the czar's influence, the *Sejm* voted on October 1, 1789, to establish an army of 100,000 troops to protect the nation's independence. Among the officers selected to lead this new force was Tadeusz Kościuszko, to whom the *Sejm* offered a commission as major general on the recommendation of several influential people including Princess Ludwika Lubomirska, the one-time love of his youth.[15] "We must all unite for one purpose," he wrote to a friend, "to free our country from the domination of foreigners, from the abasement and destruction of the very name of Pole. ... On ourselves, on our morals, depends the improvement of government. And if we are base, covetous, selfish, careless of our country, it will be just that we shall have chains on our necks, and we shall be worthy of them."[16] On a more personal level, to Tekla Żurowska he wrote: "The happiness of others is in my greatest respect and I am ready to sacrifice mine."[17]

Stationed first in Podolia and then in the Ukraine in 1790, Kościuszko was under orders to defend the nation's borders against Russian incursions. He spent much of his time training new recruits and developing infantry and artillery units, branches of the service traditionally neglected within a Polish army that emphasized the use of cavalry, but units whose importance the new general had seen first-hand in America. He also introduced a commissariat department and greatly increased the professionalism of the staff and proficiency of the troops. While in the Ukraine, he spent considerable time drawing up a plan for an army of volunteer citizen-soldiers recruited from all levels of society, a force modeled on his experience in America.[18]

While he labored to build a more efficient, balanced military force, the Four-Year *Sejm* proceeded with internal political reforms leading to the eventual adoption of a new constitution on May 3, 1791. Coming into existence as it did during a time when absolute power was vested in most European monarchs, the Polish constitution was very liberal for its time. The very first article in the document confirmed the principle of religious freedom, stating "we owe to all persons, of whatever persuasion, peace in their faith and the protection of the government, and therefore we guarantee freedom to all rites and religions in the Polish lands, in accordance with the laws of the land." The constitution then went on to abolish the injurious *liberum veto*, recognize the right to own property, and guarantee freedom and equal protection under the law for all people.[19] The latter was a very significant step because similar guarantees of freedom and equality were not established in the British Empire until the abolition of slavery more than a half-century later; they were not established in Czarist Russia until the abolition of serfdom in the 1860s; and not in the United States until the elimination of slavery at the end of the Civil War.

The Constitution of the Third of May stated that "All authority in human society takes its origin in the will of the people," whereupon it established executive, legislative and judicial branches of government much like those in the United States. While retaining an hereditary kingship as the national executive, the monarch's authority was subject to restriction by Polish law, parliament, and the judiciary. Kościuszko enthusiastically endorsed the reforms, confiding to his American friend Elnathan Haskell that the Poles "are upon the means to be respectable abroad, to give more energi for the execution of the established Laws and to destroi forever any hope for raising a *Monarchique Pouvoir*."[20] Later, to Michał Zalewski he asserted his democratic feelings unequivocally: "It is a sure fact that every citizen, even the most unimportant and least instructed, can contribute to the universal good, but he to whom the Almighty has given understanding of affairs greater than that of others ... sins when he ceases to be active. ... There should be no unfree men in any civilized state, indeed, the word 'unfree' itself ought to be banished from every legal code."[21]

The Constitution of the Third of May was a unique and radical departure from the European absolutism of the day. As such, it greatly antagonized Poland's neighbors, motivating them to action against the reformers. In the year following the constitution's ratification Czarina Catherine II, angered by Polish expressions of independence, declared war. Two Russian armies numbering more than 100,000 men crossed the Polish borders on May 19, 1792. Poland, having signed a treaty of mutual defense with Prussia in 1790, sought aid from her erstwhile ally, but received only vague, elusive responses. While the diplomats exchanged messages, the Russian troops bore deeply into Polish territory. To oppose them, Prince Józef Poniatowski, nephew of the king, could field only 45,000 men, many of them with only rudimentary training. Regardless of the odds, the outnumbered Poles resisted stubbornly. Kościuszko, serving as the prince's primary lieutenant, was active in the campaign, often commanding the rear-guard as the army retired before superior

Russian numbers. In this, the valuable practical experience he gained in the retreat from Saratoga and during Greene's campaigns in the Carolinas provided him with skills particularly important to a smaller force requiring great mobility and diligence to survive.[22]

When the prince met with a reverse at Polonne on June 14-15, Kościuszko's rear guard actions made it possible for the rest of the army to escape destruction. "Thanks to the good and circumspect dispositions of General Kościuszko," the prince reported, "our retreat was continued in unbroken order."[23] During Poniatowski's hard-fought victory at Zieleńce on June 18, the prince complimented his lieutenant for "bravery" and "extraordinary prudence." Similar praise came for his conduct at Włodzimierz on July 7, and in other rear guard actions as the larger Russian army pushed relentlessly into Poland.[24]

Aside from his military training and experience, one factor in Kościuszko's success was the strong allegiance of his soldiers, a feeling at least partially due to his treatment of them as human beings. He "taught soldiers and peasants that they are his brothers, his countrymen, that they have a common country for which they were fighting together," an observer later explained, "he aroused in them love, unbounded enthusiasm and strength which overcame difficulties ... he trained them by his example." He was frequently seen visiting the shabby huts of his soldiers, treating them with respect rather than the brutish manner that typified relationships between the officer corps and the enlisted men in most armies of the time. "Kościuszko is an unusual man," another contemporary observed, "under fire he seems to be as on a promenade, he is sensible, brave, beloved and esteemed by his countrymen and by foes as well."[25] Ladies, it was said, "adored-him because he told them courtesies and danced with them...; he disliked long faces, he considered it one's fortune to risk his life in the service of his country. He went from a ball to a battle and the next day returned to the party without losing the sight of the enemy; he found him again when least expected. He slept equally well on bare soil and in down; he shared the food of the soldier and did not consider himself Spartan enough to refuse a good supper if only his soldiers had something to eat, too.... He was not very eloquent, his deeds spoke for him, he did not possess that which we call worldly refinement, but he had something more—he had a natural charm which captivated all who approached him without a spirit of partiality."[26]

Faced with three-to-one odds at Dubienka on July 18, with Poniatowski's lines broken and the Polish army in danger of being annihilated, Kościuszko added greatly to the luster of the military reputation he first gained in America by entrenching and repelling with his 4,000 troops repeated attacks by 20,000 Russians over five days while the rest of the army retreated across the Bug River. When they and their equipment were safe, he withdrew his force in "the calmest manner and in perfect order."[27] For his conduct on this occasion he gained promotion to lieutenant general.

Despite continuing military resistance, with no chance of Prussian support the king regarded further resistance as futile and sought an accommodation with the czarina through the Confederation of Targowica, a pro-Russian alliance led by Feliks Potocki, Sewerin Rzewuski, and Xavery Branicki that favored a return to the pre-1791 constitution.[28] With the king's decision to acquiesce to Russian demands, all of the reforms of the recent constitution were eliminated, the nation once again falling under Russian rule. Further, Prussia, fearing the growth of Russian influence in Poland, suggested a second partition. Under the terms of this agreement, the Prussians obtained Gdańsk, Torun, and Wielkopolska, with 1,100,000 people. The Russians gained most of Lithuania, western Ukraine, and Podolia, including 3,000,000 people, as well as the right to station troops in Poland and control its foreign affairs, making the nation nothing more than an enslaved satellite. Only 80,000 square miles around Warsaw and Lublin, with 4,000,000 people, remained of the large nation which once stretched from the Baltic to the Black Sea, her eastern border ranging far toward Moscow itself.[29]

Kościuszko emerged from the cauldron of defeat with his honor and military reputation not only intact, but enhanced. The king praised Kościuszko's conduct, promoted him to the rank of lieutenant general, and awarded him the cross of the *Virtuti Militari*. But Kościuszko would not be seduced by these honors. Instead, he spoke out against the king's weakness, contrasting the monarch's conduct with that he had witnessed in America. "He excuses himself on the grounds that there was no money," Kościuszko wrote of the king, "but money for what? Was there no meat or bread in our country, which our citizens would have given in exchange for receipts? The American Revolution is an example of waging war without money as long as the government takes care of supplying the men with clothing and footwear."[30]

Deploring the king's action, which resulted in the near extinction of Poland from the political map of Europe, both Józef Poniatowski and Kościuszko immediately resigned.[31] "Since the changes in national conditions are contrary to my original oath and internal convictions," the latter wrote to the king, "I have the honour to request Your Royal Majesty for the favor of signing my resignation."[32] Kościuszko could not bring himself to live in a nation ruled by its enemies. Even a personal appeal from the king failed to persuade him to stay. "[W]ith tears in my eyes," Kościuszko recalled, "I answered him that we would never act against our convictions and honor."[33]

The extent of Kościuszko's emotional distress at the plight of his country is apparent in a letter to Isabella Czartoryska: "Oh, my God! why wilt Thou not give us the means of rooting out the brood of the adversaries of the nation's happiness? I feel unceasing wrath against them. Day and night that one thought is forced upon me, and I shudder when I think what end may befall our country."[34]

Determined to leave his native land, Kościuszko wrote to Felix Potocki to tell him of his plans to return to America: "Watering my native soil with my tears, I am going to the New World, to my second country to which I have acquired a right by fighting for her independence. Once there, I shall beseech Providence for a stable, free and good government in Poland, for the independence of our nation, for virtuous, enlightened and free inhabitants therein."[35] Whether these words described a genuine desire to return to America at this time is uncertain. Since Potocki was a member of the Targowica group allied with the Russians, it is probable that Kościuszko mentioned America in hope of convincing the ruling group that he would pose no threat once abroad.

Whatever the truth, Kościuszko left Poland so quickly in October, 1792, that he did not have time for a proper parting with his own family. To his beloved and supportive sister Anna he wrote:

> Permit me, my Sister, to embrace you, and because this may be the last time I shall be given that happiness I desire that you should know my will, that I bequeath to you my Siechnowicze and that you have the right to bequeath it either to one of your sons or to any one, but under one condition: that Susanna and Faustin shall be kept in every comfort until their death; that the peasants from every house in the whole estate shall not do more than two days of forced labor for the men, and for the women none at all. If it were another country where

the government could ensure my will, I would free them entirely, but in this country we must do what we are certain of being able to do to relieve humanity in any way, and always remember that by nature we are all equals, that riches and education constitute the only difference; that we ought to have consideration for the poor and instruct ignorance, thus bringing about good morals.... Embrace Susanna for me. Thank her for the friendship she has shown me. Remember me to Faustin and to your son Stanislaus. Let him give his children a good republican education with the virtues of justice, honesty and honor.[36]

Journeying south into Galicia, the Austrian partition of Poland, he tarried for a while as a guest of the Czartoryskis. There, a member of the family drew a sketch of the former general, writing beneath the image the words "Tadeusz Kościuszko, good, valiant, but unhappy."[37]

Within a few weeks the Austrian authorities, anxious lest he provoke revolution on their soil, placed him under a police order to leave the country within twelve hours. Moving on once again, he continued westward under a pseudonym aptly descriptive of his feelings, "Pan Bieda," Mr. Misery. Traveling through Kraków, he reached Leipzig, Saxony, by the end of December, still trailed by Russian agents tracking his every move. There he met with a group of fellow exiles dedicated, as he was, to the eventual freedom and independence of their homeland. Among the indefatigable revolutionary group were Hugo Kołłltaj, Ignacy Potocki, and Stanisław Potocki.[38]

From Leipzig, Kościuszko traveled to Paris where the government of the French Revolution had only recently announced its intention to support all movements for national freedom. There he hoped to solicit French assistance for a new Polish revolt, much as the Bourbons had assisted the American Revolution nearly a score of years before. At the very least he sought arms and financing for a Polish uprising; ideally he hoped for French troops and an agreement that the French navy would supply the revolutionaries through the Baltic or via the Crimea. Unfortunately, the French proclamation proved hollow. Meeting with initial ambivalence, he obtained only the offer of honorary French citizenship as a "defender of the people against despots." Nevertheless, renewing once again his quest in January, 1793, the emissary sought to arrange diversionary actions by Turkey and Sweden to draw Russian troops away from positions where they might directly oppose a Polish uprising. Promising the

French a general uprising by 65,000 troops, he also sought their assurances of support for an independent Poland. Apparently he was successful this time, receiving some assurances of French assistance in military and naval action from the Baltic, and a diversion from the Black Sea. Evidence of this appears in a note from the French foreign minister detailing such a plan to his contact in Leipzig. Before the plan could come to fruition, however, France went to war against England and that, along with internal struggles between the Girondists and Jacobins for political control, left the emissary with few friends and little support among the revolutionary leaders. Poland would be left to its own resources.[39]

Despite the setback, Kościuszko determined to continue his efforts on behalf of his native land. To Michał Załewski he promised he would not travel farther than England or Switzerland until events once again unfolded in Poland. "If they make for the happiness of the country, I shall return; if not, I shall move on further. I shall enter no foreign service, and if I am forced to it by my poverty then I shall enter a service where there is a free state, but with an unchanging attachment to my country which I might serve no longer. ... I do not see—God is my witness—how I, sincerely attached to the country, entering no intrigues, following no side except the public good, could as yet be convinced and shown the necessity of remaining in the country, I who am nothing, poor and whose voice would not be obeyed."[40]

From Paris he returned during the summer of 1793 to Leipzig where he immersed himself in planning for a new uprising. In Leipzig, however, despite their common goal the revolutionaries were not always united on the means to that end. Every obstacle gave birth to differing solutions, every opportunity brought forth contentious debate. As preparations lagged, the starting date had to be postponed several times, giving rise to fears that the plotters would be uncovered before they could act. To make matters worse, the backbone of the revolt was to be activation of the Polish military, but Russia soon determined to demobilize much of the Polish army in March, 1794. This would remove that force as a rallying point for the revolutionaries' plan to create about it a citizen militia modeled on Kościuszko's American experience. Once the regular Polish army was demobilized and scattered, the strong core equivalent to the American Continentals would be removed, increasing the likelihood that the new citizen recruits would be unable to withstand the czar's trained legions. These circumstances finally signaled a call for action.[41]

In September, Kościuszko and other conspirators met secretly in Podgórze where ringleaders in Warsaw unveiled plans for a rising by the Polish army units and citizenry of that city to eject the Russian garrison by force. Coordinated with similar activities elsewhere, this was to be the beginning of a general insurrection aimed at reestablishing Polish independence. Kościuszko, however, was not convinced, believing the planning insufficient for such an undertaking. Since the plan depended on the ability of the Polish military to oust Russian troops, he sought assurances that peasants would be offered their freedom as a means of insuring their rising to support the small regular army.[42]

To throw his enemies off the trail of the conspirators while they finalized plans, Kościuszko left on a public trip to Italy, ostensibly to visit a friend, the poet Julian Ursyn Niemcewicz, then residing in Florence. There he encountered, apparently by accident, Philip Mazzei, then an ally of the Polish king. To hide his real purpose from Mazzei, Kościuszko pretended to be wandering about aimlessly. When Mazzei suggested he return to America to claim his lands and live a peaceful life, Kościuszko pretended to agree and asked directions to the nearest port where he could sail for America. His real travel plans thus concealed, he returned as soon as possible to Leipzig more determined than ever to push his revolutionary activities forward. Unfortunately, the delay caused by his trip provided time for the Russian authorities to uncover part of the conspiratorial network in Poland and take steps to reduce the size of the Polish army that Kościuszko counted on to form the backbone of the impending revolution.[43]

On the otherwise quiet morning of March 16, 1794, Kościuszko, now forty-eight years old, and a few co-conspirators secretly crossed the border into Poland intent upon sparking another uprising. Arriving in Kraków on March 23, he immediately went to work to rouse the people to rebellion. The next day, following a morning Mass at which the officiating priest blessed his sword, he walked to the old Market Square where, surrounded by his fellow-conspirators and a battalion of Polish infantry, Kościuszko appealed to the nation. A drum roll brought the troops to attention, then in unison each swore allegiance to the new revolt.

I,——, swear that I will be faithful to the Polish nation and obedient to Tadeusz Kościuszko, the Commander-in-Chief, who has been summoned by this nation to the defense of the freedom, liberties, and independence of our country. So help me God and the Innocent Passion of His Son.[44]

Next, the Commander-in-Chief stepped forward to pledge before God to use his authority "for the single aim of defending the integrity and frontiers of the country, to regain the independence of the nation, and to establish universal liberty."[45]

I, Tadeusz Kościuszko, swear in the sight of God to the whole Polish nation that I will use the power entrusted to me for the personal oppression of none, but will only use it for the defence of the integrity of the boundaries, the regaining of the independence of the nation, and the solid establishment of universal freedom. So help me God and the Innocent Passion of His Son.[46]

The oaths taken, Kościuszko next issued his famous Act of Insurrection, a document designed to clarify the purposes of and engender enthusiasm for the revolt. The Polish equivalent of the American Declaration of Independence or the French Declaration of the Rights of Man, it called upon all of the people of the old Commonwealth—Poles, Lithuanians, all religious groups, magnates, gentry, burghers, and peasants—to join in the rebellion for their freedom, stressing their right to liberty, security, and property.[47] Calling all true Poles to armed uprising under the slogan "Liberty, Integrity, Independence," he addressed special appeals to the army, the clergy, burghers, the peasantry, and women to support a universal movement for national independence. To his countrymen he challenged:

Fellow-citizens! Summoned so often by you to save our beloved country, I stand by your will at your head, but I shall not be able to break the outraging yoke of slavery if I do not receive the speediest and the more courageous support from you. Aid me then with your whole strength, and hasten to the banner of our country. ... The first step to throw off the yoke of oppression is to dare to believe ourselves free—and the first step to victory is confidence in our strength.[48]

Wielding almost unprecedented dictatorial powers as both military and civil leader, Kościuszko established a Supreme National Council comprised of republican political leaders who would conduct daily financial and administrative affairs and attempt to negotiate foreign support. Local affairs were placed in the hands of Commissions of Order which were given the authority to punish landlords or peasants who violated laws, edicts, or the provisions of any of the commander-in-chief's proclamations. Violations could be punished by death.[49] Though decidedly undemocratic, Kościuszko viewed all of these arrangements as temporary measures necessary for the success of the uprising. It was never his intent to dictate the nation's permanent form of government. "I want to destroy the enemy," he explained. "I make certain political dispositions in the meantime, but I leave to the nation the right of decision. Let it establish a government such as will suit it best. I shall throw away my sword in the Diet Chamber, with no personal ambition, only that I may enjoy quietude and play in the garden of a small house till I die."[50]

Nor did these initial political arrangements preclude Kościuszko from basing the uprising on the ideals of freedom and social equity. Implanted in him during his youth, nurtured on the democratic philosophies of his Parisian years, and molded into mature forms in America, Kościuszko appealed to all classes of society to rally to the nation's defense, counting particularly on the peasantry to respond as the American farmers had during their revolt against England. "I will not fight for nobles only," he pledged. "I want freedom for the whole nation and for that only I will risk my life."[51]

But serious difficulties beset the infant rebellion from its very inception. Unable to call upon the authority of a legislature, a great coalition of magnates, or other existing authority, Kościuszko had to create a government, develop economic policies, solicit aid from abroad, and attend to scores of other details, as well as recruit, organize, and train an army. With so much to be done in such a short period of time, there appeared to be no end to the work. Some Polish historians have concluded that Kościuszko lacked the requisite administrative acumen to be successful as a government leader and economic planner, but given the almost total unpreparedness of the Polish nation for the uprising he certainly performed wonders in developing a working civil administration in such a short time, under such difficult circumstances.[52] A sign that these burdens wore heavily on him can be seen in a letter he sent to Gen. Franciszek Sapieha: "Let no virtuous man desire power, it was placed in my hands for this critical moment, I do not know whether I have deserved this trust, but I know that to me this power is only an instrument for the efficacious defense of my country and I confess that I desire its end as sincerely as the salvation of the nation itself."[53]

To save the nation, Kościuszko had at his command only about 27,000 regular troops, but these were dispersed about the country and could not readily be concentrated. There were another 14,000 recently assigned to the Russian army in the Ukraine, but it was uncertain how many, if any, of these could be counted on to make the long journey to a rendezvous point. Aside from these potential forces, Kościuszko felt he could count only on some 5,000 peasant militia to be raised in the Kraków area. Against this uncertain army, Russia deployed 29,000 troops in Poland, with another 30,000 in the Russian partition that could be called upon to reinforce those in Poland. Also within the borders were some 8,000 Prussians, with another 14,500 already enroute to reinforce this contingent. The odds were not good.[54]

Kościuszko "brought back from America," according to Mizwa, "a deepened love of freedom and democracy and the consciousness that even an undisciplined and ragged citizen army, if fired with zeal for a sacred cause, can win victories against a powerful nation."[55] These principles, together with the similar ideals he developed during his youth in Poland, are reflected in the new commander-in-chief's approach to rousing the country against the oppressor. Militarily, he drew extensively on his experience in America to plan for a Polish militia force that would supplement the regular army much as the citizen militia supported the Continentals during the American Revolution. Responding to his plea, hundreds of peasants armed only with their harvesting scythes flocked to his army under banners proclaiming proudly "They Feed and Defend." To Kościuszko's mind, the lack of firearms could be overcome by resolute use of the bayonet or the scythe in massed attacks covered by picked riflemen. To this end, Kościuszko ordered all male Poles between the ages of 18 and 40 to prepare themselves by drilling each week with scythes or pikes. To emphasize the importance of the peasantry in this plan, and his own egalitarian social view, Kościuszko adopted as his own personal uniform a *sukmana*, the long white cloak of his peasant scythe-bearers.[56]

Unlike many European officers, Kościuszko also proposed to treat the soldiery in his army with great humanity, both because of his general egalitarian ideals and the practical reality of raising a force sufficient in number and motivation to meet the Russians on the field of battle. "Take good care of the men," he cautioned Gen. Sapieha, "see to their victuals and comforts. Remember only that our war has its own specific character which must be well understood: our success depends in a large measure on general support and the arming of all inhabitants of our land. We should also arouse love of country in those who were previously even unaware that they had a Fatherland."[57]

On April 4 Kościuszko's impromptu army of 4,000 regulars and 2,000 peasant militia met 7,000 Russians at Racławice, near Kraków. In the closely contested battle that followed, the Russians attacked from both flanks and were on the verge of being joined by a third pincer when the Polish commander personally led 320 of his peasant scythmen in the decisive assault on the artillery at the center of the Russian line. Dressed in the flowing peasant garb of their Krakovian origins, their dreadful looking scythes glistening in the sun, the small band dashed across the violently contested field, into the muzzles of the czar's guns, and broke the enemy line. Those Russians who did not scatter in fear of the deadly blades were soon crushed, forcing the Russians into precipitate retreat leaving eleven guns to the peasant legion.[58] "The sacred watchword of nation and of freedom moved the soul and valour of the soldier fighting for the fate of his country and for her freedom," Kościuszko wrote in his report of the action.[59]

The improbable victory, one historian wrote, demonstrated Kościuszko's "excellent presence of mind, strategic skill and capacity for rapid action."[60] Another proclaimed it "a milestone in the ardurous path of social progress and a starting point that opened for the untutored masses of Polish peasants the vista of equal opportunities through equal responsibilities."[61] To future generations it would be remembered in literature, music, and art as one of the most emotionally patriotic of Poland's many battles for independence. According to Polish historian Roman Dyboski, "The blood shed at Racławice fertilized the Polish soil for the undying crop of national life throughout a hundred years of captivity."[62] But all of this was in the future. The victory won, Kościuszko seized the opportunity to call for more patriotic exertion. "Nation!" his proclamation called, "Feel at last thy strength; put it wholly forth; set thy will on freedom and independence!"[63]

Inspired by the example of Racławice the insurrection quickly spread. Warsaw and Wilno rose to throw out their occupiers, while

Wielkopolska, Lithuania, Volhynia, Lublin, and Gdańsk followed. Taking time out to organize a National Council to administer the government in his absence, Kościuszko also continued to organize his army as small contingents arrived from various provinces to bolster his forces. Unfortunately, aid from abroad failed to materialize and the Austrians, whom Kościuszko hoped to keep neutral, began to take a belligerent tone. In the face of these developments, the commander-in-chief sought to rouse the peasantry to further support by giving them a direct stake in its outcome. He did this by placing his egalitarian social ideals before them in the Połaniec Manifesto. Issued from his camp near Kraków on May 7, this historic document abolished serfdom, declared the peasantry free, and invested them with ownership of property. Although the Manifesto itself did not result in a mass uprising, Kościuszko issued other appeals, couched in emotional patriotic rhetoric, to virtually every group in society and was successful in rallying to his cause Disuniates, Greek Orthodox, Jews, Cossacks, Lithuanians, and others who came forward to support the cause of Polish independence.[64] Typical of these emotional appeals was the following:

> Lithuania! My fellow-countrymen and compatriots! I was born on your soil, and in the midst of righteous zeal for my country more especial affection is called forth in me for those among whom I began life.... Look at the rest of the nation of which you are a part.... Look at those volunteers, already assembling in each province of all Poland, seeking out the enemy, leaving homes and families, for a beloved country, inflamed with the watchword of those fighting for the nation: Death or Victory! ... Once again, I say, we shall conquer! Earlier or later the powerful God humbles the pride of the invaders, and aids persecuted nations, faithful to Him and faithful to the virtue of patriotism.[65]

A witness who observed Kościuszko during this period left a portrait of the insurrectionary leader:

> He is a simple man, and most modest in conversation, manners, dress.... He unites with the greatest resolution and enthusiasm for the undertaken cause much sang-froid and judgment. It seems as though there is nothing temerarious in all that he is doing except the enterprise itself. In practical details he leaves nothing to chance: everything is thought out and combined. His may not be a transcendental mind, or one sufficiently elastic for politics. His native good sense is enough

for him to estimate affairs correctly and to make the best choice at the first glance. Only love of this country animates him. No other passion has dominion over him.[66]

Democratic principles such as those expressed in the Połaniec Manifesto, however, did not come without cost. While many of the *szlachta* and some of the parish clergy supported Kościuszko's uprising, the Roman Catholic hierarchy and the magnate class remained aloof, offering no support to a movement they generally saw as a threat to their own rights and prerogatives. Further, a proposal to institute conscription on the French model met with little support and plans for the volunteer militia did not yield the numbers hoped for because, according to Askenazy, the peasantry and burghers "were as yet politically immature."[67] In the face of passivity, and sometimes open resistance, Kościuszko worked constantly to explain the revolt's purposes and rally the nation. In the end, his efforts were rewarded by an unprecedented increase in the army to 90,000 men, more than ever before fielded by the Commonwealth. Including the peasant militia and other local forces, the total number of men under arms approached an amazing 150,000. But lack of military arms and equipment, combined with a moribund economy and a practically non-existent treasury left the commander-in-chief unable to arm most of the troops with anything more than their own personal weapons or scythes.[68]

By the end of the first week in May it became necessary for Kościuszko to take the field again when the Russians once more threatened. Greatly outnumbered, and poorly equipped, he led but 14,000 men and 24 guns against the Russians, but found himself suddenly confronting both the Russians and a force of Prussians marching unexpectedly to their support. The combined forces of the two enemies numbered some 27,000 supported by 124 guns. To make the disparity even greater, more than one-third of Kościuszko's troops were newly recruited, largely untrained, and armed with only their scythes. At Rawka near Szczekociny on June 6 a hard-fought battle ended in defeat. Only through strenuous efforts was a slightly wounded Kościuszko able to extract the remnants of his army and retire from the sanguinary field. Nor was this the only disappointment, for in the wake of the defeat at Szczekociny the Austrians allied themselves with czar and könig to put down the rebellion, while the French revolutionary government, absorbed in its own internal squabbles, refused all of Kościuszko's entreaties for aid. In the face of these disasters, Kościuszko did all he could to keep up his country-men's spirits. "Nation!" he pleaded. "This is the first test of the stability of thy Spirit, the first day of the Rising in which you may be sad, but not dismayed. ... Nation! Thy soil will be free. Only let thy spirit be high above all else."[69]

Valiant words aside, in the face of overwhelming manpower and superior equipment there was little Kościuszko could do other than retreat to the fortifications of Warsaw. There, when a mob attacked some traitors and hanged the victims on June 28, Kościuszko, eschewing these violent Jacobin excesses, immediately placed the perpetrators under arrest, remanding them to the courts for criminal prosecution. "What happened in Warsaw yesterday," he proclaimed publicly, "filled my heart with bitterness and sorrow. The wish to punish the culprits was right, but why were they punished without the sentence of a court? Why were the authority and sanctity of laws violated? Know this that those who do not want to obey the laws are not worthy of liberty."[70] To Princess Czartoryska, who apparently wrote a critical letter regarding his dictatorial pronouncements, he provided his assurance there would be no excesses like those of the Parisian Jacobins. "How you wrong my feelings and manner of thinking, and how little you credit me with foresight and attachment to our country, if I could avail myself of such impossible and such injurious measures! My decrees and actions up to now might con-vince you. Men may blacken me and our Rising, but God sees that we are not beginning a French revolution. My desire is to destroy the enemy. I am making some temporary dispositions, and I leave the framing of laws to the nation."[71]

Similarly, when King Stanisław August, fearing lest he receive the same ignominious treatment accorded the Bourbons in France, wrote to Kościuszko offering to give up all power and place himself at the general's command, Kościuszko replied reassuringly of his respect and intentions.

My Lord King, Just when I was engrossed in the midst of so many other labors with the drawing up of the organization of the Supreme Council, I received a communication from Your Royal Majesty under the date of the 5th instant. Having read therein that Your Royal Majesty only desires authority and importance when and to the extent that I decide this with the nation, as regards my opinion, I frankly confess that, entertaining a loyal respect for the throne, I hold the person of Your Royal majesty excepted from the power conferred upon me of nominating personages to the composition of the Supreme Council. As to the nation, the conduct of Your Royal Majesty in the course of the present Rising, the restored public confidence in Your Royal majesty that was weakened by the Confederation of Targowica, the constancy with which Your Royal Majesty declares that, albeit at the cost of great personal misfortune, you will not forsake the country and nation, will contribute, I doubt not, to the securing for Your Royal Majesty of the authority in the Diet that will be most agreeable to the welfare of the country. I have written separately to the Supreme Council upon the duty of imparting to Your Royal Majesty an account of its chief actions, and this in the conviction that Your Royal Majesty will not only be a source of enlightenment to it, but of assistance inasmuch as circumstances permit. Likewise the needs of Your Royal Majesty which you mention at the end of your letter I have recommended to the attention and care of the Supreme Council. Thanking Your Royal Majesty for your good wishes concerning my person, I declare that the prosperity of Your Royal Majesty is not separated in my heart and mind from the prosperity of the country, and I assure Your Royal majesty of my deep respect.[72]

Although respecting the king's position and guaranteeing his safety, Kościuszko nevertheless kept him at arms length from the important political and military councils, fearing, no doubt, a repeat of the sovereign's duplicitous alliance with the Confederation of Targowica.

The pursuing Russian and Prussian armies, fielding a combined 41,000 troops and 235 guns, arrived on July 13 to lay siege to the city. In its defense, Kościuszko rallied 26,000 troops, of whom about 9,000 were militia armed mainly with scythes and pikes. For two long months the Poles held out against every attempt to take the city until the besieging armies were compelled to withdraw on September 6.[73] It was a truly remarkable victory. From the Supreme National Council came words of praise: "By your assiduity, your valor, you have curbed the pride and power of that foe who, after pressing upon us so threateningly, has been forced to retreat with shame upon his covetous intentions. The Council knows only too well the magnitude of the labors which you brought to the defense of this city, and therefore cannot but make known to you that most lively gratitude and esteem with which all this city is penetrated."[74]

After retreating, one of the Prussian officers paid tribute to the skill of Kościuszko's defense:

His creative power is worthy of admiration, since he, in the midst of creating an army, fought alone with it against the two best armies of Europe, having neither their stores nor their discipline. What would he not have shown himself at the head of a good army, since he did so much with peasants who knew nothing? Equally great in character, in devotion, in love of his country, he lived exclusively for her freedom and independence.[75]

After about a month's inactivity, military action switched to other theaters. On September 15 General Alexander Suvorov arrived at Brześć on the Bug River with a Russian army of 8,000. Two days later he attacked and mauled a Polish army of 10,000, opening the way to Warsaw. Kościuszko reacted by recalling Polish forces shadowing the retreating Prussians, while at the same time leading 8,000 troops out of Warsaw in an attempt to destroy the Russians retreating from Warsaw before Suvorov could join forces with them. Hoping to catch the Russians while they were vulnerable at a river crossing, Kościuszko rushed forward with a portion of his army without waiting for reinforcements to arrive. At Maciejowice on October 10, some 14,000 Russians assaulted Kościuszko's troops. In an exceptionally violent and sustained action lasting eight hours, the Polish army was virtually encircled and defeated with heavy losses, only 2,000 escaping back to Warsaw. Its commander, who had three horses shot beneath him during the battle, was gravely wounded and captured during the final Russian assault.[76]

Shortly after he fell at Maciejowice, rumor spread that his last words before losing consciousness were *"Finis Poloniae!"* [The End of Poland!]. Undoubtedly this was a fabrication. But, so widespread did the rumor become that Kościuszko later felt compelled to deny its veracity:

> Ignorance or malignity with fierce pertinacity have put the expression "Finis Poloniae" into my mouth—an expression I am stated to have made use of on that fatal day. Now, first of all, I had been almost mortally wounded before the battle was decided, and only recovered my consciousness two days afterwards, when I found myself in the hands of my enemies. In the second instance, if an expression like the one alluded to is inconsequent and criminal in the mouth of any Pole, it would be far more so in mine. When the Polish nation called me to defend the integrity, the independence, the dignity, the glory and the liberty of the country, she knew well that I was not the last Pole, and that with my death on the battlefield or elsewhere Poland could not,

must not end. All that the Poles have done since then in the glorious Polish legions and all that they will still do in the future to gain their country back, sufficiently proves that albeit we, the devoted soldiers of that country, are mortal, Poland is immortal: and it is therefore not permitted to anybody either to utter or to repeat that insulting expression which is contained in the words "Finis Poloniae."[77]

The defeat at Maciejowice effectively ended the revolt, but the victorious Russian army under General Suvorov nevertheless sacked Praga, a suburb of Warsaw, reportedly massacring thousands of civilian residents. Warsaw surrendered soon after, on November 5, 1794.[78]

Grievously wounded and unconscious, Kościuszko fell into the hands of the Russians who carried him from the battlefield and placed him under guard in the nearby manor house of the Zamojski family. "Between four and five o'clock in the evening," explained Julian Ursyn Niemcewicz, himself a captive in the Zamojski estate, "we saw a detachment of soldiers approaching headquarters, and carrying upon a hand-barrow, hastily constructed, a man half dead. This was General Kościuszko. His head and body, covered with blood, contrasted in a dreadful manner with the livid paleness of his face. He had on his head a large wound from a sword, and three on his back above the loins, from the thrust of a pike. He could scarcely breathe."[79]

Regaining consciousness the next day, he began on October 13 a lengthy, circuitous journey in great pain to St. Petersburg. Enroute the Russians displayed him like a pet animal in the villages they passed as a means of squelching rumors of his escape from Maciejowice. Along the way the column passed within about twenty miles of the Lubomirski estate where Princess Ludwika, his first love so many years before, sent gifts of clothing, books, and other comforts to Kościuszko and his fellow captives. Eventually arriving in the Russian city on December 10, Catherine II ordered him sent as a political prisoner in the Petropavlovsk Fortress on the banks of the Neva River. There, confined to a small cell with little medical treatment or food, he was under constant pressure to implicate leaders of the French Revolution, the Don Cossacks, fellow Poles, and other European governments in the Polish uprising, entreaties he refused.[80]

After several months confinement in the fortress prison's dungeons, Catherine ordered Kościuszko, his wounds still largely untreated, removed to the Grigorii Orlov Palace where he could be examined by an English physician. Though enjoying more freedom of movement about the palace, as well as a better diet and medical treatment, he remained bodily infirmed and mentally anguished. Physically, he suffered from both his wounds and illness contracted in his cold prison cell during the depths of the Russian winter. Mentally, he grieved for his country and the fate of his fellow prisoners. To the latter, he sent a portion of his own meager ration for whatever little sustenance it would afford. Day after day, month after month, he suffered under the czarina's sentence of life imprisonment. "The physical and mental forces of that upright man are nearly exhausted, as the result of the long sufferings," reported the English physician. "I am losing hopes of curing him. He has suffered so much in body and soul that his organism is entirely destroyed."[81]

While he languished in captivity, his beloved nation underwent a third partition, eliminating it entirely from the map of Europe. To Russia went the Ukraine, Lithuania, and Courland with 1,200,000 people. Prussia obtained Mazovia, including the city of Warsaw, with 1,000,000 people. Austria's share of the spoils included Kraków and the surrounding area with 1,000,000 people.[82]

Though in the end a failure, the uprising that brought about the Third Partition is celebrated in Polish history as a reflection of the will and resiliency of the Polish people. "The honor of Poland was saved by the insurrection," stated the eminent historian Oskar Halecki.[83] It is not without reason that it is referred to in Polish history as "The Kościuszko Insurrection." It was through Kościuszko's personality, prestige, and untiring efforts that the revolution occurred. It was through his exhortations, force of will, and military expertise that thousands of largely untrained and ill-equipped men took up arms and were able to hold out for more than a year and a half against the combined forces of Russia, Prussia, and Austria. Eversley, commenting on Kościuszko's strengths, weaknesses, and character in his history of the insurrection, characterized the Pole as "a man of very high qualities: calm and cool in the presence of great difficulties and dangers, inspiring great confidence in his military capacity, beloved by his soldiers, who called him Father Thaddeus, of irreproachable character, a most genuine patriot; but it may be doubted whether he possessed the power to deal with a position such as he found it in Warsaw. He had not the force of a Danton to inspire the populace with resolution, or the organizing power of a Carnot. He was more of the type of Lafayette. He had popular sympathies."[84]

He was, Aleksandr Swiętochowski concluded in his *Historia Chłopów Polskich*, "a great and wise man by virtue of intellect and heart, faultlessly noble, the most genuine of Poles, the purest of patriots, the noblest of democrats, with whom no one else can be placed on the same level in his love of and friendship for the common man—who really undertook an unequal struggle with the enemy under the motto of freedom for the whole nation, including the peasants." Though unsuccessful, Kościuszko, through his valiant and resourceful leadership in 1792, and again during the uprising that bears his name, earned for himself a place of lasting esteem in the hearts of his countrymen and became a symbol of patriotic and personal virtue for future generations.

Chapter 13

"My Second Country"

*T*he sudden, unexpected death of Czarina Catherine II on November 6, 1796, brought to the throne her son as Czar Paul I. An admirer of Kościuszko, who was treated with contempt by Catherine during her lifetime, the new czar wanted to end the captivity of the celebrated prisoner who had fallen seriously ill, but dared not release him while there was a chance he would resume his revolutionary activities. Accompanied by his son, Grand Duke Alexander, Paul visited Kościuszko on his sick bed to propose a deal. In return for the Pole's word of honor not to engage in anti-Russian activities, the czar would allow him to go free. To make the offer more appealing, Paul offered Kościuszko 1,500 serfs, 12,000 rubles in cash, a handsome cloak, and a new sword. Kościuszko rejected the offer, commenting "I have no need of a sword: I have no country to defend." In fact, Kościuszko never wore a sword after that time. Further entreaties were of no avail, but Kościuszko, feeling an obligation to his fellow comrades-in-arms, finally accepted the czar's offer when Paul agreed to set free over 12,000 other Poles held in Russian captivity.[1]

Still suffering from the effects of his wounds and the terrible treatment he received in the Petropavlovsk dungeons, Kościuszko left St. Petersburg on December 19, 1796, accompanied by Julian Ursyn Niemcewicz, his secretary and aide during the insurrection, and a single Polish soldier, Stanisław D1browski, acting as a servant. So feeble was his health that he had to be carried by the Polish soldier to the coach to begin his journey. Together, the travelers wound their way through the deep snowdrifts of the Finnish winter, through the Aland Islands, and on to Stockholm which they reached on January 26, 1797. By February 23, they were in Gothenburg where Kości-uszko hoped to take ship for England. Fearing that once released Kościuszko would again involve himself in the cause of Polish independence, Russian agents followed the travelers to report their every move to the czar. Regardless, the local population and civic officials greeted them with hospitality throughout Scandinavia.[2]

Kościuszko finally left Gothenburg on May 1, arriving in London on the 29th to an ironically enthusiastic outpouring of public sentiment from the nation he had once opposed on the battlefield. "Kosciuszko, the hero of freedom, is here," exulted the *Gentleman's Magazine*. Honors came from all sides. The Whig Club of London presented him with an expensive sword, the Duchess of Devonshire made a gift of a costly ring, the City of Bristol bestowed upon him a valuable silver serving set, while other gifts came from civic groups and individuals alike. Liberal political leaders, literary figures, artists, poets, and common citizens flocked to see one of the most famous freedom fighters in Europe. Among them was the Russian Minister in London, a frequent visitor who inquired repeatedly about Kościuszko's health as a means of keeping him under observation. "His wounds are such," *Gentleman's Magazine* reported, "that he cannot move himself without excruciating torture; he amuses his leisure hours with drawing landscapes. ... With gaping wounds, unable to walk, and with a mind ill at ease, he did not care for nor enjoy the festivities of the great and gay, of the world of fashion."[3]

On June 3 the infirmed celebrity met with a distinguished group of British medical experts who examined his wounds in an effort to speed their healing. Included in the distinguished group was Sir George Baker, personal physician to the King and president of the College of Physicians. They found that Kościuszko suffered from blunt trauma to the lower back of his head, probably caused by a blunt saber, which caused a concussion and most likely severed a nerve that caused a lack of feeling in his scalp. The symptoms suffered from this wound, they believed, would gradually diminish until nearly disappearing. More serious was a partial paralysis of the thigh and leg, and an irregularity of the bladder resulting from the thrust of a Cossack pike into his hip that severed the sciatic nerve. The physicians felt the nerve would eventually heal, but it would be a long process attended by some uncertainty. To assist in his recovery the medical team recommended regular exercise of the afflicted leg, rubbing, regular heated tepid baths increasing in duration, regular flexing of the joints, and "the use of Electricity to promote the restoration of the action of the Muscles." If these recommendations were followed, the physicians believed Kościuszko would "probably recover in a considerable degree, the use of the Limb, but the progress will be slow, particularly at first, and this he must not be discouraged by."[4]

During his stay in England Kościuszko received news that a Polish Legion was being recruited to serve with the French in Italy. Though smitten with the desire to rush to France and participate in this recreation of a Polish military presence, the wounded warrior realized that any precipitate move would break the terms of his agreement with Czar Paul and jeopardize the freedom of his companions being released as part of the arrangement. Under the circumstances, Kościuszko hoped to mislead his enemies into thinking that he planned to retire in the New World. Practical considerations also played a part in the decision to return to America. Aside from a wish to see again his colleagues from the Revolution, Kościuszko hoped to improve his financial position by collecting debts owed him by the United States government. Once these obligations were settled, he planned to invest his funds to yield a steady, if modest, income to support his activities in Europe, chief among them the struggle for Polish independence, once his associates were all released from Russian prisons.[5]

While in England Kościuszko enjoyed visits from Rufus King, the American Minister. When he finally determined to leave for America he was able to take with him the following note from King to Col. Timothy Pickering, the American Secretary of State. "I have the honor to introduce to you General Kosciuszko who seeks in America that Repose, which he has long desired, as necessary to restore and confirm his Health." The true purpose of his journey thus concealed, he left London for Bristol on June 12 in the company of Julian Ursyn Niemcewicz and Stanisław D1browski, determined to take ship for America a "fortnight" after his arrival in England.[6]

In the port city he stayed with Elias Vanderhorst, a friend from the Southern Campaign who then lived in England. There, Rev. Richard Warner left this description of the Pole:

> I never contemplated a more interesting human figure than Kosciuszko stretched on his couch. His wounds were still unhealed, and he was unable to sit upright. A black silk bandage crossed his fair and high, but somewhat wrinkled forehead. Beneath it, his dark eagle eye sent forth a stream of light that indicated the steady flame of patriotism which still burned within his soul, unquenched by disaster and wounds, weakness, poverty, and exile. Contrasted with its brightness

was the paleness of his countenance and the wan cast of every feature. He spoke very tolerable English, though in a low and feeble tone, but his conversation, replete with fine devise, lively remarks, and sagacious answers, evidenced a noble understanding and a cultivated mind.[7]

A massive outpouring of public sympathy took place, the citizens presenting him with a valuable gift of silver plate and other tokens of their respect. A military band serenaded him nightly "with martial airs from every land where the soldier's banner had waved." Then, when the time for his departure arrived, the citizens formed a procession to carry him through the streets to the ship that would take him back to the land of his earlier triumphs.[8]

The sailing ship *Adriana* slipped out of Bristol into the Atlantic on June 19 amid a tumultuous outpouring of waving hats, fluttering handkerchief's, and the shouts of thousands gathered along the docks and the banks of the River Avon. "May God of heaven, earth and sea protect him on his voyage!" the editor of a local newspaper wrote. "May the gentlest gales waft him over the mighty ocean, and conduct him safe to America, the chief, if not the ONLY asylum for the persecuted sons of freedom! He carries with him the prayers of thousands."[9]

Lt. Henry Muhlenberg stood atop the parapet of Fort Mifflin scrutinizing the diminutive sailing vessel that glided upriver toward Philadelphia. It was August 18, 1797. As the ship pulled abreast of the fort, Lt. Muhlenberg shouted a command. Cannons flamed and roared, barking forth a traditional salute of thirteen guns to honor a visiting foreign dignitary. The little ship turned slowly, heading for its moorings along a dock packed tightly with politicians and well-wishers. Resounding cheers of "Long Live Kościuszko!" echoed across the water.[10]

When the ship docked, dignitaries and ordinary citizens alike flocked to the docks to behold the hero of liberty. The crew of the *Adriana* lowered the Pole in a chair into a small boat in which oarsmen sped him to shore as the ship's crew again raised three cheers of "Long live Kosciuszko!" The reception committee unhitched the horse from his carriage and pulled the vehicle through the streets themselves in further testimony to their esteem for the visitor. Speech after speech praised Kościuszko's contributions to liberty until the guest of honor rose to assure all present that: "I look upon America as my second country, and I feel myself too happy when I return to her."[11]

Praised and applauded by the citizens of Philadelphia, as word of his arrival spread Kościuszko soon began to receive a flood of warm, congratulatory correspondence from friends and admirers. On August 31, George Washington wrote a flattering letter welcoming him "to the land whose liberties you have been so instrumental in establishing" and assuring him that "no one has a higher respect and veneration for your character than I have, and no one more sincerely wished, during your arduous struggle in the cause of liberty and your country, that it might be crowned with Success. But the ways of Providence are inscrutable, and Mortals must submit. I pray you to believe, that at all times, and under any circumstances, it would make me happy to see you at my last retreat, from which I never expect to be more than twenty miles again."[12]

"Give me leave, Sir," requested John Adams, the President of the United States, "to congratulate you on your arrival in America, where, I hope, You will find all the consolation, tranquility and satisfaction you desire after the glorious efforts you have made on a greater Theatre. On my arrival in Philadelphia I hope to have pleasure to receive you."[13]

John Armstrong, one of Kościuszko's closest friends, wrote of his feelings upon the Pole's arrival in Philadelphia in a letter to Gates: "I am much interested in Kusciusko's future fortunes. He ought to have a bed of roses amongst us. I hope Philadelphia will not entirely engross him, and if his object be (as I suppose it is) retired life I know no place so well fitted for his purpose as the banks of this river. He would find amongst us friends that love him, a people that admire him—a pleasant country—and an easy access to the stores of literature, the conveniences of life and the pleasures of the city if his wishes ever lead him thither."[14]

In New York, at a dinner in honor of James Monroe presided over by Horatio Gates, the assembled guests rose to cheer a toast: "A speedy arrival of Kościuszko; May the air of Freedom cure the wounds he received in her defense."[15] Throughout the nation, the difficult name of Kościuszko sprang readily from grateful lips, while civic groups and individuals alike sent greetings, gifts, and invitations. The outpouring of good feelings bordering on adulation impressed Niemcewicz: "Oh! it was greatful to the heart of a Polander to perceive in the honor and respect with which his chief was received, esteem and consideration for the fate of an unjustly destroyed nation."[16]

On the surface all appearances were festive, but beneath this cloak of exuberance the United States was a different nation than when Kościuszko first departed for Europe. In 1784 the Pole left behind him a nation rejoicing in newly won freedom and independence. He returned to find that nation embroiled in divisive political rivalries that nurtured a growing factionalism. Kościuszko found the nation whose independence he helped secure torn between the Federalists led by John Adams and the Democratic Republicans of Thomas Jefferson. The former, decried by the Democratic Republicans as aristocrats and monarchists, favored close alliance with England, some going so far as to advocate war against France. The latter, labeled Jacobins by the Federalists, supported the French Revolution despite its excesses and strove to maintain peaceful relations with France.

Hatreds and ill-feelings predominated in the political circles of the nation. It was not an opportune time for Kościuszko's return, especially since he and other Poles were then looking to France as the last hope to restore Polish independence. Because of this many of the more fanatical Federalists avoided Kościuszko. John Fenno, writing in the *Gazette of the United States*, condemned the public outpouring, while Noah Webster labeled such conduct "debasing." Decrying in partisan political terms the behavior of his Republican rivals, Webster wondered how men who had nothing good to say about the President of the United States could become so enamored with a foreigner. Yet in one sense perhaps it was good for the country that Kościuszko arrived when he did. His visit proved to be, to some extent, a common ground that opponents from the two factions could rally around. It is indeed a tribute to the emerging mystique of the Revolution, and to the esteem in which the young nation held him, that he largely overcame for a moment the rising tide of factional dispute between Federalists and Republicans.[17]

During his stay in Philadelphia, Kościuszko lodged in an apartment on Fourth Street where he secretly established contact with French diplomatic representatives. "I went to the general [Kościuszko] last night," wrote the chargé-de-affairs to French Minister of Foreign Affairs Charles Delacroix. "He wants to go to France. He will go there immediately by a safe way. He is observed here. This Martyr of liberty cannot speak or act, but only with the greatest precaution. He is here only to mislead his enemies. He asked me, Citizen Minister, to inform you of these facts without delay."[18]

While establishing contact with the French, Kościuszko also pursued the long-overdue payment owed him for his service in the American Revolution. If he could obtain those funds, he could invest them to provide a stable, if modest income once he returned to Europe. Within days of his arrival in Philadelphia he contacted Timothy Pickering to ask his advice on how best to invest the funds he expected. Pickering referred him to Clement Biddle, an influential Philadelphia merchant.[19]

Before his financial affairs could be set in order, however, a deadly yellow fever epidemic swept Philadelphia beginning in mid-August, 1797. Fearing for Kościuszko's safety, Dr. Benjamin Rush and several others implored him to join the thousands of residents who were fleeing the city. Letters from his Revolutionary War friends Horatio Gates and Anthony Walton White extended invitations for the Pole to leave the stricken city behind to enjoy the hospitality of their respective homes at Rose Hill outside New York City and in New Brunswick, New Jersey. Finally, on August 30, accompanied by Niemcewicz and D1browski, Kościuszko relented.[20]

A few days after his departure, Rush wrote Gates to inform him of Kościuszko's decision and explain his physical condition and desire to renew his American friendships.

> Our illustrious friend Kusiosco left this city a few days ago & is now pleasantly & hospitably accommodated at General White's at Brunswick. His wounds are all healed. One of them on his hip has left his thigh & leg in a paralytic State. Time has done a little towards restoring it. I do not despair of his being yet able to walk. He will always limp—but what then? To use an ancient play upon words, "every Step he takes will remind him of his patriotism and bravery."
>
> I take it for granted, you will pay your respects to him at Brunswick. How gladly would I witness your first interview! His Soul is tremblingly alive to friendship. He loves your very name.[21]

Traveling north by carriage, the trio stopped briefly at Princeton to see Elias Boudinot, spent the night in Kingston, then journeyed on to Ellis House on the Raritan River outside New Brunswick on the following day. There, Kościuszko found his friend from the Southern Campaign had fallen on hard times. Financial speculation in the postwar years had destroyed his fortune, forcing him to exist on the generosity of his wife's sister, Mary Ellis. "Grief poisons his family life," Niemcewicz observed, turning him into "a gloomy melancholiac, though formerly he was cheerful and sociable. ... His farm is neglected; it yields him only as much as is needed to support his family and slaves. ... The spirit of dissatisfaction and discontent is apparent everywhere."[22]

Undoubtedly his friend's condition greatly tempered Kościuszko's happiness at the reunion, but he seems to have enjoyed the visit nonetheless. Gen. William Paterson and Col. John Bayard, Revolutionary War friends who lived in the vicinity, came to visit, and when other local residents came to call, he graciously entertained them by "sketching with pencil, and painting in water-colors and India-ink."[23] Throughout the visit the Pole wore a black ribbon bound about his head "to hide the scar of a ghastly sabre cut across his forehead." Nevertheless, he "appeared to have some magnetic property about him," explained A. W. W. Evans, "for he endeared himself to all he met, and the attachment remained throughout life."[24] Eliza White, then a young child, recorded later in life the lasting image she retained of his visit. "He was simple and unostentatious in his habits, unwilling to be made the object of special attention. He pertinaciously resisted any attempt to obtain his likeness—and one day perceiving a lady stealthily endeavoring to sketch his features whilst he was lying upon a sofa, he immediately threw a handkerchief over his face."[25] Only on rare occasion did he overcome his natural shyness long enough to allow his own likeness to be sketched.

From Ellis House, Kościuszko wrote to Gates to apprise him of his whereabouts and intentions. "I am at Mr. White's house now away from Philadelphia. I propose to see you and before hand I feel great Satisfaction in Embracing you once more, that I never expectet that happines. Be pleased to present my respects to your Lady she aught to be of very amiable disposition because she is beloved by every person who know here do not forget of my old friends and acquietence."[26] Apparently Gates either responded to this letter, or one from someone else informing him of Kościuszko's visit to the White home because the guest soon wrote another playful letter to Gates reiterating his plan to visit and teasingly threatening to attack his house with the army of two at his command.

If you know well my Heart, you ought to expect that I would pay invoidably my respects to you at your House, and for that purpose I came out from Philadelphia this way. I propose to set out in three days, from General White's to go at your's and to stay their one Weak; onless you will set your dogs at me, and by force throw me out from your House. I recolect perfectly well the obligation I ow[e] to you; and respect Esteem, Veneration and afection, too strongly imprinted in my breast, not to Listened to the call of Sentyments and, to pay the common gratitude with all Cytizens of this Country for your great exertions during the War, I have only one Friend and one Servant wyth me—and with suche army I will attack your house, but will surrender imidiatly to your good, hospitable and Friendly Heart my best respects to your Lady. Hear I stop for fear you should not be Jeaulous of me.[27]

Deeply grateful for the hospitality extended during his stay, Kościuszko wrote to Mrs. White to offer his appreciation and, in his typically modest fashion, apologize for the inconvenience his visit caused her.

> I am not at rest Madame before I obtain your Pardon in full extend and force, for the trouble I gave you during my stay at your house. The uneasinesse hangs on my mind, and my feelings suffer greatly. I was perhaps the cause of depriving you a pasttime, more suited to your inclination and satisfaction than wyth me; you never was out on a visite; you was pleased to inquire every day, what I like or dislike every wysh was complied, every thought was prevented, to make my sytuation more comfortable and agreeable—let me read in your enswer of forgiveness and I beg Elisa to solicite for me.
>
> I am too much indebted to you to express in words coresponding to my obligation and gratitude lit suffice that I will never forget neither the memory will cease for a moment in my breast.

Arriving in New York, Kościuszko and his two companions shunned any public entrance, going quietly through secondary roads to Gates's home, which Niemcewicz described as "a beautiful house, decorated with a peristyle of Corynthian columns." Once they arrived, the travelers "were met at the threshold by the victor of Saratoga. He is an old man, about seventy-five years of age, still quite lively, kind, and very cheerful for his age."[28]

Kościuszko's visit to Gates mirrored his earlier stay with Gen. White, except the number of daily visitors was greatly increased as Gates invited any of Kościuszko's friends from the Northern Campaign who resided in the area to come and see the Pole. "General

Kosciuszko is, with his Polish Friend, under my roof," Gates wrote, "and is hourly visited by all the best company, which finds me in constant and unremitted employment."[29] Regardless of the time and cost, Gates continued to entertain daily, hosting Gov. Clinton, the Livingtsons, and many others—dignitaries, friends, and citizens alike.

One of the visitors, the French Duke de la Rochefoucauld-Liancourt, consigned the following to his personal diary:

> There is no heart friendly to liberty, or an admirer of virtue and talent, in whom the name of Kosciusko does not excite sentiments of interest and respect. The purity and liberality of his intentions, the boldness of his undertakings, the able manner in which he conducted them, and the misfortunes and atrocious captivity which have been their consequence, are too well known to require repetition. The consequences of his wounds, which still prevent him from the free use of one of his legs, and his rigorous confinement, have impaired his health, but it now begins to be reestablished. Simple and modest, he even sheds tears of gratitude, and seems astonished at the homage he receives. He sees in every man who is the friend of liberty and of man, a brother. His countenance, sparkling with fire, discovers a soul which no circumstances can render dependent, and expresses the language of his heart. Shall I never then fight more for my country? He speaks little, particularly on the misfortunes of his country, although the thoughts of these occupy his whole soul. In a word, elevation and sentiment, grandeur, sweetness, force, goodness, all that commands respect and homage, appear to me to be concentrated in this celebrated and interesting victim of misfortune and despotism. I have met few men whose appearance so much excited in me that effect.[30]

Others vied with Gates for the honor of entertaining the popular Pole. Mrs. Janet Montgomery, the widow of Gen. Richard Montgomery, chided Gates for keeping the "Martyr to Liberty" all to himself. "I pray you offer him my respects & wishes" for "surely there is another world where Virtue and the love of one's Country will meet other rewards than wounds and death—else why did a Montgomery die—or a Polish Hero bleed."[31]

The Polish visitors finally took leave of Gates on September 29, 1798. Traveling the short distance to the North River, "We placed General Kościuszko in a boat with great difficulty," Niemcewicz reported, "and once more embracing Gen. Gates who had accompanied us to the shore, we crossed the North River."[32] Kościuszko's friendship with Gates was genuine. The feeling was reciprocated by Gates, partly because of the Pole's contributions to the Northern Campaign, and also because of his genuine friendship for the Pole's pleasant personality and liberal political beliefs. "Kosciuszko is the only pure republican I ever knew," Gates once told the artist and author William Dunlap. "He is without any dross."[33]

Moving south toward Philadelphia, the trio stopped for about three weeks at the Indian Queen Tavern in Elizabeth, New Jersey. As soon as he arrived, Kościuszko penned an emotional letter of appreciation to Gates for his hospitality. "I cannot be at rest till I desharge part of the obligation that I ow[e] to your kindness and hospitality I received in your house—if my wishes would correspond with the feelings of my heart, you would be the most happy person upon the Glob[e]—believe me that my gratitude never will stop upon any occasion to show you, as well to Convince you of my perfect respect, Esteem and afection."[34]

The epidemic of fever in Philadelphia at last over, Niemcewicz rode on ahead to find a place for Kościuszko to stay once he reached the city. He found room in a small boarding house at 172 Third Street South, on the corner of Pine Street, accommodations Niemcewicz described as "a small room where he could receive not more than four persons at one time," chosen "because of their cheapness" as Kościuszko wished. In the two modest rooms he rented, Kościuszko met with the many people who came to seek an audience with him. Once again under the scrutiny of political enemies who swarmed about the city, Kościuszko apparently attempted to give the impression his wounds had not healed as much as they had for Niemcewicz reported that the general always received his visitors either lying in bed or seated in a large chair, a bandage wapped conspicuously about his head. Among the constant stream of visitors to the humble dwelling were many of the leading Jeffersonian Republicans of the day, and several prominent French dignitaries including the Duke of Orleans, who would eventually become King of France, and his younger brothers the Duke de Montpensier and the Duke de Beaujolais.[35]

One of the most frequent visitors to the Pole's modest home was Thomas Jefferson, then the Vice President of the United States. Although the two had met briefly during the Revolution, they now became fast friends, sharing as they did a hope that the French

Revolution would spread republicanism throughout Europe. Further, Jefferson respected Kościuszko as a champion of liberty both in America and in Poland, while Kościuszko found in Jefferson a kindred republican spirit. "I see him often, and with great pleasure mixed with commiseration. He is as pure a son of liberty as I have ever known," Jefferson told Gates, "and of that liberty which is to go to all, and not to the few and the rich alone."[36]

The two spoke often and at length about politics, both American and European, with Kościuszko hoping that French military successes against Poland's partitioners would provide an opportunity for Polish independence through a political settlement or a new Polish uprising. But his hopes that the early successes of Napoleon Bonaparte might lead to Polish independence were dashed with news of the Treaty of Campo Formo. "Kosciuszko," wrote Jefferson, "has been disappointed by the sudden peace between France and Austria. A ray of hope seemed to gleam on his mind for a moment, that the extension of the revolutionary spirit through Italy and Germany, might so have occupied the remnants of monarchy there, as that his country might have risen again."[37]

Despite the peace, solicitations arrived clandestinely from Gen. Dlbrowski and other Poles beseeching Kościuszko to return to Europe and take command of the Polish troops formed under the auspices of revolutionary France. From the French Directory, which no doubt hoped to capitalize on his popularity, came an invitation to Paris for consultations. With Europe now at peace, Kościuszko hesitated, speaking instead of his intent to visit John Armstrong, to purchase land in Pennsylvania, to settle in Virginia, or any number of other ideas that would keep him in America. Whether he was genuinely considering staying in America is unlikely, more probably he continued to play the part of a retired exile in public while secretly planning to return to Europe at an opportune moment.

Whatever his intentions, he could afford neither a return to Europe nor the purchase of American land until Congress agreed to pay the debts owed him. With Congress in session, he once again sought assistance in obtaining a settlement. Taking advantage of a letter from Washington, he used his reply to once again ask the former president for his intercession.

> I return You my warmest thanks for the Honour You have done me. If the situation of my health would admit my travelling so far, I

would immediatly pay you my Respects and my personal Homage, it was my first intention, and I hope I shall at last accomplish it.

Your High Character, Reputation and the Goodness of Your Heart, may give me the liberty to mention a circumstance concerning me and is this—From the United States, I have not received neither the procent for Fourteen years nor the Sum due to me; formerly I was independent, but now my only resource is in the Justice of Congress, having lost my Certificate and wyth my Country lost my All. I must Request Sir, You will be so kind to mention my situation to that August Body and entreat, that I may be paid my Just demand; without the trouble of making other Application.[38]

Washington replied with concern for the Pole's health, complimentary comments, but also an explanation that he was not in a position to take any official action:

I am sorry that the state of your health should deprive me of the pleasure of your company at this place and I regret still more that the pain you feel from the wounds you have received—though glorious for your reputation—is the occasion of it.

Whatever I can do as a private citizen (and in no other capacity I can now act) consistently with the plan I have laid down for my future government, you may freely Command. You will find however, contrary as it may be to your expectation or wishes, that all pecuniary matters must flow from the Legislature and in a form which cannot be dispensed with. I may add I am sure, that your claim upon the justice & feelings of this country will meet with no delay. Nor do I suppose that the loss of your certificate will be any impediment.

Your rank and services in the American Army are too well known to require that testimony of your claim and the Books of the Treasury will show that you have received nothing in discharge of it—or if any part, to what amount.[39]

Washington was correct in his assessment. On December 22 John Dawson offered a resolution to constitute a committee to investigate Kościuszko's case, stating that "as it was justice only which he sought for this brave man, he doubted not that a spirit of justice would insure its adoption."[40] Instead, the House of Representatives called upon Oliver Wolcott, Secretary of the Treasury, to provide it with instructions on how Kościuszko's accounts could best be settled. Wolcott replied on December 28, Kościuszko was due $12,280.54 in principal, $2,947.33 in interest for 1785 through 1788, and the amount of interest forwarded in Kościuszko's name to Leipzig which remained unclaimed.[41] With this in hand, Dawson presented a bill authorizing payment of Kościuszko's accounts plus interest for the years 1789 through 1797. The Senate generally agreed, but amended the bill to delete payment of the interest from 1789 through 1792 which had been sent to Leipzig. After some discussion, a conference committee determined the matter in favor of the amended version of the bill which provided $3,684.16 in interest from 1793 through 1797. This brought the amount due to $18,912.03, to which could be added the $2,947.33 retrievable from Leipzig, a total of $21,859.36. Only upon his return to Europe would Kościuszko find out that the money supposedly awaiting him in Leipzig had actually been returned to the United States Treasury years before. Upon learning this, the Pole's anger overcame his usual self-control, causing him to urge Jefferson "to publishe thos[e] letters that the public should [k]now their Characters."[42]

With the dawn of 1798, relations between the United States and France became more tenuous as the pro-British Federalist-controlled government began making preparations for a possible war. Diplomatic efforts to forge a settlement brought only the calamitous XYZ Affair which burst upon the American public in April. In its aftermath, relations were strained to the breaking point while the Federalists passed the Alien and Sedition Acts aimed at stamping out internal dissent.

Faced with an impending war against France and a domestic policy aimed at silencing his supporters, Jefferson desperately sought some means of resolving the crisis between France and America. Knowing of Kościuszko's desire to return to Europe, and French efforts to enlist him in their service, his thoughts naturally turned to the Pole as a possible intermediary. "Jefferson considered that I would be the most effective intermediary in bringing an accord with France," Kościuszko later explained, "so I accepted the mission even if without any official authorization."[43]

In the same month that the XYZ Affair became public, Kościuszko received information that Polish legions were again forming in Europe, and that the French Directory was considering offering command of these forces to him. With this exhilarating news he determined to leave for Europe, but secrecy was essential to foil his enemies and protect his family from repercussions by the Czar. To achieve this Kościuszko concocted a story that he was going to visit the mineral springs in the South, and as a cover sent Niemcewicz south on a widely publicized trip supposedly to join his friend. Only Kościuszko, Niemcewicz, and Vice-President Thomas Jefferson knew the truth.[44]

Meanwhile, Jefferson obtained the required passports for the journey. Kościuszko suggested the use of an alias, Mr. Kann, to confuse his enemies, but Jefferson changed this to Thomas Kannberg. In applying for the passport, the vice president wrote that the fictitious recipient "is a most excellent character, standing in no relation whatever to any of the belligerent powers as to whom Thomas Jefferson is not afraid to be responsible for his political innocence, as he goes merely for his private business."[45] To further confuse the issue, Kósciuszko would sail for Lisbon rather than the closer French ports. "You had the goodnes to take me under your care and protection," Kościuszko wrote to the Virginian,

> I beseech [you] to continue to the end. I must know six or ten days before I go to prepare the things and in the maner that nobody should know it. It is requisit[e] that I should have passports on the name of Mr. Kann from Ministers English, Portugal, Spa[i]n, French. ... [R]ecomend me I beg you to your friend at Lisbon to help me in every thing and as I am a Stranger and will stay few days I would wish if possible that he should take me to his house upon any Condition—not forget to recomend me to the care of the Capitain in whose Ship I will go.[46]

While Jefferson concluded arrangements for the trip, Kościuszko completed his own financial and personal arrangements. After obtaining two drafts for a total of $3,600 on Amsterdam banks, he sought the advice of Jefferson, Biddle, and Charles Pettit, a Philadelphia merchant and former comrade in Greene's army, on how best to secure a steady income without risk of wild fluctuations. Such a steady income would be needed once he arrived in Europe. Jefferson suggested the use of his own private banker, John Barnes, an offer the Pole accepted.[47]

His financial arrangements completed, Kościuszko next turned to personal matters, seeking Jefferson's assistance in placing his ideas for a last will and testament into proper English. "When ever you will have a time in the daytime for a quarter of hour I beg you would grante me to finish what I have begone," the Pole asked his friend.[48] The original version of the testament read as follows:

I beg Mr. Jefferson that in case I should die without will or testament he should bye out of my money so many Negroes and free them, that the restant Sum should be Sufficient to give them education and provide for their maintenance. That is to say each should know before, the duty of a Cytyzen in the free Government, that he must defend his Country against foreign as well internal Enemis who would wish to change the Constitution for the vorst to inslave them by degree afterwards, to have good and human heart sensible for the sufferings of others, each must be maried and have 100 ackres of land, wyth instruments, Cattle for tillage and know how to manage and Gouvern it as well to know how behave to neybourghs, always wyth kindness and ready to help them—to them selves frugal to their Children give good education I mean as to the heart and the duty to ther Country, in gratitude to me to make themselves happy as possible.[49]

The final document, rendered in more formal, legal English by Jefferson, was signed and attested on April 30, with Dawson and Barnes acting as witnesses.

As April turned to May, Kościuszko became impatient to depart. "I afraid to hurt your feelings by my reiterated importunities," he wrote Jefferson, "but I am so enxious of going away, that not one moment in a day I have a rest, if this occasion fall of going to Bourdeau, I should prefer to Lisbon to avoided of being taking by the English. The Season far advenced and rumour of this Country is very desigreable to a feeling heart as we cannot talk fully upon this Subject, I beg you was kind to put me a paper like this for information how and when I expect to go."[50]

While he waited, he made final disposition of the remainder of his personal property, giving some to Barnes to be sold. Several personal items he designated as gifts for his close friends in America. To Niemcewicz he gave the plate presented to him by the citizens of Bristol during his stay in England. Jefferson received a bear skin "as a Token of my veneration, respect and Esteem for you ever," along with a sable fur presented to the Pole by Czar Paul. It is this fur which adorns the vice president in the famous Rembrandt Peale painting found even today in Jefferson's home at Monticello, the Thomas Scully likeness found in the U.S. Military Academy, and the statue of the Virginian that adorns the Jefferson Memorial in Washington, D.C.[51]

Eventually the time came. To cover Kościuszko's departure, Niemcewicz spread the rumor that his friend had left for the south to recover his health in the medicinal springs in Virginia. To further cover the departure, Niemcewicz left three days later, heading south, so he said, to join Kościuszko. Along the way he wrote to Jefferson to apprise him of the success of the ruse. "I visited Baltimore and for the last fifteen days I am at Federal City, at the house of Mr. [Thomas] Law. Everywhere I have been overwhelmed with questions, I do not know how I have acquitted myself; I only know that the profession of a liar (to him who is not used to it) is as difficult as it is humiliating. You may be sure, however, that the secret is strictly kept, nobody guesses the truth; some think that he, in fact, is on his way to the baths, others imagine that we have quarrelled and separated. At last someone wrote from Philadelphia that you have kidnapped and concealed him at Monticello. You are then accused of rapture and violence, try to clear yourself as well as you can."[52]

The precautions taken by Kościuszko, Jefferson, and Niemcewicz appear to have been very successful in covering the departure. "Your departure is not yet known, or even suspected," Jefferson wrote to Kościuszko June 1. "The times do not permit an indulgence in political disquisitions. But they forbid not the effusion of friendship, and not my warmest toward you, which no time shall alter."[53] Nearly three weeks later he again assured Kościuszko that the prevailing opinion among the public believed he had "gone to the medicinal Springs in Virginia."[54] In fact, while rumors abounded, the truth did not become generally known until reports of Kościuszko's arrival in France finally appeared in American newspapers in early September.

Chapter 14

"The Only Solace of My Life"

When Kościuszko once again set foot on French soil at Bayonne on June 28 it was without the assistance of his servant, or even his crutches. When he heard of it, Niemcewicz considered the recovery "mysterious & wonderful." Whether it was, as Haiman speculated, the reinvigoration of his will once he found himself again in the employ of freedom, or, as his enemies believed, that he was only magnifying the extent of his wounds to gain sympathy in America, or that the wounds had actually healed to a degree sufficient to allow him more mobility will probably never be known for sure. Regardless, though still lacking his youthful zest the Pole did appear to regain much of his enthusiasm for life upon his return to Europe and it may well be this mental change which helped bring about his seeming physical recovery.[1]

Although the documentation is sketchy, as one would expect for a secret mission, it appears that Kościuszko's first efforts in France were aimed at promoting Jefferson's desire to ease tensions between the United States and France. To accomplish this he met with Elbridge Gerry, from whom he no doubt obtained the latest information on the crisis and the official and unofficial views of the American government. He also met with Dr. George Logan, himself acting as an unofficial emissary to try and diffuse tensions. At the same time he was meeting with the Americans, he also initiated contacts with the French Directory and its individual members who were known to be pro-American in sentiments. Soon, the Directory agreed to rescind its blockade of American shipping, release imprisoned American seamen, and open normal diplomatic relations.[2] The success of his efforts on behalf of his "second home" were attested to by Nathaniel Cutting, an American diplomat, who advised Jefferson that Kościuszko "has, I am persuaded, improved every opportunity of pleading our cause at the Fountain-head of Power in this Country," and his interventions had a "good effect."[3] While some, notably Federalist partisan George Cabot, complained that Kościuszko's efforts had been more of an impediment than a help, most did not share that sentiment. In fact, Richard Codman, a Federalist who was actually a witness to the events in France at that time, asserted that Kościuszko's appeals were one of the factors responsible for the change in French policy and the subsequent easing of tensions between the two nations. Further, another witness, French author Antoine Jullien, confirmed that Kościuszko's activities among "the Executive Directory contributed much to bringing France and the United States closer."[4]

For his part, Kościuszko penned the following report to Jefferson:

> The Amicable disposition of the Gouvernment of France are really favorable to the interest of the United States, by the recent prouves they give, you ought not to doubt that they choose to be in peace and in perfect harmonie with America. Before it was misrepresented by some the facts relative to your Contry, but now they are perfectly acquiented wyth yours and their interests and Mr. Logan eyewitness of the Sentyment they have towards the Nation of the United States. At present it is a duty of every true American as you, to publishe and propagate their friendship, and to Compele your Gouvernment by the Opinion of the Nation to the pacifique Measures with Republique of France, otherwise you cannot but to loose every thing even your Liberty by a conexion so intimet wyth England which increasing son influence can easily subdue and exercise son despotique pouver as before. Write me soon as possible of the effects which the news by Logan's arrival will produce in America, as well as by the Election of the members for Congress, you may rely upon my indevours here but you most work in America wyth your friends and Republicans and state their reall interest.[5]

Throughout his stay in France Kościuszko maintained close ties to the American community there, as well as corresponding with Jefferson and his many other friends in America. Yet the correspondence was of necessity frequently limited or otherwise circumscribed due to the fluctuating political situation between the United States and France. "On politics I must write sparingly," Jefferson warned in 1799, "lest it fall into the hands of persons who do not love either you or me." After discussing in a general fashion the reigning fears of possible war between the two nations, and his hopes that the American government would become a model of freedom and order, the Virginian closed with a wish for the success of Kościuszko's own cause in Europe. "May Heaven have in store for your country a restoration of these blessings," he hoped, "and you be destined as the instrument it will use for that purpose. But if this be forbidden by fate, I hope we shall be able to preserve here an asylum where your love of liberty and disinterested patriotism will be forever protected and honored, and where you will find in the hearts of the American people, a good portion of that esteemed affection which glow in the bosom of the friend who writes this."[6] Later, when the War of 1812 broke out between England and the United States, Kościuszko took advantage of the presence of English diplomats in Paris following Napoleon's defeat in 1814 to lobby the British to end the war against his second homeland.[7]

Quite often travelers or businessmen sought out the Pole for information on America or letters of introduction. One such person was the Irish patriot Thomas Addis Emmet whom the Pole recommended to George Clinton as a "great sufferer for his opinion to liberty." The letter helped the exiled son of Erin begin a new life as an attorney in New York. Another whom he assisted was Francis J. N. Neef who migrated to Philadelphia where he established the first school in America dedicated to the educational principles of Pestalozzi.[8]

Kościuszko also acted as intermediary to introduce his Polish and American friends to one another, thereby strengthening the personal friendships and good feelings between the two lands most dear to him. Sometimes this practice required diplomacy because of the decided cultural differences, while other times called for insistence. Madame Wiridjanna Fiszer relates, for example, an occasion when Kościuszko invited her to accompany him to visit Robert R. Livingston, the American Minister in Paris. Upon arriving, they found that a ball was in progress and Madame Fiszer, not being dressed for a formal occasion of state declined to enter. Rather, she insisted on staying in the carriage while Kościuszko paid his respects. Soon after entering, however, he returned with several men and told her that she would either assent to entering of her own accord or the men would carry her in. "They are not Frenchmen," he explained, "they are Americans, honest people; put away your ceremoniousness and be a good girl." With this Madame Fiszer, left with little alternative, agreed. Later she admitted to having one of the most enjoyable evenings of her life.[9]

Although Kościuszko maintained good relations with Livingston and the other American diplomats, he was happy when the American Minister was replaced by John Armstrong, his comrade-in-arms from the Northern Campaigns. One of the closest of his American friends, Armstrong named his son Kościuszko Armstrong in honor of the Pole who acted as godfather at the boy's christening in 1806. Before leaving France, the Pole bequeathed a small sum of money to his namesake as a token of appreciation and friendship.[10]

His most sustained correspondence was with Thomas Jefferson, not only because of the Virginian's assistance with his American investments, but because the two shared a close philosophical bond. "[Y]ou are the only hope of all humanity," he once wrote to Jefferson, "and I should like you to be an example to posterity."[11] When the Virginian was elected president in 1800 Kościuszko quickly wrote to congratulate him. "I most before hand pay you the first my respects as to the President of the United States. I hope you will be the same in that new station always good, true Americane a Philosopher and my Friend."[12] With his philosophical twin at the head of the American government, the Pole's joy knew few bounds, yet he was not so overcome as to forget the plight of his own oppressed homeland. "At last Virtue is triumphing," he wrote, "if not yet in the old, then at least in the new World. The people of decency and solid judgment became aware that they must nominate you for the sake of their happiness and independence and they do not err. I add my wishes to the General voice. Meanwhile remember that the first Post of the State which always is beset by flatterers, intrigants, hypocrites and by Men of bad will, should be Surrounded by Men of Character of honest talents and of strict probity.... Do not forget yourself in your station be always virtuous, a Republican of justice and probity without pomp and aspirations, in one word remain a Jefferson and my friend."[13] Later, in another letter he cautioned his friend to act judiciously but forcefully. "A statesman like you, and, above all, with your disposition and your learning, must strive to give unity of action to his nation and to establish [its] respectable and strong character.... For God's sake, do not be undecided, act with determined energy befitting a Great Man which you have to be. ... Do not deceive yourself, it is pusillanimity and indecision which destroy Nations, but never their valor and ardor."[14]

Jefferson shared the same high opinion of his Polish friend, confiding to him that "Your principles ... were made to be honored, revered and loved."[15] But, seeking more than political discussions, the Virginian also complained about the Pole's continuing timid modesty. "Your letters are too barren of what I wish most to hear, I mean things relating to yourself."[16] Upon his inauguration as president, his thoughts turned to his friend in Paris. "It would give me exquisite pleasure," he wrote, "to have you here a witness to our country and recognize the people whom you knew during the war."[17]

As the correspondence continued, Kościuszko reminded his friend of the necessity to be ever vigilant in the pursuit of liberty. To strengthen and perpetuate the spirit of democracy he proposed a national education system and the establishment of a military academy which, much like his own experience in Warsaw many years before, could at once educate young men in the ideals of democracy and the military arts necessary to sustain that freedom. He recommended that this national school be large enough to house 600 to 3,000 students at a time, and that admission be granted to people from each of the states, poor as well as rich, by examination.[18] Ironically, his vision would eventually come to fruition within the confines of the very fortress he built to secure the liberties he sought to maintain. The United States Military Academy was established in 1802, under the presidency of his friend Thomas Jefferson, along the banks of the Hudson River at West Point.

Kościuszko's continuing interest in and support of the United States was also apparent when Gen. William R. Davie, then the United States envoy to France, noting the lack of any artillery manual in the entire American army, asked Kościuszko if he would fill this void in the national defense. The Pole readily agreed. Because of his hesitancy in written English, he penned the final document in French in 1800. Davie had it translated into English and sent it to the United States Military Philosophical Society of West Point urging that its publication "would be of great importance to our country. It is perhaps the only treatise on this subject in the world." Published by Campbell and Mitchell in New York in 1808 as *Manoeuvres of Horse Artillery*, it was the first such manual in the American army, one of the first in the world, and was used extensively at West Point, various other military schools, and disseminated among existing officers, providing valuable expertise during the War of 1812. In fact, the authoritative *Historical Sketch of the Organization, Administration, Material and Tactics of Artillery, United States Army*, published in 1884, states that the War of 1812 "was declared without the Government having at its disposal any system of manoeuvers for the artillery except that of Kosciuszko." This distinction earned for its author the title "Father of American Artillery."[19]

Another of Kościuszko's suggestions was the establishment of a civilian decoration to be awarded to "those who have shown more attachment and devotion to the Republican Government, more Justice, Probity, disinterestedness, Love of their parents; For inventions in, the Arts, in the Sciences and especially in Agriculture; and at last, for all those virtues and Social qualities which alone should distinguish us one from another."[20] He had suggested such an award in Poland during the insurrection in 1794. While the suggestion was not acted on then, President John F. Kennedy created an award for meritorious achievement in civilian fields when he reauthorized the Medal of Freedom, much as Kościuszko had envisioned more than a century and a half earlier.

All of these suggestions, put forward at length and in detail in Kościuszko's voluminous correspondence with Jefferson, the Virginian acknowledged with gratitude. His concern for the future of America was, Jefferson wrote, "worthy of your philanthropy and disinterested attachment to the freedom and happiniess of man."[21] Yet, extensive as his efforts on behalf of America were during his years in France, his heart remained pained over the fate of suffering Poland. When Kościuszko returned to France from America in 1798 he arrived during a period of great uncertainty for the Polish cause. The First Coalition had been defeated, but a Second Coalition bringing Russia, Great Britain, Austria, Naples, Portugal, and the Ottoman Empire into the field against France formed in December, 1798.[22]

In preparation for an eventual return to his homeland, Kościuszko visited the ministers and representatives of governments who might be friendly toward the resurrection of Poland, lobbied for French support, and contacted all of his old comrades-in-arms and others in the Polish exile communities throughout Europe. He also took the opportunity to publicly break his truce with Czar Paul. In an open letter, the Pole returned the gifts bestowed upon him by the autocrat as part of his release from prison, while complaining of the treatment he received from the Czar's ministers.

> I take the advantage of the first moments of the liberty which I am enjoying under the protecting laws of the greatest and most generous nation, to return to you your gift which the semblance of your benevolence and the atrocious conduct of your ministers forced me to accept. If I accepted it, Sire, you must only attribute it to the irresistible strength of the attachment which I bear towards my compatriots, companions of my misfortune, and to the hope of again serving my country. Yes, I repeat it, Sire, and take pleasure in declaring it to you; your heart appeared to me to be touched by my unfortunate situation; but your ministers and their satellites did not act towards me in conformity with your wishes. And also, if they have dared to attribute to an act of my own free will a proceeding which they forced me to take, I will unmask before you and before all men who understand the price of honour, their violence and their perfidy, and they alone, Sire, should be answerable to you for the publication of their iniquities.[23]

"Through this act," Askenazy explained, "he brought upon himself the rage and fear of the partitioning Governments, and soon the latter issued orders for his capture." The Czar, labelling the Pole a "traitor," issued an arrest decree should he ever appear in Russian dominated lands, while each of the partitioning powers, now allied against the French in the Second Coalition, dispatched agents to keep him under close scrutiny in France.[24]

William Cobbett, a British journalist, saw it differently. Now that England was at war with France, Kościuszko's detractors took advantage of his residence in the lands of the enemy to attack his move as selfishly motivated, hoping thereby to incite American opinion against him and against France. "Now, here is an impudent fellow!" the Englishman wrote.

> He very willingly received presents from the Emperor and his ministers; he comes afterwards, pleads poverty, and received thousands of dollars from the ill-judging liberality of the American Congress; having pocketed this, he goes to France, whence he effects to return (he will never return any of them) the presents received from the Emperor of Russia, he boasts of the protecting laws of the most watchful, most jealous despotism, that ever human beings breathed under. Americans, remember I told you, that this fellow was no friend

of yours, and you now see him extolling the generosity of your enemy, the generosity of that enemy, by whom, he well knows, you have been robbed of twenty or thirty millions of dollars! This is an instance of the friendship of those pretended patriots; these citizens of the world.

It is very evident that Kosciusko is a mere tool in the hands of the Directory.... He is, in fact, the "Spurious Envoy" from Poland. The French Sultans have a gang of these miscreants about their heels; with whom they consult with respect to the intrigues to be employed against their respective countries.[25]

But these were the words of partisan politics. Though loyal enough to his imprisoned comrades to accept the czar's offer as a means of securing their release, Kościuszko was, throughout his entire life, deeply committed to the ideals of personal liberty and equality before the law. "[I]n nature we are all equal," he wrote, and he attempted to live these word in his life.[26] In France, he once again became intellectually stimulated in the atmosphere of revolution. In the revolt he led, Kościuszko supported the rights of the peasantry, and he once lamented that monarchs always wish "to have people obedient as the cattle that peacefully go to the slaughter-house."[27] Yet, these beliefs did not necessarily mean that Kościuszko supported all aspects of the new French Revolution. According to Józef Żuraw, "Like other leading figures of the age, Kościuszko combined his struggle with the ancient regime with the fight against its religious outlook on life. According to his philosophy, the state could only possess a natural religion. The idea of the citizen of honour of the French Revolution was directed against the traditional Christian vision of the world. He opposed to it the idea of the affirmation of the mind and rationalization of the social existence of man."[28] According to Żuraw, as Kościuszko's philosophical ideas evolved, they reflected a synthesis of rationalism and empiricism typical of Polish Enlightenment philosophers who believed in education for citizenry rather than only scientists. "In their opinion the important components of the patriotic attitude of a Pole are battle and work, weapon and pen," explained Żuraw. "This was shown by Kościuszko. His ideas, the ideas of the Insurrection, constitute the acme of the Polish Enlightenment. In the opinion of Engels, Kościuszko fought for an independent Poland and simultaneously for the universal law of equality."[29]

The situation current in France provided Kościuszko with an opportunity to once again combine the components of "weapon and pen." When the Polish Legions formed under Napoleon heard of his arrival in France they gained new hope after the disappointments of the defeats at Trebbia and Novi and the resulting peace. Instantly they dispatched earnest entreaties beseeching Kościuszko to lead them, sending along the sword of King John III Sobieski, the victor of Vienna, to the one whom the legionnaires believed their natural leader. "I want to be ever and inseparably with you," he replied, "I want to join you to serve our common country.... Like you I have fought for the country, like you I have suffered, like you I expect to regain it. This hope is the only solace of my life."[30] In a letter acknowledging receipt of the sword, Kościuszko prayed that "God grant that we may lay down our swords together with the sword of Sobieski in the temple of peace, having won freedom and universal happiness for our compatriots."[31] Despite their earnest entreaties, and his own fervent hope that these small formations of Polish troops would eventually form the backbone of a new and independent Polish armed forces, Kościuszko would not assume command of the Legions. Instead he lobbied incessantly with the Directory for aid and assurances of French support for a reconstituted, independent Poland, refusing his direct participation in the Legions or his active support of France until such assurances were proffered.[32]

Despite Kościuszko's high hopes for the eventual independence of his homeland, the French Directory saw him only as a means to its own ends, a tool to be used, if possible, to further French aspirations in Europe. Through him the Directory hoped to rally Polish troops to its colors and gain the sympathy of liberty-loving people throughout the continent. Napoleon, too, harbored similar goals. Upon his return from Egypt, Bonaparte visited Kościuszko in Paris, intent upon soliciting his participation in the next act of the European drama. But Kościuszko remained aloof, and when the Corsican staged his *coup d'etat* the wedge between him and the Polish republican widened, becoming virtually insurmountable when Napoleon ignored Polish aspirations in signing the Treaty of Lunéville in 1801.[33]

Unlike Kościuszko, many Poles supported Napoleon in the hope that a French victory would benefit their homeland. Thousands joined the Legions or other forces serving with the French Army, while esteemed leaders such as Prince Poniatowski lent their prestige and their blood to Napoleon's conquests in the hope that victory would lead to a restoration of Polish independence. Kościuszko harbored no such illusions. "Do not think," he wrote, "that he [Napoleon] will restore Poland; he thinks only of himself. He hates every great nationality and still more the spirit of independence. He is a tyrant, and his only aim is to satisfy his own ambition. I am sure he will create nothing durable."[34]

In his disappointment over French reticence to embrace the cause of Polish independence, heightened by his personal dislike of Napoleon, Kościuszko apparently flirted with the idea of returning to America. After Jefferson's election as president, Kościuszko mused about his desire "to deposit my ashes in a land of freedom where honesty and justice prevail," but nothing more came of the passing thoughts.[35] In his disgust with French perfidies, Kościuszko also considered the possibility of a new Polish revolution, issuing a pamphlet calling for the emancipation of the peasantry, the establishment of an independent Polish Congress along the lines of the Continental Congress, and the implementation of paper money as a means of financing the new attempt. All of these were ideas he brought back from his American experience, determined to use them to regain Poland's independence. Yet the publication of his pamphlet brought only closer scrutiny from French authorities.

Under the constraints of constant surveillance, the weight of a suffering nation upon his shoulders, Kościuszko grew increasingly unhappy in Paris. In 1801, on the invitation of Peter Joseph Zeltner, Swiss Minister to France, the Pole removed himself to the diplomat's estate at Berville, near Fontainebleau.[36] There, he lived an austere life despite the elegance of his surroundings and the prominence of his hosts. "His living quarters," a visitor reported, "comprised several unheated and unfurnished rooms, through which one passed to the last room where fire burned and some of the most indispensable pieces of furniture stood. Here he slept and received visitors, often while still in bed or in his dressing gown. Whoever visited him once, could freely visit him at any time without fear of embarrassing him; he did everything in the presence of his guests, as if he were alone, and as he received his friends only, he thought they would not take it amiss."[37]

Though refusing to treat with Napoleon until the French leader provided assurances of his support for an independent Poland, distinguished visitors nevertheless journeyed with regularity to Berville to meet the popular figure of American and Polish liberty. Historians, mathematicians, poets, generals, politicians, the whole spectrum of European and American society passed through his apartment, yet he retained the sense of modesty that characterized his whole life. "[H]e seems to regret," observed the English writer Mary Williams, "that great deeds do sentence great men to fame."[38]

Among the most regular of his visitors were the Marquis de Lafayette and members of the American diplomatic legation. As always, he used these occasions to keep informed of developments in America and to impress on each visitor the sad plight of his native land. His keen interest in political affairs made an impression on Francis Xavier Zeltner, nephew of his host, who noted that the Pole's heart "throbbed for the whole world."[39] But his continuing interest in politics, coupled with his seeming powerlessness to effect any change in the plight of Poland, caused a great frustration in his life. "As for myself," he lamented in a letter to Jefferson, "far from my homeland, I do nothing, you undoubtedly know the reason, I am resting in inactivity and am of no service to humanity."[40]

Among his diversions, Kościuszko enjoyed sketching, gardening, playing chess and whist, and horseback riding. His sketches he frequently presented to friends and guests as personal gifts. "I saw Genl's LaFayette and Kusciusko often," James Monroe reported while on a diplomatic mission to France in 1803. "They are the men you always knew them to be. Kusciusko lives near the barrier St. Andre not far from St. Antoine, where he cultivates his own garden."[41]

Another pleasure the retired general enjoyed was the opportunity to play for long hours with the Zeltners' children who treated him as an uncle. "All four accompanied him continually," a visitor later wrote, "filled his room with their noises, climbed to his knees and completely took possession of him; he caressed or chided them. The youngest of them all was a six-months daughter who bore his name—Thaddea."[42] The Pole also took it upon himself to act as tutor for the Zeltner children, no doubt instilling in them the same virtues he committed to writing to a teenage Conrad Zeltner:

Rising at 4 o'clock in summer and at six o'clock in winter, Your first thought must be directed towards the Supreme Being, worshipping him for a few minutes; Put yourself at once to work with reflexion and intelligence, either to your prescribed duty, with the most scrupulous exactitude, or to perfect yourself in some science of which you should have a true mastery. Be always frank and loyal ... and always speak the truth; never be idle, be sober and frugal and even hard for your own self but indulgent towards others; shun selfishness and egotism; before speaking something or answering, reflect well and reason.... Never fail to make obvious your gratitude in all circumstances to a Person who takes charge of Your happiness. Look forward to his desires, his wishes, be attentive ... always look for an occasion to render yourself useful. Because you are a Stranger in the country you must double your cares and efforts to earn legitimately the confidence and the preference over the natives by your merit and your superior knowledge. If a secret is entrusted to you, keep it religiously; in all your actions you must be upright, sincere and open, no dissimulation in any of your talk, never argue, but seek truth serenely and modestly; be polite and considerate to everyone, agreeable and obliging in society, always humane and succour the poor according to your means; read instructive books to embellish your Mind or better your heart, never degrade yourself by making bad acquaintances, but be always with persons full of morals and of good reputation; at last, your conduct must be such that everyone approves of it.[43]

With Napoleon's crushing victory over the Prussians at Jena, the Emperor again approached the aging republican during the Polish War of 1806-1807, hoping to obtain his support as a means of rallying the Poles to his side. In 1806 Napoleon attempted to summon Kościuszko to his side in Berlin, planning to use the Pole's popularity to gain the support of his countrymen for his upcoming campaign against the Russians and Prussians in Poland. But Kościuszko, sensing an opportunity to press his hopes for Poland, demanded as the price for his support (1) recreation of a Polish nation with its eastern border stretching from Riga to Odessa, its north along the Baltic including Gdańsk, and its south anchored on the Hungarian border, (2) the establishment in Poland of a government organized along English parliamentary lines, and (3) freedom for the Polish peasantry with title to the lands they worked. When Napoleon refused any commitments, Kościuszko once again declined to have any part in his grandiose scheme. Although an appeal to Poles appeared over his name in the *Moniteur* on November 1, 1806, he vigorously denied its authenticity.[44]

In frustration, and fearing the possibility that other Poles might not fully support his cause, Napoleon wrote to Marshal Joachim Murat in Warsaw in December, 1806, cautioning him, in a clear reference to Kościuszko, against "those who, before declaring themselves, demand so many guarantees" as these men "are egoists uninflamed by love of country. I am old in my knowledge of men.

My greatness is not founded on the help of a few thousand Poles. It is for them to profit enthusiastically by existing facts; it is not for me to take the first step. Let them show a firm resolve to win their independence ... and then I shall see what I have to do."[45]

Losing any hope of French support for Polish independence, Kościuszko began to consider alliance with Czar Alexander I, who ascended the throne with a reputation for liberalism. A friend of Prince Adam Jerzy Czartoryski, the son of Kościuszko's former patron, Alexander was known to harbor positive feelings for Poland, a belief held more closely when the new czar proved to be lenient in his treatment of his Polish subjects, including the appointment of Czartoryski to head czarist foreign affairs.[46]

With the defeat of Napoleon in 1814, Russian troops arrived near Kościuszko's residence in Berville. When he came upon a band of Poles serving in the Russian army who were about to set fire to a group of small homes, the Pole galloped in amongst the soldiers shouting "Stop, soldiers, stop! When I was still at the head of the brave soldiers of Poland none of them ever thought of pillage, and I should have rigorously punished the soldiers, and still more inexorably the officers, guilty of such outrages!"

"And who are you," replied the soldiers, "who arrogate to yourself the right of rebuking us in this manner?"

"I am Kosciuszko!" the Pole thundered. "At these words," a witness related, "soldiers and officers threw down their arms. They knelt down before him, and, clasping his knees according to Sarmatian custom, and in token of repentance strewing dust on their heads, they implored his forgiveness. Berville was spared."[47]

In the wake of the Russian troops came Czar Alexander. Upon arriving in Paris he met with Kościuszko, treating the aging Polish patriot with kindness and esteem. Declining any personal honors, the Pole sought Russian support for the restoration of an independent Poland and an amnesty for Polish political prisoners.[48] On April 9, 1814, Kościuszko sent the following letter to Alexander seeking to ameliorate the fate of Poles who had supported Napoleon and preserve some form of Polish sovereignty.

> I request three favours of you: the first is to grant a general amnesty to the Poles without any restriction, and that the serfs scattered in foreign countries may be regarded as free if they return to their homes; the second, that Your Majesty will proclaim yourself King of Poland, with a free constitution approaching that of England, and that you

cause schools to be established there for the instruction of the serfs; that their servitude be abolished at the end of ten years, and that they may enjoy the full possession of their property. If my prayers are granted, I will go in person, though ill, to throw myself at Your Majesty's feet to thank you, and to be the first to render homage to my sovereign.[49]

Although the provisions in Kościuszko's request seem out of character for one who so steadfastly refused to compromise Polish independence, by the time he wrote this letter the fortunes of war had turned against Napoleon and, in any event, the Pole had no doubt lost any hope of French support for an independent Poland. Then too, some historians have noted the probable influence of Prince Czarto-ryski in shaping what can be considered a compromise to preserve at least some independence for his homeland and the prospect of liberty for the peasantry.[50]

Alexander replied, ironically on May 3, as follows:

I feel great satisfaction, General, in answering your letter. Your wishes shall be accomplished. With the help of the Almighty, I trust to realize the regeneration of the brave and respectable nation to which you belong. I have made a solemn engagement, and its welfare has always occupied my thoughts. Only political circumstances have placed obstacles in the way of the execution of my intentions. Those obstacles no longer exist. ... Yet a little more time and prudence, and the Poles shall regain their country, their name, and I shall have the pleasure of convincing them that, forgetting the past, the man whom they held to be their enemy is the man who shall fulfil their desires. How satisfactory it would be to me, General, to see you my helpmate in the accomplishment of these salutary labours! Your name, your character, your talents will be my best support.[51]

The czar appeared supportive, but once again there would be only disappointment. When the Congress of Vienna met to establish a European peace following the final defeat of Napoleon, Prince Czartoryski invited Kościuszko to the Austrian capital for the nego-tiations. Hoping at last for the prize that had eluded him for so many years, he undertook the difficult journey only to witness the czar, under pressure from other European nations, abandon his promises of an independent Poland. Instead, in May, 1815, the Congress created the "Kingdom of Poland," a miniscule dependency of Russia smaller in size than the unacceptable Duchy of Warsaw created by

Napoleon. "European politics," he bitterly wrote to Jefferson, "are nothing else than an art of the best seduction. Their object ... is plunder."[52]

Completely distrusting European political leadership, Kościuszko rejected an offer from the czar to return to Poland. "A citizen who wants to pride himself on being a good Pole should sacrifice everything for his country," he wrote from Vienna, "and always be human and righteous." Having sacrificed so much for his nation, he would now sacrifice the opportunity to settle once again in his homeland. "I do not want," he explained, "to return to my country until it will be restored in its entirety with a free constitution."[53] To Prince Czartoryski, Kościuszko articulated his fears and frustrations:

> You are certainly convinced that to serve my country efficaciously is my chief object. The refusal of the Emperor to answer my last letter removes me from the possibility of being of service to her. I have consecrated my life to the greater part of the nation, when to the whole it was not possible, but not to that small part to which is given the pompous name of the Kingdom of Poland. We should give grateful thanks to the Emperor for the resuscitation of the lost Polish name, but a name alone does not constitute a nation. ... I see no guarantee of the promise the Emperor made to me and to many others of the restoration of our country from the Dnieper to the Dvina, the old boundaries of the Kingdom of Poland, except only in our desires. ... But as things go now, and from the very beginning, Russians hold together with ours the first places in the government. That certainly cannot inspire Poles with any great confidence. On the contrary, with dread each of us will form the conclusions that the Polish name will in time be held in contempt, and that the Russians will treat us as their conquered subjects, for such a scanty handful of a population will never be able to defend itself against the intrigues, the preponderance and the violence of the Russians. And can we keep silence about those brothers of ours remaining under the Russian government? Our hearts shudder and suffer that they are not united to the others.[54]

Discouraged, Kościuszko made his way westward toward France, stopping off in Soleure, Switzerland to visit Francis Xavier Zeltner, brother of the Swiss Minister to France and a government official in the Swiss Canton of Soleure. The two quickly became friends, leading to an invitation to stay. Not wishing to live in a France once again ruled by the Bourbon kings, Kościuszko accepted, grateful for the opportunity to reside in Europe's lone remaining republic.[55]

Chapter 15

"I Wished to Serve My Country"

A quiet little city at the foot of the pine covered Jura Mountains, Soleure lay in sight of the ruggedly majestic peaks of the Alps. A visitor once characterized it as "fragrant pine groves, beautiful meadows, and the most delightful views which a lover of nature can wish for." As the capital of the Canton, it also contained the amenities that commercial and political leaders required, but it was the presence of his friends the Zeltners and the peaceful tranquility of the Swiss republic that drew Kościuszko to this retirement haven.[1]

The arrival of the hero of liberty in Soleure caused considerable excitement, the citizens staging a procession in his honor, while the governing council sent an official delegation of welcome to wait on him at the Zeltner home. In keeping with his natural modesty, the Pole declined any personal honors, intent upon living peacefully as a typical townsman. Kościuszko took up residence with the Zeltner family, paying them three francs per day for his sustenance, but soon his amiable ways led to his acceptance as one of the family, giving him in his remaining years the warmth of home and family he lacked for so long. Still suffering from the effects of his wounds which made it difficult for him to get about, Kościuszko appreciated the friendship and care he found in the Zeltner home. He slept on a simple bed in a small room, took his meals with the family, and apparently allowed himself only two comforts, a pony that he used to ride quietly about the countryside and an older man who acted as his sometime manservant to assist him about and complete errands that his physical condition rendered tiring.[2]

Never losing his interest in education, Kościuszko spent some of his time reading geography and history, while devoting considerable time to the education of twelve-year-old Emily Zeltner, emphasizing subjects such as history, mathematics, and drawing. Taking great enjoyment in the activities of the neighborhood youths, he hosted parties for Emily and her friends, told stories to the frequent youthful visitors, and always had sweets to distribute to the girl and her playmates.[3]

When he felt up to it physically, Kościuszko enjoyed riding about the countryside or walking through the streets of Soleure. In town, he was frequently followed by groups of children to whom he doled out sugar-plums and other treats. Always fond of children, he arranged parties, told funny stories, played games, and otherwise spent as much time with the neighborhood's youngsters as he could. Though forsaking formal occasions, he stopped frequently during his walks to speak with merchants, laborers, farmers, and the other common folk among whom he resided. On his rides into the countryside he sought out the less-traveled trailways along the Jura, stopping occasionally to visit with the people he met along the way. "Wherever he knew of a needy family," it has been reported, "of a poor patient distressed on his sick-bed by the pangs of want, he dismounted, tied his horse to a tree, entered the cabin, and brought consolation and liberal gifts to the inmates. For this purpose he always had on his daily excursions in the saddle-bags of his horse a couple of bottles of generous old wine, which he presented to poor sufferers as an elixir of life and vigor. For long no one knew who was the tall, kind old gentleman, with the mild, beaming eyes, and the always open hand; for before the poor whom he visited had recovered from their surprise at his munificence he had already mounted his horse again, and was trotting toward the cabin of another poor man. Nor did he forget the beggars on the road, the traveling journeymen, and invalid soldiers, and never did he set out without having a handful of small coins in his pocket."[4]

Despite the outward appearance of tranquility, Kościuszko continued to mourn for the fate of his homeland. "I beg you," he pleaded with a Polish friend, "often to send me news about yourself, but above all about our dear Fatherland; it returns to my thoughts every night. From all my soul I wished to serve my Country. I have been unsuccessful and it gives me much pain."[5] Another time he lamented the final betrayal of his homeland in a bitter letter to Jefferson:

Czar Alexander promised me a Constitutional Government, Liberal,

Independent, even the emancipation of our unhappy Peasants and to make them Proprietors of the lands which they hold; by this alone he would immortalize himself, but it disappeared as smoke. I am now in the town of Soleure in Switzerland, looking at the Allied Powers which break their good faith, commit Injustices against small States and treat their own people like wolves treat sheep.[6]

In response, the Virginian invited Kościuszko to retire to America where he might live peacefully among his many friends. But the Pole declined.

I greatly and with all my gratefulness appreciate your gracious invitation, but my Country lies heavy upon my heart, and there are also my friends, my acquaintances, and sometimes I like to give them my advice. I am the only true Pole in Europe, all others are by circumstances subject to Different Powers. Perhaps you may say that this is the most unhappy country, yes, no doubt, but just for that reason it is in the greatest need of advice. Everywhere, my dear and Respectable Friend, one can be independent if he thinks right, reasons right, has a good heart, human sentiments, and a Character firm and candid.[7]

Not wishing to return to a Poland in shackles, his decision to reject Jefferson's offer meant he would spend his remaining years in his Swiss retreat. No doubt he felt this to be his final residence for about this time he also began concluding his outstanding business affairs. On April 2, 1817, he penned a document bequeathing his estate at Siechnowice to his niece, Katarzyna Estko, and her children, with the provision that the serfs on the estate be declared "free citizens and proprietors of the soil which they had hitherto cultivated, and provided also that they should henceforth not pay any more taxes in money, kind, or labor to the lords of the manor."[8]

During the summer of 1817, Princess Lubomirska, his youthful love, visited him in Soleure on her way to Italy. The visit lasted several weeks, bringing to Kościuszko a great happiness. When she was about to leave, the princess promised to visit again in the spring on her return from Italy, but the aging general asked her if she might also leave him some keepsake. She promised to send him one. Faithful to the commitment, once she arrived in Lausanne she sent him a gold ring inscribed *"L'amitié a' la vertue."*[9]

That fall an epidemic of typhoid fever swept through Soleure, making its appearance around the beginning of October. Against any eventuality, Kościuszko took the precaution of penning his will, leaving most of his funds to the Zeltner family, with a special gift for young Emily. Also remembered were the local orphan asylum and various other charities close to his heart, including a cash sum left for distribution to the poor. The sword of Sobieski, presented to him by the legionnaires serving under Napoleon, was to be returned to the Polish nation. In keeping with his personality, he stipulated that he be given a simple funeral with his coffin borne by six poor men.[10] Soon the disease made its appearance, confining Kościuszko to bed where he was attended constantly by Xaver Zeltner. The two spoke of politics, Kościuszko ruminating about the future of his homeland. Though he did not at first appear to be greatly stricken, the disease progressed until his strength began to ebb. By the evening of October 14 his condition was serious. Ranged about him, the Zeltners and a few other close friends sat in sorrowful vigil. The next day, sensing the end, Kościuszko pronounced his blessings on those present, speaking to each individually in turn. As night approached, "he raised himself up with a last spasmodic effort, held out his hands to Mr. and Madame Zeltner, greeted his Emily with a sweet smile, and, heaving a gentle sigh, sank back. He was dead."[11]

The funeral was simple, although the many mourners swelled the procession to large proportions as it wound through the streets. Six poor men carried the coffin, while a group of orphan children led the procession to Sts. Ursus and Victor Church, a local Jesuit sanctuary where his body was placed in a lead coffin in the building's vault. On the approval of Alexander I, the Polish patriot's last remains were eventually removed to Kraków where they were laid to rest on June 23, 1818, in a sarcophagus in the Wawel Cathedral among the kings, queens, and other prominent people of Polish history. The place selected for him was next to the bodies of John III Sobieski, who saved Vienna from the Turks, and Prince Joseph Poniatowski, a friend of Kościuszko who, as Marshal of France, was killed leading Napoleon's rear guard at Leipzig. Stanisław Wodzicki, in his funeral oration, noted that "echoes of admiration for him rang from humble cottages to splendid palaces; he made no distinctions between the estates under his protection." His heart remained behind. Placed in a small metal box when the body was embalmed, it was buried in a graveyard at Zuchwil under a monument inscribed with the words "Viscera Thaddei Kosciuszko." "The heart of the Polish General throbbed for the whole world," Zeltner explained, "let it, then, be accessible here to the veneration of all mankind."[12]

As word of Kościuszko's death spread, universal mourning began. In Paris, the church of St. Roche held a requiem Mass on October 31 attended by Americans residing in the city, as well as French admirers of the champion of liberty. There, the deceased was eulogized as a "great and good man, the friend of freedom," while the Marquis de Lafayette spoke in endearing terms of the man he believed had exhibited "a perfect type of courage, honor and Polish patriotism."[13] The marquis concluded:

> To speak about Kościuszko is to recall a man who was greatly respected by his enemies, even the very monarchs against who he had fought. His name belongs to the entire civilized world and his virtues belong to all mankind. America ranks him among her most illustrious defenders. Poland mourns him as the best of patriots whose entire life was sacrificed for her liberty and sovereignty. France and Switzerland stand in awe over his ashes, honoring them as the relic of a superior man, a Christian and a friend of mankind. Russia respects in him the undaunted champion whom even misfortune could not vanquish.[14]

In England, the great and small paid homage to a man once their enemy but since accepted as a champion of liberty there as elsewhere. "Among all men elevated in station who have made a noise in the world," admitted Walter Savage Landor, "I never saw any in whose presence I felt inferiority excepting Kościuszko."[15]

Word of the general's demise took a few weeks longer to reach the United States. "It is with the greatest pain," Francis X. Zeltner wrote to Thomas Jefferson,

> that I have to announce a terrible loss which we have suffered in the person of the Great and Immortal General Kosciuszko. He died in my arms on the fifteenth of this month in consequence of a violent fever against which all the efforts of art and exertions of friendship were fruitless. This great man who has honored me with his friendship and his confidence for over twenty years retired two years ago to the bosom of my family where he hoped to pass his life unless circumstances more favorable than he ventured to hope would allow the rebirth of his unhappy Country, and in that event, he would be summoned into the midst of his compatriots. A few weeks before his sickness he communicated to me the last letter he wrote to you, and a few days before his death he still told me of you, of your interesting

275

Country, of its progress in sciences, of its population, of the power of that only Republic of the World, a worthy subject of our wishes.[16]

Stunned and saddened by the news of his friend's passing, Jefferson replied in eloquent terms to the unwelcome news.

> To no country could that event be more afflicting nor to any individual more than to myself. I had enjoyed his intimate friendship and confidence for the last 20 years, & during the portion of that time which he past in this country, I had daily opportunities of observing personally of his virtue, the benevolence of his services during our revolutionary war had been well known & acknowledged by all. When he left the U.S. in 1798, he left in my hands an instrument, giving, after his death, all his property in our funds, the price of his military labors here, to the charitable purposes of educating and emancipating as many of the children of bondage in this country as it should be adequate to. I am therefore taking measures to have it placed in such hands as will ensure a faithful discharge of his philanthropic views.[17]

"Kosciuszko, the martyr of liberty, is no more!" exclaimed William Henry Harrison, a future president, when announcing the hero's death on the floor of the U.S. Congress.

> His fame will last as long as liberty remains upon the earth; as long as votary offers incense upon her altar, the name of Kosciusko will be invoked. And if, by the common consent of the world, a temple shall be erected to those who have rendered most service to mankind, if the statue of our great countryman shall occupy the place of the "Most Worthy," that of Kosciusko will be found by his side, and the wreath of laurel will be entwined with the palm of virtue to adorn his brow.[18]

Everywhere, the outpouring of grief reflected the great contributions of Kościuszko's life. But his demise did not end his influence on European and American affairs. In 1820 Kraków began constructing a memorial to Poland's loyal son, calling upon the nation he fought to preserve to deposit at a location in the city's outskirts soil from all of the battlefields upon which he fought for Polish independence. Slowly, in buckets, baskets, and wheelbarrows, brought by individuals, by groups, and by official delegations, a high mound rose to commemorate forever the contributions and sacrifices of one of Poland's most revered patriots.[19] "It was a grand memorial,"

George H. Bushnell concluded, "more fitting in character than the noblest statue, a memorial built by representatives of all parts of Poland and added to year after year by processions of pilgrims, men, women and even children bringing tiny bags of soil from their little gardens."[20] Over the years the mound continued to grow, becoming more international in 1926 when a delegation from the United States ceremoniously deposited on the mound soil from Kościuszko's various battlefields in America.

Universally admired in Europe, Kościuszko became a popular theme with continental literary figures. Poems and sonnets abounded in England, and Jane Porter enjoyed great fame as the author of the romantic novel *Thaddeus of Warsaw*. Though of only mediocre literary merit, the work, based on Kościuszko, became an immediate sensation because of the protagonist.

But it was in the United States, more than any nation except his fatherland, that the name of Kościuszko was honored and memorialized. One of the first monuments to Kościuszko in the United States was begun, fittingly, at West Point. In 1824 the Corps of Cadets offered a $50 gold medal as a prize for the best design of a statue to depict Kościuszko to be paid for by popular subscription. In 1828, under the leadership of John A. B. Latrobe, the base and column of a monument were erected near the site of Kościuszko's Garden at a cost of $5,000. Boynton described it as "A plain panelled base, surmounted by a capped and fluted column, bearing the exile's name only, tells all that marble can say, without encroaching upon the duty of every American mother, in whose heart a love of country is implanted."[21] After a long interval, a bronze figure of Kościuszko was added to the base and column in 1913.

On May 11, 1910, a huge parade witnessed by President William Howard Taft and a day-long celebration attended the unveiling of a monument to Kościuszko in Washington, D.C. designed by the Polish sculptor Antoni Popiel.[22] Today, such memorials to the Pole are legion, with busts and other replicas of his likeness adorning parks or public buildings in Boston, Chicago, Cleveland, Fall River (Mass.), Milwaukee, Perth Amboy (N.J.), and Yonkers (N.Y.), and on the Saratoga Battlefield.[23] In 1972, the United States Congress declared Kościuszko's last American residence in Philadelphia a national historic site.

During his lifetime Kościuszko possessed an insatiable desire for learning, a feeling not confined to a single discipline. He frequently advocated government support for education where the rich and poor would have equal opportunity through the use of entrance examinations. It is fitting, therefore, that the most significant memorial to Kościuszko in America is the Kościuszko Foundation. Like its namesake, the Foundation makes substantial efforts to promote education in the sciences, social sciences, humanities, arts, and culture.

Originally founded in 1923 as the Polish Scholarship Committee, it was reorganized as the Kościuszko Foundation on the eve of the 150th anniversary of Kościuszko's enlistment in the Continental Army in 1926. The stated purposes of the new organization were (1) to grant aid to Polish students wishing to study in the United States, or American students seeking to further their education in Poland, (2) to encourage and aid in the exchange of professors, scholars and lecturers between Poland and the United States; and, (3) to cultivate closer intellectual and cultural relations between Poland and the United States.

With the outbreak of the Second World War the Kościuszko Foundation expended every effort to aid Polish refugee scholars, distributing some $75,000 for that purpose. On the conclusion of hostilities the Foundation played an instrumental role in restoring materials to Polish libraries through financial grants and soliciting gifts of books, journals, and other needed items. From this effort the Kościuszko Foundation recognized the need for books on Poland, especially in the English language. The Foundation also discerned a need to pursue the approval of study opportunities in Poland, the formation of cultural and educational exchange programs, and the desirability of greater freedom for scholars. To aid in these endeavors the Kościuszko Foundation established a series of scholarship funds. Between 1952 and 1957 some 150 students received $48,122 in scholarship money. This included eight $1,000 Chopin Scholarships, one of which went to Van Cliburn, pianist at the Juilliard School of Music. Other financial support went to Eric P. Kelly whose romantic novel *The Trumpeter of Krakow* later won the Newberry Medal for contributions to American children's literature.

Throughout its existence the Kościuszko Foundation has published dozens of books and thousands of monographs and pamphlets. The Foundation serves as a clearing house for inquiries regarding Polish arts, literature, history, and culture, and a focus for international exchanges between the United States and Poland.

Tadeusz Kościuszko's legacy to the world is as multifaceted as the individual he was. On a professional level, he made important contributions to the success of the American Revolution. His first activity in America involved fortifying the island of Billingsport, in the Delaware River, and surrounding areas. His work there, which proved so durable that portions could still be seen in the twentieth century, caught the attention of Gen. Horatio Gates who asked the Pole to accompany him as an engineer to his assignment in the Northern Department. There, charged with evaluating the defenses of Ft. Ticonderoga, Kościuszko correctly surmised that if British guns were placed atop Sugar Loaf Hill they would dominate the fortress. Despite critics who branded his advice "impractical," events proved Kościuszko correct. As commander of the delaying actions during Burgoyne's movement south, Kościuszko was responsible for what many historians point to as the crucial turning point in the campaign, slowing Burgoyne's advance to such an extent that the Americans were able to reorganize and obtain the reinforcements that eventually brought victory. At Saratoga, his engineering skills created the strategic and tactical situations that made the American victory possible.

Kościuszko's masterpiece in North America was the fortress at West Point. Beginning with a rough, rocky hill over the Hudson River, Kościuszko's genius created a citadel which still exists today as the home of the United States Military Academy. So strong were the defenses he created that, as General John Armstrong concluded, "they frightened the very enemy from all temptations of even trying to take the Highlands."

Transferred to the South, Kościuszko's skills impressed Gen. Nathaniel Greene as much as they had Horatio Gates. The Pole once again proved his worth, playing a crucial part in the race to the Dan River that saved the Southern Army from destruction, receiving compliments from many civil and military authorities, and gaining praise as well for his conduct of cavalry and intelligence operations during the campaign against Charleston. The only criticism of his abilities came from Henry Lee who complained of the engineer's actions in the Siege of Ninety-Six. On that occasion Henry Lee criticized Kościuszko for failing to cut off the water supply to the enemy works, which would have necessitated surrender, and also directing his attention toward the strongest of the enemy's works while neglecting the weaker. The supposed lack of water has been debated, but most contemporaries and historians have insisted that capture of the lesser works would not have ensured the fall of the main position. The reverse course of action, the one adopted by Kościuszko, would have had that effect. The siege failed not because of faulty engineering, but for lack of time. Wasting efforts building approaches to outworks of dubious significance would only have wasted more valuable time.

Kościuszko's achievements in America were many. Praise of his works was legion. Yet the full impact of his life cannot be appreciated without a realization of the great breadth of diversity of his talents. Kościuszko was a popular figure who knew how to get along with people and elicit their best efforts. As a professional he was proficient not only in the formal engineering techniques necessary for the erection of great fortresses, but also proved adept at the improvisation necessary to be a successful combat engineer. He successfully served as commander of rear guard actions, logistics, intelligence, and as a line officer commanding both cavalry and infantry. Finally, displaying a thorough knowledge of all phases of the military service, he penned a classic artillery textbook used for many years as an instructional manual for the U. S. Army. His achievements were such that *The Blackwell Encyclopedia of the American Revolution* considered him "one of Washington's most successful foreign officers, contributing much needed professionalism to the adolescent American Army."[24]

In Poland, though his efforts met with less success, his military talents as a commander were praised by both friends and enemies, while his vision for revitalizing the Polish army resulted in many innovations taken from his American experience including emphasis on extensive training for the infantry and artillery, development of specialized logistics departments, and the recruitment of volunteer peasant battalions. Though he has sometimes been criticized for a lack of political and managerial skills, he was able to rouse the nation to rebellion, create a new civil administration, adopt exceptionally democratic reforms, and otherwise create out of next to nothing entirely new and functioning governmental systems at both the national and local levels in remarkably short time. Though the revolt that bears his name was ultimately unsuccessful, he remained in the hearts of his countrymen their *Naczelnik Narodu*, their spiritual leader.[25]

A master of his profession. A hero of two continents. What more is there to say about Tadeusz Kościuszko? While his public life and achievements are well documented, what of Kościuszko the man? What were the thoughts and motivations behind the actions of one of history's most unique figures?

The American Revolution occurred during an era in which military officers were often noted as much for their jealousy and factionalism as for their proficiency. Military hierarchies were strict caste systems; commissions and their dates jealously guarded with the demands of honor and protocol often resulting in satisfaction on the dueling field. In this world of jealousy and pompous self-gratification the most striking characteristic of Kościuszko's personality was what Colonel Robert Troup called his "unassuming manners." His unpretentious demeanor proved unique enough at that time to draw comment from many contemporaries, including Eliza White who later recalled him as "simple and unostentatious in his habits, unwilling to be made the object of special attention."

In the cause of American liberty Kościuszko was perfectly willing to sacrifice personal distinction and fortune for the good of the revolution. His professed disinterest in promotion no doubt accounts in large part for his long tenure as a colonel. While French engineers who arrived after him continually sought personal promotion, Kościuszko remained silent. There were many who felt that he rightly deserved promotion, but when the matter appeared destined to provoke controversy the Pole personally asked General Gates to have the request dropped. In January, 1778, Kościuszko wrote to Colonel Troup: "My dear Colonel if you see that my promotion will make a great many Jealous, tell the General that I will not accept of one because I prefer peace more than the greatest Rank in the World."

Kościuszko's personality exhibited what General Gates and others called an "amiable" quality. Personable and witty, Kościuszko's sense of humor contributed to the morale of the army and earned for him in the Southern army the joking title "Count of Poland." Even Kościuszko's critics admitted to his pleasant personality. Henry Lee, who criticized Kościuszko's handling of the Siege of Ninety-Six, later wrote: "Kościuszko was extremely amiable and I believe, a truly good man, nor was he deficient in his professional knowledge." Modest to a fault, Kościuszko gained a gentle rebuke from Thomas Jefferson who wrote in 1801 that "Your letters are too barren of what I wish to hear, I mean things relating to yourself." W. W. Evans remembered "the generous and kindly spirit of the man, a spirit that was composed of the lion and the lamb, lying down together in his bosom."[26]

Thought Kościuszko was often described in terms of his modesty and amiability, the characteristic which molded his personality most was his great feeling for humanity in general and the needs of the poor in particular. Reared in an environment of great diversity, he came into contact early in life with peoples of differing nationalities, religious beliefs, and socioeconomic classes. Not only did he know Poles, Lithuanians and White-Ruthenians, but he met Catholics, Jews, Uniates and Dis-Uniates, peasants and burghers, merchants and princes. His sincere human sensitivity for the feelings and opinions of others, cultivated in the diverse ethnic and religious backgrounds in the small village of his youth, led to his acceptance wherever his duties took him throughout the colonies. In the Revolutionary War, and also in Poland, Kościuszko stood ready to make great personal sacrifices, often sharing his rations and other possessions with those less fortunate. In times of great need he refused to draw his full share of rations, insisting that he wanted only enough for survival. Records indicate that he frequently furnished items to his officers and men, shoes to the workmen at West Point, uniforms to officers and soldiers alike, and clothes for neglected blacks. All of this, of course, at his own expense.

At West Point, for example, rations frequently fell below the level needed to sustain the garrison. Officers and men had to make due on reduced fare, so it was no wonder that the British prisoners confined there suffered immense hardships. Aware of their plight, Kościuszko continually sent them provisions from his own meager stores. As legend has it, years later a Polish traveller fell ill with yellow fever in Australia. A shopkeeper there took him into his home and nursed the Pole back to health. When asked why he had done so the man reported that his grandfather's life had been saved by a Pole named Kościuszko when the ancestor was a starving prisoner at West Point. The influence of Kościuszko's deeds thus reached to the far corners of the earth, traversing time and space.

Generous with his fellow man, Kościuszko had little respect for those who thought only of themselves. When Lt. Col. John Laurens was killed at Combahee Ferry, S.C., a host of men stepped forward to claim the effects of their departed comrade. Filled with indignation at their insensitivity, Kościuszko made his position clear, even in his broken English: "As to my part I wanted to be clear of intierely and to have nothing to do with any article whatsoever belonging to L Col Laurence."

In another instance involving a command problem, Lt. Timothy Whiting of the Quartermaster Department committed some transgression of discipline requiring Kościuszko to place him under arrest. Lt. Whiting refused to obey the arrest order, resulting in a court martial that cashiered him from the service. Kościuszko, the plaintiff in the matter, wrote to General Alexander McDougall urging him to mitigate the harsh sentence.

One of the most important influences on Kościuszko was the treatment of American blacks. Throughout his stay in America, but especially while serving with Gen. Greene's army in the South, Kościuszko observed the plight of blacks laboring under the inhumane system of slavery. He observed the horrors of that system in the Carolinas, with its attendant degradation of human dignity. Through first-hand observation of the plight of blacks in the colonies, and their contributions to the American cause in spite of their mistreatment, Kościuszko developed a great compassion for America's neglected class. When Col. Laurens died, though Kościuszko made it clear he wished no part in claiming the possessions of the dead man, he did attempt to secure some clothing for Laurens' slaves and to have them set free. In this will, prepared before his second departure from America, Kościuszko charged his executor, Thomas Jefferson, to use his American estate to purchase the freedom of black slaves and to provide for their education. In this, Kościuszko's efforts to mediate the injustice of slavery proved influential on the minds and actions of later generations of Polish Americans.

Nor did Kościuszko leave this humanitarian spirit behind when he departed for Poland. Following the American Revolution he returned to his native land to lead an unsuccessful revolution against Czarist Russia. The American influence on Kościuszko was unmistakable in his declarations and in his efforts to raise peasant militia, offering them their freedom for service against the nation's oppressors. As his own uniform Kościuszko chose the white cloak of his peasant scythe-bearers. On his banners, in honor of them, he inscribed the words "They feed and defend." In addition to these attempts to help his countrymen, prior to his death Kościuszko ordered the emancipation of all of the serfs on his estates in Poland. He took care to see that they all received land of their own, and further directed that they be free from all taxes previously paid to the lords of the manors. In his Swiss will he bequeathed funds to the poor, orphan asylums, and several other charities.

Still another noteworthy aspect of his personality was loyalty. While many officers regarded it as part of their privileged status to take long leaves of absence to rest or care for personal business, Kościuszko was again cast from a different mold. In seven long years of active service in the American Revolution Kościuszko took not one furlough. Indeed, in all that time there is only one recorded instance when he digressed momentarily from his duties. That occasion was his visit to Traveller's Rest, the home of General Gates, on his journey to the Southern Department in 1780. His reason was to offer his assistance to Gates's wife, then nursing a fatally ill son.

Kościuszko's loyalty was not alone confined to his sense of professional duty. A good example of his sense of personal loyalty and integrity is seen in the details of the Conway Cabal. When this became public, Gen. Gates and those about him found themselves under suspicion of attempting to replace Gen. Washington. During all of this intrigue Kościuszko never once came under any suspicion, even though he maintained his close friendship with Gates throughout.

In another instance, Kościuszko agreed to act as a second to Gen. Gates in the latter's duel with Gen. Wilkinson. When Kościuszko later found that he had erroneously signed a paper following the duel which attested to the honorable conduct of Wilkinson without like assurances of Gates's behavior, he assumed full responsibility, placing his own reputation, and indeed his life, in jeopardy to right the wrong.

Modest, amiable, humanitarian, and loyal, Kościuszko was a philosophical idealist who believed in republican forms of government and human dignity. Repeatedly one finds comments on Kościuszko's deeply held philosophical beliefs. In the diary of William Dunlap is the following: "Kosciuszko is the only pure republican I ever knew. He is without any dross." Thomas Jefferson expressed admiration for "the purity of his virtue, the benevolence of his heart, and his sincere devotion to the cause of liberty."[27]

Kościuszko believed deeply in liberty. He also believed it to be the duty of people to support the ideals of liberty even in adversity. To Thomas Jefferson he once wrote: "...it is pusillanimity and indecision which destroys Nations, but never their valor and ardor." While in Europe, Kościuszko chastised John Paul Jones for accepting a commission in the service of the Russian Navy which possessed no thoughts of liberty or republicanism. Yet, in keeping with his sense of humanity, he was also one of the first to offer Jones aid when the disappointed and humiliated admiral passed through Warsaw after leaving Russia. It was a combination of these personal traits which led Gen. Washington to write to the Pole in 1797, "no one has a higher respect and veneration for your character than I have."

Historian Ernest Cuneo summarized Kościuszko's achievements thusly: "Though the military was his first profession, Thaddeus Kosciuszko was a Renaissance man. He was a painter, an architect, a composer, a scholar and a philosopher. He was accepted as an intellectual by Jefferson. He was also a mystical visionary of human rights scarcely second to Abraham Lincoln." But the highest compliment he received came from Jefferson, who considered Kościuszko "my most intimate and beloved friend."[28] To this giant of democracy, the Pole was "as pure a son of liberty as I have ever known.

Appendix 1

Kościuszko's Will

A hero of two continents, Kościuszko resided in four separate countries, left assets in three, and penned four separate wills disposing of these assets. Given the complexities of these interacting issues, probate of his estate would take some thirty-five years and leave many confusing and misunderstood issues long after his demise and the "final" dispersal of his estate.

The complexities began during Kościuszko's return visit to America when he executed his first will, what is generally referred to as his "American Will." This document provided for the investment of his American estate, derived from back pay and allowances for service in the American Revolution, a debt acknowledged by an Act of Congress which directed the Secretary of the Treasury to pay Kościuszko $12,280.54, plus interest from January 1, 1793 to December 31, 1797.[1] Kościuszko made provision for payment of the interest on this sum to him for living expenses during his life, and the eventual dispersal of the estate upon his death for the purpose of purchasing the freedom of American slaves and providing for their education. Signed on May 5, 1798, with John Barnes and John Dawson acting as witnesses and his friend Thomas Jefferson named executor, the text of the final declaration read as follows:

I, Thaddeus Kosciuszko, being just in my departure from America do hereby declare and direct that should I make no other testamentary disposition of my property in the United States, I hereby authorize my friend Thomas Jefferson to employ the whole thereof in purchasing Negroes from among his own or any others and giving them Liberty in my name, in giving them an education in trades or otherwise and in having them instructed for their new condition in the duties of morality which may make them good neighbors good fathers or mothers, husbands, or wives and in their duties as citizens teaching them to be defenders of their Liberty and Country and of the good order of society and in whatsoever may make them happy and useful, and I make the said Thomas Jefferson my executor of this.[2]

On June 28, 1806, while living in Paris, Kościuszko penned a second will in which he bequeathed to Kosciuszko Armstrong, the son of his friend from Revolutionary War service, Gen. John Armstrong, then serving as American Minister in Paris, payment of a legacy of $3,704 from his American estate. This will read as follows:

> Know all men by these presents, that I, Thaddeus Kosciuszko, formerly an officer of the United States of America, in their revolutionary war against Great Britain, and a native of Liloane, in Poland, at present residing in Paris, do hereby will and direct, that, at my decease, the sum of $3,704, current money of the aforesaid United States, shall of right be possessed by, and delivered over to the full enjoyment and use of Kosciuszko Armstrong, the son of General John Armstrong, minister plenipotentiary of the said States at Paris; for the security and performance whereof, I do hereby instruct and authorize my only lawful executor in the United States, Thomas Jefferson, President thereof, to reserve, in trust for that special purpose, of the funds he already holds belonging to me, the aforesaid sum of $3,704 in principal to be paid by him, the said Thomas Jefferson, immediately after my decease, to him, the said Kosciuszko Armstrong, and in case of his death, to the use and benefit of his surviving brother. Given under my hand and seal, at Paris, this 28th day of June 1806.[3]

His third will, dated at Soleure, Switzerland, on June 4, 1816, disposed of Kościuszko's French properties.[4] The final testament was executed in Soleure on October 10, 1817, only five days before his death. In it, he bequeathed the largest portion of his estate to the Zeltner family, especially his close friend Emily, while also designating sums for "The poor, the orphan asylum, and several other charitable institutions were remembered with his usual munificence; and he, moreover, handed a large sum in cash to a lawyer friend for distribution among persons in straitened circumstances." This document made no reference to either his American estate or the revocation of any previous testaments.[5]

By the time of his death, his American estate was substantial. During his absence in Europe following his second American sojourn, one of Kościuszko's most frequent correspondents was Thomas Jefferson, and, not surprisingly, he turned to the Virginian for advice on investment opportunities. At the suggestion of his friend, the Pole chose John Barnes, Jefferson's private banker and a witness to his American testament, as his own advisor. Barnes invested $12,000 of the general's money in thirty shares of the Bank of Pennsylvania bearing an annual interest rate of eight percent.

Following Jefferson's term in office as President of the United States, the Virginian found himself deeply in debt to numerous creditors. In dire need of money, Jefferson was convinced to use $4,500 of Kościuszko's funds to relieve his own indebtedness. Over a period of time Jefferson scrupulously repaid all of the money, including the interest that would have accrued to it. When informed of the action, Kościuszko heartily approved, gratified at the opportunity to help his friend.

Some years later, possibly in anticipation of the banking crisis of 1814, Jefferson sold the bank certificates and reinvested the proceeds in a government subscription loan at six percent interest. Historians have generally interpreted this action as a hedge against a faltering economy. There is, however, another explanation. The war with England, begun in 1812, left the U.S. government badly in need of funds. More probably, Jefferson sought through this reinvestment to aid the United States Treasury more than to protect Kościuszko's investment. A letter from Jefferson to H.E.M. de Politica, the Russian Minister in Washington, dated May 27, 1819, offers some evidence to support this view. In it, Jefferson cites his own "situation in the interior of the country" as the reason for suggesting that Barnes handle Kościuszko's finances. He also states that it was he, Jefferson, who withdrew the money from the Bank of Pennsylvania and lent it to the Federal Treasury during the war.[6] Regardless of the motivation, it is to the credit of Jefferson and Barnes that by the time of Kościuszko's death in 1817 the original investment had grown to $17,099, exclusive of the interest which had been paid to him in Europe.[7]

Upon learning of the death of his Polish friend, Jefferson faced the problem of fulfilling his duties as executor of Kościuszko's will. On January 5, 1818, he wrote to Secretary of the Treasury William H. Crawford seeking his advice on where to submit the document to probate. "Some doubts arise in my mind," he wrote, "as to the court in which this will must be proved, and myself qualified to execute it, as it is essential that this should be done in a court which the government will think of competent cognisance of the case to authorize their placing the money under the trust. I have taken the liberty of stating the case to the Attorney General who is particularly acquainted with our laws, by whose advice and your sanction, I wish to be governed." Being then seventy-five years of age, Jefferson also confided another worry, that the probate "will occupy so long a course of time beyond what I can expect to live that I think to propose to place it under the court of Chancery."[8]

Before Jefferson determined how to proceed, in January, 1818, he received a letter from Minister Armstrong in Paris informing him of the Kościuszko's will executed in Paris in 1806 and requesting the sum of $3,704 payable to his son. Jefferson replied in a letter dated January 17 that he had not yet determined where to submit the will to probate and that he had "not decided to undertake the trust. It's execution will call for a great many minute and continued attentions, and many more years to compleat than I have to live."[9]

No sooner had Jefferson replied to Armstrong than the plot became thickened by the arrival of a letter from Xavier Zeltner claiming the departed's entire American estate under the provisions of the will of October 10, 1817. To further complicate matters, the Russian Minister in Washington soon inquired about the details of the Kościuszko will intimating that since the deceased was a citizen of the Russian-controlled area of Poland living in exile the Russian government might have claims against the estate. As if this were not enough, a fraud entered the picture, one Mr. Klimkiewicz, claiming to be Kościuszko's next of kin and therefore entitled to the entire estate.[10]

To a man of Jefferson's age these conflicting claims were no doubt all the proof he needed to convince him it was best to remove himself from the picture. Jefferson asked his friend and fellow Virginian John Hartwell Cocke to act as executor in his stead. But Cocke declined, citing the great difficulties he would encounter in carrying out the provisions of the will given the prevailing social conditions in the slave-holding state. He explained that few schools then accepted blacks, and that the popular prejudices regarding their education might harm his (Cocke's) standing among his neighbors. Without finding a substitute executor, Jefferson submitted the will to the Circuit Court of Albemarle, Virginia, near his home at Monticello.

On May 12, 1819, Jefferson entered the courthouse, arriving after the day's session had begun. Noting the famous ex-president's entrance, Judge Archibald Stuart bowed in his direction and offered him a seat upon the bench. Jefferson declined, explaining that "As soon as your Honor shall have leisure to attend to me, I have a matter of business to present to the Court." At that the judge halted the proceedings and, "by consent of all parties concerned, the matter then before the Court was then suspended until Mr. Jefferson could be heard. He pulled out of his pocket a paper, which he said was the will of his friend, General Thaddeus Kosciuzko; that the will was written in the handwriting of the testator, with which he was well acquainted, and to which fact he was willing to testify on oath." Jefferson further explained that he had been "made executor of the will; but at his time of life it was not in his power to undertake the duties of the office, and that necessity compelled him to decline qualifying. The usual oath was administered to Mr. Jefferson by the clerk, and the will was ordered by the Court to be admitted to the record."[11] Along with it went the following statement: "This instrument purporting to be the last will and testament of Thaddeus Kosciuszko, deceased, was produced into court, and satisfactory proof being produced of its being written in the handwriting of the said Thaddeus Kosciuszko, the same was ordered to be recorded, and thereupon Thomas Jefferson, the executor therein named, refused to take upon himself the burthen of the execution of the said will. Teste: John Carr, C.C."[12]

Given the realities of Virginia society, and the fact that the estate's assets consisted of U.S. government securities, Jefferson, with the concurrence of Attorney General William Wirt, soon transferred probate of the will to the Orphans' Court in Washington, D.C. In so doing, he placed probate within the purview of a federal rather than a state court.[13]

The Court delegated the handling of the estate to Benjamin L. Lear of Washington, D.C. At the further request of Jefferson, Attorney General Wirt acted as counsel for the trust until his death in 1834.[14] Following his examination of the will, Lear suggested the funds be utilized to endow "The Kosciuszko School" then being planned by the African Education Society of New Jersey. Jefferson agreed to this alternative plan, but before it could be implemented Kosciuszko Armstrong filed a bill in chancery against Lear for the $3,704 owed him under the 1806 will and appropriate interest. The case eventually found its way to the Supreme Court, which ignored the various arguments in the case and instead held that a decision on the merits of the case could only be rendered *after* the will had been duly probated. Thus, the entire matter was sent back to the Orphans' Court for proper probate.[15]

Before probate could be accomplished, Stanisław Estko filed a case against the estate on behalf of himself and others claiming to be Kościuszko's next-of-kin and claiming the general's American estate on the grounds that he died intestate in regards to his American property. The claimants were the children of Kościuszko's two sisters, Anna and Katarzyna, who married Piotr Estko and Karol Zolkowski respectively. Their claim argued that the American will was not a legal will and, even if it were, the purpose to which the money was to be put was "one which the law will not sustain," it being illegal at that time in Virginia and Maryland to teach blacks to read and write. Once again, the Supreme Court was called upon to decide the issue, and once again there was no clear decision. Instead, the Court ruled that an actual examination of the European will was necessary before any decision could be rendered, as was the establishment of the deceased's domicile, a point that might have relevance in determining under what laws the conflicting wills should be adjudicated. "We do not think the case properly prepared for decision," the Court opined, "and therefore direct that ... the case be remanded" to the lower court.[16]

At this point, Armstrong, Estko, and Zeltner joined forces in a an effort to invalidate the American will of 1798. Armstrong submitted the 1806 will to probate in the Orphan's Court, arguing that it invalided the previous 1798 testament. In reply, Lear submitted a letter from Kościuszko to Jefferson dated September 15, 1817, in which the Pole tells the former president, referring to his American assets, "After my death you know its fixed destination." Lear argued that this proved Kościuszko's intention that the will of 1798 remain inviolate, going so far as to contend that it, in fact, acted to revoke the will of 1806 and reestablish the 1798 document as the only true will. Once again, the Court remanded the case to the lower court to determine which French laws might be applicable to the will of 1806, the deceased's actual domicile, what international laws might be involved, and the nature of any other claims or claimants against the American estate.[17]

Kosciuszko Armstrong did not press his claim further, but another complication arose in 1832 when the executor, Benjamin F. Lear, died. The first executor of the American legacy received to his care an estate valued at $26,931.44. Lear astutely reinvested Kościuszko's funds in his own name so that by the time of his death in 1832 the total value of the estate stood at $31,785.27. Under the terms of Lear's will, Col. George Bomford was named executor and administrator *de bonis non* ("of goods not already administered") of Kościuszko's estate. At this point also a new attorney appeared on the scene, Major Gaspard Tochman, a veteran of the Polish November Uprising against Russia in 1830-31 who now lived in exile as an American citizen. A distant relative of Kościuszko's family, he was employed by the Estkos to represent their interests in the litigation. Tochman did not trust Bomford so he employed a legal technicality and petitioned Congress to require the Orphans' Court to require an additional bond, guaranteed by three sureties, on the estate in Bomford's care.[18]

In January, 1847, Tochman filed a petition with the court seeking distribution of the general's American assets to the Estko and Zolkowski families in Poland, the grand children of Kościuszko's two sisters. When no relief was forthcoming, he filed another petition at the beginning of August "praying that further proceedings be taken upon the former petition ... and that Col. George Bomford, administrator *de bonis non* of Koskiusco's estate, be ordered to show cause why he should not distribute the fund of the estate amongst the next of kin of Gen. Koskiusco."[19] Tochman also revived the earlier claims of Klimkiewicz. Although Klimkiewicz had already died, Tochman somehow managed to search the dead man's personal effects in which he found what he claimed was a will executed by Kościuszko in Paris on June 4, 1816, which effectively negated both the American will of 1798 and the Parisian will of 1806 bequeathing funds to Kosciuszko Armstrong. Obviously, if valid, this will would negate the claims of all the other parties except the Zeltners. To prove its authenticity, Tochman journeyed to Paris where he found the original of the 1816 will and had it authenticated. In the meantime, Bomford died in 1848 with the estate then valued in excess of $43,000, only to have the new executor, Lewis Johnson, discover that Bomford had "wasted or converted to his own use" $37,924.40 of the estate entrusted to his care.[20]

Before the revived case made its way through the courts, however, Alexandre de Bodisco, Russian Minister to the United States, attempted to interfere in the communication between Tochman and his clients in Poland by forcing members of the Estko family to sign a power of attorney against their will. The minister also attacked

Tochman directly, interposing the objection that the attorney, having been convicted of political offenses in Russia, was disqualified from conducting legal business on behalf of subjects of Russia. Further, when the representative of the Zolkowski family, Ladislas Wankowicz, a grand nephew of Kościuszko, refused to abide by the Russian minister's insistence that he disregard Tochman, the minister caused Wankowicz's property in the Russian-controlled Wilno district of Lithuania to be seized by the state. Because of this, Wankowicz, acting on the advice of Tochman, renounced his Russian citizenship, declared his intention to become a citizen of the United States, and submitted a memorial to Congress in January, 1849, asking for a special act transferring jurisdiction in the case from the District of Columbia to Maryland so the proceedings could be free of the "local influences" of the estate's executor and "to protect his own constitutional rights and privileges as a naturalized citizen ... against the like influence of Mr. de Bodisco, minister from Russia."[21] At the same time, a similar memorial asking for relief from the Minister's interference was sent to Czar Nicholas I. When no action was forthcoming, Wankowicz and Tochman submitted new memorials to Congress in December of the same year again requesting relief from the Russian Minister's meddling.[22]

With all of the various wills and interested parties now uncovered, and Tochman's personal battle with the Russian minister temporarily on hold, the Polish attorney retained the services of the Hon. Reverdy Johnson, a member of the United States Senate, to argue the case before the Supreme Court. In 1852, the complicated international litigations reached the United States Supreme Court under the innocuous legal heading of *John F. Ennis vs. J. H. B. Smith, et. al.* Ennis represented Kościuszko's Polish relatives who claimed the entire American estate by virtue of the will of 1816, while Smith, acting for Bomford's heirs, argued the case in favor of the primacy of the will of 1798 with regard to the American portion of Kościuszko's legacy. Although many questions were laid before the Court, four were critical to the disposal of the American estate. They were:

1. Were the heirs to George Bomford still liable for the funds of the Kościuszko estate? If they were not, all claims were null and void and the general's estate became the property of Bomford's heirs.

2. Did legal relatives of Kościuszko really exist? If Bomford's

heirs were not entitled to the estate, the existence of legal relatives could further complicate disposal of the estate.

3. Was the will of 1798 still valid, or had it been superseded by any or all of the wills of 1806, 1816, or 1817?

4. Presupposing favorable answers to these questions, the heirs of Kościuszko then sought clarification as to the legal residence of Kościuszko at the time of his death. This was important because his legal domicile would determine under which nation's laws the estate would be settled.

With regard to the first question, Smith argued that according to the laws of the state of Maryland, which then also applied to the District of Columbia, any change in the form of a bequest by an executor meant the estate was said to have been "administered." Thus, the defendants maintained, when the original form of the inheritance was changed by Lear's reinvestment, the legacy was no longer legally extant. Consequently Smith argued that Bomford's heirs were not liable for Kościuszko's American funds, but were entitled to retain them in their entirety. Further, the heirs noted, there was a significant difference in the bonds which they held from the Bank of Columbia and those claimed by the applicants. The Court, in the written decision of Justice Wayne, disagreed with the executors, citing several legal reasons why Bomford, as the executor of Lear, could not lawfully claim Kościuszko's inheritance even though its form had been altered by Lear and came to Bomford as a portion of Lear's estate. Bomford's heirs were liable for the sum of Bomford's last accounting prior to his death in 1848, $43,504.40.[23] With this formality concluded, the substance of the various claims became the focus of attention.

Bomford's heirs argued, in the second instance, that Kościuszko had not been married, had no offspring, and had no verified heirs to which the American estate could pass. The Polish claimants, they argued, had no proof of their relationship to Kościuszko. The Poles countered these assertions by producing decrees from the Assembly of Nobility of the Government of Grodno, dated May 7, 1843, and from the Court of Korbryn in the Province of Lithuania. Written in their original Russian, the two decrees were filed with the court in the District of Columbia. They both served to authenticate the relationship of the Polish claimants to Kościuszko, and further stated their position as next of kin, and therefore legal claimants to the general's estates. Both decrees were affixed with their respective official seals. As witnesses to attest to the authenticity and jurisdiction of the two entities, the claimants called Henryk Kałussowski and Jan Tyssowski, prominent Polish exiles residing in America who were familiar with Polish legal intricacies. Faced with this evidence, the Court ruled that the decrees proved the claimants were collateral kinsmen of Kościuszko and thus entitled to his estate.[24]

Undoubtedly the most important question that the Court had to decide was the legitimacy of the four separate wills. Bomford's heirs argued that the American estate was bequeathed under the will of 1798, and had not been subsequently revoked. If, however, it had been revoked, or if its trusts could not be carried out, they argued that the will of 1817 then bequeathed the estate to the Zeltners, thus intercepting and bypassing any claims put forth by the next of kin.

The claimants to the estate noted that the 1816 will had previously been proved legitimate under French law, and that an authenticated copy of that will was in the possession of the court in the District of Columbia. The heirs, through their attorney, argued that the 1806 will did not follow the legal forms prescribed by French jurisprudence. Furthermore, they stated that the 1816 will, regardless of former wills, included a standard clause of revocation which read as follows: "Je revoque tous les testaments et codiciles que j'ai pu faire avant le présent auquel seul je m'arre'te comme contenant mes dernieres volante's."[25] This meant that all previous wills were null and void and the new will, that of 1816, was the only legal testament extant at that time. Since no disposition of the American property was made in the 1816 will, and because the 1817 will only bequeathed certain explicit portions of the estate in general, Kościuszko's heirs concluded that the American portion of the legacy was therefore intestate. That is, the American estate not having been bequeathed, it became the property of the next of kin.[26]

The Court agreed insofar as the revoking clause was concerned and declared the will of 1816 did, in fact, supersede the 1798 will, thus making the 1798 provisions for Kosciuszko's American estate invalid. The defendants argued, however, that Clause II of the will of 1817 directed the estate to the possession of the Zeltners. The clause read: "Je léque tous mes effets, ma voiture, et mon cheval y comprise a' Madame et a' Monsieur Zavier Zeltner, les homme ce dessus."[27] The defendants argued that the phrase "tous mes effets" (all of my effects) was not qualified by the following phrase, "ma voiture, et mon cheval y comprise" (my carriage and my horse included), to mean only his personal effects. The defendants maintained that Kościuszko only intended to make sure that the carriage and horse were not overlooked along with all of his other possessions.

The claimants insisted that in the French language the word *effets* referred only to property usually found about one's person, and that when linked with other qualifying phrases, as it was in this case, the rule of *ejusdem generis* (of the same kind, class or nature) should apply. This would mean the Zeltners were only entitled to Kościuszko's personal possessions in the area of their immediate home, including his carriage and horse. The rest of the estate, including the American portion, would then go to the heirs represented by Ennis.[28]

The Court once again found in favor of the claimants noting that the use of the word *effets* could not be construed to include Kościuszko's American property. "It would be a very strained construction," the Court concluded, "to make the words, all of my effects, comprehend his personal estate in the United States." Thus, the Court continued, "the second article in the will of 1817 is not residuary and ... has no relation to the funds in controversy."[29]

There remained the question of Kościuszko's domicile for the purposes of division of property under the wills of 1816 and 1817. The Polish heirs maintained that Kościuszko had no proved domicile other than Poland, where he was born, or Switzerland, where he died. The claimants argued that Kościuszko was a resident of France at the time of his death. The French laws dealing with *intestate* legacies would give the Polish claimants possession of Kościuszko's American funds; consequently, it was important that they prove this point. The Court noted that Kościuszko, in his 1806 will, claimed that he was "at present residing in Paris." This, it held, was sufficient *prima facie* evidence of Kościuszko's domicile in France. In addition to this, in his will of 1816 Kościuszko included the phrase: "I, the undersigned Thaddeus Kosciuszko, residing in Berville, in the township Genevraye, of the department of Seine and Marne [being now], or at present at Soleure, in Switzerland." The Court ruled this further evidence of residence in France. The defendants counter-argued that Kościuszko was, in fact, an exile from Poland who hoped to return. The Court rejected this appeal. The Justices found that Kościuszko had not been forced to leave Poland by Czar Paul; rather, the Pole had voluntarily chosen to leave for political reasons. Furthermore, the Court noted that a decree of the National Assembly of France

had conferred citizenship upon Kościuszko in August, 1792. Kościuszko's legal domicile was, the Court concluded, France. Justice
Wayne also accepted the printed version of the *Code Civil* of France
as legitimate for the purposes of settling the estate. Under these
precepts, the American legacy of Tadeusz Kościuszko was ordered
transferred to his heirs as established by the Court.[30]

Thus, based largely on Tochman's efforts, the Court found that
the 1816 will effectively revoked the two previous documents, and
that since neither it nor the will of 1817 specifically mentioned
Kościuszko's American estate, he had, in fact, died intestate as far
as the American property was concerned. Thus, the American estate
would go to Kościuszko's relatives based on the laws of the location
of his domicile at the time of his death. The total amount of the
general's estate was placed at $43,504.40 including $5,680.00 from
Bomford's estate and $37,924.40 from the six sureties guaranteeing
the two bonds, plus six percent interest since June 7, 1847.[31]

Following the final disposition of Kościuszko's American estate,
some historians commented that the Pole never really intended to use
his funds to help alleviate the plight of blacks in the United States.
These writers relegate Kościuszko's American will to a state of myth.
The three succeeding wills, as shown by the Court, these historians
contend, indicate that Kościuszko changed his mind about the destination of his American funds. These conclusions are unwarranted. If
Kościuszko changed his mind he certainly would have bequeathed
his American estate to some other party or parties in one of his three
succeeding wills. He did not. Clearly, one could argue that Kościuszko always intended his American estate for its original purpose.
It appears that only the legal demands of the standard revocation
clause inserted in the will of 1816 prevented the funds from being
used for the purposes he set down in 1798. Each of Kościuszko's
wills dealt with a different portion of his estate and were intended
to be equally valid. The standard revocation clause of the 1816 will
was no doubt inserted as a matter of legal course, without a firm
grasp of what implications it might have on former wills. Proof of
Kościuszko's continued concern for his American estate is seen in a
letter he wrote to Thomas Jefferson on September 15, 1817. With an
impending sense of his death, Kościuszko wrote: "We all grow old,
and for that reason, my dear and respectable friend, I ask you, as you
have full power to do, to arrange it in such a manner that after the
death of our worthy friend, Mr. Barnes, some one as honest as

himself, may take his place, so that I may receive interest of my money, punctually; of which money, after my death, you know the fixed destination. As for the present, do what you think best."[32] This letter was written well after the will of 1816, and clearly indicates that Kościuszko still considered his American will of 1798 to be in effect.

Similarly, some historians have scoffed at the importance of the will in view of its invalidation by the Supreme Court. This is also an erroneous conclusion for the will stands not only as testimony to the humanitarian principles of its author, but, of greater importance, it has served as an inspiration to Polish Americans and others for nearly two hundred years. One need only cite the following sentiments, taken from the memoirs of Włodzimierz Krzyżanowski, to prove the value of Kościuszko's American will to succeeding generations.

> I am proud to say that the first man to recognize this [the need for education in the South], and to try to do something about it, was my countryman Tadeusz Kościuszko. In 1800 when the Congress of the United States, recognizing his services to this county, voted him $15.000 and a land grant, Kościuszko refused to accept the money or the land. Instead, he attempted to donate it towards building schools for the education of the Negroes. But his good intentions bore no fruit. The Commonwealth of Virginia immediately passed laws forbidding the education of Negroes. Kosciuszko still refused to accept the gift. This gift was invested, and by the year 1853 it had grown to $65,000. Had Virginia established schools, and named them in Kościuszko's memory, Virginia would have remembered him forever .... Perhaps Virginia would also have been able to avoid the later conflicts which raged within her borders.[33]

Clearly the ideal that motivated Kościuszko's American will survived the legal complications which struck it down. Kościuszko wrote the will in good faith and never intended that it be revoked. Rather, he expected even on the eve of his death that his original wishes be carried out. It is this spirit of humanity which has survived as a monument to its author and a goal for others to pursue.

Appendix 2

Kościuszko's Act of Insurrection[1]

The wretched state in which Poland is involved is known to the universe; the indignities offered by two neighboring powers, and the crimes of traitors to their country, have sunk this country into this abyss of misery. Catherine II, who in concert with the perjured William has sworn to extirpate even the name of Poland, has accomplished her iniquitous designs; there is no species of falsehood, or perjury, or of treason, which those governments have hesitated to commit, to satisfy their vengeance and their ambition. The Czarina, while she impudently promised to guarantee the entire possessions and the independence of Poland, has afflicted it with every species of injury; and when Poland, weary of bearing the shameful yoke, had recovered the rights of her sovereignty, she employed against her, traitors to their country. She supported their sacrilegious plots with all her military force, and having artfully diverted, from the defence of his country, the king to whom the diet had confided the National forces, she shamefully betrayed the very traitors themselves. By such arts, having made herself mistress of the state of Poland, she invited Frederick William to take part of the plunder, to recompense him for having broken a most solemn treaty with the Republic, under imaginary pretexts, whose falsity and impiety accord only with tyrants; but in fact to satisfy the boundless ambition of extending his tyranny, by an invasion of the adjacent nations.

These two powers, confederated against Poland, have violently seized the immemorial and incontestable possessions of the Republic; and for this purpose, have obtained, in a diet, convoked with this view, a forced approbation of their usurpations. They have compelled the subjects to take an oath, and to a state of slavery, by imposing on them the most grievous burthen, and acknowledging no law but their arbitrary wills, by a new language and unknown in the law of nations, have audaciously assigned to the existence of the Republic a rank inferior to all other powers, in making it appear every where, that the laws, as well as the limits of sovereigns depend absolutely on their caprices; and that they regard the North of Europe, as a prey doomed to the rapacity of their despotism.

But the remainder of Poland has not been able to purchase any amelioration of its fate, at the price of such cruel misfortunes. The Czarina, in concealing her ultimate designs, which must be prejudicial to the powers of Europe, in the mean time sacrifices Poland to her barbarous and implacable vengeance. She tramples under her feet the most sacred rights of the liberty, the safety, and property of citizens. Opinions and Freedom of thought in Poland find no shelter from her persecuting suspicions, and she attempts even to enchain the very speech of the citizens. None but traitors find any indulgence with her, and these are encouraged that they may commit every species of crimes. The property of the revenues of the public are becoming the prey of her rapacity. The property of our citizens has been seized; because the country was subdued, these plunderers have divided among them the charges of the Republic, that they might seize the spoil; and in usurping impiously the name of National Government, tho' the slaves of a foreign tyranny, they have done whatever their wills dictated.

The Permanent Council, whose establishment was imposed upon us by a foreign power, suppressed legally by the national will, and recently re-established by traitors, has by order of the Russian minister, overleaped the bounds of its power, which it has received with meanness from the same minister, in re-establishing, reforming, suppressing arbitrarily the constitutions which had just been framed and those which had been abolished. In a word, the pretended government of the nation, the liberty, the safety and property of the citizens are in the hands of the slaves of a servant of Czarina, whose troops deluge the country, and serve as a rampart to support these detestable men.

Borne down by an immense pressure of evils, vanquished by treachery, rather than by force of foreign enemies, destitute of all protection from the national government; having lost our country, and with her the enjoyment of the most sacred rights of liberty, of personal safety and of property; having been deceived, and becoming the derision of some nations, while we are abandoned by others; we citizens, inhabitants of the Palatinate of Kraków, by sacrificing to our country our lives, the only good which tyranny has not con-descended to wrest from us, will avail ourselves of all the extreme and violent measures, that civic despair suggests to us. Having formed a determined resolution to perish and entomb ourselves in the ruins of our country, or to deliver the land of our fathers from a ferocious oppression, and the galling yoke of the ignominious bondage, we declare in the face of Heaven and before all the human race, and especially before all the nations, that know how to value liberty above all the blessings of the universe, that to make use of the incontestable right of defending ourselves against tyranny and armed oppression, we do unite, in the spirit of Patriotism, of civism and of fraternity, all our forces; and persuaded that a fortunate issue of our arduous enterprise depends principally on our strict union, we renounce all the prejudices of opinion, which have divided or may still divide the citizens, inhabitants of the same territory, and children of one common country; and we pledge ourselves to each other to spare no sacrifices whatever, but on the other hand to use all the means which the sacred love of Freedom can inspire in the breast of man; all that despair can suggest for his defence.

The deliverance of Poland from foreign troops, the recovery of the entire possessions of the state, the extirpation of all oppression and usurpation, as well external as internal, the re-establishment of the national liberties and the independence of the Republic are the sacred objects of our insurrection. But to insure success to our undertaking, it is necessary that an active power should direct the national force. Considering attentively the actual situation of our country, and of its inhabitants, it appears necessary to resort to extreme and decisive measures; to wit, those of naming a commander in chief of the armed force of the nation, to establish a temporary Supreme National Council, a Commission of Good Order, a Supreme Criminal Court of Appeals, and a subordinate Criminal Court in our Palatinate. For this purpose, with the consent of the assembly, we ordain as follows:

1. We elect and declare by this act, Tadeusz Kościuszko sole commander in chief of all our armed forces.

2. The said commander in chief, shall immediately convene a Supreme National Council. We confide to his civic zeal the choice of the members, who shall compose it; and also to care of organizing

the Council. The chief himself shall have a seat in the Council as an active member.

3. The organization of the armed force of the nation shall be entrusted solely to the chief; as also the nomination of military officers of every grade; he shall also employ his force against the enemies of his country, and of this actual insurrection. The Supreme National Council shall, without any delay, fulfill the orders and dispositions of the commander in chief, elected by the free will of the nation.

4. In case the chief Kościuszko, by reason of sickness or otherwise, shall not discharge the duties of his important office, he shall name his lieutenant after having communicated for this purpose, with the Supreme Council; chief interim, and the Council shall appoint in the place of T. Kościuszko, another commander in chief. In both cases, the supreme chief of the forces, not being immediately appointed by the nation, but by the Supreme Council, shall be subject to the orders of the said Council.

5. The Supreme Council shall have the care of the public treasury, for maintaining the forces and providing for the expenses of the war; as also for supporting this insurrection. Therefore the Council is authorized to ordain temporary imposts, to dispose of all national property and funds, and to negotiate loans in this or foreign countries. The same Council shall ordain the levy of recruits, shall furnish the national troops with every thing necessary for the war; arms, ammunition and clothing. They shall endeavor to procure a sufficiency of provisions for the nation and the army; maintain order; watch over the safety of the country; and removing all obstacles and disconcerting all plans prejudicial to our great object, they shall take care that public justice be administered with promptitude and energy. They shall endeavor to negotiate with foreign powers for support and assistance. In short they shall endeavor to rectify public opinion, and rouse a national spirit, that Liberty and their country may become the most powerful incentives with all the Poles, to make the greatest sacrifices for the public good. These are the principal duties imposed on the Supreme National Council.

6. We create in our Palatinate a Commission of Good Order, by organizing it for the present in a particular manner. This Commission shall be among us, a single organ, a chief executive magistrate of the armed forces and Supreme Council. It shall be bound to execute all their orders and all their regulations, conformable to their powers.

The Supreme Council shall prescribe immediately the organization and particular duties of this commission. We on our parts engage strictly to execute their decrees.

7. The Supreme Council shall prescribe the arrangement, the proceedings and the fixed principles of the supreme criminal jurisdiction, which shall sit near the Council.

8. As in the present circumstances, we cannot conveniently choose suitable persons to form the Supreme Criminal Tribunal except those of the Palatinate, therefore we charge the Council to make choice of judges from among the persons, who, by the last free territorial dietines and elections of the cities, were designated for those judicatures.

9. The Tribunal shall have cognizance of all crimes against the nation, and all proceedings contrary to the object of this sacred association, as also of all crimes against the safety of the country. All these crimes shall be punished with death.

10. We commit to the commander in chief of our armies, the power of establishing a Council of War, according to military rules and customs.

11. We reserve to ourselves most solemnly, by the act prescribed, that none of the temporary powers, we have now established, shall hereafter either separately or collectively form any of the acts which shall compose a national constitution. Every act of that nature shall be regarded by us, as a usurpation of national sovereignty, like that against which we are now struggling, at the hazard of our lives.

12. All the temporary powers created by the present act, shall exist in full force, until we have obtained the object of our present association, that is, until Poland shall be delivered from foreign troops, and of all armed forces, opposed to this our association; and until the entire possession of our territorial rights shall be secured. Of this the commander in chief and the Council shall be bound to notify the citizens, under the most rigid responsibility of their persons and property. Then the nation, assembled by its representatives, shall cause to be rendered an account of its labors and of the proceedings of the temporary authorities, and shall publish to the world their gratitude towards the virtuous children of their country, by recompensing their labor and sacrifices in proportion to their real services. Then they will decide on their future prosperity and that of the most distant generations.

13. We require the commander in chief of the forces and Supreme

Council, to inform the nation, by frequent proclamations, of the true state of public affairs, without concealing or disguising the most disastrous events. Our despair is at its height; and the love of our country knows no bounds. The most cruel misfortunes, and the most insurmountable difficulties shall neither enfeeble nor discourage our virtue and civic valor.

14. We pledge ourselves to each other and to the whole nation, for our firmness in enterprise, for our fidelity to the principles, and our obedience to the national authorities, expressed and decreed in this act of association. We conjure the commander of our forces and the Supreme Council, by the love of their country, to employ all the means capable of delivering the nation and saving the Polish territories. By depositing in their hands the power of commanding our persons and our estates, during the combat of Liberty with despotism, of justice with oppression and tyranny, we desire that they may keep constantly in view this great truth, that THE SAFETY OF A NATION IS THE SUPREME LAW.

Done at Kraków, March 24, 1794, in an assembly of Citizens, inhabitants of the Palatinate.

Appendix 3

Połaniec Manifesto
1794

Tadeusz Kościuszko,
Supreme Commander of the
National Armed Forces

To the Commission for Order of all Lands and Districts

Never have Poles been in dread of the weapons of their enemies, as long as they were united among themselves and were able to use all their strength. It will never happen, I declare, that an army will conquer Poles if the cunning enemy through perversity, betrayal and deceit does not first destroy our will and our means of resistance. The entire course of Muscovite tyranny in Poland is proof of the degree to which this alien force has disrupted our fate by variously using bribery, mendacious promises, prejudicial exaggerations, inciting passions, inflaming one against another, blackening us to outsiders, everything, in a word, that devilish malice combined with the most perverse cunning could conceive.

In the many instances in which Poles have taken up arms against them, can this breed of brigands count a single victory over us? But the fate of Polish courage has always been that the conquered enemy has replaced the yoke on our victorious necks at the moment we stop to rest. how has such a turn of events for Poland come about? How has the nation come to groan without the means to free itself? It is thus that the cunning of Muscovite intrigue, more powerful than arms, has caused the Poles to be undone by the Poles themselves.

Moreover, the unfortunate Poles are divided by views regarding government and opinions about the law, upon which freedom and national organization must be based, and to innocent differences of opinion the criminal spirit of self love and selfish prospects added mixed obstinacy, delay, and the tendency to comport with outsiders, ending in craven submission to them.

The time has come, unhappiness and suffering are far advanced; the time of the ultimate fate of Poland, the epoch in which one goal, one undoubtable purpose, which permits no disagreement and which should unite hearts and minds and allow divided Poles to come to a general alliance, excepting those who are known traitors or those timid and insecure citizens who follow their private motives. The current national uprising aims to return freedom unity and independence to Poland, and leave to freer times and the nation's will to determine under what sort of government it wishes to live. The existence of diversity of opinions is suspended, the holy and obvious cause moves hearts strongly and collects together even those who were heretofore divided for manifold reasons.

Hence, the time, this very moment must be seized with the greatest eagerness. The enemy exerts his entire energy to prevent our using this occasion. He's using weapons, but these are the least dangerous force at his disposal. Against the host of frightened would-be slaves we oppose the massed force of free citizens who, fighting for their own happiness, cannot fail of victory, and that which has hitherto conquered us is the instrument of stealthily gnawing beasts, this loathsome Machiavellian product will be overcome by our attention, the ardor of worthy citizens and the terrible sword of justice which reaches everywhere treason or perversity harmful to the nation appears.

The fate of Poland depends on whether we crush the double power of our enemies, that is: the force of his armies and of his intrigues. I must, hence, inform the nation, that the Muscovites are seeking means to enrage the country folk against us, citing the arbitrariness of the lords, their former misery, and, finally, promising a more prosperous future with Muscovite help. Speaking thus they encourage and collaborate with the country folk in the joint plunder of the manors. These simple people, many times misled because of their distress, can and will fall into snares, and already we have seen that by seduction or force they have been put in enemy uniform.

I must note with regret that the Muscovite has often made such terrible use of the Nation. Again and again I have received complaints from soldiers and recruits, that their wives and children have not only failed to receive special attention, but that while their husbands and fathers serve the Commonwealth, they are subjected to the greatest burdens. Such matters are certainly in many places without the knowledge and contrary to the will of the landowners, but in other places it must be the result of bad will or the alien inspiration to dampen entirely among the common people the drive to defend the Fatherland.

But humanity, justice, and the good of the Fatherland show us easy and sure means by which we can avert the intrigues of domestic malice or foreign intrigue. Let us declare, that the peasants not only remain under the protection of the National Government, that an oppressed person has a prepared refuge with the Commission for Order of his province, but that the oppressor, the persecutor of those defending the country will be punished as an enemy of and traitor to the Fatherland. In this way, worthy of the justice of a glorious nation, agreeable to the kind hearted, and only lightly burdening personal interests will join the common people to the public cause and protect them from the enemy's snares. Hence I recommend to the Commissions for Order of the Provinces and the Lands of the entire country, that the following arrangement is to be given to all landlords, property holders and all their subordinate administrators:

First: Tell the common people that according to the law they remain under the protection of the National Government.

Second: That every peasant is personally free and that he is free to move where he wishes, provided he notifies the Commission for Order of his Province as to where he goes, and provided he has paid all due debts as well as the national taxes.

Third: That the common people have relief in their labor obligations so that someone who works five or six days weekly will have two days relief a week. Who works three or four [days weekly] will have one day relief a week; who works two will have one day. Who works one day a week, now need work one day in two weeks. Moreover, he who performs corvée for two, will be given relief for two. Who works singly will be given relief for single work. The leave system will last the duration of the insurrection, that is until the permanent legislative authorities make arrangements in this matter.

Fourth: Local authorities shall endeavor that the farms of those who serve in the army of the Commonwealth not fall into decay and that the land, which is the source of our wealth, shall not lie fallow, both the manors and the hamlets should attend to this matter.

Fifth: From those who are called to the general levy [pospolite ruszenie], as long as they remain under arms, no corvée will be exacted, but it will begin only with their return home.

Sixth: The landlord shall not take away from the peasant the possession of land with attached obligations. The possession of land with obligations subject to the aforesaid relief shall not be taken away from the peasant by the lord, unless previously the lord has settled the matter before the local overseer and proved that the peasant has not fulfilled his obligations.

Seventh: Should a sub-prefect steward or commissioner violate this regulation and burden the peasantry, he may be taken before the Commission and given over to a criminal court.

Eight: If a landlord (and this I do not expect) order or commit similar oppressions, they will be called to account as opponents of the goal of the insurrection.

Ninth: In return, the country folk, recognizing the justice and goodness of the Government should eagerly perform the corvée which remains, be obedient to their authorities, attend to the farms, till and sow the soil well, and when the peasants receive a reduction in their burdens for the sake of the Fatherland and when the landlords gladly accept it thanks to their love for the Fatherland, the peasants should not refuse to be hired on by the manors for a fair wage to do needed work.

Tenth: For ease in maintaining order to ensure that these instructions are carried out, the Commissions for Order will divide, as is possible in their organizations, provinces, or lands, or districts into supervisory divisions so that each division includes a farm population of one-thousand or, at the most twelve hundred. They will designate these divisions according to the name of the chief village or town and thereby they will form a network in which easy communication will be possible.

Eleventh: In each division a supervisor will be designated, a capable and worthy person, who, in addition to taking on responsibilities within the Commissions for Order, will collect complaints from the people in his charge and from the manor in case the local population is disobedient or unruly. He will be responsible for settling arguments, and if the parties are not content, he will send them to the Commission for Order.

Twelfth: The benefaction of the government in easing the burdens of the common people should encourage them all the more to work, to farm, to defend the Fatherland. Should there be those who would abuse the generosity and sense of justice of the government, would dissuade others from work, would rebel against the landlords, would refuse to defend the Fatherland, the Commissions for Order in the Counties and Districts will have to turn their diligent attention to this and immediately order the arrest of these blackguards and give them over to criminal Court. To the same degree must the Commissions for Order watch over vagabonds who desert their homes and wander about the land. All these people are to be caught and sent to the security section existing in each Commission and, after being examined, if they are shown to be vagrants and idlers they should be employed in public work.

Thirteenth: The Clergy, the especial leaders of the common people, should emphasize their obligations towards the Fatherland, which is really a mother to them. These Clergy should enlighten the people that diligent work on their own land and that of the manor is as dear a sacrifice for the Fatherland as that performed by he who with armed force protects it from the pillage and robbery of enemy soldiers; that in fulfilling his obligations to the manors, as abated by this manifesto, need do nothing more, and must only pay the debt to the landlords from whom he received the lands.

Fourteenth: Clergy of both confessions shall announce this manifesto from the pulpits of the Catholic and Orthodox churches for the next four Sundays; moreover, the Commissions for Order shall designate from their ranks (or from amongst the general citizenry dedicated to the good of the Fatherland) people who will visit gatherings in the villages and parishes and there read this manifesto aloud encouraging the people to demonstrate their gratitude for the great benefaction by sincere eagerness in the defense of the Commonwealth.

Done at the camp near Połaniec, May 7, 1794
Tadeusz Kościuszko

Translated from the Polish by
M. B. Biskupski

Notes

Chapter 1

1. Bolesław Klimaszewski, ed., *An Outline History of Polish Culture* (Warsaw: Interpress, 1984) and Jerzy Topolski, *An Outline History of Poland* (Warsaw: Interpress, 1986), *passim*.

⟩. 2. William L. Langer, *An Encyclopedia of World History* (Boston: Houghton Mifflin Company, 1972), 257; Oscar Halecki, *Borderlands of Western Civilization* (New York: Ronald Press Company, 1952), 42; Oskar Halecki, *A History of Poland* (New York: Roy Publishers, 1943), 9.

3. Langer, 257, 337; Halecki, *Borderlands*, 42-44, 107, 119-122; Halecki, *Poland*, 9, 72, 77-78.

4. Quote from Halecki, *Borderlands*, 42, 106; Halecki, *Poland*, 9, 57-58; Langer, 257.

5. Theresita Polzin, "The Polish Americans," in Dennis L. Cuddy, ed., *Contemporary American Immigration: Interpretive Essays* (Boston: Twayne, 1982), 60; Langer, 442; Halecki, *Borderlands*, 172.

6. Klimaszewski, 19.

7. M. B. Biskupski and James S. Pula, eds., *Polish Democratic Thought From the Renaissance to the Great Migration: Essays and Documents* (New York: Columbia University Press, 1990), 132.

8. James Miller, "The Sixteenth-Century Roots of the Polish Democratic Tradition," in Biskupski and Pula, *Polish Democratic Thought*, 18-19.

9. Miller, 12.

10. Miller, 12.

11. Langer, 337; quote from Halecki, *Borderlands*, 109.

12. Langer, 340, 442; Miller, 11.

13. Biskupski and Pula, 109-110.

14. Langer, 442; quote from Miller, 12-13.

15. Biskupski and Pula, 142.

16. Halecki, *Poland*, 125.

17. Halecki, *Borderlands*, 178.

18. M. B. Biskupski, "Gentry Democracy' in Polish Political Thought and Practice, 1500-1863," in Biskupski and Pula, 2.

19. Robert I. Frost, "Liberty Without Licence?' The Failure of Polish Democratic Thought in the Seventeenth Century," in Biskupski and Pula, 52.

20. Frost, 36.

21. Langer, 511, 518.

22. Langer, 511.

23. Langer, 511.

24. Mieczysław Haiman, *Kościuszko in the American Revolution* (New York: Polish Institute of Arts and Sciences in America, 1943), 1.

25. As Haiman points out, the exact date and place of Kosciuszko's birth remain a source of debate. He was baptized February 12, 1746, at the Roman Catholic church in Kossów, Słonim County, in the eastern province of Polesie. His early Polish biographers generally argued that he was born February 4, St. Andrew's Day, as Polish custom was to name children for the saint's nameday on which they were born. Occasionally, the dates of February 2 and 16 have also been cited. More recent scholarship suggests February 12 as the actual date of birth. The place of birth was probably either Siechnowicze, "the old family homestead," or Mereczówszczyzna, "which also belonged to his parents." Both were small villages near Kossów. See Haiman, *Revolution*, 1-2; Stephen P. Mizwa, "Tadeusz Kościuszko," in *Great Men and Women of Poland* (New York: Macmillan Company, 1942), 127; George H. Bushnell, *Kościuszko: A Short Biography of the Polish Patriot* (London: W. C. Henderson & Son, 1943), 5; Bogdan Grzeloński, *Poles in the United States of America 1776-1865* (Warsaw: Interpress, 1976), 42; Jan Stanisław Kopczewski, *Kościuszko * Pułaski* (Warsaw: Interpress, 1976), 56.

26. Haiman, *Revolution*, 2; Mizwa, 127; Szymon Askenazy, *Thaddeus Kosciuszko* (London: The Polish Review Officers, 1917), 3; Bushnell, 5; Jan Stanisław Kopczewski, *Tadeusz Kościuszko* (Warsaw: Interpress, 1971), 12; Kopczewski, *Kościuszko * Pułaski*, 57; Albert C. Cizauskas, "The Unusual Story of Thaddeus Kosciuszko," *Lituanus 1986*, Vol. 32, No. 1, 49.

27. Haiman, *Revolution*, 2.

28. Grzeloński, 42; Askenazy, 3.

29. Greloński, 42; Haiman, *Revolution*, 2; Mizwa, 127; Haiman, *Revolution*, 2; Bushnell, 6; Kopczewski, *Kościuszko*, 12.

30. Haiman, *Revolution*, 2; Mizwa, 127. At least one writer, Alfred Rambaud, claims that Ludwik died at the hands of "exasperated peasants" during a local rebellion.

31. Bushnell, 6; *Dictionary of American Biography*, 497; Kopczewski, *Kościuszko*, 12; Monica M. Gardner, *Kosciuszko: A Biography* (London: George Allen and Unwin, Ltd., 1920), 15.

Notes

32. Quote from Grzeloński, 43; Haiman, *Revolution*, 2.

33. Mizwa, 127- 128; Haiman, *Revolution*, 2; Koneczny, 59.

34. Langer, 511; Haiman, *Revolution*, 2.

35. Langer, 511.

36. Grzeloński, 43; Kopczewski, *Kościuszko*, 21.

37. Mizwa, 128; Grzeloński, 44; Haiman, *Revolution*, 2; Kopczewski, *Kościuszko*, 21; Kopczewski, *Kościuszko* * *Pułaski*, 58; Koneczny, 70; Gardner, 16.

38. Grzeloński, 44.

39. Mizwa, 128; Grzeloński, 43-44; Haiman, *Revolution*, 2; Koneczny, 71; Metchie J. E. Budka, ed., *Autograph Letters of Thaddeus Kosciuszko in the American Revolution* (Chicago: The Polish Museum of America, 1977), 18; Bushnell, p. 6, notes that Prince Czartoryski was Count Fleming's son-in-law.

40. Quote from Grzeloński, 44-45; Mizwa, 128; Kamila Mrozowska, *Szkoła rycerska Stanisława Augusta Poniatowskiego, 1765-1794* (Warsaw, 1961).

41. Haiman, *Revolution*, 2-3; Mizwa, 128; Grzeloński, 45; E. Bellchambers, *A General Biographical Dictionary* (London: Allan Bell & Co., 1835), 234.

42. Mizwa, 128; Grzeloński, 45; Bellchambers, 234.

43. Halecki, 260-261; Koneczny, 90-91.

44. Haiman, *American Revolution*, 2-3; Mizwa, 129.

45. Grzeloński, 45; Haiman, *Revolution*, 2-3.

46. Kościuszko to Jerzy W. Mniszech, October 19, 1775, in Dzwonkowski, "Młode Lata Kościuszki," *Biblioteka Warszawska*, CCLXXXIV (1911), 35.

47. Haiman, *Revolution*, 3; Askenazy, 4; Bushnell, 7.

48. Józef Żuraw, "Tadeusz Kościuszko — The Polish Enlightenment Thinker," *Dialectics and Humanism*, Vol. VI, No. 1 (Winter 1979), 153.

49. Żuraw, 152.

50. Żuraw, 153, quote from 158.

51. Quoted in Żuraw, 155.

52. Żuraw, 156; Tadeusz Kościuszko, *Czy Polacy mogl wybić się na niepodległość?* (Warszawa: 1967), 64.

53. Żuraw, 156.

54. Langer, 512; Kopczewski, *Kościuszko*, 27.

55. Langer, 512; Kopczewski, *Kościuszko*, 27.

56. Mizwa, 129; Bushnell, 7.

57. Bushnell, 7; Haiman, *Revolution*, 3-4; Mizwa, 129; Koneczny, 62; Gardner, 16.

58. Grzeloński, 46; Gardner, 20.

59. Quote from Grzeloński, 46; Bushnell, 7; Haiman, *Revolution*, 4; Mizwa,

129; Askenazy, 4; Bellchambers, 234; Koneczny, 70-71, 116-121; Cizauskas, 49.

Chapter 2

1. Grzeloński, 46; Kahanowicz, 1; Bushnell, 7; Haiman, *Revolution*, 4; Mizwa, 129; quotes from Budka, 13; Irene M. Sokol, "The American Revolution and Poland: A Bibliographic Essay," *The Polish Review*, XII, No. 3 (Summer 1967), 4.

2. Kościuszko to Mniszech, October 19, 1775, as quoted in Budka, 18.

3. Mizwa, 130; Haiman, *Revolution*, 5.

4. Haiman, *Revolution*, 5.

5. Quote from Lemaitre, Grzeloński, 46.

6. Quote from Lemaitre, Grzeloński, 46.

7. Grzeloński, 46-47; Kahanowicz, 1-3.

8. Most authors have mistakenly identified the destination of French aid as the Spanish island of Santo Domingo rather than the correct French port.

9. Grzeloński, 47; Kahanowicz, 1-3.

10. Haiman, *Revolution*, 5.

11. Haiman, *Revolution*, 6; Mizwa, 130; Budka, 18.

12. C. Neilson, *The Original, Compiled and Corrected Account of the Burgoyne Campaign and the Memorable Battle of Bemis Heights* (Albany: 1844), 118.

13. Armstrong memorial, Jared Sparks, ed., *Correspondence of the American Revolution* (Boston: Little & Brown, 1853), Ser. 49, I, 72.

14. Haiman, *Revolution*, 9; "The Lee Papers," *Collections of the New-York Historical Society*, IV-VII (1871-1874); Władysław M. Kozłowski, "Pierwszy Rok Służby Amerykańskiej Kościuszki," *Przeglld Historyczny*, IV, 310-314; Władysław M. Kozłowski, *Washington and Kościuszko* (Chicago: Polish Roman Catholic Union of America, 1942), 34.

15. *Dictionary of American Biography*, 497; Mizwa, 130; Christopher Ward, *The War of the Revolution* (New York: 1952), 373.

16. *Dictionary of American Biography*, 497; Mizwa, 130; Ward, 373.

17. Mark M. Boatner, *Encyclopedia of the American Revolution* (New York: David McKay Company, Inc., 1966), 783, 798-800; Haiman, *Revolution*, 10-11.

18. Haiman, *Revolution*, 10-11; Ward, 373.

19. Washington to Putnam, December 3, 1776, quoted in William Farrand Livingston, *Israel Putnam: Pioneer, Ranger, and Major-General 1718-1790* (New York: G. P. Putnam's Sons, 1901), 328. Several references to Kościuszko in the first months of his service in America refer to him as a French engineer. No doubt this confusion arose from the fact that he received French assistance in coming to America and, given his limited knowledge of English, he undoubtedly conversed whenever

possible in French with the learned officers and political leaders he encountered in and around Philadelphia.

20. John C. Fitzpatrick, ed., *The Writings of George Washington from the Original Manuscript Sources 1745-1799* (Washington: U. S. Government Printing Office), VI, 339-340.

21. Haiman, *Revolution*, 10-11; Ward, 373.

22. Ward, 373.

23. *Journals of the Continental Congress*, VI, 1006; Haiman, *Revolution*, 11.

Chapter 3

1. Ward, 400.

2. John S. Pancake, *1777: The Year of the Hangman* (Tuscaloosa, AL: The University of Alabama Press, 1977), 90-91.

3. Quote from Gregory T. Edgar, *"Liberty or Death!" The Northern Campaigns in the American Revolutionary War* (Bowie, MD: Heritage Books, Inc., 1994, 164; Ward, 398-399; Thomas Anburey, *With Burgoyne from Quebec: Travels Through the Interior of North America* (Toronto: Macmillan of Canada, 1963), 3.

4. Edgar, 164; Robert Leckie, *The Wars of America* (New York: Harper & Row, 1968), 168-169; Ward, 398-400; Boatner, 133.

5. Quoted in Leckie, 169.

6. Quote from Hoffman Nickerson, *The Turning Point of the Revolution* (Boston: Houghton Mifflin Company, 1928), 83.

7. Ward, 399.

8. Edgar, 164; Ward, 400; Boatner, 133; Anburey, 3.

9. Ward, 402-403.

10. Ward, 402-403; Edgar, 174; Pancake, 115-116.

11. Ward, 403; Edgar, 168.

12. Ward, 402.

13. Ward, 402; Edgar, 168.

14. Ward, 401-402.

15. Ward, 403-404.

16. Edgar, 168; Leckie, 169.

17. Edgar, 168.

18. Ward, 408-409.

19. Ward, 405-406.

20. Boatner, 911.

21. Boatner, 412; Edgar, 288.

22. Edgar, 181; Boatner, 412.

23. Patterson, 121.

24. Haiman, *Revolution*, 13.

25. Armstrong memorial, Sparks, Ser. 49, I, 70.

26. *Bancroft Papers*, Vol. III, 133, New York Public Library.

27. Jeduthan Baldwin, *The Revolutionary Journal of Colonel Jeduthan Baldwin 1775-1778* (Bangor, ME: The DeBurians, 1906), 101.

28. "The Baldwin Letters," *The American Monthly*, VI (1895), 196.

29. Baldwin, 102.

30. Lynn Montross, *The Story of the Continental Army 1775-1783* (New York: Barnes & Noble, Inc., 1967), 196.

31. Kościuszko to Gates, May, 1777, Gates Papers, Box 6, New-York Historical Society. The plan is not among the papers. Also see *Catholic Historical Researches*, 139-140.

32. Armstrong memorial, Sparks, Ser. 49, I, 70.

33. Kościuszko to Gates, May 18, 1777, Gates Papers, Box 6, New-York Historical Society. See also *Catholic Historical Researches*, 141.

34. Kościuszko to Gates, May 18, 1777, Gates Papers, Box 6, New-York Historical Society. See also *Catholic Historical Researches*, 141.

35. *St. Clair Papers*, I, 51; James Wilkinson, *Memoirs of My Own Times* (Philadelphia: A. Small, 1816), 173.

36. Papers of the Continental Congress, Ser. 154, I, 222-223, Library of Congress.

37. Wilkinson to Gates, May, 1777, Gates Papers, Box 6, New-York Historical Society.

38. Baldwin, 103.

39. Wilkinson, *Memoirs*, I, 171.

40. Baldwin, 104; Edgar, 193.

41. Philip Schuyler to Richard Varick, April 26, 1777, Edmund C. Burnett, *Letters of Members of the Continental Congress* (Washington, DC: The Carnegie Institution of Washington, 1921-1936), II, 342.

42. Quote from *Journals of the Continental Congress*, VII, 364; Edgar, 181; Boatner, 992; Samuel White Patterson, *Horatio Gates, Defender of American Liberties* (New York: Columbia University Press, 1941), 129.

43. Edgar, 181; Boatner, 992.

44. Kościuszko to Gates, Gates Papers, Box 6, New-York Historical Society. Original in French, translated in Haiman, *Revolution*, 19.

45. Boatner, 834, 880, 1104; Edgar, 181.

46. Boatner, 1104; Edgar, 181, 186; Edward P. Hamilton, *Fort Ticonderoga: Key to a Continent* (Boston: Little, Brown and Company, 1964), 175, quote from 176.

47. Boatner, 136; Ward, 406; Edgar, 185.

48. Edgar, 191; Boatner, 1103.

49. Baldwin, 104-105; *Proceedings of a General Court Martial....* (Philadelphia: Hall and Sellers, 1778), 115.

50. *Collections of the New-York Historical Society*, XIII (1880), 109; *Proceedings of a General Court Martial*, 115.

51. Armstrong memorial, Sparks, Ser. 49, I, 70; Edgar, 193; Haiman, *Revolution*, 18.

52. Quoted in Edgar, 193.

53. Ward, 406; *Collections of the New-York Historical Society*, XIII (1880), 58-61, 109, 115; *Proceedings of a General Court Martial*, 58-59.

54. Edgar, 175; Boatner, 135, 1104.

55. Anburey, 131.

56. Boatner, 135, 1104; Ward, 403; Edgar, 177.

57. Pancake, 151-152; Don R. Gerlach, "The Fall of Ticonderoga in 1777: Who Was Responsible?" *The Bulletin of the Fort Ticonderoga Museum*, XIV, No. 3 (Summer 1982), 137, reports that St. Clair's return for the same day listed a total of 3,842 including a late-arriving contingent of militia and 238 artillerists. Deducting the sick and detached, this left 2,089 rank and file actually available for duty.

58. Boatner, 135, 1104.

59. Anburey, 134-135.

60. Boatner, 1104.

61. Boatner, 1106.

62. Boatner, 1105-1106; Edgar, 191-192.

63. Anburey, 137.

64. Boatner, 1106; Leckie, 169; Edgar, 191-192.

65. Boatner, 1106; Edgar, 192-193; *Proceedings of a General Court Martial*, 72-73.

66. Baldwin, 40; Edgar, 194.

67. St. Clair to Washington, July 17, 1777, in Sparks, *Correspondence of the Revolution*, I, 400-402.

68. St. Clair to Jay, July 25, 1777, *St. Clair Papers*, I, 433.

69. Boatner, 1107.

70. Kościuszko to St. Clair, 1777, Library of Congress.

71. Quoted in Baxter, *The British Invasion*, 204.

72. "Journal of Du Roi the Elder," *German American Annals*, XIII (1911), 151-152.

Chapter 4

1. Boatner, 526, 1106; Edgar, 194.

2. Boatner, 1106; Nickerson, 146.

3. Boatner, 1106; Nickerson, 146.

4. Montross, 202.

5. Boatner, 1107; Edgar, 195, 197; Nickerson, 154.

6. Boatner, 1107; Edgar, 195, 197.

7. Anburey, 139.

8. Louise Hall Tharp, *The Baroness and the General* (Boston: Little, Brown and Company, 1962), 134.

9. Boatner, 526-528, 1107; Leckie, 170.

10. Leckie, 170; Edgar, 239.

11. Armstrong memorial, Sparks, Ser. 49, I, 70.

12. Wilkinson, *Memoirs*, I, 200.

13. Col. Edney Hay to George Clinton, August 13, 1777, Sparks, 49, I, 34.

14. *Collections of the New-York Historical Society*, XIII, 61.

15. Boatner, 136; Edgar, 212.

16. Montross, 203.

17. Pancake, 152.

18. Boatner, 137; Nickerson, 179-180.

19. Boatner, 137; Leckie, 170; Edgar, 239, 241.

20. Boatner, 137; Leckie, 170; Edgar, 239, 241.

21. Boatner, 137; Edgar, 239, 242.

22. Orderly book of Gen. Phillip Schuyler, June 16-August 18, 1777, p. 53, in the American Antiquarian Society.

23. Anburey, 152.

24. Nickerson, 173.

25. Edgar, 242.

26. Edgar, 242; Boatner, 138.

27. Edgar, 242; Leckie, 170; Boatner 138.

28. Quote from Nickerson, 175.

29. Quoted in Leckie, 170.

30. Anburey, 154.

31. Boatner, 138; Leckie, 170; Edgar, 242.

32. Leckie, 170.

33. Boatner, 138; Leckie, 170; Edgar, 242; Montross, 213.

34. Leckie, 170; Edgar, 242.

35. Quoted in Edgar, 245.

36. Boatner, 68-75, 138.

37. Edgar, 291.

38. Anburey, 159.

39. Edgar, 193.

40. *Jefferson Papers*, Ser. I, XIV, 148A.

Chapter 5

1. Quoted in Nickerson, 186; Wilkinson, 200.

2. Haiman, *Revolution*, 22; Nickerson, 211-213.

3. Haiman, *Revolution*, 22; Nickerson, 186-187.

4. Boatner, 138, 412, 992; Leckie, 175; Edgar, 283.

5. Boatner, 138, 412; Leckie, 175; Edgar, 289.

6. Edgar, 289-290, 292; Leckie, 175; Pancake, 152.

7. Papers, Saratoga National Historical Park; quote from Washington, ed., *Writings of Jefferson*, VII, 494.

8. George Clinton to James Duane, August 27, 1777, Sparks, Ser. 49, I, 34.

9. Edgar, 289-290.

10. Quote from Armstrong's memorial, Sparks, Ser. 49, I, 71; Upham, *Memoir of Glover*, 30, says it was Kościuszko's advice that the army be put in motion.

11. Edgar, 290; Leckie, 175; Patterson, 151; Rupert Furneaux, *The Battle of Saratoga* (New York: Stein & Day, 1971), 151.

12. Montross, 214-215.

13. Henry Dearborn, "A Narrative of the Saratoga Campaign," *Fort Ticonderoga Bulletin*, Vol. I, No. 5 (January 1929), *Journals*, 105.

14. Quote from Armstrong memorial, Sparks, Ser. 49, I, 71.

15. Quote from Edgar, 298; Wilkinson, 252.

16. Ernest Cuneo, "General T. Kosciuszko," *Saturday Evening Post*, October, 1975, 112; Furneaux, 162.

17. Trevelyan, George Otto, *The American Revolution*. (New York; McKay, 1964)

18. Chastellux, *Travels*, I, 410.

19. Edgar, 292; Ward, 504; Anburey, 170.

20. Anburey, 170.

21. Edgar, 292; Ward, 504; Anburey, 170.

22. Leckie, 175; Boatner, 138; Edgar, 296; Ward, 504-505; Anburey, 171.

23. Anburey, 172.

24. Edgar, 299; Leckie, 175-176; Ward, 505.

25. Edgar, 299; Leckie, 175-176; Ward, 505.

26. Edgar, 299; Leckie, 175-176; Ward, 505.

27. Edgar, 299; Leckie, 175-176; Ward, 505.

28. Edgar, 299-300; Leckie, 175; Ward, 505-506; quote from Misc. Papers, Saratoga National Historical Park, "Battle of September 19, 1777," 11.

29. Edgar, 300; Ward, 506; Leckie, 175-176.

30. Edgar, 300; Ward, 508.

31. Ward, 508; Leckie, 176; Edgar, 300.

32. Edgar, 304; Ward, 508, 510; Leckie, 176.

33. Leckie, 176; quote from Ward, 510.

34. Edgar, 312; Ward, 511.

35. Ward, 511; Leckie, 176.

36. Ward, 511; Leckie, 176; Edgar, 306, 312 (p. 306 says the 62nd lost 212

of 280 engaged); Bill Ward, complr., "The Battles of Saratoga: People, Places and Facts," Saratoga National Historical Park, March, 1988.

37. Boatner, 139; Edgar, 317; Ward, 521.

38. Boatner, 139; Edgar, 206; Ward, 521.

39. Boatner, 140; Ward, 522; Nickerson, 317.

40. Anburey, 176.

41. Quoted in Haiman, *Revolution*, 30.

42. Ward, 522-523; Pancake, 182.

43. Quoted in Patterson, 155.

44. Ward, 522-523; Pancake, 182.

45. Boatner, quote from 139; Ward, 524-525.

46. Boatner, 140; Ward, 524.

47. Anburey, 181.

48. Nickerson, 356.

49. Ward, 525; Boatner, 140; Edgar, 327; Leckie, 177; Nickerson, 356.

50. Edgar, 327, 329; Leckie, 177; Ward, 526.

51. Ward, 526.

52. Edgar, 329; Ward 526; Pancake, 184.

53. Ward, 526; Pancake, 184; Edgar, 329.

54. Ward, 526; Pancake, 186.

55. Pancake, 186; Ward, 526; Leckie, 177.

56. Pancake, 186; Ward, 526; Nickerson, 363-364.

57. Pancake, 186; Ward, 530; Leckie, 177-178.

58. Pancake, 186; Ward, 530; Leckie, 178; Boatner, 140.

59. Boatner, 140; Pancake, 186; Ward, 526; "Battles of Saratoga," Saratoga National Historical Park.

60. Boatner, 140; Ward, 531.

61. Boatner, 140; Pancake, 186; Ward, 532.

62. Boatner, 140.

63. Boatner, 141; Ward, 534.

64. Boatner, 141.

65. Boatner, 141.

66. Boatner, 141; Ward, 534.

67. Boatner, 141; Ward, 536.

68. Boatner, 141; Ward, 534.

69. Ward, 534.

70. Ward, 535-537.

71. Ward, 537-538.

72. Ward, 538; Pancake, 190-191.

73. Ward, 538; Pancake, 190-191.

74. Ward, 539; Montross, 225, gives the number surrendered as 5,791.

75. Ward, 538.
76. Ward, 540.
77. Quote from Bushnell, 10.
78. Quote from Bushnell, 10 and Kozłowski, *Washington and Kosciuszko,* 36.
79. Montross, 227.
80. Haiman, *Revolution,* 11; Cuneo, 112.

Chapter 6

1. Haiman, *Revolution,* 35.
2. Boatner, 278, 413.
3. Quote from Washington's letter to Laurens in Patterson, 208; Boatner 278, 413; Leckie, 179.
4. Quoted in Montross, 260.
5. Quoted in Patterson, 218; *Catholic Historical Researches,* 154-155.
6. Boatner, 278.
7. Boatner, 278-279; Leckie, 180.
8. Boatner, 278, 413; Patterson, 236-237.
9. Quoted in Patterson, 335.
10. Boatner, 278; Leckie, 179; Patterson, 235-236.
11. Quoted in Patterson, 237.
12. Boatner, 281, 413.
13. Patterson, 201.
14. Kościuszko to Mrs. Gates, January 17, 1778, Gates Papers, Box 9, New-York Historical Society.
15. Haiman, *Revolution,* 35-36.
16. Washington to Laurens, November 10, 1777, Fitzpatrick, X, 35.
17. Quoted in "General Thaddeus Kosciuszko," *The American Catholic Historical Researches,* New Series, VI, No. 2 (April, 1910), 149.
18. *South Carolina History and Genealogy Magazine,* VII (1906), 189-193.
19. Haiman, *Revolution,* 39; Laurens to Lafayette, March 4, 1778, in Burnett, *Letters,* III, 106.
20. Haiman, *Revolution,* 39.
21. Boatner, 279; Leckie, 180.
22. Gates to Israel Putnam, March 5, 1778, in McDougall Papers, New-York Historical Society.
23. Patterson, 281.
24. Haiman, *Revolution,* 56; *Catholic Historical Researches,* 155.
25. Lansing's description quoted in Haiman, *Revolution,* 57-58.
26. Quotes from Haiman, *Revolution,* 57.
27. *New York Packet,* September 17, 1778.

28. *New York Packet*, September 17, 1778.

29. *New York Packet*, September 17, 1778.

30. Haiman, *Revolution*, 62. Given Kościuszko's imperfect command of written English, it is obvious that in these newspaper articles, as in some of his American letters and reports, he has had the benefit of editorial assistance by someone more fluent than he.

31. *New York Packet*, September 24, 1778.

32. *Catholic Historical Researches*, 155-156.

33. *New York Packet*, September 26, 1778.

34. *Collections of the New-York Historical Society*, VIII (1875), 456-457.

Chapter 7

1. Montross, 325; Boatner, 530.

2. Washington to Putnam, December 2, 1777, Fitzpatrick, X, 129.

3. Edward C. Boynton, *History of West Point and Its Military Importance During the American Revolution* (New York: D. Van Nostrand, 1863), 20.

4. Mizwa, 131; quote from Haiman, *Revolution*, 42; Kite, *Records of the American Catholic Historical Society*, XLIII (1932); Dave R. Palmer, author of *The River and the Rock: The History of Fortress West Point, 1775-1783* (New York: Hippocrene Books, 1991), 132-134, 138-139, quote from 140.

5. Boynton, 56.

6. *Public Papers of George Clinton*, II, 712.

7. Quoted in Boynton, 61; Palmer, 139-140, 144.

8. Quoted in Mizwa, 131; Haiman, *Revolution*, 43; Palmer, 145.

9. Troup to Gates, March 26, 1778, Gates Papers, Box 9, New-York Historical Society; Boynton, 62; *Clinton Papers*, II, 847.

10. Clinton, *Public Papers*, III, 85.

11. Haiman, *Revolution*, 43; Mizwa, 132; Boynton, 62.

12. Washington to McDougall, November 24, 1778, McDougall papers, Microfilm Roll 2, New-York Historical Society.

13. Quoted in Mizwa, 132; Boynton, 63.

14. Haiman, *Revolution*, 43; Palmer, 132, 155, 157.

15. McDougall Papers, Book III; Palmer, 158-159.

16. Washington to McDougall, April 6, 1778, Fitzpatick, XI, 222; Palmer, 159.

17. McDougall to Washington, April 13, 1778, Washington Papers, LXXII; Sparks, V, 311; Palmer, 159.

18. Washington to McDougall, April 22, 1778, McDougall Papers, New-York Historical Society; Palmer, 159.

19. Haiman, *Revolution*, 47.

20. McDougall Papers, return by John Bacon dated April 27, 1788,

New-York Historical Society. The artificers included eight officers, one clerk, one foreman, seven sergeants, and the rest being privates.

21. Boynton, 64-65; Haiman, *Revolution*, 49.

22. Boynton, 63.

23. Boynton, 63-65; Haiman, *Revolution*, 47.

24. Boynton, 70, and quote from 73.

25. Boynton, 75-76, quoting Heath's memoirs.

26. Troup to Gates, April 18, 1778, Gates Papers, Box 9, New-York Historical Society.

27. Clinton to Washington, April 8, 1778, Clinton, *Public Papers*, III, 151; Palmer, 160.

28. McDougall to Washington, April 13, 1778, Washington Papers, LXXII.

29. Thacher, *Military Journal*, 134.

30. Kościuszko to Gates, August 4, 1778, Gates Papers, Box 10, New-York Historical Society.

31. Gates to Glover, July 2, 1778, Gates Papers, New-York Historical Society; also in Budka, 26.

32. Boynton, 79.

33. Washington to Malcolm, July 27, 1778, Fitzpatrick, XII, 239.

34. Boatner, 400-401.

35. Haiman, *Revolution*, 50; Washington to Malcolm, July 27, 1778, Fitzpatrick, XII, 239; Washington to Gates, September 11, 1778, Fitzpatrick, XII, 419; Washington to du Portail, September 19, 1778, Fitzpatrick, XII, 469.

36. Du Portail to Gates, Gates Papers, New-York Historical Society; Kozłowski, "West Point," 80.

37. Du Portail to the President of Congress, August 27, 1778, *Papers of the Continental Congress*, VIII, 54-56.

38. Washington to the President of Congress, August 31, 1778, Fitzpatrick, XII, 376-377.

39. Washington to Malcolm, September 7, 1778, Fitzpatrick, XII, 408-409; Palmer, 173.

40. Boatner, 1107; Haiman, *Revolution*, 84; Palmer, 174.

41. Baldwin, 134.

42. Du Portail to Washington, September 13, 1778, quoted in Elizabeth S. Kite, *Brigadier-General Louis Lebègue Duportail: Commandant of Engineers in the Continental Army 1777-1783* (Baltimore: The Johns Hopkins Press, 1933), 211-216.

43. Du Portail to Washington, September 13, 1778, quoted in Kite, 211-216.

44. Washington to du Portail, September 19, 1778 in Fitzpatrick, XII, 469; Sparks, *Writings of Washington*, VI, 67-68.

45. Kościuszko to Gates, October 6, 1778, Gates Papers, Box 10, New-York Historical Society.

46. Boatner, 179; Askenazy, 23; Palmer, 176.

47. Quote from Kościuszko to Gates, August 3, 1778, Gates Papers, Box 10, New-York Historical Society; Askenazy, 23.

48. Boatner, 179-180.

49. Haiman, *Revolution*, 70; Palmer, 176.

50. Gates to Washington, September 11, 1778, Gates Papers, New-York Historical Society; Palmer, 176.

51. Washington to Gates, September 11, 1778, Fitzpatrick, XII, 419.

52. Kościuszko to Gates, September 12, 1778, Gates Papers, Box 10, New-York Historical Society.

53. Kościuszko to Taylor, September 14, 1778, quoted in Budka, 28.

54. Kościuszko to Gates, October 6, 1778, Gates Papers, Box 10, New-York Historical Society.

55. Baldwin, 137, 139. According to Baldwin's diary, he arrived for visits with Kościuszko on October 14, November 23, and December 4, 1778.

56. Montross, 325.

57. McDougall to Gouvion, December 17, 1778, McDougall Papers, New-York Historical Society; Palmer, 183.

58. Montross, 325.

59. Kościuszko to McDougall, December 28, 1778, McDougall Papers, New-York Historical Society.

60. *Catholic Historical Researches*, 154.

61. Return for January 1, 1779, McDougall Papers, New-York Historical Society.

62. Kościuszko to McDougall, January 2, 1779, McDougall Papers, New-York Historical Society.

63. Haiman, *Revolution*, 74.

64. Kościuszko to McDougall, February 6, 1779, McDougall Papers, New-York Historical Society.

65. McDougall to Paterson, February 21, 1779, McDougall Papers, New-York Historical Society.

66. Washington to McDougall, February 9, 1780, Fitzpatrick, XIV, 84; Palmer, 182.

67. McDougall to Washington, April 19, 1780, Washington Papers, CIII.

68. Kościuszko to McDougall, February 24, 1779, McDougall Papers, New-York Historical Society.

69. Paterson to Maj. Richard Platt, March 2, 1779, McDougall Papers, New-York Historical Society.

70. Kościuszko to Gates, March 3, 1779, Gates Papers, Box 11, New-York Historical Society.

71. Kościuszko to Armstrong, March 3, 1779, quoted in Budka, 31.

72. McDougall to Kościuszko, March 18, 1779, McDougall Papers, New-York Historical Society.

73. McDougall to Kościuszko, April 17, 1779 and Kościuszko to McDougall, April 25, 1779, McDougall Papers, New-York Historical Society.

74. Du Portail to John Jay, May 11, 1779, Papers of the Continental Congress, 342-345; Haiman, *Revolution*, 80-81.

75. Washington to McDougall, May 28, 1779, Fitzpatrick, XV, 167.

76. Washington to McDougall, June 2, 1779, Fitzpatrick, XV, 214.

77. Haiman, *Revolution*, 81; quote from Washington to Heath, March 21, 1781, Fitzpatrick, XXI, 344.

78. Boynton, 81-82; Boatner, 1063.

79. Scammell to Heath, June 30, 1779, in Budka, 34.

80. Kościuszko to McDougall, July 1, 1779, McDougall Papers, New-York Historical Society.

81. Kościuszko to Washington, July, 1779, Washington Papers, CXIV, 1779.

82. Boynton, 81, 86.

83. Washington to Kościuszko, June 30, 1779, Fitzpatrick, XV, 341.

84. Boynton, 82; Boatner, 1063; Mizwa, 133.

85. *Catholic Historical Researches*, 154.

86. Quoted in *Catholic Historical Researches*, 153. See also Ella M. E. Flick, "General Thaddeus Kosciuszko," *Records of the American Catholic Historical Society of Philadelphia*, XXXVI, No. 3 (September, 1925), 292.

87. Angell, *Diary*, 97.

88. Reproduced in Budka, 38.

89. Boynton, 85-86; Palmer, 224.

90. *Catholic Historical Researches*, 168-169.

91. Quoted in *Catholic Historical Researches*, 154.

92. Boynton, 85-87.

93. Quoted in Grzeloński, 56-57.

94. Palmer, 206.

95. Quoted in Boatner, 1187.

96. Boynton, 11.

Chapter 8

1. Boatner, 980.

2. Boatner, 889.

3. Boatner, 982.

4. Boatner, 1036.

5. John Richard Alden, *The South in the American Revolution, 1763-1789* (Baton Rouge: 1957), 241, 243; Boatner, 1036; Ward 712.

6. Alden, 243.

7. Boatner, 1036-1037; Ward, 714; Henry Lumpkin, *From Savannah to*

Yorktown: The American Revolution in the South (New York: Paragon House Publishers, 1987), 58-59.

8. Gates to Washington, June 22, 1780, reproduced in Budka, 42.

9. Washington, *Writings of Jefferson*, VIII, 496; also quoted in Haiman, *Revolution*, 91.

10. Patterson, 305.

11. Kościuszko to Washington, July 30, 1780, Washington Papers, Vol. CXLIV.

12. Washington to Kościuszko, August 3, 1780, Fitzpatrick, XIX, 316; see also Kozlowski, *Washington and Kosciuszko*, 47.

13. Kościuszko to Washington, August 4, 1780, Washington Papers, Vol. CXLIV; Sparks, VII, 141.

14. Washington to Gates, August 8, 1780, Fitzpatrick, XIX, 316.

15. Washington to Gates, August 12, 1780, in Kosciuszko, *Free Poland*, IV, No. 2 (October 5, 1917), 24.

16. Washington to Gates, August 12, 1780, Fitzpatrick, XIX, 362.

17. *The State Records of North Carolina*, XIV, 565.

18. Haiman, *Revolution*, 99.

19. Ward, 718, 720; Boatner, 1036; Henry Lumpkin, *From Savannah to Yorktown: The American Revolution in the South* (New York: Paragon House, 1987), 59.

20. Ward, 721; Alden, 244; Boatner, 163.

21. Alden, 245; Ward, 722-723; Lumpkin, 60, 291; Boatner, 163.

22. Ward, 727; Boatner, 165; Lumpkin, 60.

23. Ward, 727; Boatner, 166; Lumpkin, 63-64.

24. Alden, 245-246; Ward, 728-729, 732-733; Lumpkin, 64-66.

25. Ward, 731.

26. Alden, 245-246; quote from Boatner, 415.

27. Boatner, 453-454, 1037; Ward, 748.

28. Ward, 731-734; Boatner, 1037.

29. Ward, 736.

30. Alden, 249-250; Boatner, 1038; Leckie, 204.

31. Haiman, *Revolution*, 99.

32. Haiman, *Revolution*, 99.

33. Haiman, *Revolution*, 100.

34. Haiman, *Revolution*, 103; Alden, 251.

35. Alden, 252; Boatner, 1018-1019, 1039; Leckie, 206; Lumpkin, 119-120; Ward, 749-751, quote from 750.

36. Quote from Haiman, 103; Boatner, 1018; Ward, 750-751; Theodore Thayer, *Nathaniel Greene: Strategist of the American Revolution* (New York: Twayne Publishers, 1960), 291.

37. Quoted in Haiman, *Revolution*, 105.

38. Quoted in Budka, 50; a slightly different version appears in Arnold Whitridge, "Kosciuszko: Polish Champion of American Independence," *History Today*, XXV, No. 7 (July 1975), 456.

39. Haiman, *Revolution*, 104; Ward, 750; Thayer, 298; Budka, 50; Greene to Col. Thomas Polk, December 15, 1780, Nathaniel Greene Papers, Library of Congress.

40. Mizwa, 134; Ward, 750; Alexander Kahanowicz, ed., *Memorial Exhibition: Thaddeus Kościuszko* (New York: The Anderson Galleries, 1927), 33; Greene to Washington, December 29, 1780, quote from Budka, 52.

41. Alden, 252; Boatner, 1018-1019; Ward, 752.

42. Boatner, 1018; Leckie, 206.

43. Greene to Kościuszko, January 1, 1781, Nathaniel Greene Papers, Library of Congress.

44. Thayer, 303.

45. Ward, 753.

46. Boatner, 1019; Ward, 753.

47. Boatner, 1020.

48. Leckie, 207-209; Ward, 755-756; Lumpkin, 123.

49. Leckie, 207-209; Ward, 755-756, 762; Lumpkin, 128-132.

50. Boatner, 1020-1021.

51. Boatner, 1021; Lumpkin, 163-164.

52. Major Morris to Kościuszko, February 1, 1781, Greene Papers, Huntington Library; also reprinted in Budka, 58, and Kahanowicz, 33.

53. Boatner, 1021.

54. Alden, 255; Boatner, 1023; Thayer, 315; Lumpkin, 165.

55. Boatner, 1023; Alden, 255; Thayer, 317.

56. Boatner, 1025-1026; Alden, 255; William Johnson, *Sketches of the Life and Correspondence of Nathaniel Greene* (Charleston, SC: 1822), I, 431.

57. Boatner, 1026-1027; Alden, 255; quote from Thayer, 319.

Chapter 9

1. Alden, 256; Boatner, 1027.

2. Greene to Washington, February 15, 1781, Sparks, III, 235; Thayer, 319; quote from Greene to Kościuszko, February 16, 1871, in Budka, 59; Kahanowicz, 34.

3. Kościuszko to Greene, February 18, 1781, Greene Papers, Huntington Library; Thayer, 319; Col. Nicholas Long to Greene, February 19, 1781, in Budka, 60.

4. Kościuszko to Greene, February 9, 1781, Greene Papers, Huntington Library.

5. Alden, 256-257; Lumpkin, 170.

6. Alden, 257-278; Lumpkin, 170-175.

7. Alden, 259.

8. Boatner, 503-506, 1029; Alden, 259, 262; Haiman, *Revolution*, 110

9. Washington to Lafayette, April 8, 1781, in Fitzpatrick, XXI, 433.

10. Boatner, 503-506, 918; Alden, 262.; Montross, 439.

11. Boatner, 503-506; Alden, 262.

12. Boatner, 503-508; Alden, 262; Thayer, 346-348; Lumpkin, 180-183.

13. Boatner, 804; Alden, 262; Thayer, 348; Lumpkin, 184.

14. Boatner, 804; Alden, 262; Montross, 440-441; Thayer, 355; Lumpkin, 187-192.

15. Lord Cornwallis to Col. Nisbet Balfour, November 1, 1780, Cornwallis Papers.

16. Montross, 441; quote from Alden, 262; Boatner, 804; Thayer, 355-356; Lumpkin, 192.

17. Marvin L. Cann, "War in the Backcountry: The Siege of Ninety Six, May 22-June 19, 1781," *The South Carolina Historical Magazine*, 72 (1971), 3-4; Boatner, 804; Lumpkin, 192, 194; quote from Lt. Col. Isaac Allen to Lord Cornwallis, December 19, 1780, Cornwallis Papers.

18. Boatner, 805; Lumpkin, 196; Johnson, *Sketches*, II, 143; Greene to Lafayette, May 23, 1871, Greene Papers.

19. Boatner, 805; Thayer, 356; Johnson, *Sketches*, II, 143; Greene to Lafayette, May 23, 1871, Greene Papers.

20. Williams Papers, No. 979.

21. Boatner, 805; Cann, 6; Thayer, 357; Lumpkin, 197-198; William Moultrie, *Memoirs of the American Revolution* (New York: 1802), II, 285, claims the distance at which the approaches were begun was 150 yards.

22. Williams Papers, No. 979.

23. Williams Papers, No. 979; Williams and Kościuszko both claim the approaches were begun at 300 yards, others cite 400 yards.

24. Williams Papers, No. 979.

25. Cruger to Rawdon, May 31, 1781, Cornwallis Papers.

26. Montross, 441; Williams Papers, No. 979.

27. Williams Papers, No. 979; Lumpkin, 198.

28. Williams Papers, No. 979.

29. Williams Papers, No. 979.

30. Cruger to Rawdon, June 3, 1781, Cornwallis Papers.

31. Boatner, 805; Cann, 7.

32. Cann, 10.

33. Williams Papers, No. 979.

34. Montross, 441.

35. Greene to Board of War, June 20, 1781, George Washington Papers; Lumpkin, 199.

36. Boatner, 806; Cann, 8.

37. Williams Papers, No. 979.

38. Montross, 441.

39. Williams Papers, No. 979.

40. Williams Papers, No. 979.

41. Williams Papers, No. 979; Boatner, 806

42. Roderick Mackenzie, *A British Fusilier in Revolutionary Boston* (Cambridge, MA: 1926); Lumpkin, 200.

43. Cann, 10.

44. Cann, 10.

45. Boatner, 806.

46. Mackenzie, Stedman, *History*, II, 369-370; Lumpkin, 200-201.

47. Montross, 441.

48. Haiman, *Revolution*, 114; Cann, 9; quote from Williams Papers, No. 979.

49. Boatner, 807; Lumpkin, 201.

50. Williams Papers, No. 979.

51. Cann, 8; Lumpkin, 202.

52. Boatner, 807; Lumpkin, 202; quote from Greene to Board of War, December 6, 1780, Greene Papers.

53. Williams Papers, No. 979.

54. Greene to Board of War, December 6, 1780, Greene Papers; Cann, 11; Lumpkin, 202.

55. Boatner, 807-808; Cann, 11; Lumpkin, 203.

56. Williams Papers, No. 979.

57. Boatner, 808; Lumpkin, 203-204; Henry Lee reported total American losses at 185.

58. Greene to Arthur St. Clair, June 22, 1781, Greene Papers, Clements Library.

59. Greene to Marion, June 25, 1781, in R. W. Gibbes, ed., *Documentary History of the American Revolution* (New York: 1855), II, 100-101.

60. Boatner, 808.

61. Williams Papers, No. 979.

62. Kościuszko to Gates, July 29, 1781, Gates Papers, Box 16, New-York Historical Society.

63. Williams to brother Elie, June 23, 1781, Williams Papers, No. 107.

64. Greene's Orderly Book, Huntington Library.

65. Henry Lee, *Memoirs of the War in the Southern Department* (Philadelphia: 1812), 98.

66. Lee, *Memoirs*, 98, 119.

67. Lee, *Memoirs*, 119. See also *Catholic Historical Researches*, 175.

68. Lee, *Memoirs*, 371. See also *Catholic Historical Researches*, 177.

69. G. G. White, *Life of Major General Henry Lee, Commander of Lee's Legion in the Revolutionary War* (New York: 1859), 207; Edward Channing, *A History of the United States* (New York: 1905-25), VI, 491.

70. Williams Papers, No. 979.

71. Haiman, *Revolution*, 116.

Chapter 10

1. *Catholic Historical Researches*, 177-178.

2. Quote from Johnson, *Traditions*, 415, as quoted in Haiman, *Revolution*, 128.

3. Boatner, 1031; Thayer, 365-367; Lumpkin, 304.

4. Greene to Burke, August 12, 1781, in Budka, 64; also in *North Carolina State Records*, XV, 606, and Kahanowicz, 35

5. Boatner, 1031, 1059; Alden, 264.

6. Boatner, 1031; Alden, 265; Lumpkin, 304.

7. Alden, 265; Lumpkin, 305.

8. Alden, 265; Lumpkin, 216.

9. Alden, 265; Lumpkin, 214-217; Thayer, 377.

10. Alden, 266; Lumpkin, 218-219; Thayer, 377-378.

11. Alden, 266; Lumpkin, 220; Thayer, 381; Boatner, 355, 1031, 1059.

12. Alden, 266.

13. Alden, 266; Thayer, 385-386; Boatner, 1032.

14. Thayer, 388; Williams to Greene, December 4, 1781, in Kahanowicz, p. 35.

15. Alden, 266; Thayer, 387-388, 401; Budka, 72; Boatner, 1032.

16. Kościuszko to Williams, undated, Williams Papers, Maryland Historical Society.

17. Kościuszko to Brown, March 12, 1782, Gates Papers, Box 14, New-York Historical Society.

18. Kościuszko to Gates, April 8, 1782, Gates Papers, Box 16, New-York Historical Society.

19. Kościuszko to Williams, March 12, 1782, Williams Papers, Maryland Historical Society.

20. Kościuszko to Williams, March, 1872, Williams Papers, Maryland Historical Society.

21. Thayer, 401-402.

22. Quote from Thayer, 397.

23. Thayer, 404-405; Lumpkin, 279.

24. Kościuszko to Greene, undated, in Kahanowicz, 5.

25. Kościuszko to Greene, September 2, 1782, Budka, 77; also in Kahanowicz, 3.

26. Haiman, *Revolution*, 98; quotes from Thayer, 391; see also Patterson, 358.

27. Haiman, *Exile*, 112.

28. Haiman, *Revolution*, 131; John Markland, "Revolutionary Services of Captain John Markland," *The Pennsylvania Magazine of History and Biography*, IX (1885), 109.

29. Haiman, *Revolution*, 132; *Catholic Historical Researches*, 179; Kościuszko to Greene, September 20, 1782, in Budka, 97.

30. Mathews to Greene, undated, in Johnson, *Sketches*, II, 353.

31. Quote from Kościuszko to Greene, December 4, 1782, in Budka, 133, and Kahanowicz, 11; Haiman, *Revolution*, 132.

32. Quote from Wayne to the President of Congress, March 9, 1782, in Johnson, *Sketches*, II, 317; Haiman, *Revolution*, 132.

33. Kościuszko to Greene, September 11, 1782, in Budka, 84, and Kahanowicz, 6

34. Kościuszko to Greene (?), undated, in Kahanowicz, 9.

35. Kościuszko to Greene (?), undated, in Kahanowicz, 9.

36. Kościuszko to unknown, undated, in Budka, 84.

37. Haiman, *Revolution*, 134; Wayne to Greene, November 2, 1782, in Budka, 84-85.

38. Kościuszko to Greene, September 5, 1782, in Kahanowicz, 4.

39. *Catholic Historical Researches*, 178.

40. Markland, 109; Armstrong to Sumner, July 27, 1782, *Records of North Carolina*, XVI, 631; quote from Kościuszko to Williams, August 8, 1782.

41. Robert Burnet to Gov. Mathews, September 5, 1782, in Budka, 79; Mathews to Burnet, September 6, 1782, in Budka, 80; Haiman, *Revolution*, 132; *Catholic Historical Researches*, 179.

42. Kościuszko to Greene, September 10, 1782, in Budka, 82.

43. Quote from Greene to Carrington, October 19, 1782, in Budka, 124, and Kahanowicz, 37; Markland, 110; Haiman, *Revolution*, 131-132; Johnson, *Sketches*, 344; Kościuszko to Greene, September 20, 1782, in Kahanowicz, 8, 37; *Catholic Historical Researches*, 179.

44. Wilmot to Greene, October 24, 1782, Johnson, *Sketches*, II, note 10.

45. William Seymour, "A Journal of the Southern Expedition," *Papers of the History Society of Delaware*, II, No. 15 (1896), 40. The author was Sergeant Major of the Delaware Regiment.

46. Markland, 110-111; Johnson, *Sketches*, II, notes 9-11.

47. Kościuszko to Greene, November 14, 1782, in Kahanowicz.

48. Kościuszko to Greene, December 6, 1782, in Budka, 138-139, and Kahanowicz, 12.

49. Lumpkin, 279; Thayer, 408-409; Alden, 267; Markland, 111; Haiman, *Revolution*, 137; *Dictionary of American Biography*, 497.

50. Haiman, *Revolution*, 138.

51. Kościuszko to Greene, December 26, 1782, Greene Papers, New York Public Library.

52. Kościuszko to Williams, February 11, 1783, Williams Papers, Maryland Historical Society.

53. Haiman, *Revolution*, 139-140.

54. Quoted in Haiman, *Revolution*, 139.

55. Kościuszko to Mrs. Greene, undated, Greene Papers, Huntington Library.

56. Kościuszko to Greene, undated, Greene Papers, Huntington Library.

57. Thayer, 411-413.

58. Haiman, *Revolution*, 140.

59. Thayer, 420-421.

60. David Humphreys, "A Poem on the Love of Country," *Miscellaneous Works* (New York: 1804), 147.

61. Henry A. Washington, ed., *The Writings of Thomas Jefferson* (Washington, DC: 1853-54), VIII, 497; Haiman, *Revolution*, 142.

62. Sparks, Ser. 49, Vol. I, 72.

Chapter 11

1. Papers of the Continental Congress, Ser. 149, Vol. III, 123-125.

2. Haiman, *Revolution*, 145-146.

3. Kościuszko to Greene, June 18, 1783, in Budka, 150.

4. Greene to Kościuszko, July 10, 1783, in Budka, 154, and Kahanowicz, 37.

5. Kościuszko to Williams, July 2, 1783, Williams Papers, Maryland Historical Society.

6. Greene to Boudinot, July, 1783, in Kahanowicz, 38.

7. Greene to Kościuszko, July 10, 1783, in Kahanowicz, 37.

8. Morris to Greene, August 1, 1783, in Budka, 156.

9. Morris to Congress, *Journals of the Continental Congress*, XXIV, 488-489.

10. Haiman, *Revolution*, 153; *Journals of the Continental Congress*, XXIV, 488-489.

11. Kościuszko to Otho Williams, February 11, 1783, Williams Papers, Maryland Historical Society.

12. Kościuszko to Washington, August 26, 1783, Washington Papers, Vol. 225; *Catholic Historical Researches*, 182.

13. Washington to Kościuszko, October 2, 1783, in Fitzpatrick, XXVII, 174.

14. Washington to Boudinot, October 3, 1783, Fitzpatrick, XXVII, 174.

15. *Journals of the Continental Congress*, XXV, 673.

16. Mizwa, 134; Grzeloński, 64; *Catholic Historical Researches*, 182-183; Haiman, *Revolution*, 157-158.

17. Haiman, *Revolution*, 158, note 29.

18. Askenazy, 8; *Dictionary of American Biography*, 497; Boatner, 229-230; Haiman, *Revolution*, 157.

19. Boatner, 398.

20. Boatner, 398.

21. Greene, *Life of Greene*, III, 522.

22. Haiman, *Revolution*, 160-161.

23. Bancroft's Revolutionary Papers, vol. II, 479, New York Public Library.

24. *Catholic Historical Researches*, 184; see also *Century Magazine*, February, 1902, 512.

25. Kościuszko to Williams, July 9, 1784, Williams Papers, Maryland Historical Society.

26. Kościuszko to Greene, July 14, 1784, in Budka, 175-176, and Kahanowicz, p. 13.

27. Haiman, *Revolution*, 143.

28. Thayer, 434; Grzeloński, 66; *Dictionary of American Biography*, 497.

29. Montross, 203.

Chapter 12

1. Haiman, *Revolution*, 120; Franklin Papers, XLVII, 209.

2. Estko to Franklin, October 19, 1783, Franklin Papers, XXX, 3.

3. Kościuszko to Williams (probably Otho Williams), August 26, 1784, in Budka, 181.

4. Askenazy, 8; Kościuszko to Congress, September 20, 1787; Haiman, Mieczysław, *Kosciuszko: Leader and Exile* (New York: Polish Institute of Arts and Sciences in America, 1946, 3; Gardner, 36-37.

5. Kościuszko to Haskell, May 5, 189, in Haiman, *Exile*, 4.

6. Askenazy, 8; Mizwa, 134; Haiman, *Exile*, 2; Bushnell, 14; Gardner, 39.

7. Kościuszko to Anna Estko, in Haiman, *Exile*, 2.

8. Kościuszko to Greene, January 20, 1786, Haiman, *Exile*, 2.

9. *Ibid.*

10. Kościuszko to Haskell, May 15, 1789, in Budka, 185; Kahanowicz, 14-15.

11. *Catholic Historical Researches*, 180.

12. Humphreys to Kościuszko, in Haiman, *Exile*, 5.

13. Daniel Z. Stone, "Democratic Thought in Eighteenth Century Poland," in Biskupski and Pula, 60.

14. Halecki, *Poland*, 203-204.

15. Askenazy,9; Mizwa, 134; Stone, 60; Bushnell, 13; Gardner, 37.
16. Kościuszko to Michał Zaleski, quoted in Haiman, *Exile*, 9.
17. Kościuszko to Żurowska as quoted in Haiman, *Exile*, 3.
18. Askenazy, 9; Mizwa, 134; Stone, 60.
19. Stone, 60-76.
20. Kościuszko to Haskell, quoted in Haiman, *Exile*, 5.
21. Kościuszko to Załewski, April, 1792, in Bushnell, 15.
22. Mizwa, 134; W. F. Reddaway, J. H. Penson, Oskar Halecki, and Roman Dyboski, *The Cambridge History of Poland: From Augustus II to Pilsudski (1697-1935)* (Cambridge: Cambridge University Press, 1941), 145, 150; Askenazy, 9.
23. Reddaway, 150, 155; Askenazy, 9; Bushnell, 15, quote from 16.
24. Reddaway, 145, 150, 155; quote from Askenazy, 9.
25. Letter from an anonymous Polish officer, quoted in Haiman, *Exile*, 11.
26. Quoted in Haiman, *Exile*, 10-11.
27. Quote from Gen. Zajlczek's memoirs in Haiman, *Exile*, 10; Reddaway, 150, 155; quote from Askenazy, 9; Bushnell, 17; Gardner, 46; Bellchambers, 234.
28. Reddaway, 151; Askenazy, 9; Gardner, 43.
29. Reddaway, 152-153; Halecki, *Poland*, 205; Langer, 512.
30. Quote from Grzeloński, 72; Haiman, *Exile*, 10.
31. Askenazy, 9, 11; Mizwa, 134; *Dictionary of American Biography*, 497.
32. Kościuszko to King Stanisław August, in Bushnell, 18.
33. Quoted in Haiman, *Exile*, 11.
34. Kościuszko to Isabella Czartoryska, in Bushnell, 10.
35. Kościuszko to Potocki, September 16, 1792, quoted in Haiman, *Exile*, 11 and Gardner, 82.
36. Quoted in Haiman, *Exile*, 15, and Gardner, 84; see also Bushnell, 20. Susanna was his housekeeper and Faustin was his servant.
37. Bushnell, 20; Gardner, 55.
38. Haiman, *Exile*, 15; Askenazy, 11-12; Mizwa, 134.
39. Reddaway, 155-156; Haiman, *Exile*, 15-16; Askenazy, 12, quote from 10; Bushnell, 21; Gardner, 57.
40. Kościuszko to Zaleski, September 30, 1792, quoted in Haiman, *Exile*, 12.
41. Askenazy, 12; Reddaway, 157.
42. Reddaway, 158.
43. Haiman, *Exile*, 17; Bushnell, 22; Gardner, 60.
44. Gardner, 63.
45. Haiman, *Exile*, 18; quote from Askenazy, 13; Halecki, *Poland*, 206; Gardner, 62-63; Mizwa, 136; Cizauskas, 56.
46. Bushnell, 24, also in Kahanowicz, 6.

47. Haiman, *Exile*, 18.
48. 20; Haiman, *Exile*, 18; quote from Askenazy, 13; Halecki, *Poland*, 206; Mizwa, 136; Cizauskas, 56; Gardner, 68.
49. Cizauskas, 56; Gardner, 65-66.
50. Askenazy, 14, quote from 16.
51. Haiman, *Exile*, 17; Halecki, *Poland*, 206-207.
52. Mizwa, 138; Askenazy, 14-15.
53. Kościuszko to Sapieha, May 12, 1794, in Haiman, *Exile*, 24.
54. Reddaway, 160.
55. Mizwa, 134.
56. Reddaway, 160-161; Haiman, *Exile*, 21-22.
57. Grzeloński, 71.
58. Reddaway, 161; Bushnell, 25.
59. Gardner, 71-72.
60. Reddaway, 161; Bushnell, 25; Bellchambers, 235.
61. Quote from Mizwa, 137.
62. Roman Dyboski, *Outlines of Polish History* (London: George Allen and Unwin, 1925).
63. Kahanowicz, 6; Bushnell, 26.
64. Askenazy, 15; Halecki, *Poland*, 207; Reddaway, 165-166; Cizauskas, 56-57.
65. Quoted in Gardner, 84.
66. Quoted in Gardner, 88.
67. Askenazy, 14; Reddaway, 166.
68. Reddaway, 167.
69. Bushnell, 30, quote from 31; see also Askenazy, 16; Reddaway, 168; Halecki, *Poland*, 207; Bellchambers, 235; *The National Cyclopaedia of American Biography* (Ann Arbor: University Microfilms, 1967), I, 54; Lord Eversley, *The Partitions of Poland* (London: T. Fisher Unwin, Ltd., 1915), 212, places Polish forces at 17,000 and combined Russian and Prussian forces at 37,000.
70. Halecki, *Poland*, 207; Reddaway, 166; Cizauskas, 57; Haiman, *Exile*, 22.
71. Haiman, *Exile*, 22; Askenazy, 16; Gardner, 79.
72. Kościuszko to Stanisław August, May 20, 1794, quoted in Gardner, 79-80.
73. Reddaway, 169-170; Askenazy, 16-17; Gardner, 95; Mizwa, 137; *National Cyclopaedia*, I, 54.
74. Quote from Gardner, 99-100.
75. Quoted in Gardner, 96.
76. Reddaway, 171-172; Bushnell, 33; Everlsey, 221-222.
77. Bushnell, 35-36.

78. Halecki, *Poland*, 208; Mizwa, 137.

79. Bushnell, 34-25.

80. Askenazy, 17; Bushnell, 34, 36; Mizwa, 139; Gardner, 114.

81. Askenazy, 17; Mizwa, 139; Bushnell 37.

82. Halecki, *Poland*, 208; Reddaway, 209; Langer, 512.

83. Halecki, *Poland*, 206.

84. Eversley, 214.

Chapter 13

1. Askenazy, 17-18; Haiman, *Exile*, 31-32; quote from *The National Cyclopaedia of American Biography* (Ann Arbor: University Microfilms, 1967), I, 54; Mizwa, 139.

2. Askenazy, 18; Mizwa, 139; Kahanowicz, 9; Bushnell, 39; Gardner, 119.

3. Mizwa, 139-140; Askenazy, 18; Gardner, 121; Anthony W. W. Evans, *Memoir of Thaddeus Kosciuszko: Poland's Hero and Patriot* (New York: Society of the Cincinnati, 1883), 20-21; Bushnell, 40; Kahanowicz, 9, says he left May 16.

4. Based on the physicians' report as reproduced in Haiman, *Exile*, 135-140.

5. Askenazy,18.

6. Mizwa, 140, including first quote; Evans, 21, second quote from 22.

7. Bushnell, 41; a somewhat different version saying substantially the same thing appears in Evans, 46.

8. Mizwa, 140, including first quote; Evans, 21, second quote from 22; Kahanowicz, 9.

9. Quoted in Haiman, *Exile*, 36; Evans, 22; Kahanowicz, 10, says the ship left June 18, and Bushnell, 41, places it on the 17th.

10. Kusielewicz, "Niemcewicz," 66-67; *Catholic Historical Researches*, 188; Cizauskas, 59.

11. Quote from Mizwa, 140; Haiman, *Exile*, 42; Bushnell, 42; Cizauskas, 59; Kusielewicz, "Niemcewicz," 66-67; Eugene Kusielewicz and Ludwik Krzyżanowski, "Julian Ursyn Niemcewicz's American Diary," *The Polish Review*, Vol. 3, No. 3 (1958), 84.

12. Haiman, *Exile*, 49; *Catholic Historical Researches*, 190; Kahanowicz, 10; Sparks, XI, 214; Mizwa, 140.

13. John Adams to Kościuszko, September 4, 1797, Bushnell, 42.

14. Armstrong to Gates, Gates Papers, Box 18, New-York Historical Society.

15. Quoted in Haiman, *Exile*, 42.

16. Haiman, *Exile*, 44.

17. Haiman, *Exile*, 42.

18. Haiman, *Exile*, 46; Askenazy, 18.

19. Haiman, *Exile*, 47.

20. Haiman, *Exile*, 42, also note 57; Kusielewicz, "Niemcewicz," 66-67; Patterson, 385; Kusielewicz and Krzyżanowski, 85.

21. Rush to Gates, September 3, 1797, Gates Papers, Box 18, New-York Historical Society.

22. Evans, 23; Haiman, *Exile*, 51; quote from Kusielewicz and Krzyżanowski, 87-88.

23. Evans, 23.

24. Evans, 24-25.

25. Haiman, *Exile*, 52-53.

26. Kościuszko to Gates, September 1, 1797, Box 18, Gates Papers, New-York Historical Society.

27. Kościuszko to Gates, September 6, 1797, Box 18, Gates Papers, New-York Historical Society.

28. Kusielewicz and Krzyżanowski, 89. Gates was actually seventy at the time.

29. *Catholic Historical Researches*, 191.

30. La Rochefoucauld, *Travels*, II, 468-9.

31. Mrs. Montgomery to Gates, October 7, 1797, Emmett Collection, New York Public Library; Patterson, 386.

32. Quote from Kusielewicz and Krzyżanowski, 91; Kozłowski, "Pobyt," 261.

33. Dunlap, *Diary*, I, 338-339.

34. Kościuszko to Gates, October 3, 1797, Gates Papers, Box 18, New-York Historical Society.

35. Kusielewicz and Krzyżanowski, 92, 94; Haiman, *Exile*, 58.

36. Jefferson to Gates, February 28, 1798, Jefferson Papers, Library of Congress; Evans, 25; *Catholic Historical Researches*, 198; Kahanowicz, 11; Mizwa, 140; Patterson, 385; Cizauskas, 60.

37. Jefferson to Gates, February 21, 1798, Lipscomb, IX, 441.

38. Kościuszko to Washington, October 8, 1797, Washington Papers, Library of Congress.

39. Washington to Kościuszko, October 15, 1797, in Kozłowski, *Washington and Kosciuszko*, 54-55.

40. *Aurora*, December 26, 1797.

41. Haiman, *Exile*, 70; *Catholic Historical Researches*, 197; Kahanowicz, 11.

42. Haiman, *Exile*, 72; *Catholic Historical Researches*, 197; Kahanowicz, 11.

43. Quote from Haiman, *Exile*, 73.

44. Kusielewicz, "Niemcewicz," p. 69.

45. *Catholic Historical Researches*, 199.

46. Kościuszko to Jefferson, undated, Fogg Collection, Maine Historical Society.

47. Haiman, *Exile*, 74.

48. Kościuszko to Jefferson, undated, Jefferson Collection, Undated, Massachusetts Historical Society.

49. Testament and accompanying power of attorney dated April 20, 1798, Jefferson Papers, Massachusetts Historical Society.

50. Kościuszko to Jefferson, undated, Jefferson Collection, Massachusetts Historical Society.

51. Quote from Kościuszko to Jefferson, undated, Fogg Collection, Maine Historical Society; Haiman, *Exile*, 76, 78.

52. Niemcewicz to Jefferson, May 27, 1798, Jefferson Papers, Library of Congress.

53. Jefferson to Kościuszko, June 1, 1798, Lipscomb, X, 47.

54. Jefferson to Kościuszko, Jefferson Papers, Library of Congress.

Chapter 14

1. Haiman, *Exile*, 84; Bushnell, 44.

2. Haiman, *Exile*, 84; Paszkowski, *Dzieje Kościuszki*, 196; 6.

3. Cutting to Jefferson, August 27, 1798, Jefferson Papers, Library of Congress.

4. Jullien as quoted in Haiman, *Exile*, 85.

5. Kościuszko to Jefferson, undated, Jefferson Collection, Massachusetts Historical Society.

6. Jefferson to Kościuszko, February 21, 1799, Jefferson Papers, Library of Congress; see also Evans, 27.

7. Askenazy, 25.

8. Haiman, *Exile*, 86; Kościuszko to Jefferson, March 10, 1806, Jefferson Collection, Massachusetts Historical Society.

9. Fiszer's memoirs quoted in Haiman, *Exile*, 86.

10. Haiman, *Exile*, 86.

11. Kościuszko to Jefferson, November 15, 1805, Jefferson Collection, Massachusetts Historical Society.

12. Kościuszko to Jefferson, August 14, 1800, Jefferson Collection, Massachusetts Historical Society.

13. Kościuszko to Jefferson, October 10, 1800, Jefferson Collection, Massachusetts Historical Society.

14. Kościuszko to Jefferson, November 5, 1805, Jefferson Collection, Massachusetts Historical Society.

15. Jefferson to Kościuszko, June 1, 1798, in Lipscomb, X, 49.

16. Jefferson to Kościuszko, March 14, 1801, in Lipscomb, XIX, 122.

17. Jefferson to Kościuszko, March 14, 1801, in Lipscomb, XIX, 122.

18. Haiman, *Exile*, 89.

19. Kahanowicz, 12; Haiman, *Exile*, 91; quotes from Mizwa, 141; *Catholic Historical Researches*, 204-206; Oliver McKee, Jr., "The Father of

American Artillery," *National Republic*, September, 1926, 30; Elizabeth Camille Brink, "Kosciuszko the patriot — Father of American Artillery," *The Coast Artillery Journal*, Vol. 75, No. 3 (May-June, 1932), 303.

20. Kościuszko to Jefferson, March 1, 1811, Jefferson Collection, Massachusetts Historical Society.

21. Jefferson to Kościuszko, February 26, 1810, in Lipscomb, XII, 365.

22. Askenazy, 19.

23. Quoted in Bushnell, 45.

24. Bushnell, 46; Haiman, *Exile*, 100; 6; Gardner, 127.

25. William Cobbett, *Porcupine's Works; Containing Various Writings and Selections, Exhibiting a Faithful Picture of the United States of America* (London: Cobbett and Morgan, 1801) Vol. X, 88.

26. Żuraw, 158.

27. Żuraw, 158.

28. Żuraw, 153.

29. Żuraw, 154.

30. Quote from Haiman, *Exile*, 100; Askenazy, 19.

31. Gardner, 128.

32. Askenazy, 19; Mizwa, 142; Bellchambers, 237.

33. Haiman, *Exile*, 101; Kahanowicz, 12; Reddaway, 212-213, 225; Gardner, 130.

34. Quoted in Bushnell, 49 and Reddaway, 212-213.

35. Kościuszko to Jefferson, undated [probably 1801], Jefferson Papers, Library of Congress.

36. Mizwa, 142; Haiman, *Exile*, 103; *The National Cyclopaedia of American Biography* (Ann Arbor: University Microfilms, 1967), I, 54; Bellchambers, 237; Gardner, 131.

37. Haiman, *Exile*, 107.

38. Haiman, *Exile*, 113.

39. Haiman, *Exile*, 108; "Last Years of Kosciuszko," *Harper's Magazine*, XXXVII, 483.

40. Kościuszko to Jefferson, May 30, 1813, in Haimen, *Exile*, 113.

41. Haiman, *Exile*, 109.

42. Haiman, *Exile*, 107-108.

43. Haiman, *Exile*, 113-114.

44. Mizwa, 142; Evans, 28, 30; Haiman, *Exile*, 103; *The National Cyclopaedia of American Biography* (Ann Arbor: University Microfilms, 1967), I, 54; Bellchambers, 237; Reddaway, 212-213; Gardner, 131-132; Cizauskas, 63; Askenazy, 21.

45. Reddaway, 213.

46. Haiman, *Exile*, 103; Reddaway, 211.

47. "Last Years of Kosciuszko," *Harper's New Monthly Magazine*, XXXVII, 479; Evans, 32.

48. Haiman, *Exile*, 104; Evans, 30; Bellchambers, 237; Gardner, 133; Cizauskas, 64.

49. Bushnell, 51.

50. Reddaway, 211.

51. Bushnell, 51-52; see also Kahanowicz, 12, and Gardner, 134.

52. Askenazy, 20-21; Haiman, *Exile*, 105; Gardner, 134-135; quote from Kościuszko to Jefferson, March 14, 1815, Jefferson Collection, Massachusetts Historical Society; Haiman, *Exile*, 104; Bellchambers, 237; Gardner, 133.

53. Kościuszko to Jefferson, 25.

54. Gardner, 136-137.

55. Mizwa, 142; *The National Cyclopaedia of American Biography*, I, 54.

Chapter 15

1. "Last Years of Kosciuszko," *Harper's New Monthly Magazine*, XXXVII, 480.

2. "Last Years of Kosciuszko," 480.

3. Gardner, 138.

4. "Last Years of Kosciuszko," 480; Evans, 33; Gardner, 139.

5. Haiman, *Exile*, fn 36.

6. Kościuszko to Jefferson, April, 1816, Jefferson Collection, Massachusetts Historical Society, translated in Haiman, Exile, 105.

7. Kościuszko to Jefferson, September 15, 1817, Jefferson Collection, Massachusetts Historical Society, translated from the French in Haiman, Exile, 106.

8. "Last Years of Kosciuszko," 482; Evans, 37.

9. "Last Years of Kosciuszko," 482; Evans, 36; Cizauskas, 66.

10. "Last Years of Kosciuszko," 482; Evans, 37; Gardner, 140.

11. "Last Years of Kosciuszko," 482. Some authors maintain that Kościuszko died from the effects of a fall from his horse, but the weight of evidence is otherwise. More likely, any such fall resulted from his weakened condition due to his illness.

12. Quote from "Last Years of Kosciuszko," 483; Flick, 296; Mizwa, 143; *Catholic Historical Researches*, 207-208; Evans, 40.

13. Flick, 296; Lafayette to an unknown addressee, February 12, 1830, *Memoires,* 11, 441; Isaac C. Barnet to Jefferson, November 30, 1817, Jefferson Papers, Library of Congress.

14. Quoted in Julian Groblecki, "Kosciuszko's Spiritual Heritage," *ACPCC Quarterly*, Winter 1977.

15. Bushnell, 53.

16. Bushnell, 53.

17. Jefferson to Francis Zeltner, July 23, 1818, in Haiman, *Exile*, fn 41, and Worthington Chauncey Ford, *Thomas Jefferson Correspondence* (Boston: William K. Bixby, 1916.

18. 46.

19. Haiman, *Exile*, 116; Evans, 41; Gardner, 141.

20. Bushnell, 53-54.

21. Boynton, 287.

22. *The Evening Star*, Washington, D.C., May 11, 1910, 1-2.

23. Flick, 297.

24. *The Blackwell Encyclopedia of the American Revolution*, 743.

25. Mizwa, 141.

26. Evans, 24-25.

27. Hoskins, 42.

28. Jefferson to A. M. Jullien, July 23, 1818, quoted in *Free Poland*.

Appendix 1

1. *Cases Argued and Decided in the Supreme Court of the United States* (Rochester, NY: The Lawyer's Co-operative Publishing Company, 1926), Lawyer's Edition, Book 14, Howard, 478 [hereafter cited as Howard, XIV].

2. The author wishes to thank Ms. Sarah Ringer of the University of Virginia Library and Mr. Shelby J. Marshall of the Circuit Court for Albermarle County, Virginia, for providing him with a copy of the original Kościuszko will and allowing him to reproduce it here in its entirety. See also Louis Ottenberg, "A Testamentary Tragedy: Jefferson and the Wills of General Kosciuszko," *American Bar Association Journal*, Vol. 44 (January 1958), 23.

3. "Armstrong v. Lear, Administrator of Kosciuszko," in Henry Wheaton, ed, *Reports of Cases Argued and Adjudged in the Supreme Court of the United States, in January Term, 1827* (Rochester, NY: Lawyer's Co-operative Publishing Company, 1918), Vol. 12, 590 [hereafter cited as Wheaton XII].

4. Howard, XIV, 481.

5. Ottenberg, 23; *Harper's New Monthly Magazine*, XXXVII, 482; Richard Peters, *Reports of Cases Argued and Adjudged in the Supreme Court of the United States, in January Term, 1834* (Rochester, NY: The Lawyers Co-operative Publishing Company, 1918), VIII, 869.

6. Howard, XIV, 478.

7. Howard, XIV, 478.

8. Ottenberg, 23.

9. Ottenberg, 24.

10. Ottenberg, 24.

11. "Kosciuszko's Will," *Scribner's Monthly*, XVII, No. 5 (March 1879), 616.

12. Quote from "Kosciuszko's Will," *Scribner's Monthly*, XVII, No. 5 (March 1879), 615. See also Thomas Jefferson to H.E.M. de Politica, May 17, 1819; statement of William Wertenbaker, Deputy Clerk of the Circuit Court of Albermarle, May 1819, now on file in the Circuit Court of Albermarle and the Library of the University of Virginia.

13. Ottenberg, 24.

14. Thomas Jefferson to H.E.M. de Politica, May 17, 1819; statement of William Wertenbaker, Deputy Clerk of the Circuit Court of Albermarle, May 1819, now on file in the Circuit Court of Albermarle and the Library of the University of Virginia.

15. Howard, XIV, 474, 481, 486; Wheaton, XII, 169, 6 L. ed. 589; Ottenberg, 24.

16. Quote from Ottenberg, 25; Richard Peters, *Reports of Cases Argued and Adjudged in the Supreme Court of the United States, in January Term, 1834* (Rochester, NY: The Lawyers Co-operative Publishing Company, 1918), VIII, 632 [hereafter cited as Peters, VIII]; "Memorial of Vladislaus Wankowicz, Grand-Nephew of General Thaddeus Kosciusko," Senate Document No. 8, 30th Congress, 2nd Session, January 3, 1849, 4 [hereafter "Memorial of Vladislaus Wankowicz"].

17. Ottenberg, 25; Peters, VIII, 863.

18. Ottenberg, 25; Howard, XIV, 479.

19. *Niles' National Register*, August 7, 1847, 368.

20. Ottenberg, 25-26.

21. "Memorial of Vladislaus Wankowicz," 1-2, 6; "Memorial of Ladislaw Wankowicz, Great Grand-Nephew of Kosciusko, and of G. Tochman, Attorney of the Heirs of Kosciusko, Praying that Measures be Taken to Protect Certain Rights of the Heirs of Kosciusko," Senate Miscellaneous Document No. 11, 31st Congress, 1st Session [hereafter cited as "Memorial of Ladislaw Wankowicz ... and G. Tochman"].

22. "Memorial of Ladislaw Wankowicz ... and G. Tochman."

23. Howard, XIV, 476-480.

24. Howard, XIV, 476, 486.

25. Howard, XIV, 481. Translation: "I revoke all the wills and codicils which I may have made previous to the present, to which alone I confine myself, as containing my last wishes."

26. Howard, XIV, 476, 481.

27. Howard, XIV, 473. Translation: "I leave all of my effects, my carriage and my horse included, to Mr. and Mrs. Xavier Zeltner, the people I live with."

28. Howard, XIV, 474, 477.

29. Howard, XIV, 482.

30. Howard, XIV, 483-484, 487.

31. Ottenberg, 26.
32. Howard, XIV, 478-479
33. Włodzimierz B. Krzyżanowski, *Wspomnienia z Pobytu w Ameryce Podczas Wojny 1861-1864* (Chicago: Polish Museum of America, 1963). Translated by Stanley J. Pula.

Appendix 2

1. Reprinted with minor alterations from Haiman, *Exile*, 131-134.

Bibliography

Documentary Sources

Bancroft Papers, New York Public Library.

Fogg Collection, Maine Historical Society.

Gates, Horatio. Papers, Library of Congress.

_____. Papers, New-York Historical Society.

Greene, Nathaniel. Papers, William L. Clements Library, University of Michigan.

Jefferson, Thomas. Papers, Library of Congress.

Jefferson, Thomas. Papers, Massachusetts historical Society.

Journals of the Continental Congress.

Kościuszko,Tadeusz. Letters, Fogg Collection, Maine Historical Society.

_____. Papers, New-York Historical Society.

_____. Will and related legal papers, Circuit Court of Albermarle, Virginia.

Lee, Charles. Papers, New-York Historical Society.

Livingston, Brokholst. Papers, New York Public Library.

McDougall, Alexander. Papers, New-York Historical Society.

Rush, Benjamin. Papers, Library of Congress.

_____. Papers, New-York Historical Society.

Saratoga National Battlefield. Misc. papers collected relating to the battle including biographies, selected quotations from published and unpublished works, bibliographies, and unpublished papers, Saratoga Battlefield National Park.

Schuyler, Philip. Orderly Book, June 16-August 18, 1777, p. 53, in the American Antiquarian Society.

_____. Papers, Library of Congress.

_____. Papers, New York Public Library.

_____. Papers, New York State Library.

St. Clair, Arthur. Papers, New-York Historical Society.

Trumbull, John. Papers, Yale University.

Varick, Richard. Papers, New York Public Library.

Ward, Bill, complr., "The Battles of Saratoga: People, Places and Facts," Saratoga National Historical Park, March, 1988.

Williams, Otho. Papers, Maryland Historical Society.

Published Sources

Agniel, Lucien. *The Late Affair Has Almost Broke My Heart.* Riverside, CT: The Chatham Press, Inc., 1972.

Alden, John Richard. *The South in the American Revolution, 1763-1789.* Baton Rouge: 1957.

Anbury, Thomas. *With Burgoyne from Quebec: Travels Through the Interior of North America.* Toronto: Macmillan of Canada, 1963. Sydney Jackman, ed.

"Armstrong v. Lear, Administrator of Kosciuszko," in Henry Wheaton, ed, *Reports of Cases Argued and Adjudged in the Supreme Court of the United States, in January Term, 1827.* Rochester, NY: Lawyer's Co-operative Publishing Company, 1918. Vol. 12, 589-592.

Arnold, Stanisław and Marian Żychowski. *Outline History of Poland.* Warsaw: Polonia Publishing House, 1962.

Askenazy, Szymon. *Thaddeus Kosciuszko.* London: The Polish Review Officer, 1917.

Baldwin, Jeduthan. "Baldwin Letters," *American Monthly Magazine,* VI (1895), 193-200.

_____. *The Revolutionary Journal of Colonel Jeduthan Baldwin 1775-1778.* Bangor, ME: The DeBurians, 1906. Thomas Williams Baldwin, ed.

Bartoszewicz, Kazimierz. *Dzieje Insurekcji Kościuszkowskiej.* Wiedeń: Franciszek Bondy, n.d.

Bellchambers, E. *A General Biographical Dictionary, Containing Lives of the Most Eminent Persons of All Ages and Nations.* London: Allan Bell & C0., 1835.

Biskupski, M. B., "'Gentry Democracy' in Polish Political Thought and Practice, 1500-1863," in Biskupski and Pula, *Polish Democratic Thought.*

Bibliography

Biskupski, M. B., and James S. Pula, eds. *Polish Democratic Thought From the Renaissance to the Great Emigration: Essays and Documents.* New York: Columbia University Press, 1990.

Blanchard, Amos. "Biography of Officers from Foreign Countries," *American Military Biography*, 1825.

Boatner, Mark M. *Encyclopedia of the American Revolution.* New York: David McKay Company, Inc., 1966.

Boynton, Edward C. *History of West Point and Its Military Importance During the American Revolution.* New York: D. Van Nostrand, 1863.

Bratkowski, Stefan. *Z czym do nieśmiertelności.* Katowice: Wydawnictwo "Śllsk," 1977.

Brink, Elizabeth Camille. "Kosciuszko the Patriot—Father of American Artillery, *The Coast Artillery Journal*, Vol. 75, No. 3 (May-June, 1932), 193-196

Budka, Metchie J. E., ed., *Autograph Letters of Thaddeus Kosciuszko in the American Revolution.* Chicago: The Polish Museum of America, 1977.

Burnett, Edmund C., ed. *Letters of Members of the Continental Congress.* 8 vols. Washington: The Carnegie Institution of Washington, 1921-1936.

Bush, Martin H. *Revolutionary Enigma: A Re-appraisal of General Philip Schuyler of New York.* Port Washington, NY: Ira J. Friedman, Inc., 1969.

Bushnell, George H. *Kościuszko: A Short Biography of the Polish Patriot.* London: W. C. Henderson & Co., 1943.

Cann, Marvin L. "War in the Backcountry: The Siege of Ninety Six, May 22-June 19, 1781," *The South Carolina Historical Magazine*, 72 (1971), 1-14.

Cases Argued and Decided in the Supreme Court of the United States. Rochester, NY: The Lawyer's Co-operative Publishing Company, 1926. Lawyer's Edition, Book 14, Howard.

Channing, Edward, *A History of the United States.* New York: 1905-25, VI.

Chastellux, Marquis de, *Travels in North America*, (New York; 1828).

Cizauskas, Albert C. "The Unusual Story of Thaddeus Kosciusko," *Lituanus 1986*, 32, No. 1, 47-66.

Cobbett, William, *Porcupine's Works; Containing Various Writings and Selections, Exhibiting a Faithful Picture of the United States of America.* London: Cobbett and Morgan, 1801, Vol. X.

Collections of the New York Historical Society. 38 vols. New York: The New York Historical Society, 1868-1906.

Cuneo, Ernest. "General T. Kosciuszko," *Saturday Evening Post*, October, 1975.

Davies, Norman. *God's Playground: A History of Poland. Volume I: The Origins to 1795.* New York: Columbia University Press, 1982.

Dearborn, Henry. "A Narrative of the Saratoga Campaign," *Fort Ticonderoga Bulletin*, Vol. I, No. 5 (January 1929), pp. 2-13.

_____. *Revolutionary War Journals of Henry Dearborn 1775-1783.* New York: Da Capo Press, 1971. Lloyd A Brown and Howard H. Peckham, eds.

Dyboski, Roman, *Outlines of Polish History.* London: George Allen and Unwin, 1925.

Dzwonkowski, R., "Młode Lata Kościuszki," *Biblioteka Warszawska*, CCLXXXIV (1911).

Edgar, Gregory T. *"Liberty or Death!" The Northern Campaigns in the American Revolutionary War.* Bowie, MD: Heritage Books, Inc., 1994.

Egleston, Thomas. *Life of Maj.-Gen. John Paterson.* New York: 1898.

Elting, John R. *The Battles of Saratoga.* Monmouth Beach, NJ: Philip Freneau Press, 1977.

Epping, Charlotte S. J. *Journal of du Roi the Elder.* Philadelphia: University of Pennsylvania, 1911.

Evans, Anthony Walton White. *Memoir of Thaddeus Kosciuszko: Poland's Hero and Patriot.* New York: Society of the Cincinnati, 1883.

Eversley, Lord. *The Partitions of Poland.* London: T. Fisher Unwin, Ltd., 1915.

Fitzpatrick, John C., ed. *The Writings of George Washington, 1745-1799.* 39 vols. Washington: U. S. Government Printing Office, 1931-1944.

Fleming, Thomas. "Kosciuszko—Hero of Two Worlds," *Reader's Digest,* April, 1976.

Fletcher, James. *The History of Poland from the Earliest Period to the Present Time.* London: James Cochrane and Co., 1831.

Flick, Ella M. E. "General Thaddeus Kosciuszko," *Records of the American Catholic Historical Society of Philadelphia*, XXXVI, No. 3 (September 1925), 285-297.

Ford, Worthington Chauuncey. *Defences of Philadelphia in 1777.* New York: Da Capo Press, 1971.

_____, *Thomas Jefferson Correspondence.* Boston: William K. Bixby, 1916.

Frost, Robert I., "'Liberty Without Licence?' The Failure of Polish Democratic Thought in the Seventeenth Century," in Biskupski and Pula, *Polish Democratic Thought.*

Furneaux, Rupert. *The Battle of Saratoga.* New York: Stein & Day, 1971.

Bibliography

Garden, Alexander. *Anecdotes of the American Revolution with Sketches of Character of Persons the Most Distinguished, in the Southern States, for Civil and Military Services* (Brooklyn, 1865), 3 vols. T. W. Field, ed.

Gardner, Monica M. *Kosciuszko: A Biography*. London: George Allen and Unwin, Ltd., 1920.

"General Thaddeus Kosciuszko," *The American Catholic Historical Researches*, New Series, VI, No. 2 (April 1910), 129-216.

Gerlach, Don R. "The Fall of Ticonderoga in 1777: Who Was Responsible?" *The Bulletin of the Fort Ticonderoga Museum*, XIV, No. 3 (Summer 1982), 131-157.

_____. *Philip Schuyler and the American Revolution in New York 1733-1777*. Lincoln: University of Nebraska Press, 1964.

Gibbes, Robert Wilson, ed. *Documentary History of the American Revolution*. New York: 1855.

Glover, John. *A Memoir of General John Glover of Marblehead*. Salem, MA: Charles W. Swasey, 1863.

Greene, George W. *Life of Nathaniel Greene, Major General in the Army of the Revolution*. Boston: 1871. 3 vols.

Greene, Jack P. and J. R. Pole. *The Blackwell Encyclopedia of the American Revolution*. Cambridge, MA: Basil Blackwell, Inc., 1991.

Griffin, Martin I. J. "General Thaddeus Kosciuszko," *Catholics and the American Revolution*. Philadelphia: 1907-1911. [Also in *The American Catholic Historical Researches*, new series, VII (April 1910), No. 2.]

Groblecki, John, "Kosciuszko's Spiritual Heritage," *ACPCC Quarterly* [American Cpouncil of Polish Cultural Cubs], Winter 1977.

Gronowicz, Antoni. *Gallant General: Thaddeus Kosciuszko*. New York: Scribner's, 1947.

Grzeloński, Bogdan, ed. *Jefferson/Kościuszko Correspondence*. Warsaw: Interpress Publishers, 1978.

_____. *Poles in the United States of America 1776-1865*. Warsaw: Interpress, 1976.

Haiman, Mieczysław. *Kosciuszko in the American Revolution*. New York: Polish Institute of Arts and Sciences in America, 1943.

_____. *Kosciuszko: Leader and Exile*. New York: Polish Institute of Arts and Sciences in America, 1946.

Halecki, Oskar. *Borderlands of Western Civilization: A History of East Central Europe*. New York: The Ronald Press Company, 1952.

_____, *A History of Poland*. New York: Roy Publishers, 1943.

Hamilton, Edward P. *Fort Ticonderoga: Key to a Continent.* Boston: Little, Brown and Company, 1964.

Heath, William. *Memoirs of Maj.-Gen. William Heath.* Boston: 1798.

"Heirs of Kosciuszko, The," *Niles' National Register,* LXXII (Baltimore, August 7, 1847), 368.

"Historical Forgeries and Kosciuszko's 'Finis Poloniae'," *Macmillan's Magazine,* XIX (London: Macmillan and Co., 1869), 164-167.

Hoskins, Janina W. "A Lesson Which All Our Countrymen Should Study," *The Quarterly Journal of the Library of Congress,* January, 1976, 29-45.

Hughes, J. M. "Aide to Gates," *Massachusetts Historical Society,* III, 1858.

Hume, Edgar Erskine. "Poland and the Society of the Cincinnati," *The Polish American Review,* I (October 1935).

Humphreys, David, "A Poem on the Love of Country," *Miscellaneous Works.* New York: 1804.

Jackson, John W. *With the British Army in Philadelphia 1777-1778.* San Rafael, CA: Presidio Press, 1979.

"John F. Ennis, Administrator de bonis non of Joseph Zolkowski et al., v J. H. B. Smith, Administrator of George Bomford; Lewis Johnson, Administrator de bonis non of Thaddeus Kosciuszko; James Carrico, Samuel Stott, George C. Bomford, Jacob Gideon, Ulysses Ward, and Jonathan B. H. Smith," in Benjamin C. howard, ed, *Reports of Cases Argued and Adjudged in the Supreme Court of the United States in December Term, 1952* Rochester, NY: The Lawyers Co-operative Publishing Company, 1918. Vol. 14, 472-487.

Johns, Joseph P. *Kosciuszko: A Biographical Study with a Historical Background of the Times.* Detroit: Endurance Press, 1965.

Johnson, Theodore. "Last Years of Kosciuszko," *Harper's New Monthly Magazine,* XXXVII (September 1868).

Johnson, William, *Sketches of the Life and Correspondence of Nathaniel Greene* (Charleston, SC: 1822), 2 vols.

"Journal of Du Roi the Elder," *German American Annals,* XIII (1911), 151-152.

Kahanowicz, Alexander, ed. *Memorial Exhibition: Thaddeus Kościuszko.* New York: The Anderson Galleries, 1927.

Kirkwood, Robert. *The Journal and Order Book of Captain Robert Kirkwood of the Delaware Regiment of the Continental Line.* Port Washington, NY: 1970. Joseph Brown Turner, ed.

Bibliography

Kite, Elizabeth S. *Brigadier-General Louis Lebègue Duportail: Commandant of Engineers in The Continental Army 1777-1783.* Baltimore: The Johns Hopkins Press, 1933.

Klimaszewski, Bolesław. *An Outline History of Polish Culture.* Warsaw: Wydawnictwo Interpress, 1984.

Knapp, Samuel L. *Tales of the Garden of Kosciuszko.* New York: West and Trow, 1834.

Koneczny, Feliks. *Tadeusz Kościuszko.* Poznań: Wielkopolska Księgarnia Nakładowa Karola Rzepeckiego, 1917.

Kopczewski, Jan Stanisław. *Kościuszko * Pułaski.* Warsaw: Wydawnictwo Interpress, 1976.

_____. *Tadeusz Kościuszko.* Warsaw: Wydawnictwo Interpress, 1971.

Korzon, Thaddeus. *Biografia z Dokumentów Wysnuta.* Kraków: 1894.

"Kościuszko," *Free Poland*, IV, No. 2 (October 5, 1917).

Kościuszko, Tadeusz, letter to Major Alexander Garden, *The South Carolina Historical and Geneological Magazine*, II (1900), 126-127.

_____, *Czy Polacy mogl wybić się na niepodległość?* Warszawa: 1967.

"Kosciuszko's Will," *Scribner's Monthly*, XVII, No. 5 (March 1879), 614-616.

Kozłowski, Władysław M. "Kościuszko w West Point," *Przegl1d Historyczny* (Warszawa), 1913.

_____. "Ostatnie lata amerykańskiej służby Kościuszki," *Przegl1d Historyczny* (Warszawa), 1918.

_____. "Pierwszy rok służby amerykańskiej Kościuszki," *Przegl1d Historyczny* (Warszawa), 1909.

_____. "Pobyt Kościuszki Niemcewicza w Ameryce (w latach 1797 i 1798)," *Biblioteka Warszawska*, 1906.

_____. *Washington and Kosciuszko.* Chicago: Polish Roman Catholic Union of America, 1942.

Krzyżanowski, Włodzimierz B. *Wspomnienia z Pobytu w Ameryce Gen. Włodzimierza Krzyżanowskiego Podczas Wojny 1861-1864.* Chicago: Polish Museum of America, 1963. Transl. by Stanley J. Pula.

Kunasiewicz, S. *Kościuszko w Ameryce.* Lwów: 1876.

Kusielewicz, Eugene, and Ludwik Krzyżanowski, "Julian Ursyn Niemcewicz's American Diary," *The Polish Review*, Vol. 3, No. 3 (1958), 83-115.

Langer, William L., *An Encyclopedia of World History.* Boston: Houghton Mifflin Company, 1972.

"Last Years of Kosciuszko, The," *Harper's New Monthly Magazine*, XXXVII (June to November 1868), 478-483.

Leckie, Robert. *The Wars of America*. New York: Harper & Row, 1968. Vol. I.

Lee, Charles. *Papers of Charles Lee*. New York: 1871-1874. 4 vols.

Lee, Henry. *Memoirs of War in the Southern Department of the United States*. New York: Burt Franklin, 1970 (reprint of 1812 edition).

"Lee Papers, The," *Collections of the New-York Historical Society*, IV-VII (1871-1874).

"Letters of Thomas Jefferson on Thaddeus Kościuszko," Extra No. 36, *Magazine of History* (New York), 1915.

Libiszowska, Zofia. "Polish Opinion of the American Revolution," *Polish American Studies*, Vol. 34, No. 1 (1977), 5-15.

Livingston, William Farrand. *Israel Putnam: Pioneer, Ranger, and Major-General 1718-1790*. New York: G. P. Putnam's Sons, 1901.

Lowell, E. J. *The Hessians and Other German Auxiliaries of Great Britain in the Revolutionary War*. New York: 1884.

Lumpkin, Henry. *From Savannah to Yorktown: The American Revolution in the South*. New York: Paragon House, 1987.

Mackenzie, Roderick, *A British Fusilier in Revolutionary Boston*. Cambridge, MA: 1926.

Malone, Dumas, ed. *Dictionary of American Biography*. New York: Charles Scribner's Sons, 1933.

Markland, John. "Revolutionary Services of Captain John Markland," *Pennsylvania Magazine of History and Biography*, IX (1885), 109-111.

McCrady, Edward. *The History of South Carolina in the Revolution, 1780-1783*. New York: 1902.

McKee, Oliver, Jr. "The Father of the American Artillery," *National Republic*, September, 1926, 30-31.

"Memoiral of Ladislaw Wankowicz, Great Grand-Nephew of Kosciusko, and of G. Tochman, Attorney of the Heirs of Kosciusko, Praying that Measures be Taken to Protect Certain Rights of the Heirs of Kosciusko," Senate Miscellaneous Document No. 11, 31st Congress, 1st Session.

"Memorial of Vladislaus Wankowicz, Grand-Nephew of General Thaddeus Kosciusko," Senate Document No. 8, 30th Congress, 2nd Session, January 3, 1849.

Metcalf, B. *Original Members and Officers Eligible to the Society of the Cincinnati, 1783-1938*. Shenandoah: 1938.

Bibliography

Miller, James, "The Sixteenth-Century Roots of the Polish Democratic Tradition," in Biskupski and Pula, *Polish Democratic Thought.*

Minutes of the Albany Committee of Correspondence, 1775-1778. Albany: 1923. 2 vols.

Mizwa, Stephen P. "Tadeusz Kościuszko," in *Great Men and Women of Poland.* New York: Macmillan Company, 1942.

_____. "Thaddeus Kosciuszko," *Daughters of the American Revolution Magazine,* Vol. 60, No. 10 (October 1926), 593-597.

Monaghan, Frank. "Tadeusz Andrzej Bonaventura Kosciuszko," *Dictionary of American Biography.* New York: Charles Scribner's Sons, 1933.

Montross, Lynn. *The Story of the Continental Army 1775-1783.* New York: Barnes & Noble, Inc., 1967.

Moultrie, William, *Memoirs of the American Revolution.* New York: 1802, II.

Mrozowska, Kamila, *Szkoła rycerska Stanisława Augusta Poniatowskiego, 1765-1794.* Warsaw, 1961.

"Narrative of Samuel Richards," *U. S. Service Magazine,* October, 1903.

National Cyclopaedia of American Biography, The (Ann Arbor: University Microfilms, 1967), Vol. I.

Neilson, C. *The Orignal, Compiled and Corrected Account of the Burgoyne Campaign and the Memorable Battle of Bemis Heights.* Albany: 1844.

Nelson, Harold D., ed. *Poland: A Country Study.* Washington, DC: The American University, 1983.

Nickerson, Hoffman. *The Turning Point of the Revolution.* Boston: Houghton Mifflin Company, 1928.

Niemcewicz, Julian Ursyn. *Under Their Vine and Fig Tree.* Elizabeth, NJ: New Jersey Historical Society, 1965. Edited by Metchie J. E. Budka.

Niles, Hezekiah. *Principles and Acts of the Revolution in America.* Baltimore: 1822.

Ottenberg, Louis. "A Testamentary Tragedy: Jefferson and the Wills of General Kosciuszko," *American Bar Association Journal,* Vol. 44 (January 1958), 22-26.

Palmer, Dave R., *The River and the Rock: The History of Fortress West Point, 1775-1783.* New York: Hippocrene Books, 1991.

Pancake, John S. *1777: The Year of the Hangman.* Tuscaloosa, AL: The University of Alabama Press, 1977.

Pausch, Georg. *Journal of Captain Pausch.* Albany: 1886. William Stone, ed.

Patterson, Samuel White. *Horatio Gates, Defender of American Liberties.* New York: Columbia University Press, 1941.

Podraza, Eugene, transl., and James S Pula, ed., *The Memoirs of Ludwik Żychliński: Reminiscences of the American Civil War, Siberia, and Poland.* New York: East European Monographs, Columbia University Press, 1993.

Polzin, Theresita, "The Polish Americans," in Dennis L. Cuddy, ed., *Contemporary American Immigration: Interpretive Essays.* Boston: Twayne, 1982.

Proceedings of a General Court Martial, Held at White Plains, in the State of New-York, by Order of His Excellency General Washington, Commander in Chief of the Army of the United States of America, for the Trial of Major General St. Clair. Philadelphia: Hall and Sellers, 1778.

Reddaway, W. F., J.H. Penson, Oskar Halecki, and Roman Dyboski, eds., *The Cambridge History of Poland: From Augustus II to Pilsudski (1697-1935).* Cambridge: Cambridge University Press, 1941.

"Report of the Secretary of State, in Answer to a Resolution of the Senate of Inquiry as to the Measures Taken by Him Upon the Memorial of Ladislaus Wankowicz, Great-Grandnephew of General Kosciusko, and Gaspard Tochman, Attorney of the Heirs of General Kosciusko, Against Alexandre de Bodisco, the Russian Minister," Senate Executive Document No. 50, 31st Congress, 1st Session.

Rogers, Horatio, ed. *Hadden's Journal and Orderly Books.* Albany: Joel Munsell's Sons, 1886.

Seymour, William, Sergeant Major of the Delaware Regiment, "A Journal of the Southern Expedition," *Papers of the History Society of Delaware,* II, No. 15 (1896).

Smith, William Henry. *The St. Clair Papers.* Cincinnati: 1882. 2 vols.

Sokol, Irene M., "The American Revolution and Poland: A Bibliographic Essay," *The Polish Review,* XII, No. 3 (Summer 1967).

Sparks, Jared, ed. *Correspondence of the American Revolution.* 4 vols. Boston, Little & Brown, 1853.

Stone, Daniel Z. "Democratic Thought in Eighteenth Century Poland," in Biskupski and Pula, 55-72.

Szyndler, Bartłomiej. *Tadeusz Kościuszko 1746-1817.* Warsaw: Wydawnictwo Bellona, 1991.

Tharp, Louise Hall. *The Baroness and the General.* Boston: Little, Brown and Company, 1962.

Tarleton, Banastre. *A History of the Campaigns of 1780 and 1781 in the Southern Provinces of North America.* New York: Arno Press, 1968.

Bibliography

Thayer, Theodore. *Nathaniel Greene: Strategist of the American Revolution.* New York: 1960.

Thomas, William S. *The Society of the Cincinnati, 1783-1935.* New York: 1935.

Topolski, Jerzy. *An Outline History of Polish Culture* (Warsaw: Interpress, 1986).

Treacy, M. F. *Prelude to Yorktown: The Southern Campaigns of Nathaniel Greene, 1780-1781.* Chapel Hill, NC: 1963.

Trevelyan, George Otto. *The American Revolution.* New York: McKay, 1964.

Trumbull, John. *Autobiography of Col. John Trumbull.* New York: 1841.

_____ *Reminiscences of His Own Times From 1756-1841.* New York: 1841, 1884.

Upham, George B., "Burgoyne's Great Mistake," *New England Quarterly,* III (1930), 657-680.

Ward, Christopher. *The War of the Revolution.* New York: 1952, 2 vols.

Warner, Richard. *Literary Recollections.* London: Longman, Rees, Orme, Brown, and Green, 1830.

Washington, Henry A., ed., *The Writings of Thomas Jefferson.* Washington, DC: 1853-54, VIII.

White, G. G., *Life of Major General Henry Lee, Commander of Lee's Legion in the Revolutionary War.* New York: 1859.

White, Israel Losey. "Truth About a European Liberalist in America—General Kosciuszko," *The Journal of American History,* 1908, 367-374.

Whitridge, Arnold, "Kosciuszko: Polish Champion of American Independence," *History Today,* XXV, No. 7 (July 1975), 456.

Wieczerzak, Joseph, "Pre- and Proto-Ethnics: Poles in the United States Before the Immigration 'After Bread'," *The Polish Review,* XXI, No. 3 (1976).

Wilkinson, James. *Memoirs of My Own Times.* 3 vols. Philadelphia: A. Small, 1816.

Żuraw, Józef. "Tadeusz Kościuszko—The Polish Enlightenment Thinker," *Dialectics and Humanism,* Vol. VI, No. 1 (Winter 1979), 151-163.

Polish History Titles from Hippocrene

Jews in Poland: A Documentary History

Iwo Cyprian Pogonowski
Foreword by Richard Pipes

Originally published in 1993, this classic historical work is now available in paperback! *Jews in Poland* describes the rise of Jews as a nation and the crucial role that the Polish-Jewish community played in this development. The volume includes a new translation of the Charter of Jewish Liberties known as the Statute of Kalisz of 1264; 114 historical maps; as well as 172 illustrations including reproductions of works of outstanding painters, photographs of official posters, newspaper headlines and cartoons.

402 pages • maps, illustrations, index • 8½ x 11½ • 0-7818-0604-6 • $19.95pb • (67.

The Polish Way: A Thousand Year History of the Poles and Their Culture

Adam Zamoyski

"Zamoyski strives to place Polish history more squarely in its European context, and he pays special attention to the developments that had repercussions beyond the boundaries of the country. For example, he emphasizes the phenomenon of the Polish parliamentary state in Central Europe, its spectacular 16th century success and its equally spectacular disintegration two centuries later . . . This is popular history at its best, neither shallow nor simplistic . . . lavish illustrations, good maps and intriguing charts and genealogical tables make this book particularly attractive."

—*New York Times Book Review*

422 pages • 170 illustrations • $19.95pb • 0-7818-0200-8 • (176)

2817017

The Forgotten Few: The Polish Air Force in the Second World War

Adam Zamoyski

This is the story of the few who are rarely remembered today. Some 17,000 men and women passed through the ranks of the Polish Air Force while it was stationed on British soil in World War II. They not only played a crucial role in the Battle of Britain in 1940, but they also contributed significantly to the Allied war effort.

272 pages • 30 illustrations,30 maps • 6 x 9 • 0-7818-0421-3 • $24.95hc • (493)

The Last King of Poland

Adam Zamoyski

One night in December, 1755 Stanislaw Poniatowski, the twenty-three year old secretary to the British Ambassador in St. Petersburg, was introduced to the Grand Duchess Catherine Alekseyevna. This marked the beginning of an affair which led to Stanislaw being crowned King of Poland in 1764. The dashing, young king was a great believer in art, education, and cultural projects. He transformed the mood and outlook of his country and brought it to a new phase of reform and independence, culminating in the passing of the Constitution in 1791, hailed in Britain, France and the United States as one of the greatest events of the century. Best-selling author Adam Zamoyski relates this rich and enthralling story of a personal dream with all the elements of grand tragedy. It is also an important chronicle of the birth and death of liberalism in Poland and the establishment of Russian power in Europe.

416 pages • b/w illustrations • 0-7818-0603-8 • $39.95hc • (676)

Forgotten Holocaust: The Poles Under German Occupation, 1939-1945, *Revised Edition*
Richard C. Lukas
Foreword by Norman Davies

This new edition includes the story of Zegota and the list of 700 Poles executed for helping Jews.

"Dr. Richard C. Lukas has rendered a valuable service by showing tha no one can properly analyze the fate of one ethnic community in occupied Poland without referring to the fates of others. In this sense, *The Forgotten Holocaust* is a powerful corrective."

—from the foreword by Norman Davies

"Carefully researched—a timely contribution."

—Professor Piotr Wandycz, Yale University

"Contains excellent analyses of the relationship of Poland's Jewish an Gentile communities, the development of the resistance, the exile leadershiɟ and the Warsaw uprisings. A superior work.

—*Library Journal*

300 pages • 6 x 9 • illustrations • 0-7818-0528-7 • $24.95hc • (639)

Did the Children Cry?: Hitler's War Against Jewish and Polish Children
Richard C. Lukas

Winner of the 1996 Janusz Korczak Literary Competition for books about children.

" . . . [Lukas] intersperses the endless numbers, dates, locations and losses with personal accounts of tragedy and triumph . . . A well-researchec book . . ."

—*Catalyst*

263 pages • 15 b/w photos, index • 0-7818-0242-3 • $24.95hc • (145)

Your Life is Worth Mine

Ewa Kurek

Introduction by Jan Karski

First published in Poland in 1992 as *Gdy Klasztor Znaczyl Zycie*, this is the story of how Polish nuns saved hundreds of Jewish lives while risking their own during World War II. This long awaited American edition includes a section of interviews with nuns and Jewish survivors which did not appear in the Polish edition.

"A welcome addition to Holocaust literature . . . deserves a wide readership."

—*Zgoda*

250 pages • 5½ x 8½ • 0-7818-0409-4 • $24.95hc • (240)

Poland's Navy, 1918-1945

Michael Alfred Peszke

Created in 1918 when Poland regained its independence lost for 123 years, the Polish Navy fought in World War II alongside of the Royal Navy. The British First Lord of the Admiralty Alexander said in 1944:

"In view of its small size, the number of operations in which the Polish Navy has taken a part is almost incredible, especially bearing in mind that some of them are continuous. Amongst these operations are Narvik, Dunkirk, Lofoten Islands, Tobruk, Dieppe, attacks on shipping in the Channel, Sicily, Italy, Oran and patrols notably in the Mediterranean, and convoy escorting. The recent work of the Polish ships in the Mediterranean has been especially brilliant."

A total of 22 Polish warships fought in World War II; 2 light cruisers, 8 destroyers, 3 destroyer escorts, 8 submarines and 1 minelayer.

250 pages • 6 x 9 • photos/illustrations • 0-7818-0672-0 • W • $29.95hc • (770)

Bitter Glory: Poland and Its Fate, 1918-1939

Richard M. Watt

"Admirably fair-minded and meticulous about the achievements and the disasters of the Pilsudski years."

—*The New York Times*

"An able political history of the Polish Republic from its reconstruction at the end of the First World War."

—*The New Yorker*

"An American popular historian writes objectively and well, and from a solid base in the existing literature, about Pilsudski and Poland's period of independence between the wars."

—*Foreign Affairs*

With remarkable skill, Richard M. Watt tells the story of the twenty-one years of freedom snuffed out by two traditional enemies of Poland.

Greatly praised by Barbara Tuchman, William L. Shirer, Alistair Horne, and J.H. Plumb for his earlier works, Richard M. Watt is noted historian and author of two other books, *Dare Call it Treason* and *The Kings Depart*. He has also written numerous articles and reviews for *The New York Sunday Times* and other periodicals. The author won the 1996 History Award of the J. Pilsudski Institute in New York.

511 pages • 6¼ x 9½ • 32 pages b & w photos • 0-7818-0673-9 • W • $16.95pb • (771)

Bilingual Polish literature from Hippocrene

Pan Tadeusz

Adam Mickiewicz
Translated by Kenneth R. MacKenzie

On the 200th anniversary of Mickiewicz's birth comes a reprint of Poland's greatest epic poem in its finest English translation. For English students of Polish and for Polish students of English, this classic poem in simultaneous translation is a special joy to read.

553 pages • Polish and English text side by side • 0-7818-0033-1 • $19.95pb • (237)

Treasury of Love Poems by Adam Mickiewicz in Polish and English

edited by Krystyna Olszer

This new volume marks the bicentennial of the birth of a poet who is second to none in Polish literature. As a full blooded Romantic, Mickiewicz left a treasure of unforgettable love poems. With over 50 poems, this beautiful bilingual gift edition contains poems addressed to Maryla (his Beatrice), as well as sonnets and verses of sensual and spiritual love in all shades of Romantic passion—"To—(In the Alps as Splugen)," "Romanticism," "The Nixie," and "The Akkerman Steppes," along with the editor's informative introduction, are all included in this collection.

128 pages • 5 x 7 • 0-7818-0652-6 • $11.95hc • (735)

Treasury of Polish Love Poems, Quotations & Proverbs in Polish and English

edited by Miroslaw Lipinski

Works by Krasinski, Sienkiewicz and Mickiewicz are included among 100 selections by 44 authors. In the original Polish with side-by-side English translation.

128 pages • 5 x 7 • $11.95hc • 0-7818-0297-0 • (185)
Also available as Audiobook: 0-7818-0361-6 • $12.95 • (576)

Treasury of Classic Polish Love Short Stories in Polish and English

Edited by Miroslaw Lipinski

This charming gift volume delves into Poland's rich literary tradition to bring you classic love stories from five renowned authors. It explores love's many romantic, joyous, as well as melancholic facets, and is destined to inspire love and keep its flame burning bright.

109 pages • 0-7818-0513-9 • $11.95hc • (603)

A Treasury of Polish Aphorisms: A Bilingual Edition

Compiled and translated by Jacek Galazka

This collection comprises 225 aphorisms by eighty Polish writers, many of them well known in their native land. Twenty pen and ink drawings by talented Polish illustrator Barbara Swidzinska complete this remarkable exploration of true Polish wit and wisdom.

140 pages • 5½ x 8½ • 20 illustrations • 0-7818-0549-X • $14.95 • (647)

Polish Fables
Bilingual Edition

Ignacy Krasicki
Translated by Gerard T. Kapolka

Sixty-five fables by eminent Polish poet, Bishop Ignacy Krasicki, are translated into English by Gerard Kapolka. With great artistry, the author used contemporary events and human relations to show a course to guide human conduct. For over two centuries, Krasicki's fables have entertained and instructed his delighted readers. This bilingual gift edition contains twenty illustrations by Barbara Swidzinska, a well known Polish artist.

250 pages • 6 x 9 • 0-7818-0548-1 • $19.95hc •(646)

Polish Folk Tales

Glass Mountain
Twenty-Eight Ancient Polish Folktales and Fables

Retold by W. S. Kuniczak
Illustrated by Pat Bargielski

"It is an heirloom book to pass onto children and grandchildren. A timeless book, with delightful illustrations, it will make a handsome addition to any library and will be a most treasured gift."

—Polish American Cultural Network

160 pages • 6 x 9 • 8 illustrations • 0-7818-0552-X • $16.95hc • (645)

Old Polish Legends

Retold by F. C. Anstruther
Wood engravings by J. Sekalski

Now, in a new gift edition, this fine collection of eleven fairy tales, with an introduction by Zygmunt Nowakowski, was first published in Scotland during World War II, when the long night of German occupation was at its darkest.

66 pages • 7¼ x 9 11• woodcut engravings • 0-7818-0521-X • $11.95hc • (653)

Other Polish Interest titles

Song, Dance & Customs of Peasant Poland

Sula Benet
preface from Margaret Mead

"This charming fable-like book is one long remembrance of rural, peasant Poland which almost does not exist anymore . . . but it is worthwhile to safeguard the memory of what once was . . . because what [Benet] writes is a piece of all of us, now in the past but very much a part of our cultural background."

—Przeglad Polski

247 pages • illustrations • 0-7818-0447-7 • $24.95hc •(209)

Polish Folk Dances & Songs: A Step-by-Step Guide

Ada Dziewanowska

The most comprehensive and definitive book on Polish dance in the English language, with in-depth descriptions of over 80 of Poland's most characteristic and interesting dances. The author provides step-by-step instruction on positions, basic steps and patterns for each dance. Includes over 400 illustrations depicting steps and movements and over 90 appropriate musical selections. Ada Dziewanowska is the artistic director and choreographer of the Syrena Polish Folk Dance Ensemble of Milwaukee, Wisconsin.

672 pages • 0-7818-0420-5 • $39.50 hardcover • (508)

The Polish Heritage Songbook

compiled by Marek Sart
illustrated by Szymon Kobylinski
annotated by Stanislaw Werner

This unique collection of 80 songs is a treasury of nostalgia, capturing echoes of a long struggle for freedom carried out by generations of Polish men and women. The annotations are in English, the songs are in Polish.
166 pages • 65 illustrations • 80 songs • 6 x 9 • 0-7818-0425-6 • $14.95pb • (496)

The Works of Henryk Sienkiewicz

Quo Vadis

Henryk Sienkiewicz
translated by W. S. Kuniczak
New Paperback Edition!

Written nearly a century ago and translated into over 40 languages, *Quo Vadis* has been a monumental work in the history of literature. W. S. Kuniczak, the foremost Polish American novelist and master translator of Sienkiewicz in this century, presents a modern translation of the world's greatest bestseller since 1905. An epic story of love and devotion in Nero's time, *Quo Vadis* remains without equal a sweeping saga set during the degenerate days leading to the fall of the Roman empire and the glory and agony of early Christianity.
589 pages • 6 x 9 • 0-7818-0550-3 • $19.95pb • (648)

In Desert and Wilderness

Henryk Sienkiewicz, edited by Miroslaw Lipinski

In traditional Sienkiewicz style, Stas and the little Nell and their mastiff Saba brave the desert and wilderness of Africa. This powerful coming-of-age tale has captivated readers young and old for a century.
278 pages • 0-7818-0235-0 • $19.95hc • (9)

With Fire and Sword
Translated by W.S. Kuniczak

The first volume of the epic trilogy, this novel has been translated and adapted for the modern reader by W.S. Kuniczak. It is a sweeping saga of love, adventure, war and rebellion set in Eastern Europe during the 17th century.

"A Polish *Gone with the Wind* . . . racy, readable to a fault . . . provides the timeless joys of a good old-fashioned read. *With Fire and Sword* should have taken its place in the general literary repertory long ago beside the works of the elder Dumas, Walter Scott and Margaret Mitchell."

—*The New York Times Book Review*

1,154 pages • 6 x 9 • 0-87052-974-9 • NA • $35.00hc • (766)

The Deluge
Translated by W.S. Kuniczak

This second part of the trilogy is published in two beautifully designed volumes. It is a superb account of the Swedish War of 1655-69, which came close to overwhelming the Polish-Lithuanian Commonwealth until the Polish people rallied to the defense of Czetochowa, found new strength and faith when there was little left to hope for, and drove out the invaders. As the structural and thematic heart of Henryk Sienkiewicz's magnificent trilogy, *The Deluge* is a masterful blend of history and imagination that illuminates the character of an extraordinary people.

"*The Deluge* is historical fiction at its best . . . This massive epic of love, war and adventure comes to life in English in an innovative modern rendering by W.S. Kuniczak . . . [it] glows with vivid imagery and unforgettable characters." —*The Chicago Tribune*

2 volumes: 1,808 pages • 6 x 9 • 0-87052-004-0 • NA • $60.00hc • (762)

Fire in the Steppe

Henryk Sienkiewicz, in modern translation by W. S. Kuniczak

"The Sienkiewicz Trilogy stands with that handful of novels which not only depict but also help to determine the soul and character of the nation they describe." —James A. Michener

750 pages • 0-7818-0025-0 • $24.95 hc • (16)

The Little Trilogy

Henryk Sienkiewicz; a new translation by Miroslaw Lipinski

Comprised of three novellas, *The Old Servant*, *Hania*, and *Selim Mirza*, this collection will be enjoyed by the thousands of admirers of the greatest storyteller in Polish literature and the winner of the Nobel Prize for Literature in 1905.

267 pages • 0-7818-0293-8 • $19.95hc • (235)

Teutonic Knights, Illustrated Edition

Henryk Sienkiewicz; in a translation edited by Miroslaw Lipinski

"Swashbuckling action, colorful characters and a touching love story . . ."
 —*Publishers Weekly*

" . . . one of the most splendid achievements of Polish literature."
 —*Zgoda*

" . . . a memorable, massive, breathtaking and compulsive read."
 —*New Horizon*

800 pages • illustrated • 0-7818-0433-7 • $30.00hc • (533)